Based on a true story

Chapter One
บทที่หนึ่ง

'Look, I think it's best if we don't stay in the same room anymore.'

'What do you mean?' asked Natasha.

'I mean, I've already booked other hotels for me for the rest of the trip.'

'What? I…I can't believe you'd just abandon me!'

Archie and Natasha travelled to Thailand as friends of the opposite sex and she was trying to do it on a shoestring budget as much as possible. That meant twin rooms were booked in each place they were staying for the two weeks of the holiday. She was shocked. There was a part of her that could understand why he'd arrived at such a decision, yet it still hurt.

'I didn't abandon you, but you have to admit that it's too hard.' Archie took a swig of his beer and looked out onto Maya Bay on the island of Koh Phi Phi, as the waves washed up on the sand in front of them. 'It's nothing personal. You're the one that said about your own space, and if I come in late again that disturbs your sleep and you get mad with me. So, I think it's best for both of us.'

On the run up to departure, she spent a lot of time on travel blogs and found many places that she wanted to go and see. It was a once in a lifetime holiday for her so she wanted to make it as comprehensive an experience as possible. Meanwhile, he didn't have a plan and was quite happy to go there and wing it, which frustrated her. She thought that he ought to have an idea of what he wanted to do too and felt as if he was trying to elbow in or mimic her discovery of Thailand. He chose not to tell her that in his opinion, she was not having the pioneering experience that she thought she was – and rather she herself was mimicking that of the blogs she'd been reading.

At the end of the day, that was her style and he had his own. He was very sociable and had no problem in finding new places and things to do and preferred to be spontaneous and go wherever the wind took him. He also had no problem in meeting new people. He'd even met a few women during the holiday and always got the third degree when he'd come back at seven or eight in the morning. With them being nothing more than friends, he couldn't understand the interrogation and hassle he'd receive on his return to the room.

Natasha got up from her cushion lounger and stormed off along the beach driving her feet deep into the warm white sand with each angry step. Archie shouted to the waiter and pulled a couple hundred baht out of his wallet to pay for their drinks before catching up with her.

'Hey, come on. Why are you so upset?'

'I'm not upset, I'm just...' He tried to catch her shoulder so they could talk face to face. 'I'm going back to the room! Leave me alone!' she snarled. Archie stood dead in his tracks as she resumed storming off around the corner into their hotel. He wasn't really prepared to stay out for the night, but then quickly appraised himself. He had money, his phone was charged, and he was dressed suitably well – better than most of the other travellers there with their 'Chang Beer' vests and elephant pants anyway. *Well, I'll just go out then*, he thought.

After a twelve-hour journey, their bus to Bangkok finally pulled into Sai Tai Mai Bus Station. Despite not sleeping at all, he felt fine. He travelled very well, and fatigue would never start to set in until he at least got to his final destination. He'd still rather have flown but was restricted because of her budget.

During the journey, she didn't sleep either. When they got on the bus, he put his noise cancelling headphones on and stared out the window. She had the window seat on the way to Krabi, so he had it on the way back. She fidgeted and nudged him several times as if trying to catch his attention, but he ignored her. When the bus stopped for a break, she stormed off into the rest station and he made his own way around. He used the toilet whilst trying not to touch any surfaces and bought a warm corn on the cob. There was no butter or salt on it like he would have at home, but actually it tasted pretty good by itself. He bought an extra bottle of water for her because he knew she never had the same kind of foresight as he did. He placed it on her seat before taking up his noise cancelling headphone position again. She waited as long as she could before finally giving in and opening it.

The driver pulled the cases and rucksacks out of the hold. Archie waited for her to collect hers before offering to share a taxi into the city. 'We're staying at different hotels, remember? How can we share a taxi?' she barked.

'Well, we still need to get into Bangkok, but…okay.'

The last few days of his holiday were spent without her. He'd go out each night and meet people to hang around with, mostly other travellers or expats. They were known as farang – as far as he understood, it was a bastardisation of the word 'foreigner.'

It was the second week of April, which was known as *Songkran*, and that was the Thai New Year. There was great meaning to it for Thai people, but for the casual outsider it was merely lots of water fights on the streets. In an attempt to make amends, he called to invite her for dinner on what would be their last full day in Thailand. They still had to travel back to the UK together after all, so they had to be friends again.

'Hey, how are you?' he asked.

'I'm okay…You?'

'I'm good.' There was a pause. 'It's our last night in Thailand tomorrow,' he continued, 'do you want to go for dinner?'

She'd been waiting for him to call. Despite how abandoned she'd felt when he booked separate hotels, she came to appreciate his reasoning and it worked out better for both of them. She'd managed to have her own space as she demanded, but it wasn't as if she was there completely by herself. She knew that if she really needed him, she could call and he'd be there. But she was very happy that he was reaching out to her once again.

'Yeah, I'd love to.' Her tone was upbeat and positive. 'Where do you want to go?'

'Well, how about that restaurant you were talking about before? Did you make it there yet?'

'No, I didn't. That'd be good. 7 p.m. okay?'

'Yeah. I'll book a table. See you then.'

They met at the restaurant and when she arrived, she wore a dress she bought from a local stall, as well as plastic safety goggles and carried a super soaker. The goggles and super soaker were obviously so she could partake in the water fights whilst simultaneously complaining how over the top it all was. She was staying on Khoa San Road, which was a Mecca for backpackers and hence was a big draw for festivities. It was a concentration of street stalls, travellers, bars, hostels and massage parlours. Although many travellers would flock there, it was not what he'd consider the real Bangkok – it was an exaggerated version of it, crammed full of Thai clichés. He stayed further down Sukhumvit Road which was a main thoroughfare through the city and things were much more civilised there. It was the hotel they stayed at when they first arrived, before they knew anything about Bangkok or Thailand.

They ordered plenty food considering it was the last night they could order real authentic Thai food, at least for a while. He'd become a fan of Pad Thai, even if it was a little obvious. He enjoyed the tamarind, flat noodles, the fresh snap of long spring onions and the succulent chicken. It was served with a carousel of condiments but he was a little unsure what was supposed to go with his dish and how much to add. The restaurant itself was beautiful and there was a musician playing traditional Thai music on an instrument that neither of them could identify. Fairy lights were suspended amongst the trees above them as they sat in the outside section. It was mostly foreign people eating there and he thought again about how authentic her discovery of Thailand really was, but wasn't about to point it out. They caught up on the past few days and shared a few experiences with one another.

'How about that girl you met when we were here the first time, did you go to see her again?' she asked.

'No, I didn't. I don't know, I just didn't really feel much towards her, and at the moment I'm still just trying to put myself back together. I really don't think I'm in a place to start something,' he admitted.

'Have you met any others?'

'Sort of…but I've just been out, you know? What about you?'

'Well, I met a guy – a backpacker. He quit his job in New Zealand and he's been travelling around South East Asia since the start of February.'

'Wow, good for him.'

'Yeah, I really admire that. I wish I could do something like that.' Archie loved to travel, but going around the world as a penniless traveller wasn't something that appealed to him at all. His positive response was merely him being agreeable and unobjectionable in an attempt to keep the peace.

After dinner, they walked back to the end of the road and he flagged down a taxi for her. It was still so hot. Even though it was well into the evening, April was always the hottest month in Thailand. That was part of the reason why Songkran involved water fights in the street, so everybody could cool off in the searing heat – other than it traditionally being about washing away bad luck and sins.

He hailed a taxi for himself and just as he got in, changed his mind about going back to the hotel. *It's my last night in Bangkok…* he thought to himself. 'Sukhumvit soi eleven please.'

Chapter Two

บทที่สอง

He'd been on that street before. Archie and Natasha went for dinner their first time in Bangkok, but she left in a bad mood after accusing him of being miserable. Perhaps he was a little bit miserable that night, but only because she pushed him to tell her about past relationships and exactly how they broke down. They were recent friends and would hang out every so often at home in Scotland. They met through a mutual friend, had a few common interests and got on well, but she'd never delved much into his past before.

It was never his fault. Whether he'd been unlucky, or he attracted the wrong type of girl, he'd collected a few sad stories over the years. It was more than his fair share, in fact. How she expected him to be upbeat after being forced to recount his heartaches was entirely unreasonable.

He skipped the place where they ate before because he wasn't particularly impressed by it. The food was okay, but the bar was a little poor. Considering he'd just ate, all he wanted was a few drinks and to take in the sights before going back to the hotel. He advanced further down the street – or soi, as it's called – and stopped in a few places for a single drink before moving on. The street was full of life. There were still a lot of foreign faces, but there were a lot of Thai too. Probably they were mostly working in the service industry in that area, but by that very nature it meant it was more like real Bangkok.

It was a street for entertainment. Not knowing Bangkok so well, it was the only place he knew where he could have a few drinks and watch the world go by. Tuk-tuks with flashing lights boomed loud music in the streets. Some of them looked dangerously overloaded and some contained people with water guns who sprayed the unsuspecting as they barrelled past over a large exhaust note. Taxis crept along and motorcycles zipped around zigzagging between the slower traffic. Smoke from the street food stands wafted its way down the road, past all the loiterers just hanging around without any clear intention.

He reached a bar which was teeming with ladies and didn't like the look of it. Archie didn't go to Thailand for that sort of thing. They hardly called out, but he could feel their eyes on him, so he ducked into the bar next door. This bar had no stools with sexy girls perched on them at the entrance, looked quieter and seemed like a much classier place. There was an outside area with a few unoccupied tables and the main entrance was set further into the building.

A big soggy mat led to the entrance and plastic sheets protected some of the more sensitive areas from the water play. He stepped through a sliding glass door onto a sodden towel and was welcomed by refreshing air-conditioned air. A few girls in pretty dresses shuffled towards him with a friendly welcome, 'Sawatdee ka.' They all made a wai with their hands. It was the prayer shape so often used in Thailand for hello as in this case, as well as goodbye, thank you, sorry and such like. It was a gesture of politeness and good manners.

One ushered him to a table, another brought him a cold towel to freshen up and another gave him a menu. It wasn't very busy, and he felt a little bit uncomfortable having women pander to him in such a way. It was hardly that he was a prude, but he was aware of the reputation of Thailand, and Bangkok, and he didn't know what kind of place he'd stepped into. The bar next door was overtly glitzy but perhaps the understated one was the dodgier one. *One last drink then I'll call it a night,* he thought.

He ordered a whisky and asked for the Wi-Fi password before noticing a girl at the bar directly in front of where he sat. She wore pink jean shorts, a strappy white vest, had two pairs of sunglasses on her head and a clear waterproof pouch hung around her neck which held her phone and some money.

He couldn't take his eyes off her. She spoke to the other girls and they all seemed to know her. Maybe she worked there and it was her day off, he thought. Either way, he told himself not to bother asking. It was his last night, so what could he do? There was no point in pursuing something when he had a flight to the other side of the world the next day. He'd already met a few girls on that holiday despite it being fairly far down on his agenda. Having just recently suffered a breakup, his intention really was just to have a holiday and relax and take some time for himself.

The girl was stunning, though. Her hair cascaded down over her slim shoulders and it was a burnt blonde. He imagined it was brown or black originally, but it had been lightened by highlights which ran through it like streaks of shooting stars in the night sky. It was her sister that worked there and that's who she had came to see. That's also who the second pair of sunglasses belonged to. She spoke to her sister in Thai:

'Who's that guy that just came in, is he a regular?'

'No, I've never seen him before,' her sister replied.

'I want to talk to him.'

'Amm, you're drunk. Leave him alone.'

She stood up and crossed to his table placing her beer down in front of him. She spoke in English: 'Can you watch my beer please. I go to toilet.' He was startled but willingly obliged. Upon her return, she sat down in front of him and introduced herself.

'Hi, how are you? My name Amm.'

'Hi. Amm?' he asked. He wasn't familiar with Thai names and wanted to be sure he heard it correctly.

'Ka. It's A-m-m,' she spelled out for him.

'My name is Archie.' She'd never heard that name before either. 'Ar–chee,' he sounded out with a huge smile on his face.

'Happy Songkran na!' She tipped her beer towards him and he clinked his glass with it.

'Nice to meet you, Amm.'

'Yes, nice to meet you too. How is your night?'

It just got a lot better, he thought. 'Yes, good, thank you. What about you?'

'It's good. I enjoy Songkran today, it's the last day. You know?'

'Yeah, it's the New Year, right?'

'Yes! So I just come to see my sister, she working here.' She craned her neck to find her and point her out, but she wasn't around.

The conversation was so natural. Her English seemed reasonably good and there was not much of a language barrier. For some reason, he felt entirely relaxed talking to her. Maybe it was the alcohol he'd already had, or it may have been the fact that he knew he was going home the next day, so it didn't matter if he messed up. He'd already decided not to talk to her anyway, so it was all just a bonus for him. She giggled at times and the coy delicate smile on her face was the absolute definition of beauty to him. She was captivating and mesmerising.

'You live in Bangkok?' she asked.

'No, I don't. I'm just here on holiday actually.'

'You come holiday alone?'

'No, I came with a friend, but she's already back at her hotel.'

'*She*? It's your girlfriend?'

'No, she's not my girlfriend, just a friend. She stays in a different hotel. We just came to the same place together, but we're not *together*.'

'But you have girlfriend mai?'

He didn't understand *mai*, but could glean what she meant from the context, even though it seemed superfluous anyway. 'No, I don't have a girlfriend.'

Something in her flashed suspicion but she tried not to dwell on it.

'Can I get you a drink, Amm?'

'Umm, yes please. San Mig light. I can?'

'Yes, you can. Of course you can.' He smiled widely at her and she giggled again. 'Come on, what is it? What's so funny?'

'Just…your smile. You make me shy!' she admitted.

'I make you shy? You don't have to be shy.'

'But you very handsome na. And your smile…I never see smile like it before.'

He lit up inside. He couldn't believe that this breathtakingly exquisite girl came to talk to him and was acting in such a manner towards him. There was a split-second cynical thought regarding Bangkok, and he had to wipe a notion out of his head. *She's too good to be true, maybe there's something up with this.* At that moment her sister walked past. 'This my sister,' she said. 'Her name Koi.'

'Nice to meet you, Koi.'

'Sawatdee ka, nice to meet you. You're okay about my sister? She a little bit drunk.' Amm crowed something at her in Thai and slapped her on the arm.

'I'm *very* ok,' came his reply.

'I not drunk, I just happy,' Amm said.

'That's good. What you happy about?'

'Happy to meet you!' She giggled her cute giggle, leaning off to the side whilst shying away behind her hands, and any doubt in him rushed away. There was no way she could fake that laugh because it was from the soul. The light in her eyes and the involuntary tilt of her head was undoubtedly sincere. She covered her mouth when she giggled, because she was slightly embarrassed at how whole-hearted it was. She couldn't help it. There really was something about his smile that just tickled her and thrilled her. 'I want to go dance!' She changed back to Thai and asked her sister if she could come.

'No, I can't. I'm working Amm. I'm with a customer.'

'Maybe he can barfine you?'

'No, it's really expensive tonight because of Songkran. Just you go with him.'

Back to English: 'I ask my sister to come, but she said she working. But we go later. Don't worry.'

They continued to talk and he discovered she was a waitress at a fancy restaurant nearby but she wasn't happy with it. The salary was quite low and it was very expensive to live in Bangkok.

'What about your work? What you do?'

14

'I'm in the Merchant Navy,' he said. 'I work on ships.' She didn't understand so he pulled out his phone and showed her some photos. 'I'm an engineer.'

They ordered another round from one the other girls, Lily. She brought them over and said something to Amm in Thai and gave him a smile. 'So…you don't have girlfriend?'

'No, I don't. Why do you ask again?'

'I just want to be sure na.' He noticed during their conversation that she embellished her speech with *na* at times. It seemed not to really mean much. He thought perhaps it was used as emphasis or just became redundant in translation. She took his hands once more and told him: 'I like you…but I don't want to hurt.'

'I promise you, I don't have a girlfriend. I'm not like that.' His eyes softened, which curled the corners of her lips into a sincere smile ever so slightly. 'Amm, I like you too…quite a lot. I'm never going to hurt you.'

There was a frailty to her in that moment and as he thought about what to say to assure her more, she started to lean across the table, lips first. He met her half way. They both had to stand up from their seats a little as they kissed over the short candle and single rose that stood in a slim vase on the middle of the table. The heat and vapour from the candle ascended into both their noses, but they didn't care.

He couldn't believe it. She was absolutely perfect to him – beautiful, sweet and charming. And he couldn't believe he was kissing her over the table about half an hour after first meeting her. All the girls saw, as well as the few other customers at the bar.

Her lips were soft, sweet and delicious. He could feel her like the key he'd been looking for all his life, and suddenly his heart unlocked. At that moment he fell in love with her. His unlocked heart somehow unravelled for her and his head spun as if his whole world was about to change. Like a sledgehammer to the face, it hit him so hard. It felt like the first day of the rest of his life.

Amm was excited and frightened and very attracted to him. She hoped he wasn't lying about being single because she fell in love with him too and it scared her so much. Koi was working on the floor above but the news made its way upstairs in a few seconds, so she had to come down and check on things. She didn't know this man or what his intentions were with her sister.

They discussed a little more in Thai and Amm asked again if she could come out. 'I want to go dance. But I want my sister come too. Maybe you can barfine her?

'What's barfine?'

'You can pay the bar and then she finish work already.'

'Oh, okay. How much is it?' he asked Koi.

'No, it's very expensive tonight because Songkran. It's okay. Just you go.' She was worried about Amm, but she'd tell her to stay close and then come to meet them later.

'How much is it?' he persisted.

'Four thousand baht.'

Archie opened his wallet, counted out four thousand baht and placed it gently on the table in front of them. 'Okay, let's go.'

They finished their drinks and settled the bill as Koi went to get changed. His change came back and Amm gave him a small lesson in Thai.

'This my friend Lily, you can tell her *khob khun khap*.'

'Khob khun khap,' he repeated. Amm and Lily both giggled and thought it was cute the way he said it. He noticed that when Amm laughed, dimples formed in her cheeks which just made to melt his heart even more.

'It's mean, *thank you*,' she said.

He left a nice tip for Lily, considering he was riding so high from his experience in that bar. They headed to a club also on Soi 11 and he paid the entry for the three of them before buying a bottle of whisky and mixers. Koi was glad she could come out and thought it was very kind of him to barfine her, especially at that price and especially just so she could come with her sister. They finally had a chance to talk and she felt quite at ease about him. He didn't seem the same as other farang. There was no condescension in his voice and he talked plainly and nicely to her which she wasn't used to. He was also funny and joked with her, but it wasn't flirty or inappropriate, neither was it derogatory. She texted some of her friends, inviting them along. When they arrived, he offered to share the bottle with them but they bought their own.

Amm stuck to him like glue. She clung on for dear life and danced like no one was watching. She seemed like a free spirit, yet she was trapped inside herself. They held each other close and she kissed him deeply and endlessly throughout the night. Kissing him made her feel better. The way his body felt against her was so good. The look in his eyes was genuine and compassionate. It was so comforting to her and what she needed most was comfort. Koi occasionally scolded her in Thai to moderate her behaviour and limit her drinks. She may have been drunk, but she was having a good time. 'I will go to meet my friends,' she said. 'They already say we will meet tonight.'

He wondered where that would leave him and supposed it would be alone, but it was okay. He'd just stay and finish the bottle with his other new friends and then go back to the hotel. 'I want you come with me,' she said.

'You want me to come meet your friends?'

'Yes.'

She spoke to Koi again, who told them just to go together since she was happy enough for that to happen now. Once they left the club, they stood outside kissing for several minutes before ambling along to an Irish pub hand-in-hand. Some of her friends worked in the area and they had already arranged to greet each other for Songkran and enjoy a few drinks and food together. Amm was only too happy for Archie to come along, since she wasn't ready to let him go yet.

They were all assembled around a big round booth in the pub. There were six chattering, excitable Thai girls and they all slid round to make space for them. The chattering continued in Thai and he felt a little bit spare but it was fine. She held his hand under the table, squeezing it every so often and checking if he was okay.

Her friends spoke to him at times and asked about his work and where he was from. Amm would answer on his behalf, with a quick look at him to check that she got it right. Despite her inebriation, she always did. They ordered drinks and food and ate and he was very happy. It was not at all what he expected after deciding to not go back to the hotel, and even though he was unable to follow their conversation, he was very glad to be there indeed.

'I will go to see my brother na. He working close here. But you stay here with my friends. It's okay?'

'Yeah.'

He didn't over-analyse it but wondered why it was fine for him to come along so far but wasn't allowed to meet her brother. Maybe it was just going to be for a minute or two, he supposed. He let her out of the booth and she gave him a kiss. 'I come back na. Wait please.'

It may have only been a few hours so far, but it was the first time he let her out of his sight, and he hated it. It was like a big gaping hole formed in his chest. When she was by his side, he felt comfortable, he even felt at home in a foreign land. But now he was just an awkward foreigner again, sitting at a table with six Thai girls he didn't know and could hardly communicate with. It wasn't easy to make small talk with them, but he made the best of it. Most of the time however, he just sat there wondering when Amm would come back. Half an hour had passed and he began to grow concerned. He told one of her friends that he was going to look for her. 'Just waiting na, she come back,' she insisted.

'Okay, I'll...just go outside to take a look.'

He stood outside for a further five minutes and wondered what to do. Did she just ditch him? Who did she go to see? Why wasn't he able to come? Taxi after taxi crawled past with the window down asking him where he was going as he stood at the edge of the road. After turning away about the seventh one, she finally appeared on the other side of the street and crossed towards him.

'Where did you go?' he asked.

'I just go to see my brother.' She could see that he was bothered by it and asked: 'What you worry?'

'Just...you were a long time. I thought you weren't coming back.'

'Ooi, sorry na.' She took his hands, wrapped them around her enticing waistline and pulled him in for a kiss. He was worried about her. Something seemed wrong and she was unsettled, but he kissed her back nonetheless. Her kisses were like nothing else he'd ever experienced, like a cross between the sweetest of nectars and the elemental essence of molten lava. Either way, he was addicted.

'Do you have a boyfriend?' he asked.

'No. I not have boyfriend. Why you say that? I have only you na.'

'Okay…' He held her in the middle of the street with a smile on his face and in his heart. He held her as tightly as he could.

Archie was astounded. The holiday was supposed to just be about chilling out and having a good time. Natasha asked him to accompany her because she'd always dreamed of going to Thailand, and as much of a confident and capable young woman as she was, she didn't want to go alone. With his particular style of work, it lended him large chunks of time off, as well as sufficient disposable income to go to Thailand without it being a life-long ambition of his. Her closer friends neither had the money or the time off. Until she asked him to go, he'd never had any ideas about going to Thailand whatsoever.

He may have already met a few girls during his trip and had a couple of one-night stands, but it was something he'd never done before. He always entered relationships and didn't ever see himself as that type of guy, but he just went with the flow, winging it and being free, following the break-up he'd just suffered.

Now he shared the most tender of embraces in the middle of Bangkok, with an incredibly beautiful girl who seemed to really feel something for him. He had to return to Scotland though, and didn't know what to do. Maybe he should just make the most of the night then walk away. He didn't fancy a long-distance relationship, although in real terms he was always bound to have a long-distance relationship because of his job, regardless of where his girlfriend was from.

They couldn't get enough of each other, though. They kissed ceaselessly and persistently. They wanted to fill up on each other, because they both felt it may be their one and only time together. Neither of them knew what was going to happen the next day, but for that moment, she was his and he was hers.

She led him by the hand back into the pub and there were a lot of other farang who looked at him in envy because of the stunning girl with a big smile looking so proud to be with him.

They sat down again and had a few more drinks whilst the chatter continued. The straps on her vest sometimes slid down her shoulders and he constantly wrangled them back up again. She never acknowledged it as she spoke, but absolutely loved how he was taking care of her. Most guys might want to take advantage of that to cop a fly look, but he was trying to protect her and her modesty. It meant everything to her.

After a while and without warning, she started to cry. The girls chattering increased as they presumably tried to console her. 'Amm, what's wrong?' Archie asked. She turned to him and he carefully swept her teardrops away with his thumb. She held his hand against her cheek as if she was trying to absorb it into her face. 'Are you uncomfortable with me being here?' he continued. 'I can go and leave you with your friends, it's okay.'

'No, don't go please. I want you stay with me.' She leaned into his shoulder and he manoeuvred her arm out of the way to maximise their contact. It was then that he felt it. Deep ridges tarnished her skin.

From her wrists up, she was scarred the full length of her forearm, so badly that he felt it. He checked the other arm and it was the same. At least now he understood perhaps why she was crying. He wished he could help her but wasn't sure how. They didn't even know one another, so what could he really do? He held her close as she sat and cried her tears away. It was as much as he could do.

It was six in the morning and he thought that he should go back to the hotel. It was obvious that she was tired too. They couldn't stay out forever and whilst it was bound to have happened at some point, it was still uncomfortable. After the pub closed, they moved to an outside bar. It was a camper van with drop-down sides and there were a few tables and chairs arranged next to it in front of a bank. Her brother ran the place and that was who she went to see. In actual fact, he wasn't really her brother, he was an old family friend from her hometown who'd helped both her and her sister to move to Bangkok. Brother was more of a respectful way of calling him and only because he wasn't old enough to be 'uncle.'

A lot of 'freelancers' would hang around at those outside bars waiting to be picked up, however. The reason she didn't take him before, was to avoid exposing him to girls vying for business, whilst she had a chat with her brother and greeted him for Songkran. But after 3 a.m. they'd all bagged off and found themselves a sponsor for the night, which meant she could take him there.

'So tomorrow you go home, right?'

'Well, today…tonight I have to leave the hotel.' She drank from a bottle of water and then gave him some.

'What are you going to do now?' he asked.

'Umm…I don't know, maybe stay here with my brother little bit.'

'Can I see you again before I go?'

She paused and thought about it. 'I want to…but, I have to go see my other sister. She is day off. But I already add my Facebook on your phone. We can talk later.'

Archie was quite the gentleman and he'd never ever just came out and asked what he was about to ask before, but he had to try. It may have been the only chance he'd get, so it was worth a shot. 'Do you…want to erm…come home with me? We don't need to do anything. You can just stay with me.' He meant it. He'd have been happy just cuddling up with her after all their kissing that night. He wanted to hold her until the sun came up, which was probably less than an hour away anyway.

She thought about it hard, but had started to sober up and her inhibitions, shyness and normal judgement started to return. She was scared that she'd never see him again and scared about him being so far from her. But anyway, she wasn't the type of girl to sleep with someone she'd just met, regardless of how strongly she felt for him.

'I'm…I like you so much na, Archie. But I cannot come.'

'Okay. It's okay, I understand.'

'I'm sorry,' she caressed his face tenderly, 'you angry with me mai?'

'No. I could never be angry with you. Really, it's okay.' There was an awkward moment whilst she battled with the decision she'd made. She really didn't want to part ways with him, especially since she may never see him again, but she just wasn't ready to go back with him yet.

'I'm actually sorry to ask,' he said, 'but I'm going home, I just had to. I hope you understand.'

'Don't think too much na,' she said with a smile. 'I understand you. I know I'm too beautiful, that's why you need to ask.' She cleverly broke the tension and lightened the mood whilst enjoying a final flirt and laugh together. It all added to her charm and appeal.

The only thing he could do from there was leave. 'So…I'll go now,' he said. 'I really hope I can see you again. But if not, you please take care of yourself.'

They both stood from their folding chairs and wrapped themselves up in one another. 'You take care too. I'm so happy I meet you,' she said.

'Me too.'

'And thank you so much.'

'For what?' asked Archie.

'For tonight. I enjoy so much, and you show me how to be happy again.'

'Well, I'm really glad. And thank you too. You've given me one of the best nights of my life.'

They kissed for a final time and eventually let go their embrace. Suddenly the unforgiving heat and stench and humidity of the place started to wash over him again. That bubble of comfort he felt around her was gone. She too ended up alone again. But maybe it was for the best, she thought. In her mind, he was much too good for her.

Whilst their bodies separated, she uttered: 'Chan rak khun,' to him whilst looking deep into his charming eyes.

'What does that mean?'

She shook her head and smiled. 'Nothing. Goodbye Archie.'

As she watched him walk away, she replied, but not out loud, 'It's mean *I love you.*'

Chapter Three
บทที่สาม

Back home in Scotland, he constantly checked his notifications and messages. She hadn't accepted her own friend request. He had to come to terms with that, but it was a disappointment he wished he didn't have to deal with. He fell for her so hard but supposed he ought to just leave it to that one fairytale of an evening. It was a great way to round off the holiday. It was just the one night, so tried to tell himself that he couldn't possibly be as attached to her as he thought he was. After a few days, he sent her a message saying: "Hi Amm. It was really good to meet you. I hope everything is going good over there. Take care and all the best."

After a few more days a message came back: "Hi. I'm sorry so late reply. I forget I add myself on your phone and I don't know who it is."

He wondered how drunk she'd been and whether she even liked him at all? Was she just out of control that night? Could he have just been anyone? Either way, he was upset about it, but at least if he meant so little to her then that'd help him forget about her. It wasn't the case, of course. She was reluctant to add him because of the distance. She'd thought about it every day since he left, but after about a week, he was all that was on her mind. She waited a while in the 'hope' that she might forget about him and wouldn't start some kind of long-distance communication. It was also harder for her to write in English than it was to talk, and she'd never had any foreigners who she'd messaged before. All of those things were daunting, but it got to a point where she couldn't ignore him any longer.

They started chatting every day. Then they started chatting all day, every day. He was still on leave and she'd just left her job but was soon to start working in a bar, because it was higher salary and she could make commission from the drinks too. She was tired of scraping things together and struggling to make ends meet on her waitress salary. She expected a decent salary by moving to Bangkok, but failed to appreciate all the other expenses she'd have. Up until then, she was still no better off than in her hometown.

Her first few weeks in the bar were tough. She loathed the customers and didn't like to talk with them. She hated the way they eyed her up and ask to take her home after buying her a couple of drinks. Amm was much too sensitive and took everything to heart. It was a sports bar

28

which was frequented by a lot of different nationalities, mostly all of them ex-pats living somewhere in Bangkok. She'd obviously had some experience serving people as a waitress, but being a hostess in a bar was something else. What's more, every guy that walked in was being compared to Archie. He was sweet and caring. He was respectful and thought about her feelings. He was also the benchmark for her and no one else came close.

He noticed that her Facebook posts became quite dark as she struggled to get her head around work and herself. Of course, they were all in Thai and he had to try to translate them online, but he got the gist of what she was saying and how she must have been feeling. They still talked all the time, although sometimes he'd have to wait for a reply when she was working. She'd send him photos of her eating after work, and photos of her and her sister out and about. He loved it. It was a completely new style of communication, courting and of life in general and Archie found that he was really drawn towards it. Although he never went to Thailand to find love, it certainly looked like love had found him.

He translated one of her posts and what he got from it was something about the world being a dark place and there being no point to life, so he had to bring it up with her. He knew about the scars on her wrists so could appreciate she had some issues and wanted to do something to try and help her or reassure her.

"Hi. I see your posts. What's going on? Is everything ok?"

"Yes, everything ok na. Don't need to worry about me. I just so tired of my life."

He thought about his reply. He checked his bank balance and called his company to ask when they were planning to send him back to sea before writing back. "I've still got leave left. I could come back to see you. But only if you want to. No pressure, just get to know each other."

Their usual all day, every day messaging ceased. She read it immediately, but there was no response and he thought he'd blown it. He should never have put her on the spot like that. A full twenty-four hours passed before the reply came: "I would love to see you. That's it."

Archie arrived at Suvarnabhumi Airport in the early evening. He headed to the taxi rank filled with a jumble of nerves, trepidation and excitement. The plan was to check in at the hotel, freshen up, then meet her at work. He received a message from her at his stopover in the Middle East, asking if he'd arrived and telling him she was so excited to see him again. It was so sweet and gave him butterflies in his stomach.

He wasn't tired. Despite having travelled six thousand miles over the course of twenty hours, he was fresh. The adrenaline filled him and pushed him far harder than any fatigue could slow him down. Upon leaving the hotel, Archie was greeted by that heat and smell and noise of Sukhumvit Road which began eroding his careful grooming and

30

aftershave. He hailed a taxi and cradled a rose in his lap as he told the taxi driver the location of her bar. He'd never been on that soi before and didn't know the place, but it was easy enough to find.

As he turned the corner, he saw a hanging sign which read 'Sport Spot' and he knew he'd reached the right place. Peering through the glass front as he pulled up, he nervously scanned for her. Amm was behind the bar washing glasses as he opened the door and was hit by the cooling comfort of the air conditioning. Of course, she'd been expecting him all night, but the sudden rush she felt from seeing him again made her knees tremble. He wanted to take her in his arms and embrace her, but he knew he probably couldn't do something like that there. It wasn't a particularly large bar and it wasn't particularly busy. A few guys sat by themselves, angled towards various TV's showing whatever sport they were following, whilst maintaining a line of sight with the staff so they could creep on the pretty Thai girls and fantasise about taking them home.

Amm came round from the bar, giggling nervously. She couldn't believe Archie flew from the other side of the world just to see her. The fact that someone would go to such lengths just for her was beyond anything she could ever imagine. She had a quick check around that no customers were watching and gave him a quick cuddle and kiss on the cheek. 'Hi, how are you?' she asked. 'How is your flight?'

'Yeah it was fine. How are you?'

Wide smiles beamed from both of their faces as she handed over her glass washing duties to one of the other girls. 'I'm good na.

31

I'm…happy to see you again.' She ushered him over to a table. 'What you like to drink? You already eat?'

'I'll just have a beer, please. And I didn't eat yet.' She returned with a bottle of Singha in a foam insulating sleeve, a menu and sat opposite him. She was shy and quiet, but it was a little bit different from before. He couldn't put his finger on it, but maybe it was because she was sober. He really worried that she didn't actually like him and she was just blind drunk that night. But then again, she didn't need to say *yes* when he asked about coming back to see her. If she wasn't interested, then surely there would be any number of excuses she could come up with to discourage him from coming.

After eating and having a couple of drinks, the conversation started to fizzle out slightly. He wanted to get out of there because he sensed that she wasn't comfortable meeting him at her work. All the girls had heard about him already so were whispering and talking about her and she hated wondering what they were saying.

'Can we go to your sister's bar? Can I barfine you?'

She thought about it. She wanted to get out of there too, but didn't want to ask him to pay for her. It was fairly normal for girls to get barfined, but they often didn't care too much about the guy, and at times it was a way to squeeze more money from them. That was the last thing she wanted to do to Archie.

'I don't know,' she said, 'it's up to you. It's one thousand two hundred. Too expensive.'

'It's not that expensive. And it was four thousand for your sister before. You just tell me what you want. If you want to go, we can go. If you want to stay then we will stay.'

'I want to go.'

When they arrived on Soi 11, Amm insisted on paying for the taxi. Her sister was glad they came so she could see how things were progressing. After meeting Archie, all Amm did was talk about him, which only intensified after she learnt he'd booked flights to come back.

They took a seat at the outside tables overlooking the road. The plastic sheets were cleared from the last time he was there and the mat was no longer soggy from the water-guns and buckets of Songkran. A few other girls came across and introductions took place. 'Oh, *this* is him, he *is* very handsome!' one of them said in English. Amm was embarrassed so slapped her arm and responded in Thai, but she was much more relaxed there. She didn't feel the eyes of her co-workers or her boss on her, just the eyes of her friends. They enjoyed a few drinks and talked and laughed and ordered food. It was such a great night for him. She really was the most beautiful girl he'd ever laid his eyes on and he couldn't believe she was sitting talking and drinking with him. Not to mention the glancing touches and how she'd squeeze his hand or thigh every now and then.

After Koi finished work, they all went to eat some street food. It may have been fate, but by some coincidence, they stayed in the exact same part of the city as he did. Their mass transit station for the BTS Skytrain was the same, but it was already late and the service had stopped for the night. They took a taxi instead to their station, BTS Phra Khanong and walked around the corner to where the street food stall was. He couldn't believe how much Thai girls ate. He had a healthy enough appetite, but they seemed to eat much more than him. And they were so slim, it beggared belief. She paid for the taxi there too and for the street food. It was all fairly cheap, but he appreciated that she paid for what she could. He did offer to pay, but she said: 'You already barfine me na.'

She scooped some water into a plastic cup and added ice and a straw for him before putting food on his plate to try. She spooned some fried rice, a few chunks of barbecue chicken and vegetables that were dripping with a brown shiny sauce. Meanwhile, she had a bowl of guay tiew, which was a noodle soup with some kind of meatball and beansprouts in it. She'd asked the vendor especially not to make anything too spicy so that he could eat it. It was still a little spicy, but he'd already tried Thai food when he was there on holiday and his palette was becoming accustomed to it. There was something else about it though; there was another element to the food he was eating. It was real Thai food because it was Thai life. No one had ever written blogs about the stall they were eating at. That's because the feeling Archie had was one which could not be quantified nor repeated. It was not for anyone to emanate, seek out or even to admire. It was a private and heartfelt moment where she included him into her daily life. It was no longer just a holiday, and Archie was no longer just a tourist.

Amm and Koi's place was a little bit far to walk from there so they wanted to take another taxi home. His hotel was back towards the BTS station, around the corner then across the road, and she asked if he wanted her to walk with him. He knew she wasn't going to stay the night and considering her sister was there too, he didn't want to split them up or take any more of Koi's time. 'No, it's okay, it's so close.' He was quite happy to take it easy with her and didn't want to push things. He was sure that it'd happen when she was ready, so it wasn't like he'd have to try and snatch an opportunity the way he did before. It wasn't going to be they're one and only time together.

'Just be careful na,' she said. 'Please...you don't know Bangkok.'

'Don't worry. I'm starting to learn now anyway.'

'Please send me message when you get home, so I know you're safe,' she instructed.

'I will. You too.'

She came towards him and he wrapped his arms around her. He hoped he wasn't too sweaty. Bangkok was a hell of a lot hotter than Scotland, and he was always a little uncomfortable in such a heat. She buried her head in his chest and they squeezed each other tight. The hug went on for a while and Archie caught flashes of Koi waiting and checking what was happening as discreetly as she could. He wasn't expecting a such long hug but was pleased that it still wasn't over. It wasn't enough though. As great as it felt to hold her, he needed her kiss too, so gently ran his fingers through her hair until she looked up at him. He leaned in and she gladly reciprocated. It was actually their first full-on kiss of the evening and it went on for several minutes as Koi patiently waited. Whilst Amm enjoyed his lips and tongue and the safety of his arms around her, she was also terrified, and thought about all the things that could go wrong. *Surely he has someone else. I can't be the only one. Maybe he's already married,* she thought. Being in his presence filled her with delight, yet she couldn't help feeling uneasy. The more she fell for him – the more terrified she became. She was so scared of being hurt again.

Chapter Four

บททีสี

He spent some time seeing more of Bangkok during the day. He only spent about four full days there in total during his first holiday, so there was still so much to see. Essentially though, he was merely killing time until he got to see her again. He asked if he could barfine her once more so that they might spend some more quality time together. Since she hadn't been working there very long, she didn't want to barfine too often. He could appreciate that he supposed, but felt a little disappointed. She missed out on her commissions from the night before and despite having a great night with him, she still needed to make money.

He didn't get a kiss when he arrived, but she was at work, so it was understandable. Perhaps it was okay the first night, because she was still so shocked that he'd come all that way just for her. It did seem however that it may have been more than that. Somehow, she seemed more distant and wasn't as warm, but he had to give her the benefit of the doubt.

She had on a flowery dress, bold red lipstick, and pearl earrings peeked through her hair every now and then. Her shoulders were too skinny and like the white vest she wore the night they met, her straps kept making a getaway down her shoulders. Somehow, he didn't feel like he was able to reinstate them as he did before.

They ate some food and had a few drinks, but she was continually looking over her shoulder for something, or someone. He didn't have her full attention like he usually did. When customers came in, she greeted and seated them and would take a drink order. She'd disappear at times whenever the bell in the kitchen rang so she could take food orders out. Of course, he knew she still had to serve others, but when she sat with him, she was still looking round elsewhere. He felt uncomfortable, but didn't know what else he could do.

As she began to get drunk, she asked him for more and more drinks. She asked for drinks for all the other girls too and he didn't want to refuse her. He'd been introduced to them and they all said he was handsome, but now that he was 'friends' with them it was very hard to refuse drinks. Meanwhile, his bill grew and grew, yet he was trapped. Where else could he go? He had to stay there so that they could get a chance to talk, but she just ended up drunk and more aloof with him whilst being friendlier to customers. He thought that's just how it was and he'd have to endure it until she finished work and they could be together properly. It was perhaps a less desirable side of his new style of life, but he had to be patient.

She found a carrot in the kitchen and brought it to the table. He did find it incredibly cute as she sat gnawing and crunching at it like a bunny rabbit. She offered him some too and wouldn't take no for an answer. 'It's good for you na,' she said. Whilst force-feeding him the carrot, there was a farang behind her who was clearly drunk and started becoming loudmouthed towards everybody, but mostly the staff. He spoke some Thai and Archie was quite impressed, but that's the only thing he was impressed with. The guy complained at the top of his voice about how he'd had an argument with his Thai wife and how all Thai women were the same. She was a 'bitch', a 'stupid cow' and a 'fucking idiot'. One of the girls, Natty, tried to appease his bad mood which didn't seem to go down too well with him.

'And what are you going to do my little fuck toy?'

'Okay, you drinking too much. I think better you go home now,' she said.

'You're just the fucking same as her. Think you can tell me what to do? Who the fuck are you?'

Amm watched over her shoulder as Archie could take it no longer. 'Where you go?' she asked, as he walked past her.

'Right, come on mate, that's enough. I think you should leave.'

'And who the fuck are you?'

'Just someone trying to have a quiet drink and enjoy my evening, but you're making a scene and embarrassing yourself.'

The to and fro between them persisted for a moment and Amm didn't know what to do. She was so frightened of this man, and frightened for Archie, but she was frozen at the table watching with nervous anticipation. Natty stood with Archie and as they argued, the man tried to grab her. 'You come with me then, I want to fuck you tonight.'

Archie intercepted his hands and pinned them behind his back. All the girls stood up from their respective tables, as did Amm. He took the guy outside and told him he wouldn't let him go until he calmed down.

'Alright, I'm calm! Just let me go you cunt!'

'Well, say it a bit nicer and then I'll let you go.'

'You're dead, you dickhead.'

Archie used his leg to push him away hard as he let go of his arms. The man stumbled for a few yards before tipping over and scraping his face along the street. Archie hunkered down as he entered fight mode. Meanwhile, the guy got up and ran at him, swinging on the move. It was easy for Archie to dodge him and he fell flat on his face again, all of his own accord – well, perhaps with a little nudge from Archie. The manager was at the door and shouted for Archie to come back inside, to which he complied. She shut and locked the door until the guy became bored and walked away.

'Oh my God, so crazy guy!' said Ploy the manager. 'Thank you so much for your help. If you not here, I don't know how we can get him out! Let me buy you a drink.'

Now that the coast was clear, Amm rushed to check on him. 'You okay mai?' She hung her arm around him whilst inspecting him closely. Her eyes were glassy, as if she was about to cry. 'Why you do that? You make me worry!'

'Don't worry. I can handle myself.'

'Sit down na, I get you drink.'

The manager had already poured him a large whisky and Amm brought it over placing it down next to the discarded bottom half of a carrot. 'Don't do like that again. I worry too much, you know?'

'How come you're so upset?'

She looked deeply and desperately into his eyes but didn't answer.

As the bar was closing, he helped her clear up a little and helped the manager lock up. She thanked him again for his protection. 'Well, if you need a security guard, maybe you can give me a job?' he joked.

There was street food around the corner and at the end of the block. After his display, all the girls were interested and wanted to come along too, but Amm chased them away. It was a strange night, but in a way, he enjoyed it. It was part of his experience beyond being a tourist in Bangkok. Maybe drunk and abusive ex-pats were normal day-to-day occurrences. Archie was just relieved to have Amm to himself at last, but it was already late and they didn't have much time to spend together before she had to go home.

Sweat began to form on his brow and crept down the side of his face as he sat on a plastic stool by the side of the road. He'd enjoyed the air conditioning of the bar, but now he had to suffer the searing heat once more. It was already after 2 a.m. but it was still much hotter than the hottest day of a Scottish summer. Meanwhile, Amm was still vacant and he couldn't place it.

'What's wrong with you tonight? Is everything okay?' he asked.

'Yes...okay.'

As they ate, she used tissues from the table to blot the sweat that would bead on his brow. It was an amazing feeling. It was a level of care he'd never felt before, but she just wanted to make him comfortable – as much as she was able to anyway.

'Amm?' She looked across at him from the other side of the table. Sukhumvit Road was behind her and as loud motorbikes with big exhausts raced past, he could smell the charcoal from the street food stand whilst fragrances of galangal, chilli and garlic also roamed in the air.

'Yes?'

'I really like you.' She smiled. 'I mean...I *really, really* like you.' Suddenly his perspiration increased somewhat. 'So erm...is it too early to ask what our status is?' She looked confused.

'I don't understand.'

'I mean, are we boyfriend and girlfriend?' She looked away from him.

'I like you too...so much. But I don't know.'

42

'Well…do you have feelings for me?'

'Yes, I have,' she said quickly without hesitation, 'but…I'm no good girl.'

'What do you mean *no good girl*?'

'I mean, when you know the real me, you will not like me.'

His mind whirred. What things has she done? Has she followed the stereotype of an impoverished Asian girl? Was it about her self-harm?'

'I think that's up to me to decide though, right?'

'But I'm no good. You are too good man. I'm no good for you.'

'What is it? You can tell me.' He rested his fork and spoon at the edge of his plate and took her hands as the table rocked on the uneven paving stones. 'Please tell me.'

'Not yet. I'm sorry. I tell you later. But when you know the real me, you will not like me.'

Before returning to Thailand, he dreamt that Amm had a daughter. It came from a photo on Facebook of her with a young girl who was actually her neighbour. In the dream, she told him the young girl was her daughter and that she wasn't good enough for him. There was something eerie and unsettling considering what she was now telling him. But if it was a daughter, then he'd already came to terms with it when he woke up and still accepted her. He put the dream down to a little bit of apprehension of being so impulsive to fly back just to see her. Aside from that, every other worst-case-scenario had also already been considered in his head but he loved her and knew that his feelings wouldn't change.

'I want to go home now,' she said.

He held her hand as they stood awaiting a taxi but she withdrew it to play with her phone, although she didn't actually do anything on it. In the dark of the taxi however, she leaned her head on his shoulder and closed her eyes. He could feel her gentle breath on his arm. Only then did she reach for his hand and squeeze it tight. 'Are you okay with me?' he asked softly. 'If I make you feel uncomfortable, then I can leave you alone. I'd rather not, but it's okay. I don't want to make you feel bad. You just need to tell me.'

'It's not *you* make me feel bad,' she replied.

'Then what is it?'

'It's *me* make me feel bad.' She sat up again and faced him. He cupped her cheek in his palm and she turned to putty. She melted into his hand and let out an involuntary whimper. The man next to her was perfect, but she was far from perfect in her head.

'Do you want to see me again?' he asked.

'Yes. I want to. But if you don't come, I will understand.'

'So long as you want me to, then I'll be there. Every time.'

She dropped him off at his hotel before continuing around the corner and along the road to her place. He wanted to kiss her. She wanted to kiss him too, but they both hesitated. Before he knew it, the taxi was stopped in the middle of traffic and he had to get out. He attempted to pull out his wallet to give her money for the taxi, but she point blank refused. 'Thank you for tonight,' he said.

'Thank you Archie…for everything na.'

Chapter Five

บทที่ห้า

He woke up early and pottered about the hotel room. They had arranged to meet at 1 o'clock, go to the movies and have a look around the mall together. He sent her a message asking how she was and how she slept. She'd been online but didn't read it and his heart groaned. What the hell was he doing in a country six thousand miles from his own, chasing a girl who couldn't figure out if she was interested or not? But it was already too late for him. He was already trapped. Like a rabbit in a snare, the more he struggled the worse it got.

A message came later saying that she felt sick and wasn't sure if she could make it. It was an alarm bell for him. It was her day off and she'd agreed to spend it with him. In fact, she asked whether she could, yet it suddenly sounded like she was making excuses. He didn't want to react to it too much or put her on the spot about her intentions. He'd already asked her whether or not he should just leave her alone, but for some reason she didn't want him to go.

"We can meet later about 4. I go to hospital first, see doctor."

"Oh ok. Are you alright?"

"Yes, ok. Just feel sick. But I meet you later don't worry."

The meeting point was at the BTS station, just a couple minutes walk from the hotel. It would be even faster, if not for the big intersection that he had to risk his life crossing just to get there. Red lights were seemingly advisory in Bangkok rather than anything else. The lanes of traffic came from one direction, then another, then another. Even if he had the right of way to cross, he'd still walk very swiftly to the other side whilst scanning diligently.

4 o'clock came and went. The station had entrances from both directions and on both sides of the road, so he thought maybe he was standing at the wrong one. He walked between all the exits and couldn't see her at all. He tried to call but couldn't get through. Instead, he got some automated woman speaking in Thai, which of course, he couldn't understand.

It was 4:50 when she arrived; looking flustered and annoyed and talking on the phone in Thai as she came up the escalators. There was no real greeting, she merely looked at him and waved passively as she continued walking and talking. It was completely rude. She bought two tickets from the machine and handed him one without saying a word. They passed the ticket barrier and he followed her up the stairs and stood next to her at the platform. By this time, he felt utterly

47

awkward, as if he was some kind of stalker just following some poor girl around, except Amm knew fine well that he was there. When the train arrived, she was still on the phone. It wasn't until after a couple of stops that she finally hung up.

'So how are you feeling now?' he asked.

'Today I can't stay long time. I have to meet my sister, it's her birthday. We can't go to see movie. Just look some shop then I go.'

No, 'hello, how are you?' he thought, and she didn't even answer his question. But she didn't look particularly sick anyway – in fact she looked fantastic. But he'd just waited around all day long for her to tell him that they can't even spend much time together. He was devastated and frustrated, but it still never crossed his mind to walk away from her. Something kept him there. Something made him accept the poor treatment she was dishing out. Perhaps it was a big deal to travel somewhere so far away just to see if there was a chance at something happening. If he didn't try his absolute hardest then the whole escapade would have been a complete waste of time and energy. He had to persevere and give it his all, so long as she was still willing to meet.

They reached the station for the shopping mall and got off the train. She placed another call whilst passing the ticket barrier and they made their way inside. Once she was off the phone, she began to talk with him again. 'My sister come now. You remember her, you already meet Koi.'

'Yeah, okay.'

'Because then we go together to see my other sister.'

'Okay…' He looked at her beautiful face and thought about how all she'd said since they met was about how she couldn't stay and how she was going somewhere else. It looked as if she was just squeezing him in. He didn't feel important, and more than that, he felt like a burden. They managed a little bit more small talk as they waited for her sister to arrive. He asked about how many sisters she had and it turned out it was four. She didn't have any brothers, and neither did she have a dad in the picture. She never knew him, and apparently didn't want to.

They sat on a plinth next to a pop-up marketplace at the entrance of the mall. Each week or so, they'd have a different theme with different retailers; one week it'd be ladies' shoes and handbags, the next it was Japanese toys, the next perhaps sports apparel. People came and went and it hurt him to think they were presuming he and Amm were together. Yet, despite sitting inches from her, he felt a million miles away.

When Koi arrived, they talked only in Thai as they walked in and out of shops, and he was excluded. The mall had only been open a few months and was still very bright and shiny inside. It was colossal and split into different sections, but it seemed like they knew exactly where they were going. They ascended escalator after escalator and part way up, there were doors outside to a roof garden with a water feature and an outstanding view across the city. He'd never seen anything like it, and in a shopping mall no less.

'You want to look outside mai?' she asked.

They entered the garden and it was incredible. Water trickled from artificial rocks and led into ponds, there were terraces paved with fake grass and vegetation like the middle of a jungle. Other people were milling around and taking photos with the backdrop of Bangkok behind them. She posed for photos alone and it was Koi that encouraged her to take some photos of them together. For some reason she wasn't keen, but agreed nonetheless. It was awkward, and he didn't know if it was acceptable to put his arm around her. She wore a stunning blue dress with an oblique cut across her shins. Her olive legs stood next to him in his casual clothes because he got ready at lunchtime and he felt uncomfortable and ungainly next to her.

Once the photo opportunity had lapsed, they headed to eat some food. It seemed that the revised plan of a *quick look-round* before escaping to see her sister had gone out the window along with the original *movie and a look-round* plan. At least they met somewhere in the middle, he supposed. He spoke with Koi and she asked him about his work and why he wanted to come to Thailand. The conversation was mainly between Archie and her whilst Amm spectated.

'So, what you do after here?' Amm finally asked.

'I don't know. Maybe I'll go to take some photos. I was thinking of going to Benjasiri Park.'

'Yes, it's nice there. Just close to here too.'

'But I need to go back to the hotel to get my camera first.'

'Oh. Why you don't bring it with you now?'

'Well,' he hesitated, 'because I thought we were going to the movies and stuff. I didn't think I'd have to find something else to do.' She cringed at herself as she remembered how she'd given him the run-around all day.

He didn't know what else he could do to prolong the meal, or even if he wanted to.

'You don't need to wait, you can go,' he said plainly. 'I'll get the bill. I know you're meeting your sister.'

'No, it's okay, I wait with you. How you go home? You take taxi?

'No, I'll just get the BTS.'

She suddenly became concerned over him. Perhaps she noticed his flat tone or how his face and whole mood seemed to drop during the meal because of her dismissive attitude towards him – or perhaps it was pointed out to her.

'Okay. I walk you there na. And then we go to get taxi.'

They descended the many escalators and walked the smooth white floors between designer shops and towards the exit. Through the sliding door they were met with flashing lights and booming music which was being piped all around the outside of the mall as dusk started to set about the Bangkok sky. The hustle and bustle of the BTS station lay close as he tried to establish where they'd part ways for the evening. Suddenly a hand slipped into his. She held it as they walked out and a sudden euphoria flooded him again. It may have been heightened by all the sights and sounds of the place which were still exciting and novel to him. Whatever it was, he felt ecstatic, if not a little bit confused. *She must just be shy,* he thought. *She probably just needs time.*

'I take you to BTS na.'

He smiled at her and she shied away from him a little. Looking and touching him all at the same time was quite a lot for her to handle.

'It's okay. I know where I'm going. You should just go for your taxi. I know you stayed longer than you wanted to. I don't want you to be too late.'

'No. Not late.'

They stopped in the middle of the concourse at the watershed between BTS and taxi directions and he could feel the grip weakening from her as Koi gave a little bit of distance to be polite. He gave her a hug and kissed her cheek. Koi smiled from the fringes as Archie tapped his own cheek and asked, 'What about kiss for me?' It was meant as a joke, but he was really hoping that she'd oblige. She didn't know what to say and Koi came to her rescue. 'Just wait time. You wait time na,' she said warmly. There wasn't much else he could do. It was hard to understand however considering the kissed all night the first time they met, now he could hardly get a kiss on the cheek.

'Send me message when you home, okay?' she said. 'Enjoy your picture.'

'Thanks. I hope you have a nice time with your sister.'

'Thank you na.'

He watched them walk onto the escalator down to street level, out of sight beyond the moving steel steps, before making his way to the station.

By the time he reached the hotel, he felt exhausted. He switched on the TV but he wasn't watching. He just wanted some noise in the room with him because he had nothing else. She had gone away again and he was becoming tired of the continual rejection. *She* was the one who said she'd *love* to see him again, not just *like* to. She said she had feelings, so he couldn't understand her behaviour at all. He thought about it perhaps being a Thai thing. He had no experience of dating a Thai girl before and no knowledge of others who had ever done so. It may have just been normal for all he knew. Showing moments of affection interjected with icy coldness and distance. It was tantalising, but it worried him. He had a lot riding on her and at the very least, he wasn't even having a holiday, he was just dedicating all of his time trying to be with her. Having an additional ten days in Bangkok, he could have achieved so much more than he currently was.

By the time he reached the park, it was already closing. He'd wasted time feeling sorry for himself and trying to summon the energy to leave the hotel again and that took a while. He was beginning to realise that he was not having as good a time as he had hoped by coming back to Bangkok. He was expecting that first night he spent with Amm every night, and for them to get closer and closer still. It certainly was not going that way at all.

He walked slowly back along to Sukhumvit Road, passing an alley at one point. It was full of lights and activity. It was hard to make his way on the street because people were milling about and pop-up bars occupied the pavements. Girls sat there and sized him up as he went past and he had no idea what he'd stumbled across. With a quick cursory glance, he realised it was some kind of red-light district all packed into one street. Pausing from his walk was a mistake, as he was approached by some girls who tried to get him to have a drink. The girls he thought, were not so beautiful, but probably sufficiently attractive for one thing.

Not that it was an option for Archie, but he wondered what it would be like just to go to a bar there and take another girl home. Deep down it wasn't what he wanted though. Even if it was a legitimate woo and if he'd manage to charm someone enough to go back with him, the biggest problem was that she wouldn't be Amm. Another issue would be that he'd perhaps be tempted to walk away from her, when his sole purpose of the trip was to get to know her. He couldn't come to Bangkok and sleep with random girls, because that would just make him a sex-tourist, he thought. He always kept high standards of behaviour and integrity for himself, so it's a level that he never wanted to stoop down to. He knew plenty of guys were doing that kind of thing, and it was fair enough, he supposed. If he were to do that, then it would completely defeat the whole purpose of him being in Bangkok. But with all that he was going through and the things he was learning, he was seriously starting to question himself and his virtues.

Just then, he picked up some stray Wi-Fi from one of the bars and a message pinged on his phone. It was a photo of Amm with Koi, her other sister and husband, in a restaurant for the birthday dinner. He wondered how she could be eating again, because he still felt full from the food they had together. Nonetheless, if he had any reckless thoughts, that photo wiped them right out. He had to stay true to himself. He politely declined the invitations from the girls on the pavement and walked all the way back to his hotel to spend the night alone.

Chapter Six
บทที่หก

After previously failing to take any nice photographs at all, he wanted to head out during the day to attempt it once again, starting from Benjasiri Park. Sure, the photos maybe wouldn't be as nice without the twilight and twinkling lights, but it didn't matter. He'd brought his big SLR camera to Thailand and hadn't even taken a single picture yet. It was also something to do again to fill the day until she was at work and he could see her. It'd been a few days since her sister's birthday and he'd been to her bar a couple more times, but nothing much happened. He'd go and eat and drink and run up a huge tab. They'd go to eat again after the bar closed and share a taxi home. Amm was rarely warm to him, except on the ride home. For those eleven precious minutes, they were isolated and alone and only then was she herself. They never kissed anymore however, which was incredibly discouraging for him.

In the daylight, he could see the area he passed the last time he went to the park as it lay dormant in the afternoon sunshine. He imagined all the people who'd copped off and all the hangovers that were being suffered as people were waking up. He didn't want what that place could offer, but he *did* long for someone to be with him at night and someone to wake up next to. Lately he'd felt more lonely than usual. The first visit with Natasha was just for a good time with no expectations and he enjoyed himself then. He'd already lost that agenda about taking care of himself and didn't realise how much he was forgoing all of his own feelings just to try and coax Amm out of her shell.

After leaving the park, he walked back along to Sukhumvit Road and towards the BTS. There was a pub close-by and he decided to stop for a quick refreshment since he'd been out walking around all afternoon, filling his camera with evidence to justify his presence in Thailand to everyone back home. It was an English style pub with a mix of mostly English, American and Australian ex-pats of all ages. 'Pint of Guinness please.'

He watched the dark liquid as it began to fill the glass and wondered how it would be after travelling all the way from Dublin to South East Asia. His dad used to tell him that Guinness couldn't travel. He had a pint in Dublin one time whilst he was still training for the Merchant Navy and remembered how delicious it really was. He thought that surely, they must have another place to produce it, but then the price suggested that perhaps it *did* come all the way from Ireland.

He waited for it to settle before lifting the glass to his lips. It was good. Or maybe he was just very thirsty, but either way he enjoyed it.

A man flopped his rucksack down and wearily took the seat next to him. The stranger ordered a beer and seemed obviously flustered as he spoke to Archie: 'Excuse me,' the accent was American, 'you don't happen to know any good translation services, do you?'

'Oh, no. I'm sorry, I'm just...' he had to think how to word it, 'here on holiday.'

'Oh, okay. No problem. I've just been running around all day. I have this big document to translate for my lawyer. I'm divorcing my bitch of a wife.'

'Sorry, I can't help you.'

The man persisted to talk at Archie, seemingly in the need to vent his frustration about his soon-to-be ex-wife, and at life in general. After a few minutes, he asked about Archie. 'So, what brings you to Bangkok? You're on holiday alone?' It wasn't a totally uncommon thing to find people travelling through Thailand alone, but those types were usually the backpackers around Khoasan Road, and of course the sex tourists.

'Well, yeah. I was here just over a month ago, and then I sort of met someone. So I decided to come back and just see if it goes anywhere, you know?'

'She's not a bargirl is she?'

'Well...' Archie hesitated, still not accustomed to the terminologies and typecasts found there, although it was already fairly obvious.

'Does she work in a bar?' he offered.

'Yes,' Archie said, 'just started actually. I didn't meet her there though.' Archie wanted to add that stipulation as if there was some significance to it.

'Oh man, be careful. Nothing but trouble. You'll never find a good girl in a bar. Take it from me.'

They continued talking and Archie discovered his new friend was Steve from California, who was undergoing a messy divorce as his wife had cunningly acquired property and land at his expense and put it in her name. That meant he had absolutely no claim to it whatsoever. Archie learnt that whilst a foreigner could buy a condo outright, they couldn't own any land. It was quite interesting for him to hear. It seemed like a pretty easy way to con someone if he'd had no choice but to put their property in his wife's name.

Archie was sure there must have been scams running, but knew Amm wasn't doing anything like that, so there was no way he'd associate her with the warning Steve gave him. He remembered that first kiss and the hours that followed and how that kind of tenderness could not ever be faked. She'd never asked him for money and always paid for what she could. He was a mix of despondent and hopeful. Surely, she felt something for him. But what if she didn't anymore? He had a few more days left to find out, he supposed.

Steve continued to talk and kept ordering drinks for him. It appeared like he really needed someone to talk to and Archie didn't mind helping out a fellow human being in distress. Plus, he was being supplied with drink, so he was okay. Before he knew it, he'd drank nine pints, and on an empty stomach. A few hours had passed and the sun was on its way down. He had to think about making a move so he could go to see Amm. First, he'd need to go back to the hotel to drop the camera off; shower and change, and he supposed he should eat something too. He politely concluded his conversation with Steve and wished him the very best of luck, but didn't hold out much hope for him.

He resumed walking and went a short distance along to the mall and BTS station where he'd been before with Amm. Instead of heading straight back to get ready, or at least get something to eat, he was on the prowl for some perfume for her and wandered around the mall knowing that there had to be a Dior counter there somewhere. He could feel a buzz in his head, but actually he was doing okay considering the amount he'd had to drink. He was surprised at himself, but he'd experienced it there before and generally found that he could drink more in Bangkok. Maybe it was the heat – he guessed he probably sweated out most of the alcohol, or because he made a conscious effort to drink a lot of water in that climate. If he was in Scotland, he'd be drunk for sure after nine pints. He couldn't decide if it was a good thing or not.

After doing a few circuits, he finally found what he was looking for. As he had a quick look at the counter, he was approached by a salesperson. She was very pretty and had a nice smile, but not as nice as Amm's, of course. 'Hello sir, how can I help you?'

'Yeah, I was interested in this Miss Dior.'

'Oh, yes, it's so popular right now for all young ladies. Is it for your girlfriend?'

'Yes,' he said simply. *Umm, sort of,* didn't seem like an appropriate response. He was being positive. He paid no heed to Steve's story of woe and was delighted to be buying something for Amm. He had to convince himself that it was going well and that everything he was doing was going to be worthwhile.

The lady was interested and asked a little about him. He explained briefly about how he'd met Amm and came back just to see her. She thought it was incredibly romantic and found him lovely with his constant smile. There was no doubt that whoever was about to get a perfume bought for her was very lucky indeed. She took a card and sprayed it twice before waving it in the air a few times. As soon as he sniffed it, the scent invoked a feeling in him. It took him back to that moment holding her outside the pub on the first night. He recalled the feeling that ran through him and it was one of romance and kissing and intimacy and he was sold.

He really didn't feel like catching the BTS so took a motorcycle taxi to the hotel instead. It was fast and there was plenty of natural cooling. With the buzz in his head, it was certainly more fun to dart and zip through all the traffic and assemble at intersections like the start of a bike race. He grabbed a sandwich and a bottle of water from the convenience store next to the hotel and consumed them in his room. It was already later than he'd planned, but he thought that may have worked to his advantage. He was always hanging around and waiting for her so it may have been better to arrive a little later for a change. That'd surely make her wonder where he was and make her miss him. It was a Friday night, so it'd be busier too and she probably wouldn't feel so crowded, funnily enough.

When he arrived, Amm was already with a customer, so he headed inside not wanting to disturb her. He ordered some food, because the Guinness had washed out his stomach, and the sandwich seemingly vapourised as soon as it went inside him. As he waited, she made a brief escape from her customer to come and see him.

'Hi, how are you?' she asked.

'Yeah, I'm good. How about you?' He produced the bag from under the table. 'I bought you a present.'

'Yes, I'm okay. Can you give me it later please? You eat already?'

'I just ordered something.'

'Okay. I'm just with customer na. I hope you understand. It's just my work.'

'Yeah, it's okay. Don't worry,' he smiled warmly. 'I will eat soon anyway; I'll wait for you until you're not busy.'

He offered to order her something to eat too, but she said she was fine before disappearing back outside to her customer. He didn't like it. Not one bit. But he had to remind himself that it was just her work, and how else can she make decent money? The job was to flirt and fraternise with punters so she could get commission, it was as simple as that. Basically, she just had to talk shit, humour the patrons and look pretty. Not to mention add as many drinks as she could to the customer's bill. Part of the reason she wanted to entertain someone else was because she also didn't want to run up a huge bill for Archie again. She was beginning to feel very guilty about that so wanted to squeeze someone else's wallet for a change, because at the end of the day she still needed the money.

His food came. By the time he was finished, she still hadn't come inside to see him again and he felt quite spare and uncomfortable, so decided to go to her sister's bar. At least he had friends there so he wouldn't be alone. He did know the girls at Sport Spot, but they were expecting Amm to go to him and didn't want to tread on her territory, which meant he was left alone if not for Amm.

When he arrived at Viva bar, he was greeted by a few familiar faces but didn't immediately see Koi. He was beginning to get friendlier with a few of the girls there too. One of Koi's close friends, Wanisa approached him. She thought he was very handsome, but respected the fact that he was involved with Amm. It didn't mean she couldn't sit with him and talk with him and get a few drinks out of him, of course. She ordered a red wine for herself just as Archie received message from Amm: "Where you go? I'm so sorry, it's just my work. Please understand me."

He replied: "It's ok. ☺ I just came to Viva because you were busy. I'll come back later."

"Are you going out tonight? Who did you meet? Is my sister there?" He was a little surprised with the barrage of questions.

"She's upstairs, I'm just sitting with Wan. I don't want to go out somewhere else, I just want to see you. I'll come back later." With his forced positive attitude, he was trying to be cool with her work even though it wasn't easy. The fact that she'd sneak away to message him after he left showed to him that she *did* care though.

"Did you buy her some drinks?" Amm asked.

"Yes, I bought her one so far. Why?" He remembered about the perfume and sent another message: "Also I left your present with Lily." He didn't want to trail it around Bangkok with him.

Wan sat with him with the aim of getting to know him better. It was her intention to help, because it was generally better for all sisters to support each other. She liked him. He spoke politely to her and asked about her too, rather than just talk about himself and how amazing he was. Archie was a breath of fresh air. She asked where Amm was and said that she expected them to come together, but he explained that she was with a customer. Koi came down from upstairs and spoke to Wan in Thai. There was some pointing and gesturing but he couldn't glean anything from the context.

After a couple of drinks with Wan, he received another message from Amm: "I think my customer go soon. When you come back?"

"Ok, I'll come back soon. I'll just finish my drink."

He turned to Wan, 'Her customer will go soon, so I think I'll go back.'

'Okay, it's good. You want me to come with you?'

He thought about it. It might be better if she was there, just in case he was left a little spare again. Perhaps it'd take a bit pressure off, or even eliminate any awkward silences between them. Wan was very friendly and it seemed that she would be able to help his cause, so he agreed. 'Okay, let's go.' He knew it meant a barfine, but he didn't mind. She herself was very happy to go since it was a slow night at Viva and she could escape work to hang out with friends instead.

'I just go to change clothes. Please wait for me. Ten minutes.'

They took a tuk-tuk along to Amm's bar and there was a dispute over the fare by the time they arrived. Wan barked at the driver, gave him sixty baht and told him to 'go away,' but in less kind words. The tuk-tuk driver was obviously trying to extort money from a stupid farang who'd appeared to have found his companion for the night. Amm's customer was still there and Archie started to feel fed up. But at least he was in the vicinity and he'd just have to wait for him to finish up and then he could have her back again. Amm came in to greet him again and spoke with Wan in Thai. She told her it'd be better if they went to another bar first then came back later, since her customer decided to stay longer.

Archie was tired of all the running around and messing about, yet he still persisted. At least the barfine paid off and he had Wan there, so he wasn't just wandering around the Bangkok city streets like a stray dog. *It's just her work,* he told himself again. It was made somewhat better in seeing that she was physically uncomfortable with him being there. The look of shame in her eyes was obvious. He could tell that really, she didn't want to send him away, but she hated Archie seeing her flirting with another man even more.

The other bar was just one block away and had an all female band on the stage. It was bigger than Amm's bar and quite a fancy place. There were comfy red leather couches around the place and it was bathed with blue and lilac lighting. Archie and Wan found a quiet corner to have a couple of cocktails and talk more. 'You know,' she said, 'most girl, they hate to work in the bar. But we have to do it. We do only for money, we have family.'

Archie's eyes wandered the room and saw all the girls paired up with foreigners – mostly considerably older than them and the rest just somewhat older. They hung on the shoulders of the guys and encouraged them to buy drinks. They gave off a party-going façade which seemed utterly shallow and false. The whole thing stunk to him, but that was just how it went. Older men don't mind to part with their cash, so long as they can have a beautiful young girl on their arm. And the girls did it so they could make them believe that they'd go home with them, just in order to get more commission and more money to send back to the family. Most of the girls there were just straight up hostesses, but of course there were some of them coming to arrangements with customers for 'extra-curricular' activities. But then there were other bars in other neighbourhoods where *all* the girls were available to take home.

As the evening progressed, he became increasingly concerned about Amm and the guy she was with. Watching the goings-on there made him sick. He felt even sicker to imagine Amm hanging off that scrawny, pasty piece of shit.

Before heading out, Archie managed to assemble himself a good feeling but that was all gone now. He didn't blame Steve for making him late, because he could have stepped away at any time. His plan to arrive later to make her long for him more had obviously backfired though. Arriving later only allowed her to be available for someone else.

'What's wrong with you?' Wan asked.

Archie shrugged his shoulders and she could tell. It was adorable to her that in a bar full of beautiful ladies, enjoying cocktails with another beautiful girl, all he wanted was to be next to Amm. 'Okay, let's go back. We go to see her. If she still busy, we just wait there, it's okay.'

Amm's customer was still there and it looked like a friend had joined them. He stared them down and tried to listen in as he walked past. They of course had no idea of his connection with her, as the guy lorded himself about trying to impress her.

Amm saw them return and it wasn't long after they sat down before she came charging inside. She was unsteady on her feet and didn't seem as composed as usual. 'Why you come back here??' She didn't ask him delicately or privately. She asked him out loud so all the other customers inside could hear. Wan spoke to her in Thai, obviously trying to diffuse the situation, but she was not for accepting it.

'Why you come here??' she yelled.

'Well, I thought that was the plan?' he replied calmly. 'You said we'd go to that other bar for a while, and then come back.'

'You should not come back here! I don't tell you to come back!' She became increasingly flustered and agitated, stumbling into the tables and chairs as she moved around. Her customer was craning his neck to look for her from his table outside. Archie tried to approach her so they could talk more discretely, but she was trying to avoid him. She did circles around the tables and chairs before heading outside again with Archie, Wan and Ploy the manager following close behind. Now her customer noticed something was happening and stood up. 'YOU GO HOME!' she screamed at the top of her lungs.

Archie had to walk past her customer as he attempted to catch up to her. The guy tried to stand up to Archie and told him, 'I think you should leave her alone, mate,' as if he was some kind of tough guy. But he was a rat of a man and Archie knew he could squash him very easily if he wanted to.

'Well,' he retorted with a firm derisive tone, 'I think you should mind your own fucking business. This is between me and her.' Archie was disgusted as he knew the guy obviously just thought he was some customer she'd rejected.

He caught up to her and took her gently by her scarred arms.

'Amm, what's going on? What did I do wrong? You can talk to me.'

She broke free of his mild grip and started to strike him as hard as she could. She beat him over and over again, thrashing with all the might that she had in her thin arms. Tears and hysteria started to pour out of her with each blow. 'I don't want you come here!! I want you go home!!'

By that time, Wan and Ploy started shouting at Amm and her behaviour. All the other girls slipped away from their customers to see Archie holding her gently by the hips as she continued a barrage of punches and slaps. He stood there quietly taking it all. 'Why you come here??' Wan intercepted and tore Archie away as Ploy was screaming at her. Her customer could see that Archie had some support with Wan and the manager and the other girls, so finally realised there was maybe something more to it than he'd assumed.

Wan hailed a taxi that was mercifully passing at the perfect time and bundled Archie inside. 'We go! She is crazy! I don't know why she do like that!' She gave the driver some directions. 'I never see like that before! How she can do that to you? She is no good!'

Archie was destroyed. Wan continued to talk to him – partly comforting him and partly complaining about Amm in disbelief, but all he could hear were the crushing words ringing round and round like a nightmarish echo in his head. All he could feel were the blows around his face, head, neck and chest. Yet, the punches and slaps were not even a fraction of the pain he felt in his heart.

They made their way back to Soi 11 because she could always find friends there. It was just after closing time for Viva so Wan tried calling Koi but she didn't get any answer. As their taxi took a right-turn across Sukhumvit road, she spotted Koi eating at the side of the road. She leapt over Archie and lowered the taxi window, shouting to her as they continued down the soi, trying to tell her what happened. They eventually managed to reach each other by phone, but by that time Archie and Wan had arrived at a club. She wanted to take him away from Amm, but that was the entirety of her hasty plan so far. Perhaps a nightclub was not the best place to overcome what just happened, or then maybe it was. Essentially, she didn't know what else to do with him.

Archie was lost. He was distraught. Now he stood in a club filled with agony, whilst teardrops fell from his eyes. He was embarrassed about whether people could see him cry, and felt like a complete fool about Amm. Why the hell did he fly to the other side of the planet just to get that? He felt so stupid.

They had a table close to the stage and she spoke to some of her friends as they came and went, but it was just the two of them. Of course, she had no idea that she'd brought him to the same club Amm brought him on the first night they met. But it was a big draw in that area so it was an obvious choice.

They ordered a bottle of whisky and Wan tried to distract him from what happened. She moved her alluring body next to his and danced with him. Archie went through the motions, but didn't feel much like dancing. Although, he certainly couldn't deny that it was nice to have someone close and taking care of him. She got closer and closer still as they held each other. Her body felt nice against his and he enjoyed the comfort she gave him.

The music, whisky and heartache flowed through him like torrent waves and in one moment, their eyes met in the dark of the club. She leaned in to kiss him. If Amm hadn't happened then he'd have been happy to kiss her. In fact, he'd have been more than happy. Wan was beautiful and sweet. She spoke to him tenderly with her soft, sexy voice and her waist felt supple and soothing. But he couldn't escape Amm. As Wan closed in on him, he tilted his head forward and rested his forehead on hers, leaving mere millimetres between their lips. 'I'm sorry. I can't.' He shifted his head to over her shoulder, wrapped his arms around her and held her tight. 'I'm sorry. It's not that I don't want to, but I just can't.'

'No, it's okay. You don't be sorry to me.'

It wasn't really part of her plan but she just couldn't help it. Something about how broken he was made her want to console him in any way she could – never mind the fact that she *did* find him very attractive, not just in looks, but in personality. He deserved more, and for a moment she wanted to give it to him. She wasn't offended or upset. In fact, she thought even more of him for turning her down.

'You are the dream,' she said.

'What do you mean?'

'You are real gentleman. I never see someone like you before. Amm don't know what she do tonight, and she don't know what she lost. I'm so sorry for that.'

Archie placed a kiss on her forehead and held her close again. 'Thank you,' he said.

'For what?' she asked.

'For being here. For taking care of me tonight.'

Chapter Seven
บทที่เจ็ด

Archie awoke face-down on the bed, soaked in sweat, with a massive thump in his head and an unrelenting dryness in his mouth. He looked around his hotel room and he was alone. He was also fully dressed. The fridge door was wide open and there was a trail of shoes and socks on the floor which led from the door to the bed. He didn't manage to put the keycard in the slot by the door, so there had been no air conditioning all night, which was why he'd sweated so much.

After the club, he and Wan had something to eat and each took a taxi home. He suddenly recalled the events of the previous night and a rush of agony tore through his whole body. It was like a bad dream to him, except he knew it was real enough. He wondered if he'd made a mistake to reject Wan, but either way, the moment was already gone and it didn't matter one way or another.

He checked his phone and found a long message full of auto-correct errors, typos and nonsense from him to Amm, explaining how he felt and how hurt he was. He didn't remember writing it. It wasn't even written in a nasty way, it was still full of care and politeness. He was soft and pleading and merely described how she'd ripped his heart out and tore it into a million pieces. He could have been angry; he could have scolded her or called her names. He had every right to do so, yet he didn't. She read it, but there was no reply.

After a while, he got up and went for a shower. He stood for an excessively long time with the heavy drops pelting him. He wished he could vomit to expel everything from the previous night – not just the alcohol – but he couldn't. He felt sick for sure, but he mostly wanted to find a way to purge himself from what he was feeling. He increased the heat little by little to see how hot he could take it. If he couldn't vomit, then maybe he could melt the feeling away, he thought. But that didn't work either.

There were only two days left until his flight home. He thought perhaps he ought to just hide in his room until it was time to go, because he simply couldn't face anything else. The massive amount of alcohol from the whole of the previous day left a huge upset in his stomach. He watched TV and considered having something to eat but found it difficult to move; as if experiencing full mental and physical shutdown.

His phone rang, which forced him to eventually move. It was Amm. He didn't know whether he should answer or not but as soon as it stopped vibrating, he regretted not picking up. He was given a second chance when she rang again. Archie had no idea what he was going to say, or what she might have to say to him. Perhaps he could get an apology and that might soften the blow before he went home forever. Or at the very least he'd have a chance to tell her goodbye. He picked up.

'Hello?' she said tentatively.

'Hi.'

'Archie…how are you?'

'I've been better,' he admitted.

'About last night…I don't know…I'm just…I have problem na.' She prepared what to say before the call but suddenly words failed her – in both Thai and English.

'I have…broken head. You know…I'm so sorry about what I do.'

A door opened on Amm's end of the line and he recognised the other voice. It was Koi speaking very sternly indeed. She obviously heard that Amm was awake and wanted to have a firm word with her.

'Archie…I can call you back?'

He shrugged his shoulders and then realised she wouldn't be able to see that. 'Yeah,' he conceded.

'Okay, I call you again na. Call soon.'

Broken head or not, Archie wondered whether he should forgive her. He cursed his soft heart and the way he didn't have it in him to hold any resentment against her. It was something, he thought, that she had the decency to call and apologise. His heart may have been shredded into a million pieces but he was gathering up each piece just to hand back to her again.

About forty minutes passed before the call back came and he had almost given up waiting.

'Hi,' she said. 'I'm sorry, I just talk with my sister.'

'Yeah…'

'I want to say, I'm so sorry for last night. I don't know if you still want to see me again. But my sister say, maybe you can come for dinner. She will come and my other sister.'

'Where?' he asked.

'Come my work?'

'Come to your work again? I don't think so.'

'Please. I hope you will come. I'm sorry I cannot day off, but now I have problem with my boss about last night too.' He thought about it for a while. He wanted to point blank refuse, but was unable to materialise a 'no'.

'Please Archie. I'm so sorry. I don't want you go. I want you come see me. Pleeeeeaaase.'

He regularly had trouble matching her actions with the things that came out of her mouth, but he thought he may as well go. He was already at rock bottom, so supposed he had nothing else to lose. 'Okay. What time?'

'7 o'clock. It's okay for you?'

'Yeah. And you won't have a customer?'

'No, tonight no customer, just waiting you for dinner.'

'Okay. Just...please...don't do something like that again.'

'No, I will not. I never do again like last night. I'm so sorry...'

Archie slept a few more hours and by the time he woke up it was already time to get ready. He didn't have time to consider whether or not to go. Part of him thought about just not turning up, but he could never do that, not after agreeing to go. He didn't know if it was completely stupid of him. The previous night he considered it to be over, but when she called, he thought there might still be a chance. If there was, he had to go and find out.

When he arrived, she greeted him warmly. Amm had been hiding behind the bar avoiding customers whilst waiting for him. She ushered him to a table and Koi was already there. She had in her hand a small paper bag which had a couple of bracelets inside. One had an anchor on it, which was a nod to his work, and the other was a smart leather one with a steel clasp which complimented the style of his watch. He was so surprised and impressed. It really seemed like she wanted to make it up to him. The gifts were not just random things she'd picked up, they seemed very well thought out. If he could pick any two, he'd have picked the same.

Some of the girls gathered around during the gift giving just to look on. They were all rooting for him. In the times he'd been there and spoken to them, they'd enjoyed that level of respect and politeness that Koi and Wan had found. He was never sleazy or inappropriate, and he was focused only on Amm. 'And I wear your perfume tonight,' she said. 'Thank you so much na.' She tapped the corner of her neck and invited him in. 'You can smell.'

All the girls giggled and wooed when he nuzzled his nose into her neck. She shuddered hard down her spine, but it was a good shudder. It was a shudder that made her feel whole and loved and appreciated. His warm breath on her neck was a pleasure that she was avoiding and trying to deprive herself of. She did feel a compulsion to grab him and make him linger in the nook of her neck some more, but she had to resist.

Whilst they waited for her other sister to arrive, he ordered food for them as well as extra food for her workmates to snack at as they were passing. They were served by Lily, who he'd started to become more familiar with. She was working at Viva the night he met Amm, and remembered seeing him there. She thought he was very handsome and that Amm was very lucky. She moved to Sport Spot because it was much more casual and she didn't have to wear a fancy dress every night.

Archie was aware of there being some kind of affiliation between the bars despite them having different owners. That was what led Amm to get the job there through her sister, and allowed Lily to change bars too.

Amm and Lily knew each other well, but weren't especially close. Lily and Koi were close however, as they had already worked together for a while at Viva. The manager Ploy, was also Lily's aunty who had recently returned to work after the relationship with her boyfriend and sponsor came to an end. He was sending her money every month so that she didn't need to work, but she also genuinely loved him. When she found out she wasn't the only one he was sending money to and not the only one he was fucking, she couldn't accept that. She was happy to have his financial support, but for her, love and commitment were always more important.

A few beads of sweat started collecting on his brow. 'You hot?' she asked, whilst pulling some tissues out of the dispenser on the table. She blotted his brow tenderly and delicately. Whenever she did that it felt like sheer bliss to him. She then took a small powder out of Koi's handbag, scrubbed some between her hands and applied it to his face. It was the first time he'd ever had his face powdered. It was quite unusual for him, but there was no way he was going to tell her to stop. He hoped it wasn't just an over-correction because of guilt. He prayed it was the real treatment and the normal way in which she wanted to care for him. He started to justify the previous night to himself, even though it still hung around in the air like a huge black cloud. Maybe she just had to blow off steam and get that out of her system. Perhaps that night was the catalyst they needed to get their relationship on the right track.

When her other sister arrived, he was introduced to her. 'This my sister, P-Joy.'

'P-Joy?' he asked.

'Yes,' she nodded and smiled. The 'P' prefix was associated with those who are older or who you want to show respect to in Thai culture.

As they drank and ate, he noticed what a great trick the powder was as it really seemed to stop him from sweating. P-Joy talked to him and her English was very good. They got to know each other and she very quickly approved of Archie. She liked the way he looked at Amm and could see the way she responded to him. At one point, Amm was fetching more drinks at the bar and Joy was at the bathroom. Koi spoke to him, 'My sister Joy, she like you. It's good for you. You know, Amm she listen to her for everything. She not listen to me same because we only half-sister. But she and Joy full sister.' Archie perked up as things finally seemed hopeful. That old adage of *what's worth having never comes easy*, came to mind. Maybe that was the case with her, he thought.

The night wore on and P-Joy had to go home to her husband. Koi left with her, which meant it was just the two of them alone. The other girls had made themselves scarce too so that they could have some time alone. They seemed to really click that night. There was no uncomfortable searching for something to say. They somehow understood each other better and everything was a lot more natural than ever before. Amm began to soften around him as they were left alone.

80

She couldn't hide behind her sister or friends any longer and she didn't want to.

She had to not judge Archie by her past experiences. Her previous boyfriend, who she was madly in love with, had a wife and kids. When she found out, she fell to pieces. That's when she started to cut herself. She couldn't understand how for more than two years, he managed to keep her on the side. The fact that she was never anything more than the mistress was too much for her to handle. Her boyfriend knew from the start and just made a complete fool of her. He let her talk about marriage and the future whilst having absolutely no intention of following through with anything.

They drank more and Amm got closer and closer, but they were almost out of time as the bar was about to close. The night had been perfect for him and it was better late than never, he supposed. It was just a great shame that he had only one more day in Bangkok after reaching that point with her, but there wasn't a great deal he could do about that. He thought about taking her to a club as a way to extend the evening, but also, he didn't want to go. He just wanted to stay somewhere quiet with her and talk, or just sit and look into her eyes or snuggle her.

They went for some street food. She ordered for him like usual and placed things on his plate. 'And what's that?' he asked pointing at something on her plate.

'No, it's not for you. So spicy. I think you cannot eat it,' she smiled.

'Okay, I'll listen to you.'

He wasn't very hungry because dinner was big and he'd picked at things throughout the night too. He mostly sat drinking water and watched with admiration as she did such a simple thing as eat. Her phone was on the table and she chatted with her sister, tapping the screen with her pinkie whilst balancing chopsticks on her fingers and a soup spoon in the other hand. She kept the phone flat on the table, in a way that he could see easily who she was talking with and he appreciated that. They stayed for a while longer, just chatting and drinking and enjoying each others company.

Eventually, she got up and paid for their food. 'Okay, I think I go home now. I'm so tired.'

'Okay,' he conceded. Of course he was upset that the evening came to an end, but at least he'd thoroughly enjoyed himself and the whole experience had been positive for a change. In the taxi, Amm held his hand tight and at times placed it between her legs if she had to write back to Koi. She still wanted to feel him touching her and despite it being quite high up between her legs, it was not a sexual thing at all, it was a comfort thing. The inside of her upper thigh was smoother than silk and he had never felt such soft skin ever before. As they approached the hotel, she enquired about his accommodation: 'You like the hotel mai? It looks so nice. I see it everyday, but I never go inside.'

'Yeah, it's really nice. Room is very nice. Big, clean, new. I like it.'

'That's good. Umm,' pressure had been building up in her bladder for a while, 'I think, maybe I need to go toilet na. They have in the lobby?'

'Yeah, they do.'

She paid the taxi, and at the point where he usually got out alone, she followed him out. He didn't get ahead of himself though, she was just going to the toilet and then she'd take another taxi back to her place. They'd been drinking after all and then sat outside for a while, so she was probably in great need. Plus, it was a chance to satisfy her curiosity. Not just from the fact that she passed it every day, but because it was a glimpse into Archie's life too.

They entered the hotel and the bellboy recognised him, gave him a nod and smiled warmly as usual. He spotted Archie's companion but politely didn't draw any conclusions about it. Amm headed to the toilet and Archie sat patiently on the duck egg velvet corded sofa opposite the lady's room.

She was there for several minutes. And then a few minutes more. He started to grow concerned and got to his feet. He felt very conspicuous indeed in the big echoing lobby in the middle of the night. No one else had come or gone and he was sure there was no one else in the toilet at that time of night. If there had been, they would have surely been finished by that time too. He started to knock softly on the outside door. 'Amm? Are you there?' He tried again. 'Amm?' He pushed the door open ajar. She stood at the mirror with tissues at her face as she cried uncontrollably. He didn't know if he should intrude on her, but he couldn't just stand there and let her shed tears alone. 'Amm, I'm coming in, okay?' He knew he spoke loudly and clearly enough for her to hear, whilst trying to not alert the staff. 'Okay?' If there was no objection, he supposed it was alright. He entered the lady's room and she looked at him through her wet brown eyes. 'What's wrong?' he asked.

He approached her slowly and made it obvious that he was going to hold her. She was as volatile and unpredictable as ever and he didn't want to upset her any more. He was preparing for another beating, but there was no one else who he'd rather be beat up by. 'Come here.' He pulled her in close and held her tightly as she cried her tears away. 'Will you tell me what's wrong?'

'Nothing…just me. I'm so stupid girl. I'm no good girl.' She looked up at him. 'I don't know why you like me. I'm no good for you.'

'I think I'll decide that. What's this all about? You know you can tell me anything.'

'Just me. I'm broken head.'

'Stop being so hard on yourself.' He nuzzled her head into his chest and continued talking over her shoulder as he held her tight. 'You know, you make it hard for me. I see you crying and acting like this and you don't tell me what's wrong. It makes it difficult for me to give you the right advice. But what I can say is that no matter what's happened, or even if you've done bad things before, it doesn't mean the rest of your life has to be like that. Just because your past has been bad, it doesn't mean the future needs to be.'

'Now's your chance, Amm. You could take control. And if you're not strong enough to do it alone, then let me help you. I'll support you and protect you.' He broke their embrace so that he could look her in the eyes. 'Your happiness...it's so important to me. I'll do anything I can to chase the dark clouds away and bring sunshine into your life.'

The warmth of his words and smile was enough to dry her tears.

'Why you always so good to me, Archie?'

'Just because...I want you to be okay. I really care about you.'

She was clearly troubled and whilst most men might have taken that as a sign to clear off, Archie did not. He fell in love with her the moment their lips touched across the table at Viva bar. There was no way he could just run from her, that wasn't him at all. 'You want me to call your sister? Maybe she can come to pick you up? Or I can take you home.'

'No.'

'So...what do you want to do? If you feel upset, you should just go to sleep. Things will seem better tomorrow. Believe me.'

'I don't want to go home.'

'You want to go out? We can take a taxi back.'

'No, I don't want to go somewhere.'

Archie ran out of ideas. 'So...what do you want?'

'I don't want to go somewhere else. You said I should sleep…I want sleep. Maybe I can just stay in your room? It's okay with you?'

Archie had no idea of her intention but was worried about taking advantage of the situation. In her current state, he knew nothing was likely to happen and that was fine. He just wanted her to feel better. If he wasn't okay with any of it then he should have ran away a long time ago. He couldn't be presumptuous, so planned to sleep on the sofa and she would sleep alone in the bed. He wanted to take care of her, so it had to be that way. It didn't seem like a *I want to stay with you tonight*, she just said that she wanted to sleep, and he supposed as quickly as possible. No doubt she was exhausted and upset and couldn't face even the fairly short distance home. Her state of mind was more important to him than his wants and needs, even though he burned like wildfire for her. 'Of course you can stay. I will sleep on the sofa.'

They made their way to the room he opened the door and dropped the keycard in the slot. The air conditioning unit and lights clicked on. 'You think…it's okay if I take a shower?' she asked.

'Yeah, sure you can.'

Whilst she was in the bathroom, he looked out a t-shirt and a pair of fisherman's pants that he bought during his island visit last time. They were a one-size-fits-all type of thing, so she'd be able to fit into them alright. He hadn't worn them yet that trip, and thought about how far he'd come from a carefree tourist in Thailand in such a short time. Things had gone from nothing to serious so quickly. It was funny, he thought, since he was actually deliberately trying to *not* get involved with anyone when he came, but he'd already thoroughly fucked that up, he thought. He told her about the clothes as she was in the shower and left them by the door.

It took all his might to stay around the corner as she emerged from the bathroom with only a towel wrapped round her perfect slender body. Holding her hair up and with beads of water still rolling over her soft olive skin, it was a good thing that Archie couldn't see her. Drops of water shed from her and landed on the floor as she picked up the clothes and went back inside to put them on.

It was hardly the most flattering of outfits, but for Archie she was amazing. She looked cute and charming. It was a closeness to her which he'd obviously never experienced before, but had been longing for. He didn't want to revel in the freshly made-up Amm who was falsely upbeat and trying to party at work, because so many had seen that one. Archie wanted to immerse himself in the one that was currently trying to put her hair up into a bun in the full-length mirror next to the bathroom door. He was very happy that she decided to stay, even if nothing was going to happen, because he just loved to have her close to him and under his protection.

She watched him take a pillow from the bed and place it on the sofa. 'I can sleep there. You pay for the room and you don't sleep on the bed. It's no good na,' she said.

'No, you are my guest. I want you to be comfortable. Don't worry.'

He quickly went for a shower and by the time he came out she was already in bed, but not yet asleep. He went across to tuck her in and stroked her forehead soothingly for a while before softly placing a kiss on it. Each stroke that she enjoyed seemed to wipe away some of her anguish. He wanted to kiss her lips hard and throw the covers off her, yet his huge desire was only outdone by how much he cared for and loved her. She was right there, but he had to not touch her.

'Goodnight Amm. Sweet dreams.' He had to swallow the *'I love you,'* from the end of his sentence. He was more than willing to admit it of course, but he didn't want to load her up with more things to think about.

'Goodnight Archie.' He always liked the way she said his name. It wasn't just because of how he felt about her; there was a certain sweetness to it because of her accent. It wasn't *Archie*, but more like *Ah-chee*. It was adorable.

'Thank you na,' she said, 'for everything. You really take care of me so good.'

She felt another compulsion to reach out and pull him close, but she was much too scared to do it. And the way he tucked her in actually made her feel so comfortable and secure that she didn't want to move.

He switched off all the lights and stared at the ceiling above the sofa for a long time before drifting off.

Sleep eluded her. She felt guilty for stealing his bed, and was preoccupied with the events of the night. Staying over wasn't really her intention, but when she was in the nice comfortable and well-appointed lobby, something inside her compelled her to stay. Following her episode in the lady's bathroom and Archie's pep talk, she certainly wanted to remain by his side somehow, because he was always able to make her feel better.

The idea of sleeping with him was obviously on her mind, but she wasn't very experienced and was also not in the habit of jumping into bed with someone. From the lobby to the room was too fast for her. She could feel the restraint he exercised whilst tucking her in though, and even though she still wasn't ready for him at that time, the way he behaved made her want him more. Amm knew that Archie was being wholesome and polite and understood that she would have to be the one to make the first move. Whilst he was over her and stroking her head, she felt the onset of desire, but didn't have the courage to make an advance on him. As an hour or so had ticked round the clock, not only had she acclimated to the surroundings, she'd gotten used to the thought of something happening between them. Now she was left feeling restless in bed and craving him.

She got up to pace around the room a little. In her travels, she went to the fridge and had a drink of water. The stirring and the light of the open fridge door woke him from his light slumber and he sat up. 'Hey. You okay?'

'Little bit,' she said.

She came across and sat next to him on the sofa. 'I think you can sleep in the bed na.'

'I'm okay here. Don't worry.'

'But…I want you stay in the bed. Just stay next to me.'

'Oh, okay. Only if you're sure.'

'Yes, I'm sure.'

They settled in and both felt much more comfortable. Now, neither of them could sleep though. He turned onto his side to look at her and swept some hair off her face. She couldn't help the smile that emerged. Something about his touch was so tender and gentle – it was always bliss when his hands were on her. She turned to lean on her side facing back at him. They watched one another as if trying to find things on each others faces in the low light that they hadn't ever seen before. It wasn't awkward in the slightest though. They were both exactly where they wanted to be.

'Are you not tired?' he asked quietly.

'Yes. I'm tired. But…I can't sleep.'

'Yeah. Me too. Something on your mind?' he asked delicately.

She considered opening up, until her train of thought was overridden by another: 'So…tomorrow night you go home?' He nodded regretfully. 'Are you…you think you come back here?'

'Well…it's up to you. I only came back here for you, so you have to decide. You don't need to tell me now. I'll go to work for a few months. You can think about it. And if you want me to come back, I will.'

'Yes. I want you come back,' she immediately replied.

'You don't need to decide now. You can think about it.'

'But I already know I want you here.'

He smiled from the very origin of his soul. She was broken, but Archie had the right stuff to mend her. The only times she'd felt fine was when she was alone with him. Whenever she stopped over-thinking things, she knew exactly who she was and how she felt about him.

He couldn't help it, but he placed a small kiss on her lips as they lay inches from each other. She gave him one back. More small kisses went back and forth for a while before slowly intensifying. Archie caressed her face in his hands as the kissing escalated. She began to remove her t-shirt, interrupting the kissing for a couple of seconds. He pulled her in close and there was no longer any gap between them in bed.

She was worried about him going away again and wanted to give him something of a parting gift. She didn't want him to look at, or think about other girls when he was away. How was he supposed to do that if she had only been bad to him and never achieved such a level of intimacy? Not to mention how he was all she wanted at that moment too. He stretched over to his bedside table for a condom. He'd put them there at the start of the trip, but as the days went, he thought he'd never get to use them at all. He was probably the only farang to stay in Bangkok for so long and never had a need for them so far.

Archie and Amm were not just having sex. It wasn't even just making love. It was comfort and caring and a culmination of his faithful longing and her raw despair and desire for him. It was the apology she wanted to give him and the compassion he wanted to show her. He wanted to fix her and show her that there were real men in the world and that he was just that for her. It was the joy and contentment that they both had been searching for.

Afterwards, they lay awake for a while in one another's arms whilst the dopamine was still coursing through their bodies. As Amm was on top of him, she pressed her ear against his chest. 'What you doing?' he asked.

'I just listen your heart,' she said. 'I just check you still alive.' She laughed innocently at her own joke.

'I'm alive for sure. I've never felt more alive in my entire life.

Chapter Eight

บทที่แปด

Sun peeked round the skyscraper next door and broke into their room. Archie woke up to use the toilet and when he came back, he noticed her phone flashing and buzzing and then stop. There were dozens of missed calls, but he couldn't read the Thai writing so didn't know who it was. He settled into bed again and she stirred. Her eyes were still closed, but she reached for him and pulled his arms around her. Her phone flashed and buzzed yet again. 'Amm,' he said softly, 'your phone.'

'Huh?' she murmured.

'Someone is trying to call you. Many times.'

She reached over and grabbed it. 'It's my sister.'

Amm sat up in bed with the covers bundled up in front, but her back was exposed. The smooth line of her spine led down to her soft cheeks, which were somewhat enveloped by the mattress. He could make out two dimples at the bottom of her back which he didn't have the chance to notice the night before. She spoke in Thai for a while and Archie heard his name once or twice. Amm didn't tell her sister that she wasn't coming home or where she was. Koi had been up half the night worried sick, but had to console herself and assume that she was with Archie. She trusted him, but didn't expect Amm to spend the night. It was still quite early for her to do such a thing she thought, and it was a little out of character.

After hanging up, she slumped back down and rolled towards him. Through bleary eyes, she admired his handsome face, as a fresh smile shone from it uninterruptedly. She really wanted to tell him good morning, but somehow felt embarrassed. The words seemed to stick in her throat and she choked heavily on them.

'How was your sleep?' he asked.

'Yes, it's good. This bed so nice.'

'Oh, just the bed?' he joked.

He brought her some water before she even realised how thirsty she was. The cool liquid felt good as it rewetted her palette and trickled down her throat. She knew she had to get up, but really didn't want to move. She didn't want to leave Archie's side, but of course she had to go home. Koi gave her a reprimand for letting her worry all night, so she had to take some food to her to make up for it. 'Can I go to shower?' she asked.

'Of course you can. You don't need to ask me.'

'So…tonight you can come to see me? I'm sorry I have to work again. But my boss still angry.'

94

'Okay. I understand.'

'Better if you come early.' She reached for his hand and squeezed it tight. 'What you do today?'

'I need to pack my bags,' he said regretfully.

'What time your flight?'

'3 a.m. tomorrow morning.'

Misery washed over him as he felt it was so unfair that he had to leave. It was incredibly frustrating to have those perfect nights with Amm only on the night before he left Thailand every time. It was as if he ought to fly somewhere else and come back frequently for a couple of days at a time in order to increase the frequency of great nights with her. That was ridiculous, of course, but it was just a thought that ran through his mind.

He walked her out of the hotel and towards the motorcycle taxi stand at the end of the block. 'So…I'll see you tonight,' he said.

'Yes. See you,' she said with a bright smile. 'I'll send you message na.'

Amm was already getting on the motosai so it was too late to give her a kiss, unless he wanted to get very close to the driver as well. He didn't know whether she'd be comfortable with it either. Now they were out in a public place, maybe she wasn't at ease with letting everyone see just yet. In fact, she *was* ready for it, but in the end it didn't happen.

He went to sleep for another hour or so. He was exhausted physically, mentally, emotionally. It had been a trip of extremes – extreme emotions, expenditure, alcohol consumption, disappointment and then elation. In a way it was great. Even with all the lows, then came the highs. It was a kind of life he'd never experienced before. He'd just been living a very normal and standard existence up until then. Now he truly was living, he thought.

After waking up, he felt he should start preparing his luggage, but simply couldn't bear the thought. Rather than packing, all he wanted was to find her a red rose as a parting token. He searched online for florists and made his way to the closest high-end looking one.

A small bell hung on the inside door handle and it jingled as he pushed the door open. In the middle of the shop was a huge display, stacked with all different types of flowers. Despite the shop being cool, there were a few chiller cabinets – the type you'd expect to find in a supermarket, containing milk, cheese or butter. There were thick plastic curtains on them so he supposed the flowers in there were the more rare and expensive ones. All the writing was in Thai and he was a little concerned that he wouldn't be able to ask for what he wanted. He supposed he could just try to point at what he wanted though.

It was expensive for Thailand, but the variety and price compared to home was outstanding. It seemed inadequate going all the way there just to buy her a single red rose, but he wanted to keep it low-key. Yet, at the same time he wanted to get her a real quality one. The rose he bought for her when he first came back was just from a street vendor next to the BTS station and it was a little feeble. It was all he could do with the time available to him that day though.

The assistant asked him something in Thai and when he asked for, 'A single red rose, please,' she went through to the back. Someone else came out who was able to speak English. After repeating his request, she came to the stack of flowers in the middle. Archie was dressed well and she could appreciate he was trying to make a romantic gesture with a single red rose, rather than it being all he could afford. She excused herself for a moment, retrieved another half dozen or so from the back and invited him to choose one. They were just slightly fuller and more beautiful than the ones out front and he appreciated her consideration. After selecting his favourite, the florist clipped the thorns off, wrapped the stem with a beautiful smooth grey paper and tied a bow around it. She only wanted to charge him the same as the price posted out front, but he rounded the price up anyway and attempting to say *thank you* in Thai: 'Khob khun krap.' There was a stack of business cards on the counter and he lifted one off the stack. 'For next time,' he said.

Upon his return to the hotel, he reluctantly packed his bags, leaving aside just his change of clothes for the evening as well as a change of clothes for travelling. Because of his job, he always felt like he was living out of a suitcase and disliked it more and more. Sure, from the outside it seemed very glamorous, with flights to different places all the time, but the reality of it was that he just wanted to stay in one place with someone he loved. He enjoyed the job though and really couldn't ever imagine himself in a nine-to-five. It just didn't fit him well at all. With a run-of-the-mill job, there would be no way he could just up and fly to Thailand when he felt like it either. Of course, when he was at work, he really was away, but that's just how it was and to him it was worth it.

He was almost finished getting ready and received a message from her: "Hi. Where are you? What time you come?"

"I'm leaving the hotel soon. See you there."

When he arrived, it was obvious that she had been patiently waiting for him. The single red rose managed to keep its hydration in the heat of the day and during the taxi ride there. He presented it to her and she smiled and smirked.

'Archie, you so sweet na.'

'It's not much. I just wanted to bring you something.'

'Yes. I like it. Thank you so much.'

'What are your favourite flowers?'

'Yes, I like rose so much. But pink, it's my favourite colour.'

'Ah, okay. Sorry.'

'No! Not sorry. It's beautiful.'

'Next time pink…okay?'

'Yes,' she tilted her head and smiled at him, 'next time.'

He didn't want to drink too much considering he had a long way to travel come the early hours, and didn't want to stink of alcohol, or generally feel lousy for the flights. Conversation was a little awkward and neither of them really knew what to say. It was a different type of awkward than it had ever been before, though. He knew he had to work for a few months and they'd only just started out. Despite the previous night, they were really in their infancy and didn't know if their bond would last the time apart. She was still potentially unstable too. At least he felt that they were finally on the right track and was delighted they reached the point that they did. It enabled him to go home with a positive feeling, which he didn't think would be possible just a few days beforehand. His persistence and patience seemed to have paid off and he was tremendously glad that all his efforts finally amounted to something.

Amm knew she had feelings for him, but she was still in turmoil with herself. One of the reasons she'd been acting out was because she felt so much pressure about the whole situation and didn't know how to handle it. It was very overwhelming for her to know that he was there just to see her. It would have been much better for her if he was just working and living there, then they could hang out and see where it went, or rather, there wouldn't be a deadline for their time together. They'd have some days to themselves and just meet up whenever they were free. Knowing there was a time constraint was very uncomfortable because she was unsure how to cope with her feelings, not to mention how she really didn't want to end up wasting Archie's time or fall short of his expectations.

Since she'd started working in a bar, she felt ashamed of herself too. Granted, it wasn't that every single customer was a dirtbag, but it was still a degrading job. Most of the girls were repulsed by customers too, but they seemed to cope with it better than Amm. They all just had to do what they had to for money. With a normal job, their salary would be so small and the work would probably be much harder. Putting aside the effects of alcohol on the body, to sit and drink in a bar was hardly *hard work*, and they could make so much more money doing that. It was a twisted way of life, but that's just how it was – and a common reality in South East Asia. Amm had real trouble reconciling with the job and especially hated Archie seeing her there.

She really didn't want him to go. He'd been strong, calm and devoted to her and she'd never been treated quite so well before. He protected her and built her up, but now he had to go far away.

Ultimately, there were aspects of each others jobs which neither of them liked, but they had to accept it and let time play it out.

'So, when you will go back to work?' she asked.

'I'm not sure, but when I get home, I'll tell them I'm ready to travel. I think they've got a ship lined up for me in about two weeks. But sometimes it changes.'

'Okay. But you have internet there?'

'Yeah. It's not the same as normal internet, usually it's very slow, and sometimes there's no signal.'

'Okay. But…we can chat mai?'

'Yes, we can.'

He kept an eye on the time as it began to run out. His flight was at 3 a.m. so he wanted to leave the hotel about eleven o'clock. He still had to swing by Viva to say goodbye to Koi and the girls there too.

'After you finish work, you come back here, right?' Amm asked.

'Well, yeah. Like I said before…only if you want me to.'

'Yes, I want.' She reached for his hand and held it softly under the table. 'I will wait for you.'

He didn't want to ask her to wait, but he did want to know whether she would or not. The fact that she came up with it all by herself made him very happy indeed. 'Okay,' he said with a smile. He wanted to tell her that he loved her, but knew he had to keep it cool and keep his composure, but it eroded him like crashing waves against tall cliffs. Holding that in was like an itch that he just couldn't scratch. He'd learned how to handle her during each occasion they spent together and knew that professing his love would pile the pressure on. He always had to be patient with her and this instance was no different. He was trying to be very careful about how he left it and needed her to feel comfortable and happy, rather than stressed about whether she needs to say it back to him and the implications thereafter.

They talked a little more, but soon it was time to go. He called Lily over to settle the bill. Whilst they'd been sitting there, Amm had pulled his hand between her legs in that way that she liked and was very upset that he had to remove it. It left a cold spot.

'Are you go home now?' Lily asked.

'Yes.'

'Okay. So nice to see you. See you next time ka,' she said politely.

101

'Yes. And…you please take care of her for me.'

He felt a thump in his throat and a moistening of the eyes as the words tumbled out of his mouth, but he had to be strong. He felt like crying, because deep down, no one knew what was going to happen. Maybe that would be the last time he ever saw her. Maybe after a few weeks, she'd get bored of waiting. Or maybe she did truly love him and they'd have to suffer the time apart until he could return. In any guise it wasn't easy. He couldn't ever remember being so continuously close to tears or crying whenever he was in Scotland. He was just a normal guy going about his business and living his life. But the goings-on of Bangkok brought it out of him – a full spectrum emotions, thoughts, disappointments and joy.

Archie said his goodbyes to some of the other girls and of course to Ploy. Amm saw him to the door, at which point Ploy told her to see him off properly and that she could take her time. They left the bar hand-in-hand and ambled along to the end of the soi. She was glad, because she wanted to be out of sight from the other girls in order to give him a goodbye kiss. He held her tight where the soi met Sukhumvit Road, with the usual swarm of cars, taxis, trucks, motorbikes and hundreds of people passing by. Whilst they locked lips, she didn't mind if other people saw, because their kiss was more important than her modesty. The sky overhead was filled with swirling dark clouds and it looked like the city was due for some heavy rainfall. Some people walked past and stared, thinking that it was still a little early to see that sort of thing in the middle of the street. She didn't care though whilst he didn't even notice.

'Safe flight na. Tell me when you get to airport, and when you get home please.'

'Yes, I will. You take good care of yourself Amm.' He caressed the side of her face and she kissed the inside of his hand. She was trying hard to not cry, but her eyes were welling up. When she blinked her gorgeous eyelids, tears were pushed out and ran down her soft cheeks. He wiped the teardrops rolling down her face before placing one last kiss on her forehead. 'I'll see you when I'm back,' he said.

He hailed a taxi and she stood waving at the side of the road as he drove away from her. When he arrived at Viva bar, he saw Koi and broke down embarrassingly. He was quickly hurried into a corner table where he was the least conspicuous and she offered him some tissues. 'Ooooii. No, don't cry. You man, you not cry.'

'I know, but I'm going to miss her so much. I don't want to go.'

'No, it's okay. You don't think too much na.'

All the girls understood him and thought that it was incredibly touching that he would cry after his goodbye with Amm. They were pleased that he came to say goodbye too. Over that time, they'd started to value him as a customer and then as a friend. With his type of personality and all the things that had been going on, they looked out for him and were protective over him. And even when things weren't going well, he didn't try it on with anyone else, or go somewhere else to find easy companionship with a rent-a-love for the night. He could have slipped off into Bangkok and got up to all-sorts, yet if he wasn't with Amm, he was with her sister. Of course, the night where Wan tried to kiss him was never brought up and would forever remain just between them. Everyone could see his actions and his persistence with Amm and it made him stand out from all the other guys that would pass through there.

Some of the girls had been to temple that day and bought a couple of souvenirs for him to take home. There was one small white Buddha in a plastic case and a red bracelet with black beads. They all fussed over him to put the bracelet on his wrist next to Amm's ones, and to present the Buddha, whilst enlightening him about the rules for keeping it – not to cover it or put it in his pocket and such like.

Amm walked slowly back to the bar. She really wished he didn't have to go. She really wished she had more time with him, but there was nothing else they could do. She was annoyed with herself for the way she'd treated him and was filled with a sense of dissatisfaction, but knew it was all her own fault. It was a quiet night in the bar and as she looked around, it just felt entirely like something was missing. She suddenly became overwhelmed and had to rush to the toilet so she could cry out of sight of everyone. Even though he was still only about a kilometre from her, she felt his departure so hard and her heart was breaking in a way she never expected. The bar seemed so plain again. He had left her alone. There was no sparkle and no anticipation of him turning up – not for a long time at least.

She sent him a message as he sat in Viva: "Thank you for everything you did to me. You are good man, but I'm not good for you. Have a good flight and take care. And thanks for flower."

"You are good. Don't say that. You're so special Amm and I'm very happy I met you. Please take care of yourself when I'm away. I will miss you so much."

The farewell drinks in Viva were being poured very generously indeed so he'd already exceeded how much he wanted to drink before his flight. Some of the other girls came and went, but he sat mostly with Koi.

'Archie, I want to ask you. You love my sister?'

'Yes, I love her. From the bottom of my heart, I love her.'

He sat in Zone 3 at Gate D7, waiting for his flight to board and watched some of the other passengers as they trickled along from the terminal. It was easy to pick out all the backpackers and the sex-tourists and honeymooners and once-in-a-lifetimers and knew he was carving out his own kind of category. It was bittersweet. Archie was both content and disappointed. He hadn't planned any of it, but it just seemed to unfold in such a way. He was concerned about how much he'd have to spend on flights in the future, but then he couldn't put a price on something like love. He had to just shoulder the cost, because he did not want to simply turn around and say *she's very far away, it's not worth the hassle.* If she was his chance at true love then he'd give everything he owned just to be with her.

105

He sent her a message: "Now I'm waiting to board my flight. I'm going to miss you so much. I really wish I could stay longer."

The bar was just closing and she was helping to shut everything down for the night, but dropped it all when she saw his message. "It's ok. Don't worry. I will wait for you. Have a safe flight na. Tell me when you at home already. I hope you will come back to me soon. X"

Chapter Nine
บทที่เก้า

'Archie? Did you see this?'

'What?'

It was morning coffee break and he sat in the engine control room. One of his colleagues liked to check the headlines on their basic news service and spotted something he thought would be of interest to him.

'There's been a bomb blast in Bangkok.'

'What??'

Archie launched from his seat and across to the computer. *Dozens killed and more injured in deadly bomb attack*, read the headline. His eyes scanned the words faster than he could really read them. He panicked, but tried to pacify himself with the fact that Bangkok was a big city. The chances of her being anywhere near to a bombing must have been very slim. It was a Monday morning, and she usually had Mondays and Tuesdays off. He read on more and then froze as a blind panic tore through him again. *Erawan Shrine*, he read. He knew that on her days off she'd often go to temple with her sister, but sometimes if they didn't want to go so far afield, they'd go to Erawan Shrine. It was close to shopping malls, and they sometimes went there to look around or have something to eat. There was every possibility that she was there.

He bolted up to his cabin to take his phone and check his messages. He connected to the ships internet and painstakingly waited for the slow connection to refresh. He hadn't spoken to her that morning, because he usually never had much time before going to work. His normal morning routine was shower, breakfast, coffee, then he'd pick up his boilersuits from the drying room and get changed. Sometimes at lunchtime they'd chat, but usually they would talk the most in the evenings, for him – which was after work for her. *Last active 16 hours ago*, was on the screen. It was very unusual. Like most girls, she was constantly on her phone. How could she possibly not have been online for that length of time? He sent some messages and they were not delivered to her phone which made him grow even more concerned.

He messaged Koi. When there was no reply for a few minutes he tried to call. Often, the connection was quite poor and it was not possible to actually have a conversation, but he had to try. She missed the call, but picked up the messages.

"Yes, she ok, I already talk with her. Don't worry. Everything ok."

"Ok. Thanks Koi. Where is she now? She didn't reply to my messages."

"Now I think she stay at the room, sleep more."

"Ok. Take care. And try to avoid public places like that, until they know more about who did it."

"Yes, ok. Thank you for think about me na. You too take care. Have a good work."

He went back down to the control room where the adrenaline and panic gradually drained from his body, making him feel like a burst balloon. At least he heard from Koi, but still felt uneasy until he could hear from Amm herself.

'All okay?' his colleague asked.

'Yeah, seems to be. I couldn't get her though, just her sister. She says she's fine though. But…she could have been there today. It's her day off and sometimes she goes there. I just totally freaked out when I saw that.'

'Don't worry, at least she's safe.'

He found it very hard to concentrate on his work after that and his productivity was somewhat reduced. At lunchtime he ran upstairs to check his messages again. She'd replied by that time.

"Hi Archie, today I'm so lucky. My sister stay with her friend, so I think I will go to shopping and go Erawan shrine alone. But I'm tired and want to sleep longer so I don't go. I feel so scared." She sent a

109

lot of crying emoticons and stickers. She was really shaken up about it, but was relieved.

"I'm so glad you're ok. I was so worried when I saw the news. I really panicked. Don't worry about it now. Just stay away from public places please."

She didn't reply again for the rest of the day. He supposed she probably just needed some time to calm down. At least he'd seen that she was online again, but she obviously didn't have anything more to say to him.

The next day it was all quiet from her. She hadn't been online and she hadn't even received Archie's messages. It was unlike her. They usually sent messages everyday just to ask how each other were, and he'd tell her a little about his work. He left it for a few days more before messaging Koi again. "Now Amm she stay in the temple one week. She is ok, but she cannot play phone there. Also me, I not talk with her. But she is ok. Don't worry."

Amm was freaked out because had she not decided to go back to sleep for a little longer, she'd have probably been there. She might have been killed by the bomb, or at least severely injured. She thought it was a sign. She had been increasingly spending time with more and more guys by letting them barfine her. After all, she was incredibly beautiful and attracted a lot of attention. So many men wanted to have her, and whilst she was working it was as if she was assuming a character. She liked to be taken out because they'd take her somewhere else rather than the bar. She could go and eat well and have a nice time on rooftop bars or luxury establishments and pretend to be someone more than a lowly bargirl.

Being apart from Archie was truly hurting her, so she started pulling away from him emotionally. Of course, she still cared about him and thought about him, but in the time that had elapsed since they last saw one another, she'd been unable to process her emotions for him. She got more drunk each night and took more and more customers out. Staying at the bar was even more unappealing considering she could still remember how Archie would walk through the door like her knight in shining armour. So if she could somehow escape that reminder, it was better for her.

At times, she'd gotten herself into sticky situations where the only way to escape was to *kiss* her way out. It was her own fault for being the character she was and partying and flirting. She was too good at her role.

She just wanted to party all the time to mask the way she really felt. It was a way of distracting herself from the things going on inside her heart and mind. If she wasn't out partying then she'd sit and remember him. To miss him was to feel pain and she was trying to do all she could to avoid that. A few guys had asked her to go home with them and she'd told them an outrageous price as a joke – humour was one of her techniques to handle awkward situations. When many of them had said yes, the lure of that money became so tantalising for her. She still didn't agree, but after being offered huge amounts of cash on a daily basis, she eventually became desensitised to the idea.

She tried to wait for Archie, but she just couldn't. She wasn't strong enough. She'd often imagine him helping her clear tables at the end of the night, or eating food together, or riding in the taxi with his hand between her legs. She couldn't do those things anymore so tried to displace that by following other options, and it didn't matter because it wasn't really her. She became a warped and twisted version of herself.

Considering how lucky she felt to have not been there when the bomb went off, she was compelled to go to temple to make merit. Perhaps there was a way to make amends for the way her life was going. Amm was disgusted with herself, but she didn't know what else she could do. Her mother was sick and needed medicine and hospital bills paid for. Koi and Joy paid their part, so Amm ought to as well, she thought. She'd never dream of asking Archie for help. She also knew only too well that the 'sick mother' was a standard story that a lot of Thai girls claimed just to get money from guys. Koi was strong enough to do the work and not take it to heart, but she didn't let guys take her out as much, not unless they were well known and had already become friends and it was clear that it was just for hanging out and nothing else.

Amm wanted to cleanse herself and pray for something else to come along and suddenly make her life better. She meditated and prayed all day long. She didn't talk with anyone outside because she wanted to stay as pure as possible. That way, by the end of the week, karma would bring her the clear option and path out of her misery. When the week was over, unfortunately a new path never presented itself and she was faced with the reality of returning to work. It was not the path she wanted, but it looked like it was the only one available to her, so she'd just have to get on with it. The only way she could stop feeling so much shame was if she blocked it out. So that's exactly what she did.

She let guys take her out and if they tried to kiss her it didn't matter; she just went with it because she didn't feel it. If they wanted to have sex with her, she told them the price and just went with it because she didn't feel it. She wanted to find somewhere dark to hide, and in the hotel rooms or condos of strange men was the darkest place she could find. She lost herself, and in doing so forgot about Archie, although not completely. But whatever feelings she had for him had to be put to one side. Of course, in her mind, he was always different from all the men she was going home with because she always considered him to be too good for her.

Their communication resumed once more, but at a much lesser level. Sometimes it'd take her a long time to reply, because if she was with a customer, there was no way she ever wanted to talk with Archie. It's not even that she was trying to hide or avoid him. It was more that she simply could not communicate with him whilst she was doing those things, because it was another Amm. Archie was disappointed of course, but respected her space. He thought perhaps she'd just ran out of things to say. Being apart for a few months, surely the conversation was bound to run dry – especially when their mother tongues were different. On her days off she was a little chattier, but then those days off became less and less. She'd arrange to meet guys every day of the week because she could make even more money as well as not needing to worry about paying for food that day.

Archie's trips were supposed to be three months long, but sometimes it wasn't possible. There were often delays in reaching port, or drifting for some time – either waiting for the cargo to be bought or sold. That's how tankers are at times. And then sometimes the guy who was supposed to replace him wouldn't be available and he'd have to stay longer. His three months elapsed in early October, which would have been great timing because his birthday was in the middle of the month. The ship wasn't due to make port until mid-October however, but that still seemed fine. Amm's birthday was at the end of November, but he wanted to go home to spend time with his parents and do some shopping first. He had a lot of ideas about what birthday presents to buy, and he especially wanted to buy her some Scottish things.

They were approaching New Orleans and arrival was exactly on his birthday, then he was to go home the next day. Once they arrived, the usual port operations kicked in and the ship was bustling with agents, officials, loading masters and others. Some of the other officers were gathered in the mess room after all arrival activities came to a conclusion. 'So, who wants to go ashore?' the Chief Engineer asked. He looked towards Archie first, as he was the closest to him.

'There's no point in me going,' Archie replied, 'someone else should go, because I'm going home tomorrow.'

At that moment, the captain walked in and interrupted him. 'No, I'm sorry Archie, you're not going home. I just got an email, your reliever's not coming. They're sending him to another ship. Sorry.'

'Oh, fantastic. Happy birthday from the office,' said someone else. They all empathised because they were quite literally in the same boat when it came to going home. They could all relate to his disappointment.

'So, when will I go?' he asked the captain.

'Maybe next port.'

'Do we have any orders yet?'

'No, we don't.'

He had to break the news to his parents. They were expecting to take a drive to the airport the next day and pick up their son, but it wasn't to be. He had to tell Amm as well, but it took her two days to reply. "It's ok. Don't worry na. Just tell me before you come."

After that port stay, they proceeded out to anchor in the Gulf of Mexico with no prospects for cargo and remained there for ten days. He was just hoping everyday that orders would come and they'd go back into a port somewhere along that coastline. When they came, it was for Algeria, which meant a crossing of the Atlantic – another two and a half weeks. Algeria was hardly the best place to execute a crew change either, but considering they had to enter the Mediterranean, he thought he'd get off whilst the ship was passing Gibraltar. It was a very common place for vessels to change crew, pick up supplies and provisions, or take on fuel. Once the vessel was underway, he talked with the Captain.

'So, when am I likely to get off? Can I go from Gib?'

'Yeah, I've already asked them about it, and it looks like Gibraltar, but…the next again crew change is due just after Algeria, and you'll go with them. So, it *will* be Gibraltar, but…outbound.'

It was dragging on and on and pushing closer to Amm's birthday all the time. He thought he'd be very safe when he arrived on board. He had a clear six weeks between finishing his stint and Amm's birthday, but now there was a chance he might miss it. He was so frustrated, but that was the job at times. The main thing that was unsettling him, was the longer he spent from her, the easier it might be for her to forget about him. He was desperate to pay off and make it back to Bangkok in time for her birthday because he wanted to make it so special for her. Then she'd be swept off her feet and admit how much she loved him and they'd live happily ever after. He wanted her to forget about her problems and just realise all the potential they had as a couple. All the while, he had no idea what was really going on.

Archie paid off five days before her birthday. He then spent three days at home gathering gifts for her and catching up with his parents. They were very surprised and a little concerned that he was going back to Thailand so quickly after coming home, but he explained that he was trying to make it for her birthday. He planned to stay a month and managed to secure a long-stay discount at the hotel where he stayed before, close to her place. They saw that he'd booked three times before – albeit the first two times were just a couple of days each, but he looked like a serious return customer, and they were quite happy to have him fill one of the executive studio rooms for a month. If he went for that length of time, he'd surely have plenty opportunity to get to know Amm without there being the same time constraint as before. Subsequently, he'd be home in time for Christmas with his parents too, which was a big plus for them because the few preceding years, he'd spent Christmas and New Year at sea.

Amm video called him one time after getting home and he was so glad he had normal internet again. It was already 8 o'clock in the morning in Thailand and she hadn't been to sleep yet. He knew what things he was doing whenever he got home at that time, but tried not to think too much about it. He also knew that when Thai girls got together, they can talk and eat all night long without any issue, so tried to not jump to any conclusions.

She seemed excited to see him and kept posing for him in the camera and giggling. Truthfully, she *was* excited, but she'd still detached herself from him. Even though he was her special one, it was almost as if she was talking to a customer. So many conversations or messages had gone from her to guys arranging 'dates' and she was more or less doing the same with Archie as they discussed the plans for her birthday.

He was due to arrive the night before her birthday. She told him she didn't want him to come to her work and that they'd just meet at the restaurant on the day. He could understand and didn't want to set anything off again by going there. By now however, she'd established quite a substantial fan-base, so she didn't want anyone real to go there.

Archie laid all her presents out on his bed as he prepared his suitcase. He thought maybe he'd gone a bit overboard, but then again, he really wanted to spoil her. He felt bad that he was arriving much later than he told her and wanted to thank her for being patient. Of course he worried about her working at the bar, but he really believed that she was just sitting and maybe flirting a little – as much as was necessary. The Amm he was with before told him that she'd wait, and was already certain that she wanted him to come back. If only he knew that the Amm he first met had vanished somewhere between the nightlife and designer handbags and obligations to her mum. The Amm he once knew and fell in love with was lost somewhere in Bangkok.

Chapter Ten

บทที่สิบ

He checked in at the hotel and as hard as it was, he didn't go to see her. After all those months apart, it was all he wanted to do though. Koi had moved bars and wasn't working at Viva anymore. It was on a soi he'd never been to before but Amm gave him the location and advised him to go there instead. He took a motorcycle taxi and as they went down the soi he could see a lot of massage parlours. Masseurs sat at the entrances and some of them ate food from takeaway containers whilst the others tried to tempt passers-by with a massage. Sure, there were plenty of legitimate massage shops in Bangkok, but he got a weird feeling from the ones he was passing by.

The bar was down an alley and the motosai went past it at first because his driver had also never heard of the place. When he entered, it was more or less a normal place. It looked like an American style sports bar, akin to, but much bigger than Amm's bar. Archie could see dozens of staff, but there were hardly any customers at all. Given how remote the place was, he wasn't surprised at all. The door was very close to the front of the bar and he was enthusiastically greeted by the girls there.

'Hi, I'm looking for Koi? Is she here?' One of them shouted over to the corner of the mezzanine floor behind them as the rest speculated as to what their connection might be. Koi emerged and greeted him warmly with a nice smile and a hug.

'Oh, so good to see you! How are you?' she asked.

'Yeah, I'm good. A little tired, but I'm okay.'

The week before was also Koi's birthday, so he decided to pick her up a perfume in duty free on the way there. He presented the small bag and she asked what it was. 'That's for your birthday last week.' She was excited and opened it in front of all the girls there whilst expressing in Thai that he was her *sister's boyfriend* rather than an admirer of hers.

'Oh, how you know? I always want to try this one, but it's so expensive! Thank you so much na Archie.'

'You're welcome.'

'You eat already?' she asked. 'You want to order something?'

She handed him the menu and it was all foreign food, which was fine by him. The travelling had built up his appetite and thirst. 'What about you, are you hungry?'

'No, I'm okay, I eat already. But I want to buy you drink na.'

120

After ordering something, she led him to a table on the mezzanine. They talked and got caught up with each other as some girls came to have a look at him before being chased off by Koi. They finalised the plans for the following night and she asked him if he knew the restaurant they were going to meet at. It was on Soi 11, but he'd never been and never seen it. It was on top of a skyscraper and occupied the top couple of floors, which was why he had never stumbled across it before. 'Tomorrow I meet you and I take you there,' Koi said.

'Good. Because I need you to help me take some of her presents. It's a lot to carry.'

'Really? You buy her so much?'

'Err…yeah. It's quite a lot.'

'No, you don't need to buy her too much na.'

She knew Amm had been going out with men and spending an awful lot of time with them and she had always reminded her about Archie. Yet, Amm promised she wasn't doing anything other than going out to dinner, going to clubs and hanging out. Koi was worried, and whilst not wanting to tell her what to do, she advised her that if she had no intentions of waiting for Archie then she should let him go. She had heard things from some of the girls, but Amm insisted it was all untrue.

Archie alighted the BTS train and let the hoard of people filter down the stairs. He was keen to find Koi and supposed she was there on the

121

other side of the ticket counter, so he carefully made his way towards the barriers. Koi was quite short, but he could pick her out as she stood waiting for him. He was so glad to see her. Partly so he could offload some of the presents and partly because he felt so conspicuous carrying all of that around by himself. During the day he'd been to the same florist that he'd visited for the single rose before. He remembered Amm said her favourite flowers were pink roses, so he arranged a bouquet from there – twenty-three – it was her twenty-third birthday after all. Down on street level, Koi said it'd be better if they got a taxi. Considering all they had to carry, it was much too far to walk. The taxi slowly navigated along the busy soi, avoiding the street carts and the tourists and the ex-pats out to find alcohol and a honey for the night.

They took a right turn and pulled up at the building where a doorman opened the taxi for them. Once they got out, he shone a torch in the back to make sure they had everything. It was a normal routine for him, usually for a mobile phone or wallet, but on that occasion it was particularly necessary.

It looked like an affluent condo building or a hotel and Archie was a little confused. He could see no signs of any restaurant. It wasn't until Koi led him around the back of the building that he spotted a separate lift which would take them to the restaurant. It dawned on him that they were at the restaurant Amm used to work. He knew it was a very high-end modern gastronomy affair and suddenly the pieces fitted together. Fortunately, she still had a lot of friends working there and they had secured her a fantastic table.

They emerged from the lift and Koi led him along a corridor where nothing but a few dim floor lights illuminated the way. It was dark to enable patrons to see the fantastic night-time view of Bangkok through the windows. They walked past a small artificial garden complete with a park bench, before being greeted firstly by the massive forced draught of a huge pedestal fan and then by the front of house staff. Koi was instantly recognised and showed to the table in the corner looking out over the city. They placed the bags down and Amm got up to greet him. She wore an elegant pink dress and a big floppy black hat. Her hair was darker. She'd let the highlights go and it had more or less returned to her natural black. There was no doubt that she looked absolutely incredible.

He was a little overwhelmed as the anticipation finally left his body, yet he kept his composure. He'd yearned for her for so long and he finally got to be with her again. She gave him a short and jaded hug and he wished her a happy birthday. There was already some food and a bottle of wine at the table as well as her other sister P-Joy and one of her closest friends. Behind them sat the twinkling lights and cityscape of Bangkok that he was becoming so familiar with. It was nice to see it from a new elevated perspective, thirty-two floors up.

First came the gift-giving; starting with the flowers, since they were the most obvious. 'Pink roses…your favourite,' he said. 'There's twenty-three…one for each year.' It was a very thoughtful thing and she loved them. The bouquet was full and flawless. At the time they first met, that alone would have been more than enough for her, but she could hardly remember those days. There had been a lot of water under the bridge since then and it seemed like a long time ago indeed.

Archie cleared the Dior counter of his department store in Edinburgh of several items. He used to work in that shop whilst he was studying, albeit not in the cosmetics department. But everyone was familiar with each other there and he had great pleasure in recounting his romantic story, just how he did at the Dior counter in Bangkok. As a favour, she packed all the items carefully in a special padded Dior box and gift wrapped it so beautifully, as well as providing him with a few samples for himself. Amm had great satisfaction in unwrapping it. She pulled out each item and looked towards Koi. He could gather that Amm was asking if she'd helped Archie to pick everything out, because she couldn't believe how right he'd got it. Of course, Koi told her that she didn't help him at all and he'd obviously selected everything by himself.

Archie always paid close attention to her whenever they were together; what make-up she used and how she wore it. He paid attention to every single item she browsed when they'd go shopping. By closely scrutinising the slightest changes in her facial expressions, allowed him to evaluate what she liked. That included the things she rejected, the things she liked and even what she liked but couldn't afford. That's how he knew exactly what she wanted.

Next there were earrings and a pink charm bracelet with a single charm on it – an anchor. It corresponded with the anchor bracelet she bought him, albeit much more elegant and expensive. There were other items from home such as a picture book of Scotland and a teddy bear with a kilt. She loved everything so much but remained standoff-ish. Joy told her in Thai that she should kiss him, but Archie heard her reply something like *not until I'm drunk*, or *I'm not drunk enough*. Archie knew the Thai words for *kiss* and *no* and *drunk*. Add that to the gesturing and body language, and it's not hard to figure out what was said.

Her sister and friends (including the waitresses) were all amazed at the gifts too, and started to take photos of everything. They all posed for selfies with her presents and seemed more excited about the gifts than she did. He made allowances for her again considering it had been about five months since they'd seen each other. He thought she needed to acclimatise to him again. Anyone might have thought it rude that she continued to ignore him and that she didn't even thank him so far.

One of Amms' waitress friends handed him an iPad and it took him a second to realise that the menu was on it. That was a first for him, but not the only one for that moment. The menu was highly unconventional. All the dishes had inventive names, arty photos and descriptions which didn't make it much clearer either. Archie was well travelled enough to have an idea about food, but this was another level to him. Since he wasn't sure what to order, he left it up to her. He assumed she'd have a good working knowledge of that menu after all. He picked a wine though, because that menu he could understand.

Eventually she started to ask him a little about his work, but she didn't talk about anything that had happened whilst he was away and evaded any questions pertaining to that. They stayed there for a few hours, picking away at food and taking photos and drinking. The wine was starting to weary him after all the travelling, and it was hardly as if he managed a good sleep the night before. Being there and having to wait a day to see her built up the suspense and the tension for him. Finally paying off the ship after an extra month and a half plus the associated stress that brought; followed by running around Edinburgh to find all the gifts, repacking his bags and flying out to Bangkok, hardly made for a very restful week for him either.

After finishing their food, not one, but two cakes were brought out. Her sisters brought one, but her friends had also arranged one too. Everyone sang for her and when it came to blowing out the candles there was a big pause. She put her hands together in a wai and prayed. As he sat next to her, he watched her. Although her eyes were closed and she was partly hidden under her big floppy hat, he could tell that she was praying hard. Candlelight flickered off her beautiful button nose and cheeks, her new bracelet, and also caught the shiny golden letters of the Dior bag that she'd positioned on the empty seat at the other side of her. People from other tables looked on in wonder at the beautiful girl who had obviously been spoiled by her kind and handsome suitor and the magnificent fancy time they were all seemingly having. She opened her eyes and blew out the candles.

After the meal, they headed back downstairs to the Bangkok city streets. It was quite an entourage, with Archie, Amm, her sisters and friend carrying all the gifts. They made their way down Soi 11 and met up with some more of her friends before going to a bar. In all, there were seven beautiful girls with him and it was quite the spectacle. He'd never experienced anything ever quite like it in Scotland. Of course, it's not as if he had something with all of them, but certainly when he arrived at the bar, all the men looked at his party of friends, then looked at Archie, and were dumbfounded with jealously. Girls already in the bar thought that he must be someone worth knowing since he could lead such a group of women around. All eyes were on him and he couldn't deny that it felt good.

During dinner, he was concerned about the continuous order stream so decided to give her some money to pay for the drinks that were about to follow. At the restaurant it was like a bottomless pit style and he was sure that the drinks order would go the same way too. The meal itself was already very expensive, what with the upmarket Asian-fusion cuisine and a few bottles of wine. He thought it'd be better to give her some money so that she knew that was as much as he wanted to spend for the rest of the night. Archie still had no real concept of Thai budgeting. It was certainly a generous amount, more than adequate for a good night out. In actual fact, the money he gave her for drinks alone was a little more than her monthly salary when she worked at that restaurant, yet only about a quarter of what she made from the bar – salary, commission and tips only. Not including the extras.

She began to loosen up in general, but still wasn't very warm to him. He thought perhaps it was rare for her to have all her friends together like that so he was happy just to let her enjoy it. It was her night – it wasn't about him. He soothed his fraught mind by thinking she actually didn't need to invite him along; she could have blown him off and just said it was girls only. But then again, if she did that, who would pay for it all? Still, it could have been worse again. At least at the restaurant it was just her closest people. She could have invited everyone else there too and she knew that he'd never refuse her.

All those things circled his head as he was starting to over-analyse the night. He decided just to have a few drinks and go with the flow. Surely by the time she woke up, she'd realise what an incredible birthday she'd had courtesy of him and she'd appreciate it then. It was just a shame that he could never realise the reason he had to make excuses for her was because she was completely ungrateful and not treating him the way she ought to at all.

The last stop was a street bar to have a few more drinks, but some of her friends and her sister Joy had to go home. Meanwhile, her friends from the restaurant had finished work and came to meet her. They ate street food and continued the party. There was yet another cake which appeared from somewhere, so it was adorned with candles, sang over, prayed over and then eaten. Archie began staring into space and it hadn't gone unnoticed by Koi. She spoke frankly to Amm to remind her that he was still with them and that she ought to show some gratitude. For two minutes, she fussed over him, put some cake on his plate and refilled his glass. The cake was Tiramisu, and he wasn't a huge fan, but he ate it anyway. He had nothing else to do after all and wasn't satisfied in the slightest. He felt as if he was going backwards with her. Perhaps if they were alone again then he could get the real her and they could have some real exchanges and quality time. He had to hope and hold out for that.

Eventually, it was time to go home. This time it was Koi that told her she should kiss him, but she didn't feel like it. She was bent out of shape. All the presents and the money, she'd managed to get without doing anything. She got it just by him being in love with her, so if she didn't have to do anything then she wouldn't. She'd ignored Archie most of the night because she still didn't want to realise the feelings she had for him or face the shameful things she'd been doing behind his back. It would be easier for her just to keep him at a distance and keep herself closed off. She forgot about how she was attracted to him, because affection became a sordid thing for her. Her lips, hips, hair, eyes and all other parts of her anatomy were no longer the parts that made her what she was, they were nothing more than work equipment now, and she was currently on her downtime.

He gave her a cuddle and went in for a kiss without being forceful. She dodged it and only hugged him back.

'I love you, Amm.' He couldn't help it. The words just fell from his mouth. It was obvious for everyone to see and she already knew it too.

'Okay, goodnight. I'll send you message tomorrow.' It was the most dismissive reply in all of existence. It was as if she never heard it at all.

She still didn't even thank him for the evening.

Chapter Eleven
บททีสิบเอ็ด

Amm took the next day off so that she could wake up whenever she felt like it. She was expecting a big hangover or a late night at least. Archie sent her a message: "Hi. I hope you had a good time last night. What you doing today?"

"I don't know. Maybe I'll go shopping. Just relax day today. What about you?"

"I'm not doing anything. Do you want to meet?"

She did. And she didn't. She felt out of control with him. She wanted to be around him because he always made everything nicer, but he just reminded her of the things that she'd done. It was hard to control the way that the real Amm responded to him too. She had to keep her real self suppressed however, because she was an over-emotional, sensitive mess, whereas the working Amm was strong and independent and couldn't be affected by anything. Dropping the front and being real was simply not an option.

"Ok. We go to mall? We can go to see movie," she suggested.

They exchanged a few more messages to arrange what movie and what time, and he met her there. Koi was there too, which he wasn't expecting, but it was okay, he supposed. They sat down with their popcorn and drinks and watched the trailers. It was a mix of English and Thai films – all of which were unknown to him. Amm sat closely next to him and for once, there was a sense of them being a couple. All of a sudden, a song came on with images of The King and everybody stood up. She tugged at his arm. 'Stand up, Archie.' He was a little surprised. He had no idea that everybody had to stand before a movie to show respect to The King. He liked it. He watched the images of their kind, benevolent and beloved King and actually felt quite moved. Amm stood in revered silence as did everyone else.

During the movie, she was sweet and fed him popcorn or lifted the juice up to his lips and he couldn't understand why sometimes she liked to take care of him. But at least it was sometimes – albeit only when it's completely dark or when there's no one else around. He thought about why she was ashamed of him without realising it was because she was ashamed of herself.

After the movie, they looked around the shops and she still had money leftover from the bar. She did offer to give it back to him but he told her to use it for shopping, so bought herself and Koi some clothes. Once he'd handed it over, he'd already written it off anyway.

It felt almost normal to get dragged around shops and hold a girls' handbag as she tried on clothes. He'd had a couple of girlfriends before and whilst one of them was quite serious, it certainly felt like quite a while since he'd accompanied a girl in such a way. Given that so far, most of the experiences with Amm had been quite extreme and unusual, it was mundanely comforting for him.

They eventually exhausted their mall activities so headed to take a taxi back to their home BTS station, Phra Khanong. Across the road from his hotel there was an open-air market, but it wasn't selling goods. It was a food market with stalls of every type of cuisine on offer: Thai, Japanese, Indian, French, burgers, seafood, pizza, sushi, whatever you fancied, it was there. There was also a bar at either side of the market so it was possible just to go and drink, but given the food culture in Thailand, it was unusual to drink without eating. She ordered some food but Archie wasn't hungry. He sat with a beer, soaking up the atmosphere, until it turned very heavy very suddenly.

'Archie? I want to ask you.'

'Yes?'

'Why you love me?' She had a serious look on her face.

'I don't know. Why is the grass green?' he retorted. She didn't understand the turn of phrase and he could tell. 'I can't explain, I just do,' he continued. 'It's not just because you're beautiful. I just…I feel something when I'm with you. We have a connection and I know you feel something too…otherwise you wouldn't have come to talk to me that night. And if I didn't meet you, I'd have gone home and maybe

133

never came back here. I think…' he struggled to keep it toned down, 'I think it was meant to be that we met.' He'd gone over that speech a few hundred times in his head whilst lying alone in his cabin at night. He wasn't quite prepared to have to recount it there at the food market though, so he missed a few things out.

'But it's better for you if you don't love me.'

'Why do you keep saying that?' Koi got up to make herself scarce and give them some privacy.

'Because you don't know me. We don't know each other. You need to learn about me and then you will know. I'm no good, you know?'

She was like a broken record and Archie was growing incredibly tired of that line. 'So give me a chance then.'

'Why you come back here?' she asked.

'Well…' he was becoming tangled up in her imprudent questions, 'so we can get to know each other better. I'm staying for one month, we have plenty time to get to know each other.' The repetition of such conversations was beginning to really wear him down. How could she really question him about why he came back? That was so unfair. It just looked like she was forever making excuses to shun him and they were doing nothing but going in circles. 'This is what we talked about. You're the one that said you wanted me to come back.'

'But I think it's no good for you. I think you just say love, but you not really love me.'

Her words were unbelievably hurtful. It seemed that he'd hit a wall with her now and really couldn't see any way over, round, through or under. It wasn't her place to tell him how he felt about her. It was only what he felt inside, and what he felt was that he was madly in love with her.

If she hadn't ambushed him with her question then he might have had a chance to answer her better. He'd have told her it was because when they met, the real her was soft and tender and timid and shy, but somehow got the courage up – drunk or not – to talk to him. It was about how he held her outside the pub when she said that she had only him and was upset at any suggestion otherwise, and how he wished he could have stayed in that conversation and embrace forever. It was about the way she would place his hand between her legs. It was about how – no matter how badly she wanted to treat him or how much time and space was between them, something kept bringing her back to him.

He'd thought about it whilst he was away. Being concerned as he was about everything, he drew comfort from the fact that if she'd found someone else, or even just lost interest, then she'd surely stop messaging him. It's not as if he was sponsoring her in some way. Perhaps he went over the top with the birthday gifts, but it was only because he was so excited to go and see her again and wanted to make it as special as he could. And the birthday gifts were just gifts, pure and simply.

'Okay, I think we go home now.' Yet again, he was rejected and somehow felt that he was never ever going to get a kiss from her again, never mind anything more.

'Well, what about tomorrow, are you still off?'

'No, tomorrow I work again. You can come if you want to. Up to you na.' Her tone was dry and passive.

'Yeah, I'll come.'

She gathered her things and Koi had already made her way back to the table to start doing the same.

'Goodnight Amm. Let me know when you get home.'

'Goodnight. See you tomorrow na.'

He went home alone once again. He opened the door to a beautiful but empty hotel room once again. He tried to fill the emptiness with a TV blaring a language he didn't understand once again. It was still early evening, but the sparkle of Bangkok was already beginning to shine outside his hotel window. Lights started to come on in the dusk as a dark musky blue began to penetrate and dissolve the orange glow of the daytime. He questioned himself hard. He had a month there and didn't know how he was going to fill it. He had a feeling however, that it wouldn't be with Amm. It was just a shame that she was all he wanted.

He looked through some photos from the first night they met, to the night she made it up to him before he left last time, to the photos she sent him whilst he was away. She continually dangled a carrot in front of him and took it away at the last moment. He was good to her, he did everything right, so what the hell was the problem? She was obviously attracted to him, she was the one who approached him after all, and it wasn't even about her being drunk. Most of the time when someone is drunk, it's just the inhibitions that go and they have the freedom to do something they are too reserved to do whilst sober. And as much as she was trying to push him away, Amm would always reply to his messages, she'd always think about him and she'd always compare other guys to him. She fought every second of every day with herself over that.

But without work she can't eat, she won't have anywhere to sleep and she can't help her mum. Life was tough and she had to do things that she didn't like just to survive. She loved Archie, but he made her feel better and worse about herself at the same time. He always looked at her like she'd never done anything wrong in her life, whilst she knew what depraved things she was doing. The distance when he went away was unacceptable for her too. She wanted him close to her and available whenever she needed him, and if she couldn't have that then they may as well not be together. She didn't want to miss him or remember how they did things together, she wanted it everyday or not at all. That's why he was stuck in limbo, because she was. It was too hard for her to just tell him to go, since that was the last thing that she wanted to do. In a way, it was as if she was treating him badly in the 'hope' that he'd just give up on her.

She never did send a message to say that she was home. Then again, neither did he. A small part of him wanted to go out. Maybe he could head to that street he saw when he went to take photos before and just find a nice bar – or a not-so-nice bar – and simply drink his troubles away. Perhaps he could find himself a smooth-skinned petite friend for the night. Anything had to be better than staying alone again.

In the end he went nowhere. He remembered when he was younger and before going out at night, there was that excitement about whether or not he was going to meet someone – the anticipation of sexual congress. He didn't have that excitement because pointless sexual encounters were no longer a desire of his. Even if he could find someone else to keep him company, it wouldn't be right. He was mature enough to know himself and not need to seek simple physical gratification. What Archie wanted was to love and be loved.

He went across to the shop and bought a bottle of whisky. Back in the room, he dropped a few ice cubes in his glass and splashed the whisky over them. Usually he'd never drink it with ice, but then that was the same for beer too. In Thailand they would add ice to beer and it was very strange to him. But it was so hot that a cool and slightly watery beer was better than a warm one. Everything was different and he had to adjust. He thought he was doing well and that he was on the brink of a great love, but he was starting to think maybe it'd be better if he just went home and never came back again.

A well-timed message came through from a friend asking how he was doing. He brought him up to date and explained exactly what was on his mind. Archie still considered Amm as his true love, but it was pointed out to him that if she really was, then he wouldn't have so much hassle. Archie's friend told him to be patient, but to forget about her because if she really loved him, she would never treat him in such a way. He made excuses for her of course and said it was just her mental health and what kind of man would he be if just walked out on her when deep down she needed him?

"Well, man, that's her issue and if she's broken, unfortunately, it's not down to you to fix her. If she doesn't want to be fixed then you'll never do it. And you'll just keep giving yourself away for nothing. I'm telling you, she's not the one. But she's out there. You'll know when, because it won't be a battle, it'll just be comfortable and nice. Everything will fall into place and it'll just work. This girl is putting you through hell. You can't honestly tell me that's real love."

He felt a little bit more hopeful after his heart-to-heart with his friend but it did seem that romance was dead in Bangkok. He was frustrated that on paper he was perfect, and yet she couldn't accept him. He thought about all the sleazebags cruising lady bars or go-go joints. Those guys were engaging in debauchery with no consideration of any consequences, but he reckoned they all had a smile on their face every single night. They never ever had to suffer any heartache and it seemed upside down to him. Sure, he wouldn't ever pay for it, but when you take into account the presents, the expensive restaurants, not to mention the nights spent at the bar where Amm would run up a huge tab partying, he was actually spending so much more without getting anything but pain in return. Yet he'd endure it just so he could stay in her presence and continue being the 'virtuous' person that he was.

With a hire-a-honey, you know how much the night will cost you at the very start and that was it. Both parties knew what would be the outcome of the evening, there was no fear of rejection or her flipping out. Chasing a real girlfriend was nothing but an emotional, psychological, physical and financial drain. It didn't matter if you can manage to buy her the right makeup without asking, or brought her the same number of roses as her years on the earth, because romance was nowhere to be found.

Bangkok had seemingly taken his integrity and dulled his spark. He went there with no preconceptions about anything, but it had more or less destroyed him. He checked his bank account and was shocked at how out of hand he'd let it get. He felt so stupid for following her whim when all she did was shun him. At times, he thought maybe it was better to feel hurt rather than nothing at all, but the fullness of the city left him empty inside. Perhaps feeling nothing would be better, because the pain and regret was crippling him.

Never before had he been so defeated and elated and excited and crestfallen all at the same time. That was the effect Bangkok had on him. Maybe Amm wasn't the one after all. It was only day three of his month there and he knew he had no problem in finding a good time. Whether that was spent in bars, temples or just escaping to the beach was up to him. Perhaps he'd change his style and just revert to his carefree holiday mode. Or perhaps he'd give her one last chance. Ultimately, he hadn't decided – but either way he wasn't done with Bangkok yet.

Chapter Twelve
บทที่สิบสอง

Archie woke up early and sat on the balcony. He listened to the sounds of Sukhumvit beneath him, as cars and trucks and motorbikes went past. BTS trains thundered up and down the track every few minutes. For the out of town train, he could always see the reflection of it in the building opposite before it passed by his balcony. The overhead bridge was layered with grime from exhaust fumes and rain. The sun battered down yet he was still in the shade, but supposed after a couple of hours it'd be over the building and too hot to stay out there.

He checked his phone and there was not a single message from her. It looked like she wasn't up yet, but that probably wouldn't change even after she woke up anyway. Life was unfair, he thought. He didn't blame Amm of course, but if he was actually living there, then perhaps they'd have the time just to get to know each other properly and it wouldn't be so intense. Meanwhile, he wouldn't have to stay in a hotel whilst missing time away from his family and friends. Sure, he'd made some friends, but he didn't really have anyone else there. Everything was pinned on her, but she blew hot and cold with him so often. She was a rollercoaster that he was starting to get sick from, but he still didn't get off.

It wasn't that he could wait forever, though. There was nothing more that he could do to prove his feelings for her, or be better to her. He came to regret giving her such an extravagant birthday. Had things been good between them then it would be fine, but the way she acted made the whole thing feel seedy to him. It's well known about foreigners coming across to Thailand and finding some girl to shower with gifts and money and then suddenly she's their girlfriend. A majority of which were older and perhaps divorced and with no hope of finding a beautiful young thing in their own country. But in Thailand it was much easier and acceptable; anything was available for the right price. Besides, it wasn't as if that was working with Amm, because she was hardly warming to him in proportion to the amount of things she got from him – quite the opposite in fact. What he was clinging onto was the belief that there was a soft loving core, deep down in her that still burned for him, and that's what he wanted to coax from her. If only he knew how.

He headed back inside and was comforted by the room's air con. It was set to twenty-six degrees, and whilst it felt cool after being outside, he knew that would be a scorcher of a day back in Scotland. Bangkok was a new side of himself which, despite everything, he was enjoying. He was familiar with the BTS, taxis and shops. He knew his way around and began to learn where the good places to go were, including off the beaten track. He really took pleasure from that. Of course, he'd seen a lot of the world and was already very well travelled, particularly from work, but this was a different style. Going to or from work he'd have a day, or maybe two maximum, and it was never enough time to reach a level of familiarity anywhere near to what he had with Bangkok. Being with locals obviously took it to another level too. All his other previous holidays were mostly spent on a resort, by the beach or pool and just chilling out. Never before had he ever been so far into the nitty-gritty of any other city.

The evening came round and he was ready to go out. He had lazed about the room all day, topped up his sleep a little, checked Facebook and watched TV. He flirted with the idea of not going, or giving her some kind of excuse as a cry for attention. But he was simply weak for her.

He hailed a taxi and as the driver weaved in and out of traffic, narrowly avoiding motorbikes, he realised he hadn't sent her a message to say he was on the way. He didn't have any internet outside so it was already too late, but supposed it might just be better to turn up unannounced anyway. As he turned onto the soi, a sense of foreboding filled his stomach; or perhaps it was just hunger. Since he'd only been in the room all day, he hadn't eaten anything other than some snacks that were left over. He was beginning to grow concerned over the sheer amount of alcohol he'd consumed. Archie could handle a drink, but it was never as regular and unrelenting as it was in Bangkok.

As he stepped inside the bar, she was nowhere in sight. He took a seat and expected that she was perhaps in the toilet or the kitchen so waited a few minutes. She definitely said she was working that day. Lily came to greet him, handed him a menu, then stood eagerly awaiting his order. When she returned with his beer he decided to ask, 'Where's Amm?' She looked a bit perplexed and wasn't sure how to answer. She didn't know whether she should make something up or just be honest. Whilst deciding, she realised it'd been too long a delay so she just told him the truth.

'She already go out. With customer.'

His face dropped. Lily understood that he was expecting to meet her there and felt bad for him. She'd been on the outskirts of all the goings-on so far. She knew everything that had happened and was also well aware of all the things Amm did whilst she was supposedly waiting for Archie to come back.

'I can sit with you?' she asked.

'Yeah, sure.'

She smiled timidly and slid her stool a little bit closer to him before sitting down. She admired him. Not because of the things that he'd done and the presents he'd bought for Amm, but there was just something else about him. He had a casual and comfortable style and it captivated her.

'Do you want a drink?' he asked.

She was a shy girl and took a while to reply. Yes, she certainly wanted a drink, but she didn't want to take advantage of him. She also didn't want him to see her as just some other bargirl. 'It's okay, you can have a drink,' he said.

'Okay. Thank you ka.' She made a quick wai with her hands and smiled shyly.

Archie checked his phone and drafted a message before deleting it. *Oh, what's the point?* he thought. Lily returned with her drink and sat down again.

'Its okay, Lily, you don't need to sit with me, just have your drink, relax.'

'No, I want to. If you're okay?'

'Yeah, okay.' He wanted to know more about Amm's activities but also got a sense that they may close ranks to outsiders and wondered whether or not there was any point to ask. Nonetheless, he had to try. 'So, what about Amm? She said she'd be here tonight. Who did she go out with?'

'I don't know him. I see him sometimes, but I never talk with him. But I think I don't like.' She swept her long sleek hair demurely behind her ear and stared at her bottle of light beer. 'I don't like talk to customers.'

'So how can you work in a bar and not talk with customers?'

'I don't know, I just need to work. And my aunty is manager. I have to work here.'

'Hmm, okay.' He still stared mostly at his phone, willing a message to come from Amm. 'Well…did you eat something? You want to order some food?' He could tell that she was having trouble with his accent so he made an eating gesture with his hand. Being as she was and not talking to many customers, she didn't have as much practice with English as some of the other girls, and she'd never heard a Scottish accent before Archie.

'No, it's okay. Maybe later.' Having the experience that he did, he knew Thai girls liked to eat all the time and could tell she was just being polite.

'I'm sorry she not wait for you. I don't know why she do it. In Thailand, no have someone same like you.'

It sounded to him like she may have been flirting, but he put it down to the language barrier and supposed she was just being sweet in an attempt to comfort him.

'Thank you.'

She stole glances at him whilst he wasn't looking, alternating between him and the drink he bought her. She thought he was very handsome. Most of the girls in the bar did. He was quiet and she searched desperately for something to talk to him about.

'You know, I remember first time you meet Amm,' she said. 'That night I work there in Viva bar. I see you.' She searched for more words. 'And I see Amm come to talk with you.'

'Ah, yeah, I think I remember seeing you. It was Songkran and you all had the same dresses on though.'

'Yes.'

'But I wasn't really paying attention to other people.' She didn't understand, but just nodded anyway.

Lily kept him company whilst he ate his food. He did feel like a bit of a pig in front of her because he was so famished from not eating all day, but then he was also past the point of caring what others thought. He so often didn't get what he wanted, so at least he could stuff his face and it wasn't worth worrying about it. The more they talked, the more Lily began to relax. He was genuinely the first customer that she'd felt comfortable talking with. Archie was more than just a customer though. She remembered all the food and drinks he'd bought her before without demanding her presence or anything in return. Of course, he thought she was very cute and gorgeous and wanted to do something just to help her out, because he so often saw her sitting alone in the corner. She only ever really spoke to her aunty Ploy. But it hadn't gone unnoticed by Archie, the frequency in which men approached to buy her a drink. He could see and feel her wince in her seat but agree with a stunted smile since she didn't have much choice.

'Archie, I want to tell you na…just be careful about Amm.'

'What do you mean?'

'I mean…' she thought how to express herself in Thai, before translating into English, '…I don't want her hurt you.'

'Well, it's already a bit late for that, but…do you know something?' She was a little bit torn. She wanted to come clean to him about Amm's exploits but they were friends too – it was a betrayal. But then, if Amm wasn't doing Archie wrong, she wouldn't have been put in that position at all.

'Just, she have a lot of customer. But she not same like before. She quiet like me before, but then it look like…she go crazy. And she go outside with many customer.'

'Go outside…like what?'

'She go with customer and they will pay her.' Her gaze was firmly in her beer bottle. 'She will stay with them.'

'Ah…okay.'

'She do it many times.'

He was entirely calm, because it was hardly a shocking revelation for him. Lily may have confirmed his worst fears, but he'd already gone through all the motions whilst he was at work. He came up with every scenario but always tried to reassure himself. Amm said repeatedly that she was no good, but he didn't believe her. He remembered she said that when he knew the *real her,* he wouldn't like her. He'd came to peace with it all. There was every chance that she'd been with guys for money before – she was a stunning girl after all. Or perhaps she had kids or something. Those things didn't really bother him though. So long as the sleeping with guys was behind her. As it happened, she'd never actually done anything like that until she started working in the bar, and until after Archie had left the previous time. But if she was still doing that, then he didn't know whether he could accept that, or *should* accept that. The point was – she told him that she'd wait, but she lied.

He supposed that there'd reach a point where he'd have to give up on her. There was only so much she could push him away before he ran out of power to push back. He was devastated enough from the night before and then turning up for her not to be there was yet another blow. Learning she was out with a customer was more or less the final nail in the coffin. Perhaps that point of giving up may well have been reached.

Lily was nice to talk to. What a difference it was just to have someone calm who he could have an actual conversation with. Being able to talk specifically about Amm was great too. He could talk with his friends at home, but none of them could ever fully understand the situation there and the whole way of life. Lily understood. She was there to listen when he really needed it, and he appreciated the insight she gave him. Even with the other girls he was good friends with and who cared for him, he always got a sense that they were being careful about what they said, or that they weren't revealing all that they knew. It wasn't even so much that they were deceiving him, but more that it wasn't their place to say. To talk about people behind their back was very un-Thai. Even if they knew something, it was not the done thing to talk of others business behind their back. Lily was interpreting it another way though, and chose to be honest and truthful, because for once, he deserved it.

The night wore on and Archie got the bill. He didn't know what to do after there. He didn't fancy going out but just couldn't bear to be by himself and go back to the hotel alone again. The emptiness of the room was like an insult to him, it was salt in the wound. He was a young, attractive, kind and funny guy. Why the hell should he have to endure such a hard time? What had he done to deserve such suffering?

During the whole time in the bar, Lily didn't eat anything. She sat with him all night and she was happy. It was the first night she'd ever enjoyed at work. What's more, it was the first time she'd sat with someone who didn't try to touch her or ask her what her favourite sexual position was, when she lost her virginity or if she liked *boom-boom*. Archie was something completely different.

One thing she left out from the story of seeing him the first time was how she was struck by him. He came into the bar alone and quiet, with a charming smile, bought a whisky and sat down. Although he was quiet, it wasn't a shy quietness; it was more of a powerful stillness. Some guys came in and sat alone, but they looked awkward or anxious whilst they tried to figure out a game plan or choose which girl he wanted to chat up, whereas Archie just looked calm, comfortable and collected in his thoughts.

It was the first chance Lily ever had to catch him alone and the latent adoration she had for him turned into tangible feelings the longer she sat with him. Of course, she still felt conflicted about Amm, but she thought she didn't deserve him. If Lily herself had a chance with him then she wanted to take it. Amm had wasted her chances over and over again. Both Lily and Archie had come to such a conclusion that night.

'So...where you go after here?' she asked.

'I don't know,' he shrugged his shoulders, 'maybe just home. But I'm a little hungry again. Too much beer.' He smiled, patting his stomach and she giggled. 'Are you not hungry? You didn't eat anything all night.'

'Yes, I'm hungry, but it's okay. Maybe I can go for something outside, maybe just somtam, because I don't have too much money.'

'Well, that's why you should have let me buy you something. Or maybe you don't like to eat at work?'

'No, it's okay. Thank you ka,' she said smiling.

'What about now then? Do you want to go for some food?'

She already knew the answer but feigned a contemplation. 'Umm…if it's okay…yes, maybe we can go to eat?'

'Okay, you can tell me where you want to go.'

'You can eat Thai food mai?' she asked.

She didn't want to eat at work and for the other girls to see and start talking. To sit down and have drinks with him was normal, but to eat food with him was something a bit more. Even though she was so hungry, she declined his offer so long as they were at the bar.

She took him to a restaurant which was open twenty-four hours. He'd been there before, the last time being with Wan after his very drunken and upsetting night where he was Amm's punching bag. There were a few other couples – Thai girls with foreign guys as well as a few groups of younger revellers. It served all kinds of food, not just Thai, so her question about being able to eat Thai food seemed a little bit redundant. He did order a Thai dish though, considering he had western food at the bar. She ordered a couple of dishes, asking each time if it was okay. Of course, he said it was fine.

It was noisy there due to the inebriation of some of the other diners. One other guy was particularly crass and discussed rude things out loud for all to hear. Archie checked on Lily because he wondered if she was also hearing what he was. She hadn't been paying attention though and in actual fact seemed a little glum and quiet. He wondered if she was uncomfortable. It was a normal thing for girls to take a customer out after work and get some free food, but she hadn't ever done it before. If she ate after work it was only ever with her aunty, or maybe other girls from the bar. It was something else that was bothering her though.

'Lily, are you okay?'

She tried a smile and then when she looked in his compassionate eyes the smile became real.

'I'm okay, little bit.'

'Why little bit?'

'No, I'm okay ka.'

'Then…why are you so quiet since we arrived?'

Her mind was preoccupied when they walked in the door. She could see the couples there and wished that Archie was hers, but she knew he really loved Amm. She was jealous and upset. She felt very unlucky in life. She hated working at the bar and would rather just stay in her hometown and have a simple job. But being an attractive young girl, her family pushed her to go to Bangkok to earn a 'good' living. It was not at all a life that she enjoyed, though. On top of it all, she really *wasn't* making a good living because she hated talking to customers.

'I just thinking,' she said.

'Okay.' He didn't want to pry because it was hardly like they were close, but he felt that she was the kind of person that needed some encouragement considering she was always so withdrawn. Archie wanted her to feel comfortable and relaxed if she was to be around him, so tried a little bit more. 'Is there something I can do?'

'No. It's okay. It's my problems.'

'What problems?'

She looked around to see whether the food was coming, but that restaurant was always so busy, which meant the service was slow. It was more the opening hours, location and variety of food that made it so popular.

'Lily, you can tell me. We are friends. Maybe I can help you. Even...it can help to talk about your problems.' He wanted to reciprocate the courtesy she'd extended to him that night by listening to him bellyache about Amm. She was still quiet but he smiled and encouraged her a little more.

'Just...I not pay my rent this month. And now my aunty stop helping me. She just tell me tonight.'

'Oh, okay. And how much is your rent?'

'Six thousand.'

He was surprised. He wasn't so familiar with the cost of real places in Bangkok and thought about how he'd spend in excess of twenty thousand baht on an average night in the bar if Amm was there. That night of course had been a quiet one and his bill was very unexceptional. He took out his wallet and kept it discretely in his lap, so as not to give any onlookers the wrong impression. He counted out thousand baht notes to himself: *One, two, three, four, five, six.* Maybe he was being a little bit ridiculous, he thought, but at the same time, she was sweet and hadn't demanded anything from him. Most of all, she was there to talk to when he really needed someone. He'd be glad that his money went towards something useful rather than just on alcohol. 'Here, you can pay your rent.'

'Huh?? You give me??'

'Yes.'

'No. I cannot. Archie, it's too much. I don't want to take your money. I cannot. It's your money na ka.'

'But if Amm was there tonight she'd have been getting drinks for everyone again. You know how much my bill is usually. I just want to help you.' He rolled the notes into his palm and she held his hand timidly before accepting. 'And I don't need anything from you. I just want to help you because I see you're unhappy and I don't like it. Now we are friends. And friends help friends.'

'But it's okay for you, really?'

'Tell you what…just take it and pay your rent now, and then if you want to pay me back some time in the future then you can.'

'Okay. Thank you so much ka.' She made a wai with the notes between her hands. 'I will pay you back.'

With one worry alleviated, she still didn't feel good. She didn't particularly enjoy being in Archie's debt. It wasn't that she'd feel obliged towards him, but she was worried about his opinion of her. Lily didn't want to be seen as a cheap girl or appear as if she was after his money. It was her intention to set herself apart from other bargirls so that he might notice her. What she wanted most was his affection and his love, but someone else had it, even though she was horrible to him. It wasn't fair, she thought.

She remembered to cheer up, and when the food arrived, she lovingly placed things on his plate for him to try, just like Amm used to. It was the best feed she'd had for a while and she was truly grateful. Archie appreciated the restraint that she'd shown at the bar knowing how hungry she really was, which was part of the reason he wanted to help her. She didn't try to force things out of him. It was good behaviour, and good behaviour ought to be rewarded, he thought. It was more relaxed now too, because there in the restaurant, they were just a guy and a girl enjoying some food together. No one there knew them and wouldn't cast any aspersions about what they were doing. The main reason he invited her out to eat though was that he simply dreaded leaving the bar and going home alone.

They shared a taxi home. Her place was in the same direction but was closer than his. It was way down a soi from Sukhumvit Road, and was much more like real Bangkok, he supposed. He caught a glimpse of her building as he dropped her off and it was a little peek into her life. Also, he wanted to see what six thousand baht a month could get you.

'Thank you for keeping me company tonight,' he said. He took her hand before she got out the taxi and placed a kiss on it. She wanted him to pull her in close and hold her. She wanted him to kiss her the way he kissed Amm in the bar that first night. That looked like real, raw and tender passion. She'd never seen anyone kissing in the bar before and whilst she was a little shocked, she was also incredibly envious. There was nothing more she could do that night though. She got out the taxi and stood by the scooters lined up in front of the building to wave him goodbye.

A few minutes later, she sent a friend request and a message: "Thank you so much for tonight and for food. I really enjoy. And thank you for help me. I hope I can see you again soon." It was what she wanted to say to him face-to-face before getting out the taxi, but she was much too distracted by the touch of his fingers and the tenderness of his lips on her hand.

Once he came back into Wi-Fi range, he got her message and wrote a reply: "I'm sure you'll see me again. Thanks for being there too, I had a nice time. Goodnight Lily, sweet dreams."

Chapter Thirteen
บทที่สิบสาม

Days passed and he'd heard nothing at all from Amm. He had however been speaking with Lily, but nothing too intense. Her spoken English was reasonable, but written was more difficult for her. She was always worried that Archie would see her grammar and spelling mistakes and that she'd appear un-intellectual. At least whilst talking, the word was out then already gone. It can't be viewed or checked again. Of course, some words that are spoken do carry such a weight that they can last for a long, long time. The things Amm had said to Archie for example.

He still pined for her, but just spent some time with himself. He explored new parts of Bangkok that he'd never been to before and it was nice for him just to have a holiday again. After just two days spent alone and out of bars, he'd recovered quite well and felt ready to go back for a drink somewhere and have a catch up with some people. Lily had been asking him to come along but he didn't want to. Amm was back at work so he wanted to avoid her. The last thing he wanted was to appear needy or desperate by always hanging around when there was a whole Bangkok metropolis to explore. If she couldn't appreciate him then that was up to her. Of course, she knew what a great man he was, but she couldn't accept love again since she believed that nothing lasted forever. She'd more or less written off any chances she and Archie had.

He was still friendly with her sister Koi and thought about going to Viva. She'd moved back there because the other bar was much more saturated with staff which made it more difficult to get drinks. It created somewhat bitter competition between her and the other girls, so she decided to revert to Viva, where all her friends were. She'd rather have a happier life and less drama for a little less salary, when in the end she could make up the difference with drinks anyway.

If he was going to go to Viva, he'd have to keep it brief though. After becoming friendly with so many of the staff, he always felt obliged to buy them all drinks and he wasn't a person who could easily say no. His spending had been outrageous, so he had to make an effort to calm things down.

He sent Koi a message and she encouraged him to come along for a drink and a catch up. They were joined by Wan, who had a day off, but was in the area. She swung by for a chat, only to find Archie there too. They talked a little about Amm and were apologetic about her actions, whilst trying to offer some sympathy.

Meanwhile, Lily asked him once more if he could come along, but he explained that he didn't want to go if Amm was there. "Tonight I'm just hanging out in Viva. Koi and Wan are with me. It's a shame you're not still working here." She understood, but felt very disappointed. She had to figure out a way to get out of work for some time so that they could perhaps spend some time together. Since her rent was already paid for the month, she plucked up the courage to talk to some customers and started to get more drinks. Her aim was to build up some money so that she could pay her own barfine and make herself available for Archie.

Having worked with Koi and Wan, Lily was very close with them. She sent a message to Koi asking about him and it was apparent that she had a thing for him. She did remember Lily asking her who the man was with Amm and that she said he was very handsome. Whilst Archie sipped his whisky, there was some discussion in Thai about taking him to see Lily. Koi didn't mind if she played a part in bringing Archie and her together because she was really disgusted with the way Amm had treated him. She wanted him to be happy too because she knew all the things he'd done just to be there and all the lengths he'd been to, just for all his efforts to be dashed so cruelly.

'Archie,' Koi said, 'how about we go to Sport Spot? But we don't go to see Amm, we go to see Lily. She my sister too.'

He thought about it for a while and then Wan interjected, 'Maybe you can barfine her and we can go out somewhere?'

He did want to see Lily and it was essentially the only way to do so. And he definitely wanted to go out with them rather than stay in the bar again all night – or even worse, go home alone early. It'd also give Amm a taste of her own medicine and she could perhaps feel jealous that he was going out with other girls.

'Okay, let's go,' he said. 'So, I need to barfine you?'

'No, it's okay, I will pay. Tonight so boring anyway, no customer. Better if we can go out and enjoy.'

Koi didn't mind to pay for herself because she felt he'd already spent so much on a member of her family; it was the least she could do. Plus, she knew she'd be rewarded with a good night out anyway.

Their taxi pulled up outside Sport Spot and Archie felt a little bit sick. It was a place he thought he'd never need to come back to, but he found himself there yet again. Doubt suddenly started submerging his mind about whether or not it was a good idea to meet up with Lily. What if she was just the same? Amm seemed like a sweet, shy and timid girl when they first met and everyone knew all too well how that panned out. But then again, what else would he be doing that night?

From inside the bar, Lily saw them emerge one by one from the taxi. She looked towards Amm to see if she'd noticed, but she was busy. She greeted them at the door and sat them down as discretely as she could, but as soon as Koi's voice bounced around in the cool dark interior, Amm knew she was there, and could see who she was with.

161

Archie didn't look over to Amm and it felt like a knife in her chest. He went to sit down without even acknowledging her existence. It wasn't even that he was being callous by ignoring her – he just simply couldn't look at her. She knew she had no right to be upset and it wasn't his fault, but there was still a part of her that adored him, and to think that he maybe no longer cared was quite upsetting for her.

It had always been a bolster to know how he felt about her. Whilst she was so occluded and confused about life, having Archie love her made her feel like there was still some hope. It felt as if there was some way out or another way to go. If that was gone then there really wasn't anything else good left in her life at all.

She excused herself from her customer mentioning that her sister had just arrived. They spoke for a while and Koi just let her know that they wanted to take him for a drink and maybe go out, since they didn't want him to be left alone and abandoned. Amm knew the relationship Lily had with her Koi and Wan so didn't draw any particular conclusions about that. When she returned to her customer, she wished unendingly that it was Archie sitting opposite her again. But she'd insulted him and rejected him a few too many times.

They hung out a little before Archie paid the barfine for Lily. They went out to a nice restaurant to have dinner. Lily sat next to him because she felt much too shy to be opposite him and be in his gaze all the time. Plus, she'd be closer to him and could help him with the food and put things on his plate again. It was something he found so sweet. Of course, he was more than capable of feeding himself, but it was just a level of tenderness that he'd never encountered before he came to Thailand. It was nothing to do with servitude of women for him, it was just caring and cute, he thought. Having first choice of food and being introduced to new foods as well as her guessing what he'd like and what he probably wouldn't, was something really pleasing to him. It was all part of his Thai experience.

They moved to a bar for a couple of drinks but Lily said she wanted to go out dancing because she'd usually never have the opportunity. Thankfully it was a different club than usual and he was glad of that. He wanted things to be different this time, so to repeat old patterns didn't appeal to him at all. Lily found that she was so relaxed around him and the alcohol was gently ebbing her shyness away. She got more playful and giggly as the night progressed and there was more glancing of their bodies and tender touches whilst they danced. When Archie touched her, it felt like electricity or flames shot through her body. She felt so alive and at ease, whilst feeling somewhat wild. She was crazy for him. Since the very first time she ever laid eyes on him, she was addicted. She never entertained the thought of them being together since she thought she'd never get the opportunity. But now things were starting to go in her favour and she was so excited that it was finally happening.

For him, he was starting to feel something for her too. He wasn't sure if it was just a rebound reaction to Amm. He craved some physical comfort for sure, but it was more than that. He could go out any night and no doubt find someone to go home with – especially in Bangkok, but that wasn't the kind of thing he was looking for. As Lily danced next to him with her long sleek black hair and her gorgeous motion, he was undoubtedly enchanted. It wasn't even about the way the flashing lights skimmed around the delicate curves of her body. There was a naivety to her. It was a purity and innocence which captivated and enthralled him. He wanted to take her in his arms to protect her from all of the bad things in the world and preserve that innocence. He didn't want her to become spoiled and warped – like Amm, or like many young Thai girls were.

Naturally, he understood that he had to be careful about transcending the feelings he had for Amm onto Lily, but she had a tenderness all of her own. Perhaps it was time to really forget about Amm and find someone who was able to be her true gentle self around him and treat him the way he ought to be treated.

Koi and Wan could see the progression between them through the night. Even with Wan's fondness for him, she stepped back, because it was obvious that Lily felt very strongly. Wan had other male 'friends' too, so didn't want to end up giving him the run-around. She was quite happy to keep him as a good friend.

After the music stopped and the lights came on, they made their way outside. Obviously, it was time to eat again, so they headed around the corner and ordered some street food. He wasn't particularly hungry, but it was a mandatory part of any evening in Thailand. After the food, they all piled into a taxi together. Wan stayed on the same soi as Lily but a few hundred yards away, then further out was Archie's hotel, and then a little bit further again was Koi (and Amm's) place, of course. Archie sat in the front which Lily was disappointed about, but he didn't really think it through. She was also a little disappointed that she didn't have him all to herself at any point that night. She wanted to maybe try to hold his hand or at least talk a bit more privately with him. She'd been urging him to come to see her, and whilst she could appreciate why he didn't come, that night was her chance to spend some more alone-time with him. She consoled herself with the fact that they had been out and she had an amazing time. Certainly, she felt like she had made progress with him, but was still worried about Amm. Worried about betraying her friend, worried about his residual feelings for her, worried about the reputation she might get in the bar for stealing someone else's man – never mind the fact that he was by no means *Amm's man.*

They dropped Wan at her building and she thanked Archie for a fun night before saying something to Lily in Thai. He didn't get what it was but it sounded important and advisory. After a few hundred more metres, it was her turn to get out, but Archie was so far from her. She just politely and shyly made a wai, thanked him for the evening too and got out the car. She stumbled a little bit as she walked behind the line of scooters to her building. Archie told the driver to wait until she got inside before driving away.

By the time he got to the hotel, there was a message waiting from Lily. Although she'd started writing it immediately after getting home, it took her several minutes to figure out what to say and to check it through as best as she could for any errors.

"Thank you so much for tonight. I really enjoy. You are so nice and lovely and I am happy I can meet you."

He crossed the lobby as the soles of his tan boots squeaked quietly on the pale marble towards the lift. "You're welcome Lily. I'm also happy that you came out with us tonight. It was nice to hang out with you." He continued, "Remember to drink some water before you go to bed so you don't have a big hangover tomorrow."

The message struggled to send until the doors pinged open onto his floor. "Ok ka," she replied. "Thank you for think about me. You too hope you not hangover tomorrow."

"Thank you. I'll be okay. But I have been drinking too much since I arrived, maybe I need to take a break! Haha."

"Yes, you have to take care yourself. For me."

It was the first real sort of admission she made regarding her feelings. He closed the door to his room and switched the lights on as he read the message over a few times. *That's deliberate, that's not just bad English or something*, he thought. He didn't know how to respond, but he was pleased about it. A glimmer of hope passed through him. He may have still stupidly ached for Amm and still hurt about the whole thing, but now a beautiful sweet girl was making advances to him. It was very encouraging, when all his thoughts up until then had been very dark indeed. After a few minutes, he replied asking: "Will you go to sleep soon?"

"Yes, just take shower then sleep."

"Ok. Goodnight Lily. Sweet dreams."

"You too sweet dreams. Dream of me please." *Oh, for sure she wants me*, he thought.

He jumped in the shower himself. It was always so hot in Bangkok, but regardless of the heat, it was always dirty too. It wasn't pure and clean like at home in Scotland. But that was more of an observation rather than a complaint. You would expect that of such a busy city. Bangkok had more people in it than the whole of Scotland, after all.

Once he was settled into bed, he decided to look through her profile. He wanted to spy on her a little and check for past boyfriends or admirers. He wanted to see who commented and who liked her photos. From her last message, it was obvious that she liked him. If something was to happen, he really didn't want to make the same mistakes again.

It was difficult to sleep. He thought about Lily, Amm, home, money, his liver. It was all excessive, everything. Whilst his head was doing circles, his phone flashed and buzzed, it was Lily again. "Can we go to dinner? Only me and you please. I will pay my barfine. If you free just tell me please. I hope you can."

Well, Archie thought, *a girl asking me out for dinner? There's a first*. He couldn't help it, but a wide smile beamed across his face as he lay alone in bed. Whilst he was trying to figure out whether or not she was a rebound, he realised that she most certainly wasn't. If he fucked

167

Wan that night, that would have been a rebound. If he went out to pick up a random girl, that would be a rebound. But building a connection and being inundated by a romantic excitement for Lily was not a rebound in the slightest.

He wondered if he should wait to reply or not, but guessed she'd been trying to pluck up the courage for the last hour or so and didn't want to keep her in suspense. Besides, he was still awake and there was no need to play games with her. "Yes, I'd like to go for dinner with you. I'm free tomorrow if you want. Is it okay for you?"

"Yes," came the immediate reply.

Chapter Fourteen
บทที่สิบสี่

They made their arrangements for dinner and agreed to meet at the end of her soi. The traffic was unbelievable that night. He sent a message just before leaving to tell her he was doing just that, but after a few minutes they caught up with the jam and hardly moved at all. He'd experienced Sukhumvit traffic before, but never as heavy as that. He had no internet on his phone because roaming was prohibitively expensive, so would just use Wi-Fi in the hotel or in bars. It was usually all he needed, but as he sat impatiently in the long line of vehicles, he was agitated not being able to tell her that he was running late. He could probably walk it and get there faster, but it was so hot. He didn't want to be sweaty by the time he arrived and then feel uncomfortable during the whole date. He'd made an effort to groom himself nicely, and walking the remaining distance would just cancel out all that effort.

The traffic didn't let up at all, and ten minutes late became twenty minutes. Twenty became thirty. They continued to creep forward, but he was growing very concerned that she might feel as if she was stood up. He wondered how long she might wait before going home. He wondered whether she'd sent him messages or tried to call, only to not get through. 'I'll walk from here,' he told the taxi driver. After paying the man and checking for motorbikes zipping between the cars, he opened the door and Bangkok greeted him – the heat, the noise, the heavy exhaust fumes from the traffic. There was perhaps less than a kilometre to go and he walked a little briskly whilst trying to look ahead and think cool thoughts. He could feel beads of sweat begin to gather on his forehead and at the top of his back, but he had to keep his pace.

He approached her soi, and lo and behold she was sitting there peacefully. A street vendor had taken pity on her and let her borrow a chair as she waited for her date. She wore a red velvet dress, her hair was up and she sat cross-legged with her phone in her lap. She was breathtaking. Her simplistic beauty stood out like a vision amidst the urban throng. 'Lily!' She was startled and looked up to finally see him. Relief washed through her like a waterfall. She didn't know how long she had to wait, but she'd have probably waited all night for him to come. The anticipation built up and built up but finally he was there. 'I'm so sorry! The traffic is so bad!'

'Yes, I can see. Tonight have too much traffic.' The queues of vehicles were also evident at their meeting point, but she didn't mind at all.

'So, I was planning to take a taxi but I think it's better if we take the BTS,' he suggested.

'Yes, it's better.' She stood up from her seat and thanked the street vendor, which gave him a quick chance to surreptitiously wipe his brow.

'Khun suay mak krap,' he said.

'Thank you ka,' she giggled nervously. He'd looked up how to say *you are very beautiful*.

They arranged to go to Asiatique, which was an attraction along the Chao Phraya River. It was a mock-up of a dockside with 'old' warehouses under a pretend trading company with shops and restaurants and bars. There was also a Ferris Wheel which ascended into the Bangkok twilight which he really wanted to go on.

The BTS also happened to be packed and there was hardly even room to stand. It really wasn't what he wanted, considering he already felt hot – to be jammed in a long tin can filled with other hot bodies. Lily looked nervous and he wanted to make her feel comfortable. He used humour to put her at ease whilst flirting at the same time. There was no doubt that he was attracted to her, in fact he thought she was stunning, but he wasn't in the habit of swapping from one girl to another like the flick of a switch. For the sake of his sanity and health and wellbeing, he had to make a concerted effort though. He wondered whether he was doing the right thing to take a chance on someone new, but it was better than staying alone in the hotel. It was certainly much better than pursuing Amm any more, or cruising bars looking for a hook-up. Besides, there was no good reason for him to turn down an invitation to dinner from a beautiful girl.

The train buffeted side-to-side on the tracks and he nudged her at times because of the lack of space. 'Oh sorry, miss.' He joked with her and made out as if they were strangers. The train rocked again and threw her into him. He caught her and steadied her with his hand on the small of her back. She zinged and popped with energy like a firework going off. 'Oh, excuse me,' he said with a cheeky smile. Since the train was so busy, she tried to stifle her giggle but it just made her look even more adorable.

People started to gradually alight the train and the breathing space increased somewhat. That only lasted until Siam station however, where they had to change trains, and the concentration of people increased once again. It was a bit of a mad scramble whilst people crossed the platform, and she looked unsure where she was going. He stayed close and guided her with his hands on her hips and it was bliss to her. They were taking the train all the way to the river; thereafter they'd take a boat down the Chao Phraya River. As much as it was about getting there, it was also part of the date in a way. He never had to ride a boat in Scotland just to take a girl for dinner. It was another thing that just added more magic to the place for him.

It was quite a long queue for the boat, but it advanced quickly enough. She'd never been on it before and was very excited. It may have just been a short hop down the river, but it felt like an adventure to her. He helped her step aboard before effortlessly transferring from pier to vessel. Stepping on and off floating things was a skill he'd honed over years and his sea-legs were obviously very good. They climbed down the steep narrow stairs into the cabin where he encouraged her to pick some seats. She took photos with her phone and pointed out things to him that piqued her interest, which just so happened to be numerous and often. 'So, this same like your work?' she giggled. She knew it wasn't, since he'd already shown her photos, but it was a boat in the water.

'No, my one is a little bit bigger.' The boat splashed through a little wake and she enjoyed the bumpy sensation. She liked to think that she was getting a taste of being waterborne like Archie was so often.

Before long, they arrived at the pier and he again helped her alight onto land. They were overwhelmed with coloured lights and bustle and people. Restaurants lined the riverfront, whilst people strolled up and down the artificial boardwalk. It was such a beautiful and picturesque place. An anchor adorned the boardwalk and some people were gathered around it for a photo opportunity. She wanted a photo too and asked him if they could wait for it to become free. She enjoyed all the nautical references so far and rather than be negative about his job, she wanted to take pride in his career. She clung to the anchor like a little monkey and giggled freely as he took her photo. She felt silly and out of place but could see a smile on Archie's face, which was exactly what her intention was.

As they walked together, he thought about holding her hand. It just seemed the appropriate thing to do at that time and place, yet he refrained. He thought they still weren't quite there yet. 'Where you want to eat?' she asked.

'I was late…so you can choose.'

'Anything, it's okay for me na.'

'Lily, it's fine, you can choose.'

'No, it's okay.'

They walked around and he encouraged her to check some menus. They reached one restaurant which was, as most of them were, half inside and half outside. It looked like it had quite a nice ambience and the food looked reassuringly pricey, without being too much. He guessed you had to pay a premium just for the location too, but it was all worth it.

'What about here?' He checked the menu and it had a mix of Thai and western food. 'They have Thai food here,' he said.

'Okay,' she said with a smile.

He followed her slender figure to the table and felt proud of himself. He was happy to have met Lily and happy to be in such a place with her. When he spent time with her before, that was just hanging out, even going to eat and going to the club. But this was a formal date for sure and the night belonged to them. Although not one hundred per cent there yet, he felt he was moving on from Amm. She was still there at times when he forgot himself and he'd feel a smack of foolishness. But then again, he knew he didn't do anything wrong, he was nothing but kind and caring towards her. It was her loss. It had to be. And her loss was Lily's gain.

Lily was so keen on him and it would have been really foolish of Archie to reject her invitation. He couldn't live in fear of being hurt, because he might miss out on something amazing. He also knew what effect living in fear had on Amm, and there was no way he'd let himself emulate her in any way. As he sat opposite Lily, he was enormously glad to be there with her.

As his fixation of Amm started to fade, his eyes were being opened to how beautiful Lily was. Men looked at her as they walked past their table. Women did the same. She sipped tenderly at the wine he ordered. She wasn't much of a wine drinker and always viewed it as a sophisticated person's drink. She had always wanted to try, but she'd never felt the occasion to be fitting before. Now the time was right for her. As she held the glass, her pinkie extended out, so even though she was still a novice, she certainly looked the part.

Lily exuded a simple grace and elegance. Of course, she'd done her hair and makeup nicely for him, but she was just a down-to-earth and straightforward girl. There was no complex make up routines and expensive clothes; she looked extraordinary with very little. Her most endearing quality however, was that she never realised how authentically beautiful she truly was.

A gentle breeze gusted intermittently and flicked her sleek long hair around as they browsed the menu. She ordered a steak, much to his surprise. For a start, Buddhists weren't supposed to eat beef, he thought. He remembered Amm didn't eat it for that reason. But then that was Amm and not Lily, they were not the same and it didn't matter anymore. There were a couple of steaks on the menu and she chose the same one as him, but only after checking that it was okay first. He also knew it wasn't about her being unobjectionable or imitating him, because she revealed her choice first.

After the food, she asked him tentatively if she could order another drink. 'Can I have…whisky, please?' *Oh my God!* thought Archie, *a girl who eats steak and drinks whisky. This is the girl for me.* He was thoroughly surprised and impressed.

When he got the bill, she was shocked at the price. Before letting him pay, she checked it through a few times, convinced that there had been a mistake. She took a photo on her phone to send to her aunty Ploy, because she'd never had such an expensive meal in her life. Whilst it may have been a bit more premium than the average restaurant, it hardly broke the bank for him. It was certainly much more than anything Lily had ever experienced before, though.

They took a walk, browsed shops and fooled around a little. They were enjoying each others company. 'Lily, do you want to ride the wheel?' He couldn't come all the way there and not ride it. Not only was he developing feelings for her, he was already very much in love with

176

Bangkok, so if he had a chance to see it from up high then he'd want to take it. There was no one else who he'd rather see it with too. Lily was scared to go, but didn't have the courage to tell him. She wanted to make him happy and never ever wanted to tell him *no*. Whilst she may have had a fear of heights, she was more frightened of letting him down.

The capsule rocked slightly as she stepped aboard. She let out a shriek, yet she was still giggling; she just didn't expect it to move. They sat down and she still felt alright, but as soon as it started to move, that feeling wore off. She went stiff as a board and quieter than a mouse. Archie began to take some photos of the city and marvel in the sight before checking back on her. He could tell something was wrong.

'Are you okay?' he asked.

She took a while to reply. 'Yes, okay.'

'You err…don't look okay.'

'I'm scared to go high,' she finally admitted.

'Oh God, Lily. You're scared of heights? Why didn't you say something?'

'I don't know. I just think that it will be okay when I'm here.'

The wheel stopped as they were at the top to change over another capsule. It wasn't particularly busy because it was just an average night and more of a novelty than anything else. Below the wheel was a small outdoor track for go-karts and as much as he wanted to try that too, he couldn't really imagine Lily getting into a go-kart with her short velvet dress on. Back in the capsule, there were more pressing matters of course. 'Just don't look down,' he said. 'It's quite safe though. Nothing will happen to you.' She looked up at him with her big deep brown eyes and felt a little more at ease. 'You should have told me first, Lily. You can tell me, you know? That's why I asked you.'

'I know. But I see you want to go.'

'But we are here together. So we choose *together* what we want to do. We are fifty-fifty, it's not like I'm your boss or something.'

That was the kind of talk which always made him stand out, particularly in Bangkok – treating a woman as an equal and valuing her feelings and opinions rather than demanding from her, just because he's splashing the cash. The capsule started to move again and she flinched with her whole body. He reached out for her hand as he sat next to her and held it so as to comfort her. Suddenly, all her worries and fears subsided, because all she could feel was Archie's secure hand enveloping hers and how their fingers were wrapped together. 'I'll try to tell them to stop when we go past. You want to get out?'

'No, it's okay, I'm okay now. I can do.' She didn't want to break the hand holding and with that being the only thing on her mind, she didn't even notice the height anymore. If it took for her to be scared stiff for Archie to start holding her hand then she supposed it was worth it. She wanted to rest her head on his shoulder too, but didn't know how he'd react.

The wheel continued round a few more times and the view of the city was incredible. They could see all the way up the river. Temples were illuminated, floodlights shone columns into the sky from somewhere and the lights of the city twinkled with wonder.

She may have felt better after Archie calmed her down, but when they got out of the capsule, Lily was certainly glad to be back on solid ground again. 'Okay, let's get you a drink then after your ordeal.' She didn't understand *ordeal*, but agreed nonetheless.

Usually she only got between eighty-to-ninety percent of what Archie said. Sometimes it was down to his accent, sometimes about the words he used. He'd already started to alter the way he spoke since his previous visit. Spending time exclusively with Thai people, he recognised how they talked and would modify his grammar and vocabulary to be more easily understood. There were still times however, when the most appropriate word was also a difficult one, but he couldn't help that. What he did do of course, was let Lily know that she could ask him again if she didn't understand. With more practice she was bound to improve and it'd also help her feel better, as well as develop her ability to share her feelings and opinions, which was important to him.

He had an idea to start to learn Thai, but all the courses required weekly attendance for a few months. Archie never had that amount of time to spend continuously in the country. The alternative was a basic crash course, but the thought of spending ten solid days in a classroom didn't appeal to him, when he could be out having fun and enjoying himself. He was there to enjoy, not to learn. As it was, he could muddle through and check out the odd phrase here and there. Generally, the level of English in Bangkok was enough to negate his need to learn any Thai properly. But rather than her feel bad about her English, he told her it was him who was at fault for not speaking the language of the country he was in.

Lily adjusted back to ground level as they zig-zagged their way through the exit gates. Beneath the steel superstructure and bright beaconing lights of the wheel, there was a bar on top of a repurposed blue shipping container. They ordered some drinks and she asked if she could order something to eat. He couldn't believe that she could eat more since they both had the same steak and he was still full. Given how slim she was too, he had no idea where she put it. But that seemed not to matter, because she hid it somewhere, and as shallow as it was, he was glad of that. 'I can order something more, is it okay?' she asked.

'Yes, it's okay. You can have anything you like.'

'Thank you ka, Archie.'

They also ordered a tower of beer and the waitress brought over a tall Perspex light up container filled with beer, a bucket of ice and two glasses. She used tongs to drop cubes of ice into their glasses and they rattled around, surrendering some water onto the bottom and sides. Despite the waitress's best efforts, the beer was poured very frothily indeed, but it didn't really matter. Lily ordered a spicy glass noodle salad. She fed him some but it was much too spicy, and he had to wash away the burning chilli sensation from his mouth with beer as she happily ate the rest.

Archie was delighted. He rarely enjoyed that kind of casual relaxed time with Amm. Even if he managed to find her at a calm point, he was always on edge, like walking along a precipice, inches from severe peril. It was how spending time with someone ought to be. Seeing new things together, trying new experiences, enjoying some food and drink and learning their fear of heights too, perhaps. The setting was magnificent as they sat at their vantage point on top of the container. It was Lily who was the real spectacle however, and she set the whole occasion off. He thought about what his friend said regarding it not having to be a battle and that's exactly how it felt with her.

As she gingerly balanced food onto her spoon and lifted it to her quiet lips, his feeling inside changed. Something clicked about Amm and he could let her go. He thought perhaps he'd need time or to take it slowly with Lily, but he realised it wasn't going to be a gradual thing. It was like the parting of a rope under massive strain and the load on the other end fell fast into oblivion. Finally.

'Archie?'

'Yes?'

'Thank you for come to see me tonight.' She put her fork and spoon down. 'I'm so happy now. You are very good to me.' She wanted to convey her feelings, but didn't know how to find the words. She was struggling for them in Thai, never mind in English. She was in love with him, but didn't want to scare him off. She had to know whether or not he could let go of Amm, but the concern she had about betraying her had already long departed. There was no way she'd let him get away because of that. She didn't do it in a sneaky way, even Amm's own sister was with them when they started to hang out and played a key role in them coming together. But if there was any chance that she could be with him then she wanted to grab it with both hands and never let go.

'You're welcome Lily. And I'm happy too.' He put his beer down and wiped the condensation off his hands with a tissue. 'I think I made a mistake before. But now I'm spending time with the right girl.' She lit up from inside and shone brighter than the lights from the wheel above them.

'But...I see you really love her. Did you still talk with her or something?'

'No, we don't talk anymore. And yes, maybe I did. And maybe it looked like I was so in love, but it's because if I love, it's always one hundred percent.' Archie wanted to calm her concerns, because if Lily was his chance at moving on, he didn't want any leftover lingering of Amm to ruin that. He also knew how to adjust his dialogue and use words that she'd be able to easily understand. 'Me and Amm, we don't have anything now. I don't love someone ten percent, or fifty-fifty. I give everything. So also...when I stop, I stop. And now I stop with her.'

'Okay.'

Their seats were quite slouchy, but he leaned forward to take her hands across the table. 'Maybe the reason I met her...was so I could meet you.'

She smiled the truest smile ever. 'Yes, maybe it's why.'

They didn't quite finish the tower of beer, but that was okay. He took her hand to lead her down the stairs from the container and didn't let go when they reached the bottom. It had already been established in the capsule, and he had no intention in rescinding it. They browsed some more of the shops and markets because they still hadn't seen the whole place yet. There were interesting boutique shops, clothes shops, novelty and souvenir shops. He wanted to buy her something small just as a memento of their first date, but she insisted she didn't want anything. She didn't want him to spend any more money than he had to. The food and drink and everything was great, but she didn't need something from a shop. She already got more than she could ever hope for from her evening and the feeling from that night would last forever for her.

Her feet started to strain and she became tired as they had just about seen everything there. She had received a message from her aunty whilst they were on top of the container, but didn't check it until they were leaving. Unlike most girls who would constantly play with their phone, she wanted to give him her undivided attention. For Lily, there was nothing more interesting to look at than him anyway. Archie was her priority and whatever else might be happening in the world could wait.

Ploy told her that a lot of the girls from Viva had turned up at their bar. The original plan was to go back there for a nightcap, but she no longer wanted to go. It wasn't that she wanted to hide her and

Archie, it was more that she expected Archie to be hijacked and the attention wouldn't be on her anymore. She was much quieter than the other girls, so she'd just end up fading away into the background, she thought. Archie would never let that happen now, of course. That night changed things and he realised what he felt for Lily. There was nothing about latent feelings for Amm being transferred to her; it was all about Lily on her own merit and by her own sweet uncomplicated personality. She was the most adorable and sweet lady he'd ever had the privilege of being with.

His feelings manifested very rapidly over the evening, because it had simply been perfect. It was always his way though, to fall very hard and fast. Somehow everything with Lily just felt so much in line. He came to realise that *real* love was not just about loving someone, but having them feel the same for you too and being brave enough to show it. It was all intensified for him by the fact that he was overseas and his senses were being continually bombarded with new and interesting things. Bangkok was as much a part of the relationship as any girl was – the sights and sounds, the restaurants and bars, the traffic and trains and malls and markets. Despite still officially being a tourist, he felt like he was home – natural in his surroundings, at ease and familiar with the city.

'Archie, where you want to go now?' She wanted to revise their plan. 'My aunty tell me a lot of girls from Viva there now.'

'Oh, okay.' He understood how she felt, and didn't want to divide his attention from her in any way either, because as much as he cared for those girls, they didn't give him what Lily did. It would be a shame that he didn't turn up and show Amm how happy Lily was and how great they were getting on together. Then again, she probably wasn't even there, he guessed. 'We'll go somewhere else, close to there. And then I can take you to meet Ploy after.'

They took a taxi back to Sukhumvit and stopped at a bar a couple of blocks away. It was only about an hour before closing time and the herd had already started to thin. A live band was packing up whilst music played gently through the speakers. The dim light of the bar caught her eyes and made them sparkle. Sitting side by side in a booth, she felt the time was right to lay her head on his shoulder at last. It was well received. With one hand on her lap, he enjoyed the sublime texture of her red velvet dress, yet he supposed what was underneath felt better still. He didn't want to push things, but placed a kiss on her head as she rested there, which seemed to wake her up. 'Can I ask you something?' he said. She lifted her head and looked up at him expectantly with her big brown eyes. 'If I kiss you...will you kiss me back?'

She thought about the best way to respond. She didn't want to seem uncivilized by shouting out *Yes please!* as was her initial compulsion.

'Maybe...better if you just try...'

Her hand slid along the red velvet to meet his and he leant in. Their lips touched. He could still sense the chilli from the salad she had at the previous bar, but it now tasted so sweet. Between their lips was chilli and whisky and something else too. It was the taste of each other, of course.

It wasn't just her lips that he was kissing however, because he touched every corner of her being. She felt somehow weightless, as if she was suspended in mid air. The kiss sealed it for him too. Not only was she the very first girl he ever met that liked whisky and steak, but her every single action was entirely enchanting. She was subtle and willing and innocent. There was a purity to her which he wanted to both protect and enjoy. In their secluded corner of the bar, they kissed one another slowly and tenderly until the lights came on. As the harsh fluorescent light hit the back of her eyelids, she was startled, as if awoken suddenly from her dream. Lily then drifted back down from the clouds into the booth with Archie, until she realised her dream was now her reality too.

He took her and her aunty home. By no accident, Lily and Ploy stayed on the same soi, and in buildings next to each other. Her aunty got out first, Lily was squeezed next to Archie in the middle anyway. They kissed for a moment. She didn't care if the driver saw it, she wanted more of him. He was all she wanted and she'd never felt a desire like it in her life. 'Thank you again na, Archie. You make me so happy. I'm very happy I can meet a man like you in my life.'

'Goodnight Lily. Thank you too.'

'Send me message when you get home na ka,' she requested.

'Yes, I will.'

Upon arrival at the hotel, his phone started to ping with messages from her:

"Thank you so much. I'm sorry about in the wheel tonight."

"I want to see you tomorrow please, if you can. I hope you will."

"Did you get home yet?"

"Goodnight and have a good sleep na."

The messages were spaced a minute or so apart as she eagerly awaited his reply. He wrote back whilst making his way to the lift. "Yes, I'm just back now. I had a great time. Don't worry about the wheel! But you should have told me! And you will see me tomorrow for sure. Sweet dreams XXX"

"Sweet dreams for you too na XXX"

Chapter Fifteen

บทที่สิบห้า

Lily couldn't sleep. Whilst lying in bed in her small and simple room, her legs and feet throbbed. Never before had she ever walked so much and she really wasn't accustomed to it. But each blister and ache was well worth it; she wouldn't take them back for anything. Her date with Archie was the best night of her life and she prayed it was the start of something good. When she was around him, she somehow felt completely herself and relaxed. She had no impression that he could ever harm her or even be inappropriate with her, which was exactly what she'd learned men were like from working in a bar in Bangkok. Comfort and confidence filled her when she was in his presence and she'd never experienced such a feeling ever before.

Usually she was much too shy, but whilst she still retained her normal shyness, there was an energy which came from deep inside and propelled her without even thinking about it. She wasn't ashamed to ask him out and thought nothing of waiting so long on the street for him to arrive.

Archie himself didn't have a particularly restful night. He felt good, but he felt like it wasn't enough. As soon as he dropped the keycard in the slot by the door, the room came to life and yet it seemed completely empty. He hated loneliness. He had to stay alone at his work so many nights and so often, without anyone to talk to, let alone hold. If he was on leave and slept alone, it felt entirely like a waste of a night for him. He truly longed to share his nights with someone.

He wished she could have at least stayed with him. But at the same time, he knew he wouldn't have been able to keep his hands off her. In many ways, he was glad that she wasn't a girl that he could so easily take home. Deep down he knew it was too early for her so he had to wait for her to come to him. He could of course let her know she was welcome, in a nonchalant way, so as not to put pressure on her. Then it'd be up to her and he'd know by then she'd already made her mind up.

But life is short, he felt. Being at sea gives someone a certain understanding beyond most land-lubbers. People often take for granted the nights spent at home or with loved ones or merely doing something they enjoy. Because when that is taken away from you for months at a time, you begin to appreciate the full value of every moment spent ashore and in the real world.

Then came the worry about him going back to sea again, and whether she would wait for him. There wasn't much point in getting ahead of himself though. He still didn't know if they were together or not, although he was about ninety per cent sure.

"Good morning," came her message, "how are you today?"

He'd just sat down to breakfast, which was another occasion of loneliness that he hated. As simple as it was, he longed to wake up next to someone else and start the day together with them. Breakfast with someone was not just eating, it was a continuation of the intimacy.

He sat with a plate of breakfast and his phone at the side, next to his cup of coffee. The hotel restaurant was merely a breakfasting restaurant and was down on the fifth floor. The building was arranged in a hollow square which formed a courtyard in the centre. The pool, gym and sauna were also on that level. The ceilings of the restaurant were very high and a full windowed wall enabled you to watch out over the pool. Of course, nobody was swimming at that time, as the sun began to peek over the roof on one side and into the square. The restaurant had a couple dozen people there for breakfast at that time, but it was so large that the place still felt very quiet. It was always occupied but not busy, and he liked that.

There was a table of what he guessed were Japanese businessmen right next to the window. He could hear them conversing as one held a newspaper over his crossed legs and the rest played on their phones or simply ate breakfast. There were a few westerners, mostly couples, then the occasional singleton like himself. They were dressed in elephant pants, vests and with flip flops on however, which he always found unappealing. He wore cargo shorts and a normal short-sleeved t-shirt for breakfast. He didn't like seeing men in a dining establishment with bare upper arms. Women were okay, though, because that was a normal for a lady to wear a vest. There were two Asian families, one with young kids and another with teenagers. He couldn't figure out exactly where they were from, but thought perhaps Singapore and Korea.

He was pleased that she was the first one to message. It wasn't like with Amm, where he'd have to send a message and nervously await the reply. Archie did want to message as soon as he woke up but was scared that he'd disturb her sleep. There maybe was a part of him that wanted to check if she'd message first too. He wrote back: "Good morning. I'm good thanks. How about you? Good sleep?"

"No I not sleep good," she told him.

"Oh, why?"

"Because just miss someone ;)"

"Oh really? I wonder who that is?"

Archie's eggs, sausage and fried rice cooled a little whilst he and Lily flirted and got down to the business of date number two. She was desperate to see him, but wanted to get another couple hours of sleep. They agreed to meet for lunch and a movie but he didn't really know what was on. Whilst at sea, he would always miss the trailers or previews to upcoming films so usually never had any idea what was showing at the cinemas. He asked her to pick something and check times, but she didn't care what movie. She didn't care even if they did see a movie, she just wanted to be next to him, no matter what.

They met at the shopping mall entrance next to the BTS station. It was an easy and obvious place to meet, and it had been a place he waited for Koi with Amm before. He was getting frustrated about not having any internet outside, so the purchase of a second cheap and cheerful Thai phone was on the cards too. There was free Wi-Fi at the mall but it was a bit of a hassle to connect to. She was running a little late, but he knew he had to extend her the same courtesy by waiting. He was certainly in no doubt about whether she'd turn up or not. Having been so tired from the previous nights walking, she overslept a little. There was no way that she'd allow herself to skimp on getting ready though, because she had to look her best for him. And that she did.

She wore a yellow vest and jean shorts as she moseyed over the concourse towards him like a ray of sunshine from the hips up. Her smooth slender legs paced forward and her arm was bent at an angle carrying her small handbag. A huge smile erupted on her face the moment she spotted Archie. Her ears and cheeks would lift to reveal her sparkly white teeth and wide smile, she just couldn't help it. He gave her a quick hug and kiss on the cheek. She would still get embarrassed, but it was fine. Actually, she'd have felt upset if he didn't. She wanted to be claimed by him. Out of all the other pretty girls who stepped off the train, she was the one he was waiting for and that's exactly what she wanted.

'So, did you decide on a movie then?' he asked.

'No, maybe we can go to look. But maybe I fall asleep!' she giggled. She had an unadulterated, unfiltered, goofy, from-the-belly cackle. It was joy at simple things and another endearing element of purity to her which he treasured.

'Okay, well we don't have to see a movie, we can go to eat and go shopping? Did you eat anything yet?'

'No, I not eat yet.' He was about to ask if she was hungry, but he was sure of the answer, so asked a more pertinent question instead. They walked through the mall and he saw a lot more of it than before. Lily hadn't been there much because it was a fancy and expensive mall, and as such, it was not a place that she'd have any occasion to go to. Ploy took her a couple of times before for a spot of window shopping, but that was all.

There were a couple of buildings to it, but they made their way to *The Helix*. Past the rooftop garden where he'd stopped at before, it ascended just exactly as the name suggested– a giant elliptical corkscrew wound its way skyward with many restaurants along the way. They picked one and sat at a table next to the window. The view was down Sukhumvit road with the BTS line below them. Men worked on the building opposite, seemingly dangled precariously on planks of wood or whatever else was available. They were welding and hammering under the shadow of a crane, building another skyscraper to soar into the Bangkok skyline. It was still nothing more than a shell with green netting surrounding it and he looked forward to seeing how it might turn out in the end.

They browsed the menu and she asked if she could order a cocktail. 'Start early?' he asked.

'I like this one,' she pointed out. 'It's so pretty!'

Most of the menus in Bangkok had pictures with them. That was handy for newbies wondering what *Larb Moo Tard* or *Tom Yum Gung* was. She was attracted by how attractive the drink looked and didn't even check what was in it, but he was more than happy to let her try. Sometimes in Thailand, appearances meant more than something having actual substance but appearing ordinary. Things ought to look good in a form-over-function sort of way. The name was also interesting and that was actually the main thing which caught her attention. 'Love never dies?' he read out.

'Love never die,' she repeated and giggled.

'Are you trying to tell me something?' he teased.

Archie was having a great time. Lily was so naive and genuine. She had an inquisitive mind, but it seemed like she'd never had the means to explore anything before or never had anyone who knew the answers to the questions she had.

Her hometown was a small place in North East Thailand – a region known as Isaan – and she had led the typical sheltered life growing up. Yet there was more to her than a simple farm girl, or a simple bargirl for that matter. She wanted to better herself and learn and experience more. He took joy in explaining things to her, even if they often were run-of-the-mill to him. It was a great joy of his to enrich her world, expand her mind and satisfy her curiosity. The way in which she was continually captivated was incredibly endearing to him.

Archie opened her eyes to the world, but without any condescension or arrogance. Of course there was the physical attraction between them, recently an emotional one, but there was an intellectual one too. The previous night made his world turn back around in an instant. He had something to hope for and look forward to and every moment with her was precious.

They descended *The Helix* hand-in-hand and walked around the shops. He remembered when he stopped at the Dior counter to buy a perfume for Amm, and thought that perhaps he should buy one for the girl who was much more deserving of it. He wanted to spoil her, but also wanted to be very careful about giving the wrong impression and setting a bad precedent. But buying perfume was not just a present for her. Plain and simply, he loved the smell and wanted whoever his girlfriend may be to have that fragrance, so that he could enjoy it on her. He slowed down as they approached the counter and began to browse. 'You want something?' she asked.

'Maybe...' he admitted. He was looking at the lady's perfumes after all, 'I think I will buy a present for somebody.'

'Buy for your mum?' That was the innocence he so loved about her; humble and in no way presumptuous.

'No. Somebody else...' By the cheeky look in his eye, she began to catch on. 'Somebody who's holding my hand right now.'

She couldn't deny that she was tantalised by the thought of such fancy goods, but didn't waver from her usual: 'No, it's okay, it's so expensive.'

'Why don't you just have a look?' He took a bottle and sprayed a little on her wrist whilst a young and immaculately turned out effeminate man came to offer them assistance. They talked in Thai and it looked like Lily was making excuses to leave. It was all the more reason for him to want to buy her something. 'It's okay, Lily. Take a look and if you want something, I'll get it for you.'

The man took her across to their demonstration area where he immediately and enthusiastically bombarded her with his pitch about what was 'in' for that season, as he tried to reach his sales target. Lily still wasn't sure, but nevertheless, the man applied some cream to her face and rubbed it into her soft cheeks whilst all she could do was giggle out loud from atop the tall stool. It attracted the attention of his other colleagues, one of which had served Archie before. Of course, he recognised her because he was in the same place, but he was surprised she recognised him too, considering how many customers she must have served since then.

'Hello sir, how are you? Nice to see you again.' She came across to him and saw that he was with Lily. She asked her in English, 'How did you like the perfume, madam?' Of course, Lily was confused, but thought perhaps she was just asking whether or not she liked the smell of it. She had no idea that the lady presumed she was the recipient of Archie's previous purchase. Thankfully the moment passed and there was no need to explain or make excuses, but yet again it was another annoying reminder of Amm.

In the end, he bought her a perfume, a mascara and a lipstick. When she asked about the price, she was shocked and wanted to back out, but he insisted. She'd never had a chance to have such nice things before, but if she was going to be with him then she ought to know how to start. He wanted to bring her life up little by little because he felt like she deserved it, certainly more than anyone else. He knew deep down that she did have aspirations and it was his intention to help her realise them without her asking.

The way he saw it was that he'd reached thirty years old with a good job and everything else that someone might expect, including a nice car, expendable income and no further desire to spend money on material things for himself. The thing that was missing from his life was a partner, so he wanted to do all he could to make that happen too. He worked hard for his money and there was no reason why he couldn't use some of it to put a smile on her face. Yet, it's a very fine line between spoiling someone to make them happy and paying for their affection. That line was particularly blurry in Bangkok too. He may still have been rushing it a little and buying her things early, but that mindset came about from his work. He had to cram as much as he could into the time spent there.

They looked in some clothes shops and whilst she tried on some things, she claimed that nothing was right. He knew she was just being polite, but was hardly going to argue about it. Meandering through the mall with Archie in one hand and a Dior goody bag in the other, she couldn't be happier and wanted for nothing more.

She was due at work that night, but the thought of sitting there being leered at by men was dreadful – for both of them. He didn't want to go and he was reluctant to barfine her. He'd already spent a lot on barfines, and it was a sheer waste of money. But the thought of not spending the evening with her was quite daunting. She also didn't want him to go to a random bar and was tormented by the thought of some other girl having the same reaction to him that she did – or Amm did. He was to be hers and hers alone. What if there was a more beautiful girl who took a shine to him? Or maybe one with bigger boobs, or better at English and who could chat him up?

'Tonight, I don't want to work. I think I will barfine.'

'Okay.' He wasn't sure if she was asking or not.

'I will pay myself. I don't want to go. I want to be with you.'

'Really? You have the money to pay?'

'Yes, it's okay. Because you already pay my rent. And I have been working. And I will talk to my aunty, maybe she will help me.'

'Okay, well, that's great. Just try to think where you want to go.'

Usually her aunty Ploy wouldn't let her dodge work, but she was also very in favour of something taking off between them. Lately, Lily had become a bit of a burden to her by not making money or missing rent, but if she and Archie got together then she knew Lily would be taken good care of.

Ploy was also friendly and had the chance to get to know him during all the time he'd spent at Sport Spot. She could see his character, particularly the time when he was being assaulted on the street by one of her employees and how he didn't react badly to it – or at all. Or more, he didn't react in the way she'd expect another man to. Yet, it wasn't about him being weak. If anything, to be able to take blows from the girl he loved without manhandling her back, or even raising his voice, was a strength beyond any. She'd never seen such control and restraint in a man. She also remembered the way he threw out the idiot who started causing trouble, so it wasn't at all that he was weak. Ploy had been a long time in bars and knew the ropes better than most. She was older and wiser, which also allowed her to recognise Archie as the best thing that could ever happen to Lily.

After being on several dates, the rumour mill had started to churn. Lily's sudden absence from work had not gone unnoticed. Whilst out with Archie one night, she received some messages from the girls telling her that Amm was asking around about her. Of course, she had no right. Lily was her own person who didn't owe Amm anything. She certainly pushed Archie away so much, thus relinquishing any entitlement she had to his fidelity. That same night, he received a message from her: "Hi Archie. Long time no talk. How are you? You're still in BKK?" She knew full well that he was.

Lily had told him about the messages she got too and began to feel uncomfortable. As much as she just wanted to be with him, it was very important for Thai people to 'save face'. She didn't want people to think that she'd stolen him from under Amm's nose, which was the farthest thing from the truth. There was no stealing, but human nature is such that the discarded toy suddenly regains all its value when you see someone else playing with it.

Archie and Lily had been meeting for a week, and after the first few nights Archie told her that he'd pay her barfine. She'd already proved her intention by paying for the first few and it was the only way that they could continue spending time with each other without Lily coming into money issues again. They had a cursory chat about other options for her, but she didn't know how her family would react. They talked vaguely about her going to college, but she really wasn't sure. They hadn't been together long and it was a big commitment. What if she started college and then Archie left her? She'd have to drop out, but by that time it might be hard for her to get her job back because it would already be filled by the next incomer from Isaan.

She was getting accustomed to the two-way communication which Archie was implementing. Being assured that her thoughts and feelings mattered was taking a while for her to get used to, but she did manage to intimate to him that there was no need to hurry and perhaps it'd be better to wait until the next time he came back. By that time of course, despite not having had the *'are we boyfriend and girlfriend?'* conversation, they most definitely were.

It may have been going fast but it didn't feel *too* fast. They had a real sense of comfort with one another. It wasn't the same as dating someone else where there were still many aspects about their life which were unknown. Lily was a simple girl with no ulterior motives and

Archie was a genuine and loving man. They reached a level of union quickly, but it was all natural and comfortable.

After the night of messages, they decided that she ought to go back to work. She still had to continue her job in the interim and the bar needed the staff too. She didn't like to be the centre of attention, so if she went back to work then perhaps people would stop talking about her. Amm knew of course that Lily was interested in Archie and that they had been spending time together. Her sister also told her. It was hardly a great secret, but Koi did find herself a little bit caught in the middle, yet she was fine with that. She liked Archie a lot and still wanted to be friends with him, as well as wanting to see him happy. So if she could set him up with her non-biological sister instead, then why shouldn't she?

Chapter Sixteen

บทที่สิบหก

There was only one week left before Archie had to return home and subsequently to sea. He had to spend some time with his parents and friends before going back. Not to mention that after all the trials and tribulations it was as if he needed a holiday from the holiday. His time there was certainly more than just a holiday of course. Most people would collect a few souvenirs, some photos and perhaps a few repeatable stories, but Archie was falling in and out of love, then back in love again, riding the BTS like a local, he knew where all the shops were for whatever you wanted, he had his second phone with a Thai SIM card and he even got his haircut whilst there rather than waiting until he went back to Scotland.

It was more of a transition than a holiday, and he loved every second of it. Even all the low points that Amm gave him, on reflection, it felt like living. And without those lows, he'd never be able to fully appreciate the highs. He found that Bangkok had enhanced his life considerably. Even though it didn't turn out as he first expected, that wasn't necessarily a bad thing.

He was feeling the time constraint begin to loom over him once more however, and the fact of the matter was that he had a flight back home to catch. He and Lily had not yet spent the night together and he felt that it needed to happen. They'd been spending some real quality time together but without spending the night together it was still like they were just hanging out. He'd now invested his time, energy and heart into Lily and she was his new hope and happiness. He wanted to substantiate things with her before he had to go away again. Knowing he'd be gone for a few months, he'd need something to keep him going during that time too. To wait until he was back was not acceptable for him. He knew he couldn't push her, but perhaps a nudge might be okay. It was very unlikely that she'd be the one to make the first move anyway, he supposed.

Lily met him at the outdoor food market across from his hotel. It was her day off, and she'd spent it at home, cooking and conversing with Ploy. Archie was the hot topic, of course. She had never eaten there before but was keen to try. It was still so hot, but at least the market had large outdoor fans with some water spray to help cool the place down. Being surrounded by buildings on all sides, it didn't get much natural breeze – like an urban gorge. 'Do you want to go somewhere after this?' he asked.

'I don't know, I'm a little bit tired, and I don't want to drink too much.' She took the tail off a big shrimp with her spoon, before splitting it in half. 'If my day off, I don't like to get drunk, I just want to relax.'

'Okay, well, what about the cinema or something?'

'Yes. If you want.' She didn't sound keen.

'You don't want to?'

'No, it's okay for me, but maybe it's late already. I feel like I don't want to sleep late.'

'Oh, okay, you want an early night? But what about me?' he joked. She had an idea of what she wanted from the evening but didn't know how to go about it. 'What about a movie in my room? And then you can go home to sleep.' It was the ideal invitation. She could take it or leave it. If she didn't want to, it'd only be the movie that she'd rejected. And even if she wanted to go home after the movie, he supposed he'd just have to accept that.

'Okay. Good idea.' Her response was suddenly much more enthusiastic. She had no idea how to make an excuse to go back to his room and even though she wasn't sure if she'd manage to stay the night, she could go there and see how she felt. She always knew she was safe with him and she wouldn't get herself into a difficult situation. Her aunty Ploy had a very long talk with her when she first arrived in Bangkok about those kinds of things, and an invitation back to the room for *anything* most likely was an invite for sex.

She was definitely attracted to him, but was very inexperienced. She'd only actually slept with one guy before, her Thai boyfriend, when she was a teenager. Now she'd been working two years in Bangkok and during that time she'd never slept with anyone at all. Until she started spending time with Archie, the thought had never even crossed her mind.

They walked back across the road after stopping at the shop for some supplies. He knew she'd get hungry later, so bought some food and snacks and water as well as a few drinks to take back to the room for movie time. He surreptitiously bought things for breakfast too – enough for two people, should she not feel like leaving the room to eat, or if they woke up too late to attend breakfast – in the eventuality that she stayed. They walked hand-in-hand up the stairs of the overpass which crossed Sukhumvit Road. A beggar was laid out in the corner on top of some cardboard with an old battered 7-11 cup which was most likely fished out the trash. Archie scooped some coins from his pocket and dropped them in. He had no use for coins, other than perhaps the BTS, but he'd always end up with a big heavy pocketful and liked to empty it now and then. He also got rid of his scrappy twenty-baht notes. It wasn't much, and she was aware of that, but Archie's act of giving to a less fortunate person at random, took her by surprise.

Lily had a charitable manner, but never found herself in the position to help others. She was used to making merit, by bringing charitable donations to monks, but those were for religious purposes. It was the fact he gave to a stranger that he just happened across on the way home which she found truly endearing. She realised that maybe he *was* being completely genuine when he helped her for rent that time. Regardless of what his intentions may or may not have been with her, she was certainly glad that they'd made it to the point they were now.

They crossed the marble lobby to the lift. The staff looked on discreetly as he finally brought a girl home. They had been surprised it took him so long – especially being a single male traveller who'd now stayed with them a fourth time. Of course, there was the one night with Amm, but he'd been staying three weeks so far that trip and never brought anyone back yet. Lily looked like a real girl. She laughed and smiled earnestly, her clothes weren't trashy, neither was her make-up, and she hung on his arm with real adoration for him. It wasn't like hanging on as others might to feign or force affection, it was more that she wanted to follow him wherever he may go.

The hotel staff also enjoyed having him as a guest. Every now and then he'd buy some treats to bring them back for them. If he was getting home late, he'd bring an energy drink and a snack for the slumbering guard who was doing the nightshift outside. It was just small touches, but they always made a difference. The women behind the desk were always envious of the Dior bags and bouquets of flowers he'd appear with, and then disappear with, after putting a nice shirt and trousers on. They obviously assumed he had been wooing someone and all thought it was sweet. Now they got to see the girl who they thought was the recipient of all those things, except she wasn't.

The doors opened onto his floor and he led her to the room. It was big for a hotel room, with a living area, kitchenette and a full bathroom with shower cabinet and a separate bathtub. He even had a washing machine and a space for drying clothes on the balcony, which was an essential for staying a month. Basically, it was the same as a condo or apartment, except he could go for breakfast every morning and someone would come to clean every day.

The décor was very upmarket. She'd never seen somewhere so fancy, other than in magazines or TV. It was certainly an impressive and comfortable place for her if she wanted to spend the night, and a far cry from her primitive place. The TV was on a swivel base and had been pointed towards the bed. He swung it round to face the sofa and switched it on. As he began loading the fridge and the cupboard with his provisions, she sheepishly sat down in front of the TV, next to the sliding balcony door.

Whilst avoiding a normal full-blown sweat, he still felt a little bit grimy from being outside and wanted to take a shower. He knew at least snuggling was going to happen, so the last thing he wanted was to worry about was how fresh he was.

'Just make yourself at home. You don't need to ask me if you want something, just take it.'

He removed his shoes and placed them by the door. Her silver pumps were already there at random angles and he squared them up perpendicular to the wall, next to his. 'Are you okay, do you want something just now?'

'No, I'm okay ka,' she said timidly. 'But...maybe I can go to toilet?'

'Yeah, of course you can. You don't need to ask permission,' he smiled. The bathroom door clicked shut and he lifted the remote for the TV to adjust the volume. He wanted to give her as much privacy as he could.

First, her feet needed to be washed. Wearing pumps or sandals in Bangkok always left them dirty and she hated having dirty feet, especially in Archie's clean and fancy room. Lily had to decide whether to use the shower, or the bath. There was a shower head in the bath, so that seemed more appropriate. She then wasn't sure which towel to use since they were new and fresh and nicely folded on top of the towel rail. She was scared to touch them, so just used toilet paper to dry them and dry off the floor after herself. Meanwhile, he'd picked out a pair of shorts, a t-shirt and a pair of underwear to put on after his shower. She emerged cautiously into the room and Archie was standing at the TV. He'd plugged his hard drive in and was browsing movies, just to collect some suggestions though, because he wanted her to pick. He looked at her and smiled. 'Hey. You okay?'

'Yes, I'm okay ka,' she smiled nervously back.

'I want to take a quick shower,' he informed her. 'You can look through the movies and choose one.' The screen displayed a list of movie titles that she didn't recognise and it made her anxious. Of course, the film was just a pretext to bring her back, so he didn't actually care about which movie she'd choose. Lily put pressure on herself unnecessarily though, since she was trying her best to do everything right to make him happy and win his heart.

All her life she'd followed what her family said, what her aunty said nowadays and even when she had her boyfriend before, she always followed what he said. Never before had she been in the position to make decisions. Archie empowered her and valued her input. It may have just been a movie, but it was unfamiliar for her to be asked what *she* wanted.

'Here have TV also?' she asked.

'Yeah, I think there's one or two movie channels, some music channels too, and normal Thai TV.' He switched the source and handed her back the remote. 'You can look. I'll just go and shower.' He could see her uncertainty as to what to pick, 'Anything is okay for me, Lily,' he smiled reassuringly.

He dashed into the toilet for his shower, trying to be as fast as he could. The volume was still up and he could hear her flicking the channels. She stopped on a Thai network showing a soap opera and began watching. Archie heard the shouting of Thai celebrities and the sensationalist wailing of the leading lady, interspersed with cheesy dramatic music. It took just a few minutes to complete his shower and change and when he opened the door, she immediately changed the channel to resume browsing. She reacted like she'd been caught red-handed, as if watching a Thai drama was such a bad thing for her to do.

'Wow, you so fast!' she said.

'Yeah, well…I was so lonely in there, you know?' Her goofy giggle filled the room. 'Why did you change the channel? You can watch that if you like.' He came across and sat next to her. 'Lily, you don't have to be shy or hide what you like. You should be yourself around me. Please.' She smiled at him. 'You should be yourself *all* the time actually.'

'Thank you ka. Archie, why you so sweet to me?'

'Err…because when I'm a baby my mummy dipped me in sugar.' She laughed out loud and it was contagious and endearing. It filled his soul with joy.

'Okay. Tell your mummy thank you na,' she smiled. 'I think I want to look for movie,' she continued.

They navigated their way to the movie channels and one was just starting. It was an American movie set in Bangkok, the second in a series. It was full of ludicrous and far-fetched ideas of what a tourist might encounter in Bangkok, but then again, he thought about the things that he'd been through and although they weren't all as comical as those in the movie, he'd certainly been through a lot in a relatively short time spent there. 'Oh, this is a good movie!' he said. 'Have you seen it before? It's set in Bangkok.'

'No, I never see before. I don't watch too much English movies.'

He poured himself a whisky and coke and opened a wine cooler for her. There were some grapes in the fridge and he put some in her glass just to make her plain drink a little bit special. They settled in to

210

watch the movie and although she didn't understand everything, she still found it very funny. She snuggled adoringly and seemed to fit perfectly into him. His arm was around her and as each minute passed, she seemed to slide more and more into him. He fed her some snacks and she sipped her drink gently.

After a while, the movie suddenly cut off and went to public service announcements. The screen went blue with some kind of government badge. Auld Lang Syne started to play, but there were Thai words set to it. Archie was quite confused as to what was happening, and why a Scottish song was on the Thai TV channel. 'Oh, what happened? They cut the movie!' Archie laughed because he knew the next scenes included vandalism, drug use and ladyboys. 'So what was the point in showing the movie at all if it's going to be cut in Thailand?' It was only then he realised it was an American movie channel which was cabled in to the hotel for the foreign guests. 'So...what do we do now? Find another movie or something?' he asked.

'No, it's okay.' She rubbed her eyes sleepily. 'I feel a little bit tired.'

'Oh...okay.' Archie had to think fast. He wasn't expecting movie time to finish part-way through the movie, and needed to figure out his next move quickly. He'd just been lost in the embrace of her and was content enough with that. 'I thought I had more time for snuggling,' he admitted. When she sat up, her hair was all around her face so he swept it behind her ears. Like magnets, they were both drawn suddenly and strongly to each other and started kissing passionately on the sofa.

They kissed and kissed and a feeling of real and imminent desire rose in him. He swept her hair behind her ear, so that he could kiss her neck. She softened like a box of chocolates left out in the Thai sun all day long. She couldn't help her reaction to him. No one had ever kissed her on the neck before, and it felt so good. She'd never been a big fan of sex before, but she wanted it. Any intention of going home was completely out of the question for her. She found it hard to talk whilst his lips explored her neck because she was shuddering hard, but she tried her hardest to get her request out. 'Archie...' she uttered, '...I want to stay with you tonight. Is it okay?'

He stopped kissing her for a second to take her gaze in his eyes. 'Of course it is. There's nothing in this world I want more than that. I hate being away from you.' He knew he had to be the one to orchestrate the correct circumstances for her staying over, and was so glad that his plans worked out.

He began to move the straps of her vest down, one by one, whilst still kissing her. She didn't want it on anymore so she removed it completely. She'd been waiting for the right person and up until then she hadn't found him. Of course, it wasn't her first time, but it almost felt like it was. Everything that he was doing and the way he made her feel was completely new. How he kissed, the length of time and the sincerity she sensed in his lips was incredible. She didn't feel just like an object for him to enjoy, she was experiencing a pleasure that she never knew existed. The mounting tension had built up in her for quite some time without paying any attention to it. Now, all at once, she felt it flooding her bloodstream. Her pupils dilated, her breathing and heart rate intensified. She could smell the freshness of him from the shower as well as the whisky and coke on his breath.

As she continued to surrender herself to him, he unhooked her bra. She didn't want to reveal herself there however – it had to be perfect. Since spending time with him, she had a vision of how it would be and the sofa was not part of it. She stood up holding her bra in place, with the straps hanging at the back. She made her way to the bed and asked him: 'Can you close lights please?' He dashed to the door and switched off all the lights. The TV was still on and it illuminated the sofa, but there was no time to switch the public service announcement off. It created a little ambiance anyway, with the blue glow gently cast around the room. Dull enough for it to be dark at the bed, but still light enough for them to just see each other. They kissed more as she dropped her bra and he made his way down her neck and onto her chest. The sensation was truly amazing for her.

Lily had a flawless body which Archie yearned to get himself fully acquainted with. He was so glad it was finally happening, and so glad that it'd came about naturally. He could tell she wanted it as badly as he did, which was so important to him. Nevertheless, he wanted to check with her. He wanted her to know she was always safe with him, 'If you're not comfortable, you can tell me,' he told her.

'No…I want.' Hearing her muted whimpers and knowing that he was the object of her desires was a huge turn on for Archie. It had to mean something, and this meant everything. It's exactly what he'd been looking for – something much more than empty encounters, or purely physical exchanges.

He pulled the covers back, removed his t-shirt and shorts as she removed her shorts too. He softly laid her down and she arched her back in anticipation. He lifted her stomach up towards his intrepid lips; they made gentle but positive contact, whilst roaming her soft skin. He continued exploring the whole of her slender feminine figure. She felt more confident with the lights off. Even with her incredible body, she was still always that same shy girl with the goofy giggle. But she certainly felt comfortable with him.

Eventually, he climbed on top of her to match her eyes with his and he eased himself inside. She was so neat that he had to wait for her to soften a little more before she could fully receive him. Once they were there, it was pure ecstasy. The way she yielded to him was incredible. She gave herself to him fully and truly and she'd never felt so connected to someone ever before. Neither had he.

The movie eventually cut back in but they were no longer watching. They didn't need it anymore because they were making their own Bangkok story. It was fortuitous that it cut out when it did, otherwise they wouldn't already be where they were. Of course, it seemed as if it was inevitable and it would have just delayed things, but when it felt this good, any delay would have been a sheer waste of time.

Her body ascended to somewhere it had never been before. It was a place of comfort and joy and love. She had no idea how long it had been going on, but it felt like an eternity to her – like the beginning of the universe and the creation of all precious things in the world. Whilst not wanting it to ever stop, she also wanted to reach that point of natural conclusion. She'd never had it before and didn't know what to expect, but had full confidence that Archie would be able to take her there. She was young in her previous relationship and satisfaction never ever happened for her. Her boyfriend was by no means a great lover. In a way, she saw sex as something to endure in a relationship and just let the man do because it was a woman's duty. She never knew she could enjoy it, and enjoy it as much as this.

He kept his face close to hers and told her to keep looking at him. He wanted to watch her wondrous deep brown eyes and see the effect he was having on her. 'Look at me…' he'd repeat tenderly. The shy girl was turning into a fully fledged lady and called out involuntarily. She just couldn't help it. She bit her bottom lip a few times but between the moans and groans she would utter, 'Chan rak khun.' The young lady came of age as she filled the hotel room with sound. She wasn't embarrassed though, because all that mattered and all that existed at that moment were the two of them.

Afterwards, he pulled her gorgeous naked body on top of him in order to cradle her lovingly. The light from the TV continued to glow and bounced gently off her sensuous curves. Her slim slender legs tapered their way along his until their feet met. Her head was on his chest as she started to worry about what she said. *Chan rak khun*, means *I love you*. She supposed he didn't know what it meant because she didn't think he'd have ever heard it before. What she failed to appreciate was that he *had* been told it before. He didn't know what it meant at the time, but spotted it when he was looking up phrases. After Amm told him on their first night, he wrote down the sound in his phone and eventually found out what it meant. He also found the corresponding phrase *pom rak khun*, which was the equivalent for a man to say to a woman.

His heart was still beating hard and her head was lifting up and down on his chest. He asked her affectionately: 'Do you mean it?' She turned her face up to look at him, confused at first. 'Do you mean what you said?'

She realised her secret was no longer a secret but she didn't care, it wasn't something that she ever wanted to take back, so just nodded. 'Okay,' he kissed her on the head and gently stroked her long sleek hair. 'Pom rak khun too.'

Chapter Seventeen

บททีสิบเจ็ด

Amm was barfined for the night. It was a prearranged thing, so there was no need for her to go into work at all. The owner of the bar had a friend coming from the USA who was some kind of businessman looking for a bit of company whilst he was in Thailand for 'business.' He was in his late-fifties and of course had a wife and two grown kids.

She'd been out to the mall in a pre-emptive shopping spree. What started as a way to support her family became more of a way to indulge herself, and buy expensive things to try and mask the revulsion of what she was doing and the self-hatred she had. On the way home, she stopped off at Koi's bar for a drink and a chat. It was already starting to get a little bit late, but then again, she still had time. Her 'customer' wasn't arriving from Hua Hin until ten-thirty at night. He'd been golfing for a few days and was on his way back to have some sex with a girl about the same age as his own daughter.

Before reaching home, she wanted to pick up some food from the market at Phra Khanong. At least she could enjoy that by herself. It usually wasn't like a normal date where she'd be wined and dined and given compliments all night. It was just about getting drunk and going to bed with a strange old man – the drunker the better, lest she remember it. She got off the BTS station next to Archie's hotel and walked through the condo complex to the open-air food market. She ordered some Japanese food and checked her phone. There was still a couple of hours before meeting, which was just enough time to eat and get ready, then his taxi was going to pick her up back at the BTS station. She didn't want to give out her actual address, although her boss knew, so it wouldn't be so hard for him to find out if he really wanted to. It was better for her customer to stop at the BTS station anyway, because he didn't want to go through all the filthy backstreets of Bangkok just to pick up some whore.

As she waited for her food, her attention drifted from her phone and she looked around at some of the other people there enjoying food and drink and a nice social time. Much to her horror, she spotted a couple of figures walking off together just at the edge of the market. It was Archie and Lily. Her heart sank. She saw a glow and smile in Lily which she'd never seen before. Usually she would sit quietly at work with a despondent look on her face. What Amm was witnessing couldn't be farther from that. Lily laughed and looked at Archie in a way that Amm once did. In the noise and hum of the market, she could pick out Lily's goofy cackle as it echoed round the urban gorge like a massive slap in the face.

It was too much for Amm to handle. That should have been *her* hanging off his arm and the smile should be on *her* face, not Lily's, not anyone else's. But she only had herself to blame. She willed her food to arrive quickly so that she could get the hell out of there. Not that they saw her or was aware of her presence, but she just had to go somewhere – anywhere else. As soon as the food was ready, she paid quickly, jumped on a motorcycle taxi and went home.

Every step felt like a mountain as she climbed the stairs to her floor. The bags of luxury things she'd bought felt like a ton weight in her hands and she had lost her appetite completely. Being so flustered, it was a struggle to unlock her door, but once she got in, she threw her bags down, screamed and cried. She bawled her eyes out for a few minutes, until she could calm herself down.

She found herself on the floor next to her bed, desperate to message Archie. Maybe she could distract him, or remind him of her existence, because it seemed like he'd forgotten about her already. It hurt like hell. She wasn't mad at Lily – she could understand her actually. But that didn't stop her from being insanely jealous, of course. Maybe if she sent a message, Lily would see it and ask why Amm was still talking to him. She might be able to create a problem between them and wipe that smile off Lily's face. She wasn't sure what she could say, but wrote out a few messages:

"Hi. How are you? I just saw you tonight across from your hotel. Hope everything is ok."

"Hi, so I see you are with Lily now. I hope you can be happy with her."

"Hi Archie, where are you? What day you leave Thailand?"

In the end, she sent nothing. She knew she had no right to interfere with him. If she felt bad it was only because of her own actions and she had to find a way to deal with it by herself. She still felt like she wanted to scream, yet she knew she couldn't scream loud enough to let out the frustration that she felt.

She checked the time and realised she'd wasted it sitting on her bedroom floor, which left her in a hurry to get ready. She didn't eat, but she didn't want to anymore. If she had an empty stomach then she could end up being even more drunk and that would be better. She could just lie back and pretend it wasn't happening to her. She opened some wine and started to drink it straight from the bottle as she got ready.

She dressed up all fancy and put a nice white dress on. She looked amazing, but on the inside, she felt far from that. The contrast between her pure white dress and the mess she was within was tangible. It approached ten-thirty and she knew she ought to be on her way already. She headed for the door and almost forgot one last thing. Dashing back into the room, she spritzed herself with a little bit of Dior, the one that Archie bought her. It was the most precious thing she had, except perhaps the bracelet he bought her, which she wore all the time. All the

220

other things guys had bought her meant nothing, and at that time she felt as if she wanted to burn them all.

She locked her room and carried her heels down the stairs with her, slipping them on at the front door. Around the corner was a motosai stand and she rode to the BTS station where he was already waiting. Her phone had been ringing in her bag but she couldn't hear it because of the traffic. She eventually arrived and saw a private taxi waiting with its hazard lights on under the *BTS Phra Khanong* sign. She came up to the car and tried to look inside but couldn't see past the tint of the windows. She tried to open the door but it was locked. He rolled down the window to address her: 'Are you Amm?'

'Yes, I'm Amm.' He had a sneer and general look about him which truly repulsed her.

'Well...I've been waiting for you. You're late.'

'Oh, sorry na. Only five minutes. Don't worry!'

'Get in.' The driver unlocked the doors and she fumbled with the door handle before practically falling into the car. 'What the fuck is this? Are you drunk?'

'No, I'm not drunk, I just like to party, okay? Let's go to party and get drunk.'

Her customer was not impressed with her ungracious attitude. It was very un-Thai, and that was exactly what he came for – a nice subservient Asian lady who hardly had the wherewithal to stick up for herself. But Amm was falling apart.

They went to a fancy rooftop bar. The guy just wore a crappy polo shirt and slack-assed slouchy jeans with granddad shoes. She didn't like the way he was dressed at all. Archie was always sharply dressed. Mostly, she'd found that guys dressed like slobs in Bangkok. Since it was hot, that was like some excuse to get out of wearing nice shirts and trousers. They'd just wear shorts and flip flops to a restaurant, and she hated that. Archie was hardly the style icon, but he was always immaculately turned out. That came from the job too. He would spend his time away covered in and smelling of oil with no one there to see him at all. Consequently, whenever he was on leave, he liked to make an effort with his appearance.

When they were ushered to the table, she asked for a menu in Thai. 'Did you eat already?' she asked. It wasn't that she cared, but she intended on eating so it was just a hint that she was going to order food. There was just something about his whole demeanour which seemed to exacerbate the bubbling already in her blood. It really prickled her to look at him or hear his voice.

'I had something before I left, but I've been in the car a long time.' He closed his menu and sat it on the table. 'It's a bit late for me to eat though.'

'Oh, why? You can't eat so late mai?' She knew older men couldn't eat at night otherwise they'd suffer from indigestion or other age-related things.

He was annoyed at the remark, because he knew what she was referring to. 'No, I don't want to eat,' he said, 'but you can order something if you've really got to.'

'Okay, thank you na ka, boss!' He wasn't sure if she was being sarcastic, but she totally was. She followed up with: 'Maybe you like to diet? It's better for you, don't eat too much na.'

She ordered in Thai so he wouldn't understand and couldn't object until after it was already too late. Seven dishes. She didn't care. They ordered drinks which she consumed way too fast. The place and the view were both amazing, but everything looked dark for her. She couldn't enjoy anything anymore after spotting Archie and Lily together. That image was all she could see over and over in her mind. The way Lily – the girl who never laughed – cackled out loud, so much so that it echoed around the market, and how close they walked together. It wasn't fair. Archie looked good too. It seemed to Amm like he'd been for a haircut and she liked it. It looked like a slightly different style and she wished she could compliment him on it. He'd given her so many compliments before but she never even accepted them, let alone returned any.

A couple of dishes arrived, then another couple, then another. 'What the hell is going on here? How many people did you order for?'

'Tonight, I not eat anything yet. You said I can order, right? You can try some.' She didn't want to put food on his plate for him to try like she'd do with Archie, and like Lily was now doing. She didn't care if he tried or not. She couldn't decide exactly what she wanted because of her lack of appetite, but she knew she had to eat. She was restless and agitated so didn't care what she ordered. It was not at all what her customer was expecting.

He was under the impression that she was a nice friendly girl who knew how to party, but the one in front of him was brash, uncouth and rude. He wanted to sit there, talk about his rounds of golf, brag about all the things he had and furtively put down her culture and race – yet he was in no way in control of the evening.

'Look,' he said, 'you're being rude, I think you need to calm down. I don't know if this is normal for you.'

'Oh,' she replied with derisive tone, 'I'm so sorry siiiiiiiir!' Please don't angry with me.' She made a wai with her hands. 'Yes, maybe I'm not normal girl, or maybe you don't know Thai lady. We need to eat every time na.'

'Okay…but just calm down. We'll have a few drinks and have a nice time.'

'Yes, sir. You are boss.'

She quietened down without calming down. There was nothing but mayhem in her head and she certainly didn't want to be there. She *really* didn't. A few moments passed without incident as she pushed her food around the plate. She picked at it a little but simply couldn't stomach anything. The drinks were still going down hard and fast though. He also couldn't help but notice all the expensive food she ordered and didn't touch so far.

'How's the food?' he asked.

'Yes, it's okay.'

To see it lie on the plate being wasted really aggravated him. 'I thought you said you're hungry?'

'Maybe, but I don't want this,' she said.

'And you only figured after the...' he quickly counted, '...seventh plate?'

'Oh, sorry boss, it's my wrong. I'm so sorry sir.'

'Maybe you can take it home to feed your brothers and sisters?' It was meant as a joke, but it was a low blow from a foreigner with a superiority complex. She did not find it funny at all. 'Never mind, it's not your fault you're stupid.'

'Arai na?' She asked *what?* in Thai. She hated being called stupid – it was the worst thing that anyone could call her. 'No, I not take it home, I don't have anyone.' Amm seethed. She was right on the edge, about to snap. The displeasure of all her experiences were rolling into this one. The guy encapsulated all that was wrong about foreigners. He thought Thai people were lower than him, the country was a mess, standards were poor, yet he still enjoyed spending so much time there.

'Really?' he replied. 'I thought maybe you'd have a skinny waster Thai boy waiting for you at home whilst you're out making the money.'

'What I just tell you? I said I have no one!' Her voice was raised as her patience ran out. That last comment crossed the line for her and the bubbling of her blood suddenly boiled over. How fucking dare he comment about her personal life. 'What about your wife??' she retorted. 'She know what you do tonight??'

225

'What the fuck? Shut up you little whore! Don't talk about things above you.'

'Yes, because you are farang, you above me. But you are like a low person. Old man.'

'Fuck you bitch! I've never been talked to like this before. You need to remember what you are!'

'Yes, I remember who I am!'

With that, she got up. 'Where the fuck do you think you're going?' He grabbed her tightly by the arm and jerked her back towards him. 'We had plans for tonight.'

'You can cancel. Go and call your wife. I will not stay with you. I never stay with you. You think I like you, old man?? I hate you!!'

He let go of her because they were creating a scene, of which the context was starting to escape, had it not already been apparent. She ran towards the lift and he followed her. Some staff members wondered whether to follow or not. It wasn't their business, but also it was happening in their restaurant and there was still a big bill outstanding for their table. Someone did go to fetch the manager however.

She pushed impatiently for the lift until he grabbed her and turned her round, pinning her against the lift doors. 'I'm going to fuck you tonight, whether you like it or not.' She wished she could summon one of those mega screams that she wanted earlier to blast this guy out of her face, but she knew it wasn't in her so she just stayed quiet. 'Now,' he said, 'you stay here, I'll go to pay, and then we'll go back to my place. And then you can go back to whatever fucking paddy field you came from.' She stayed silent. 'Okay?' he asked.

She looked around and was still alone with him. 'Okay.' She had no intention of going with him, but thought she'd just comply until she could plan an exit strategy. 'I will stay with you, but…you need to pay me first.'

She hurriedly stuffed the money into her bag, and whilst he made his way to the cashier to settle the bill, the lift doors opened behind her and an exit strategy presented itself. She stepped backwards into the lift, ran out the building and straight out onto the road. She was desperate for a taxi. So desperate it seemed that she almost got knocked down by one. The driver shouted at her and she came to the window to apologise and ask if he could take her away. He could see that she was in some kind of distress, so he obliged. Amm didn't know what she was doing, she was out of control. She took the money, but that was her boss's friend. She was in big trouble for sure. That was probably her job gone. Maybe she could return the money and just explain that she was having a bad night and say they just had a disagreement. She'd claim anything so that she could get away with it, but thought there was no chance.

She told the driver her destination but it was too far for him. They settled to take her half way, just back to Sukhumvit and then she'd get another taxi from there. She thought about going to see Koi, but couldn't face going to a lady bar. Although she really needed her sister, she just decided to go straight home.

When she opened the door, her bags of shopping still lay dishevelled on the floor and her food lay there cold with condensation inside the plastic. She wasn't sure if she could manage that scream that she wanted, but gave it a try anyway. Amm screamed and screamed until her voice ran out and she fell on the floor in a mess of tears. She wanted to die. She couldn't stand the feeling inside her, it was all too much for her to cope with. If only there was some way for it all to be over so that she didn't have to feel pain anymore. With every ounce of herself, she hated what she'd done for money – money which was supposed to help her mum and instead she'd squandered. She hated how people treated her. But most of all she hated what she'd done to Archie. She could probably manage the rest of her feelings if it were not for him. He tipped her over the edge with guilt and self-loathing, and seeing Lily enjoying the nice time that she should have been having was the last straw for her.

She rushed frantically to the bathroom and found a razor blade. It felt like a while since she'd cut herself. She opened it and sliced across her wrist. She changed hands and sliced the other one and watched the blood issue from the incisions. Dropping the razor on the bathroom floor, she lay down hoping to bleed to death. She didn't feel better, but then she didn't feel any worse either. Tears streamed from her sullied eyes whilst she wished Archie would come and scoop her up. Whenever she was with him, she felt safe and secure. She would feel okay with herself, until the demons in her head spoiled everything for them. Amm had to push him away because she loved him. But despite wanting to protect him, she couldn't ignore the fact that all she wanted was to lie in his caress, listening to his heartbeat once again.

The only heartbeat that was with her was her own – much to her regret, but with each beat, more blood pushed out of her wrists. She wished she hadn't done it. If there was any chance for him to respect her, she supposed that was not the way. But she didn't know what else to do.

Eventually, the adrenaline started to subside and she started to come to terms with what she'd done. She called Koi, who was still at work. Amm supposed it wouldn't be long until she finished, but she kept trying continuously. She did consider calling Archie, but thought she didn't have any place to disturb him, not to mention that she ashamed to let him see her like that. She also knew he was with Lily that night, so if he didn't answer, she didn't want to come to the conclusion that they were in bed together. She knew his hotel was just across the road from the market and knew what that meant, but would rather leave it as a suspicion rather than have to face the truth. Him being a mere five minutes away just made her feel worse. But as close as he was, she felt a million miles from him. She knew full well that it was her who put the distance between them though. Her older sister Joy, lived on the opposite side of Bangkok, but she'd already be asleep, because she had a normal office job, handling bookings for a hotel group. Her salary was modest but she had a husband with a good job, so what she earned was just for her and her mum. All the big financial commitments were met by him.

At Koi's work, it started to get quiet so she slipped away to check her phone. She had twenty-seven missed calls from Amm and immediately knew what that meant. She called back and Amm was still in the bathroom, but had propped herself up against the wall and packed her arms with tissues. The bleeding had reduced but not stopped. The previous times had taught her to raise her arms to help stop the bleeding, so once the first surge of emotion had subsided, that's exactly what she did. Slouched next to the sink, she leaned her arms over the edge of the basin. Blood was smudged on the porcelain and trickled down the drain. Her beautiful white dress was absolutely ruined. That was a shame, she thought, if it even mattered. She picked up the phone.

'Amm! What have you done??'

'I'm sorry. I did it again.' Salty tears rolled down her soft gorgeous cheeks as they started to turn pale. The makeup that was so nicely done a few hours before was smeared and smudged. Koi ran to the manager and explained that she had an emergency. Wan caught on too and came with her. They caught a taxi and told him to step on it.

They burst into the room. 'Amm! Where are you?'

'I'm in here,' came a fearful voice. The way the blood was all over her dress, the floor and the raspberry ripple pattern in the sink, made it look even more horrific. Koi and Wan were hysterical, but had to get a handle on the situation. 'We need to go to the hospital,' Wan said.

Amm felt weak from the loss of blood and the general atmosphere of the night. She didn't want to go, but she was no longer in a position to make decisions. 'There's no taxi that will take her like that, we have to change her clothes,' said Wan again. They achieved that whilst keeping her arms up and keeping her calm. Amm got a fresh t-shirt and a long sleeve loose denim shirt. They managed some rudimentary bandaging and the long sleeves would hide her wounds somewhat. They walked her downstairs and caught a taxi.

When they reached the hospital, she was taken in immediately, treated for blood loss and had the wounds fixed up. The doctor could see the previous scars and tried to reach out to her.

'Miss, I can see that this isn't your first time.' She looked away from him. 'I know you don't feel like it now, but there is help out there for you. This is very dangerous. Maybe the next time you will not have your sisters to bring you here. Maybe the next time you won't be so lucky.'

'Good,' she said.

'I recommend you seek some psychological help.' He gave her some information on the matter, but she wasn't interested. She knew what she'd done and *what she was* as that guy had put it. Everything was brought on by herself, that was her karma and she felt there was nothing she could do to change it.

During the taxi ride there, Amm told them everything that transpired that night whilst the taxi driver eavesdropped. Of course, she finally had to admit to them what she'd been doing, but by that point they already knew. They both felt guilty about playing a part in putting Archie and Lily together if that was the result. But they never could have envisaged that. Koi thought she was past all of the self harm already, but she could see how everything culminated in one disastrous, distressing night for her.

Her customer wasn't even particularly rude, not any more than they usually were anyway. She would ordinarily find a way to not react, and just smile and nod. She was getting six weeks restaurant salary for six hours of 'companionship' was a great incentive for that. But sitting there nodding and smiling whilst she was being insulted was impossible after seeing what she saw. She was at maximum already and just erupted. But there was one thing she knew for sure, that was the last 'customer' she'd ever entertain.

Chapter Eighteen
บทที่สิบแปด

After the most perfect night of her life, Lily woke up next to the man she loved. She then realised that she didn't tell her aunty Ploy about staying over and hoped she wasn't worried sick all night. She'd talked with her about the whole situation whilst cooking and eating the previous day, and in fact, her aunty encouraged her to stay. Even though Archie was different, Ploy advised her that he was still a man and he had needs. So long as Lily was comfortable, then she shouldn't hold back, because if she would not be the one to meet those needs, then she'd lose him to someone else who would. She knew that it'd been a while for Lily too, coupled with the shyness, so just wanted to give her the encouragement that she needed.

Of course, Lily had no problem with the idea, but she was simply nervous and apprehensive about whether she'd be able to satisfy him or not. It then became a thing in her head. Eventually, her own desire became more than her apprehension however. They'd only been together for about a week. It wasn't so long, but also, after spending every evening together, it was not exactly too early either, especially considering the way she felt for him. Nevertheless, Ploy was expecting her to stay over.

As they lay together in the days' early radiance, she thought about checking her phone and knew she'd have to charge it. She just couldn't bear to leave his embrace though. It was already morning and supposed another hour or two wouldn't make any difference to Ploy in the long run. He stirred as she adjusted her position from next to him to on top of him again. The sun shone hard through the windows at the sofa, but the curtains at the bed were still shut. They still had their privacy. 'Good morning na ka,' she said.

'Good morning,' he replied. 'Oh…' he checked around the room, 'did I wake up yet?' She didn't understand. 'Maybe I'm still asleep, because you look like the girl of my dreams.' He knew he was being cheesy, but it was an acceptable cheesy, and well received by her. Archie's body felt warm under her and she placed her icy hands on him. 'Oow, your hands are so cold!' he shrieked.

She laughed, knowing full well what she was doing. 'Yes, I don't know why, my hands always so cold when I'm sleeping.' Her self-consciousness crept back in and despite what they'd spent the night doing, she still covered her naked body with the bed sheets. He went to quickly rinse his mouth out and when he returned, she pretended to not let him back in bed.

'Sorry, last night I cannot sleep, so now I will sleep more, okay?' Her hair was still sleek and fanned out over the pillow and he didn't know how she managed that. He'd been with a few girls over the years but never did they look so perfect in the morning.

'Ah, okay. I'm sorry I disturbed you. Maybe you don't want me to disturb you again?' He pretended to make his way back to the bathroom.

'No!' she exclaimed earnestly. Even though she knew he was joking, the thought of him leaving was still no laughing matter for her. Plus, she was still a bit of a rookie when it came to flirting and couldn't help but slip back into her serious self sometimes. He always teased and joked with her, which she really enjoyed, because he was always sweet with it. She'd never had fun like that with anyone before. She was trying to improve so that she could do the same for him.

'Okay, well…' he said whilst slipping under the covers, 'is it okay if I disturb you again now?'

They stayed in bed for a couple more hours and made love a few more times. Each time, her self-consciousness started to subside. She even started getting up to use the toilet without covering herself, yet she still locked the bathroom door. There wasn't much time left before breakfast at the hotel was finished so he had a look in the fridge to see what he could make from the ingredients he bought the night before. They had the option to go out somewhere too, but he wasn't sure if she needed anything in the way of makeup or a change of clothes before going out. He thought maybe she'd have to go home first, but didn't much fancy the idea. He wanted to have breakfast with her, but he was already very hungry, considering he'd been a busy boy overnight and again in the morning.

Since Lily was hoping for it, she had the mind to bring some spare underwear, essential make-up and such like with her. She didn't have a change of clothes, but she'd only been in them for a couple of hours, just to meet him, eat and then cross the road to the hotel. And sitting there outside with the big fans and water spray, she was comfortable enough, considering she didn't feel the heat the same way as he did.

'I think I need toothbrush,' she said, as she stood at the bathroom mirror.

'Well, yeah. I didn't want to say, but…you do,' he called through, teasing her from the kitchenette. 'There's one more just there.'

'Really? Why you have one more toothbrush?' He appeared behind her and held her tenderly by the hips.

'Some girl must have left it. Can't remember which one though.' She remarked something in Thai at his joke. 'No,' he said smiling and showed her, '…it's from the hotel.' It was just in a plain plastic package so it wasn't particularly obvious, especially for someone who was not accustomed to frequenting hotels. She brushed her teeth whilst he went for a shower and they both got ready to leave. He did invite her in, but she said she didn't want to get her hair wet. 'Maybe I can wear shower cap?' she suggested.

'Oh yeah, that's sexy!' he chuckled. 'Anyway, the way we do it, it'll just come off!'

On the other side of Sukhumvit Road, there was a large coffee shop which was open twenty-four hours. They took a leisurely walk there for brunch. They sat next to a full-height window which had a see-through blind pulled down to keep some heat of the sun out, whilst not obscuring the sights of Bangkok. It wasn't until then that she checked her phone. It was dead as expected, so she plugged in her power bank. It was essential for Thai girls to carry a powerbank because they were continually chatting and Facebooking and Instagramming. After a moment, she was able to switch it on. They'd already ordered at the counter and Archie was waiting for the pager to go off. There were a couple of messages from her aunty of course, just checking that she was in fact with Archie, and there were some from Koi. They seemed more urgent, so Ploy had to wait:

"Hi, I just want to tell you, Amm saw you and Archie tonight. Then when I went home I found her with her wrists cut. Now she's in hospital. I should never have helped you. I hope you're happy."

Koi sent follow-ups at irregular intervals: "She almost died! This is because of you!"

"They had to give her a transfusion, she lost so much blood. If I didn't come when I did, then maybe she'd be dead."

There were a few photos too. It was a big habit of Thai's and most South East Asians in general, to use phones to document things. Of course it came about with technology, but the way it was used was perhaps a little different than in the western world. It was related to the sensationalist news and over dramatic soap operas, and a general penchant for tragedy and hardship. If something was happening then somebody would be filming. If there was someone being recorded helping, then most likely they were the second person to arrive. Koi sent photos of Amm slumped on the floor and the blood all over her dress, the blood all over the sink and floor, and a few photos of her with doctors and then in the hospital bed.

Archie checked on Lily and she was quiet. That was okay, he thought, because she had to have some time to catch up with her phone. He guessed it was probably the longest she'd ever gone without looking at it. The pager went off so he made his way to the counter to collect their food, and by the time he came back she was crying. *Oh God, not more unexpected crying,* he thought. He remembered the first night at the pub with Amm and her friends, and that should have been his sign to run. What the hell was this now?

'Lily, what's wrong? Has something happened?'

'I don't know…I should tell you or not.'

Oh fuck, here we go again. 'Lily, you can tell me anything,' he said bravely and softly, whilst taking a gulp.

'Amm…she hurt herself last night. She see us at the market.' She opened the photos and showed him. 'Koi said…it's my fault.'

'Oh my God…is she okay?'

'Now she stay in hospital.'

238

There was a pause whilst the crema silently split on the top of his coffee, the condensation rolled down the side of her fruit juice and until they could both digest the news. 'But Lily, it's not your fault,' he said. 'You know she has many problems about her feelings.' With a single finger, he lifted her chin gently, encouraging her to look in his eyes. 'This is not your fault.'

'But maybe I should not –'

'What? Shouldn't have started seeing me?'

'No. I don't know.' That was definitely not the conclusion that she'd reached, but she still felt in some way responsible. Naturally, Archie was horrified and it filled him with such sorrow to hear about what Amm had done, especially because it proved that actually she did care about him. But she'd already made her choice. It *was* a choice. If she was with Archie then none of that would have happened – the 'customers' and the previous night. There was not a single fibre in his being that would ever blame or scold Amm for doing that to herself, but at the same time, whether she saw them together or not, it was in no way down to either of them.

'So…you can't be with me, in case Amm cuts herself? She didn't want me. She pushed me away many times and I tried with her. You know exactly what happened.' He gathered some tissues from their tray and wiped the tears from her face. 'She missed her chance, and that was because of her. It's not your fault Lily.' He lifted her chin again to look her in the eye, as teardrops continued to roll out of them. 'So does this change anything about us?'

'Huh?' She didn't understand the question so he had to simplify it.

'Do you change your feeling for me because of this?'

'No.' She neither hesitated nor wavered. Of course she was upset, but there was no way that she would let it affect things. She just really hated that her friend couldn't accept it and felt the need to do that. It hurt her to have Koi blaming her too. It was going so perfect between Lily and Archie, and whilst it didn't cause a rift between them as such, it just gave her a bad taste in her mouth.

'Do you remember what you told me last night? About your feeling for me?' he asked.

'Yes.'

'Do you still feel it?'

'Yes.'

'And me too. I love you Lily.'

'Me too, I love you. So much na,' she re-emphasised.

After a few minutes, she regained her composure and Archie encouraged her to start eating. 'Come on, your food is getting cold. Eat something please. For me.'

After brunch, Lily went home to talk with Ploy. She agreed whole-heartedly with Archie, and reassured her that it wasn't her fault. Later, she plucked up the courage to message Koi. Thankfully she'd calmed down and subsequently apologised for blaming her, because she knew full well it was only Amm that was involved. But she felt guilty for her part too and may have lashed out a little. Since Amm had rejected Archie time and time again everybody thought that she didn't have any feelings for him, except that wasn't the case at all.

Archie sent Amm a message himself, saying how upset he was to hear about what happened. He also reiterated the doctor's advice about professional help. Whilst he'd managed to displace her very nicely with Lily, it wasn't as if he'd stopped caring for her. Perhaps even, he'd still always have a love for her, but he just had to change how he perceived her. He and Lily discussed visiting her, but Koi said it probably wasn't a good idea.

Meanwhile, the owner was informed about the goings-on of the previous night, first from his friend and then from Ploy. The whole thing was forgotten about. Ploy made out that he'd been insulting and made her feel so bad about herself, including the sexual threat, that she went home and slit her wrists. His friend wasn't particularly happy, but her boss had also used her 'services' before and held her in too high regard to make any further problems for her. He certainly didn't want to get rid of her anyway. And the fact she cut her wrists meant that he must have been a real pig to her. He wasn't to know about any other aspect of her state of mind that night, and never would he find out.

Amm was out of hospital later that day and had to stay at home. She was also given some time off to recover, which meant Lily had to work more. The prospect of going back to the bar was unpleasant for her but she saw it as a way of making up for any part she may have played. She dreaded going and was concerned about what the other girls would say or think of her, but in fact, everyone was supportive. Everybody knew the tale of Amm and Archie, and given the chance themselves, they'd have snapped him up in a second too. It just so happened that Lily was the lucky one. They merely found themselves together in the right place at the right time and it flourished from there. Those were the facts, and everyone was aware of them. She never did anything underhanded or played any games, yet she still couldn't shake her feeling of unease about it all.

Sometimes, she just wished she could go back to her hometown and help out on the farm. That was a nice life there. *Slow life* they called it. In her hometown, there was no lady bar scene, nobody was cutting their wrists, she could eat for cheap, drink alcohol only if she felt like it, whilst being able to sleep early and wake up late. That's all she wanted, but her family wouldn't let her. She had to stay in Bangkok to make money, even though she really wasn't making much at all. And by the time she'd paid her rent, ate something and sent something back home, she had nothing left for herself. There was no money to go out or buy something, and no means for recreation or enjoyment. All she did was work and sleep. Bangkok was like prison for her and she felt trapped without a life of her own. But if she went home, she'd be able to survive on much less money and probably still be able to contribute to her family in some way.

All she knew was that she wanted out – especially after being with Archie. She didn't want to talk to customers even more, because they were dirt compared to him. And she particularly didn't want him to worry about her and what she was doing, seeing as he'd been through it all before. It wasn't fair on him.

They were running out of days, but each one was spent together. Without Amm at the bar it was much more relaxed, so long as they didn't remember why. Lily never bothered him for drinks or asked for drinks for the other girls and they never asked him either. They respected him and besides, they'd had a good run of insane partying which was driven by Amm and her false personality at the bar. They could all appreciate that nights like those were unsustainable. He'd still buy a few drinks here and there of course, but mostly he'd just chill out and talk to them when they were free. Lily always made herself free of course, so it was *almost* like they were going out, but the drinks he bought her, she'd get some money back on. That was *sort of* alright he thought – strange, but alright. They were together though, and that's all that mattered.

Their new after-work habit was to take Ploy to eat, then go back to the hotel together, dropping Ploy off on the way. It felt much more natural and less manic than the activities before. It just worked.

The dreaded flight home was approaching however. The thought of leaving her was almost too much. Even though Archie and Lily had professed their love for one another, there would always be something in the back of his mind wondering whether or not she'd still be there for him by the time he got back.

Chapter Nineteen
บทที่สิบเก้า

He joined a new ship much to his displeasure. It was beginning to be a real drag. The original idea of going to sea was for the adventure and to follow in his father's footsteps. As he was growing up, much of Archie's school holidays were spent on his dad's ships. Big machinery always fascinated him. Not only did he have an inquisitive mind, he had an affinity towards it too. When he was even younger again, he would disassemble his toys and reassemble them, just so he could see what was inside and how they worked.

The job was no longer the same as it was in his father's time however. On top of the scarce shore leave and no alcohol policy, there were so many rules, regulations and paperwork. Seafarers were merely numbers and only provided with the minimum. There was barely any pleasure left in the profession since that'd been pushed out by commercial pressures. But it was a living, and everybody needs to

244

work. The main thing he still enjoyed was the fact that he could take a few months off twice a year. Being completely free like that was by far the greatest advantage of the job. Those months were his to do with as he pleased and he could travel anywhere he liked. Of course, all his travels were now focused in one place, but that was fine. The job allowed him to spend time in Thailand and to maintain the new lifestyle that he had developed.

It didn't mean the time away wasn't hard though. When he was still young, free and single, it was okay but now things were different. It may have only been about two weeks that he'd actually spent with Lily, but he felt he was onto something good. He wasn't sure if he'd still want to continue a career at sea if he started a family. His dad did, but that was the best living he could make for them. He appreciated everything his dad had to put up with to provide for them and never ever thought any less of him for being away so often. He remembered fondly the homecomings and reunions with his dad, and the song his mum used to sing to him in anticipation: *Clap handies, clap handies, till daddy comes home. Sweets in his pocket for Archie alone.*

If he somehow had a chance to stay at home whilst he raised a family then he'd rather do that though. By then, he'd have no interest in travelling any longer, he'd just want to settle down. He already wanted it. Perhaps Lily would be the one he could do it with.

He truly loved her. It was a completely natural and tender understanding they had with one another. They could so innocently laugh and joke and flirt (she was improving) and he loved the way she soaked up all the things he told her. She was like a wild flower growing in a beautiful plain, whilst still being a blank canvas. There was so much to her, yet she was still so far from her full potential. It wasn't even that he wanted to shape her into a woman for him – despite the fact she hung onto his every word and was impressionable enough, that it would be entirely possible. He wanted to give her the means to grow and be herself in the way that she wanted. He wanted her to bloom in sunshine, and for her masterpiece to take shape on her own terms. That was how much he loved her.

The trip passed without incident. There were no bomb blasts, no one-and-a-half month extensions or anything else to report. They talked continuously throughout his trip. She sweetly arranged times through the day when she could give him her undivided attention – when she woke up, before work, and after work. There were also many other times in-between, if she wasn't busy. She set another clock in her phone and would always keep track of what time it was where he was. She learned his normal work schedule and knew when he was likely to be eating or relaxing. Of course, whilst he was in port it was always unpredictable, but usually at sea he'd follow a steady routine, so long as everything was running well. If he changed time zone, he'd update her and she'd adjust her second clock to keep up with him and his actions.

The internet wasn't great, so it was not really possible to have a video call, but they often still liked to try. Even a few seconds were nice, until the screen would freeze and the call was dropped. She wanted to assure him that she was safe and sound at home after work too, not just from the safety aspect, but from the fidelity side of things. He was out there working hard and she didn't want him to worry about where she was, what she was doing, or who she was doing it with. A video call would also give them a fresher image of each other, and a more natural one than the carefully selected selfies she sent him. Messages and pictures could never really replace the sound of each others voice too, or how she'd throw her head back when he made her laugh. Her laugh and smile were like medicine to cure all ill-feelings he encountered as he traversed the ocean deep. She was the remedy to all his woes.

Lily wasn't really much of a selfie-taker, she was too modest for that, but she wanted to keep sending him photos. Perhaps it was a little insecure of her, but she thought she ought to maintain a supply of beautiful photos which would keep her in the forefront of his mind. Photos or not, it was hardly likely that he'd forget her, but he certainly wasn't complaining. There was nothing better for him than to finish work and receive a photo of her with a little bit about how her day was. Her English was improving and she'd been studying online because she wanted to be able to talk with him more effectively. Most of the girls got practice at work, but that didn't appeal to her. She would still avoid customers.

He flew straight to Thailand from the ship, and her excitement was through the roof. She'd done well and organised a nice condo for them to stay in. Even though she wasn't sure at first how to go about doing it, she wanted to do it for him. Of course he was welcome in her place, but she was embarrassed about how simple it was. What's more, he wanted to give her a bit of luxury too. He wanted their time together to always be as special as possible. Her room may have been a little cramped for the both of them too.

Eventually, he supposed, they'd buy a condo or at least rent long-term, but it was still early days. He'd been looking online for a place and sent emails off to enquire, until she took over the search. She knew she'd be able to find more options and that the price quoted to her would perhaps be a lesser one than they'd charge him, so long as she didn't reveal that she had a farang boyfriend who'd be paying. Double pricing was a very real thing in Thailand and being lumped with a premium bill based on your origin was a harsh reality of farang life there. She cared enough to want to protect his pocket and did all she could to help him. Lily diligently travelled around Bangkok before work in order to view places, take photos to send to him and negotiate discounts.

There was a great condo available in the area he stayed before. It was in the condo complex across from his usual hotel and next door to the food market. Sure, it was still close to Amm he thought, but then again, Phra Khanong was also *his* part of Bangkok. It was the first place he ever stayed in Bangkok; he knew it well and felt comfortable there. Why should he have to change just because of her? The place was just a couple minutes walk to the BTS, he could always get a taxi outside, there was a convenience store, plenty of places to eat and everything else they might want close-by.

She got up early that day anticipating his homecoming. Sleep was a big pleasure of hers, but she could hardly manage any the night before since she was so excited. Her first task was to take a motosai to buy a small bunch of flowers for him. Later, she rode the train all the way to the airport. She'd never been before. If she travelled to her hometown it was always by bus, and she'd never been anywhere else in Thailand, never mind abroad. When he left last time, his flight was in the middle of the night, as usual. He checked out of the hotel and spent the evening in her room. The said their goodbyes there, before catching a taxi to the airport. Despite her protests, he didn't let her come with him, since she'd then have to travel back alone in the middle of the night.

She'd only ever seen airports in movies, and Suvarnabhumi was colossal. The thought of going there alone was quite daunting, but she couldn't *not* go. She wanted to see him the second he got off the plane because it'd already been too long. When she alighted the airport link train, she had no idea where she was or where to go. Everything was signposted, but she didn't know what information she was looking for, so that didn't help her in any way. She grew more and more concerned that she was lost and maybe she'd end up being late for him. Suddenly, Lily appreciated why he didn't let her go back alone at night since she felt alarmed enough at potentially being lost during the day. There was a slight panic started to set in, but she told herself to stay calm.

Archie had advised her to take a taxi there, but it was more expensive and she wanted to be as frugal as possible. But if she was going to end up being lost, it may have been worth shelling out. The passengers thinned on the platform as the train thundered out of the station. A few more stragglers like herself were hanging about and she managed to find someone to help, who explained where she had to go.

Upon arriving in the terminal, Lily was overwhelmed. She was confronted by several long escalators, having no idea where they led. There was non-stop hustle and bustle with masses of people loitering around or forming lines at car hire or tour counters. Archie wrote her a detailed message about how to get there and she followed it strictly. He'd never taken the train himself, but he had to look it up online. He forwarded the link and reiterated it simply for her, whilst hoping the information was still up-to-date. He also tried to urge her to take a taxi one last time, but she insisted that she'd be fine by train. That was how she tried to protect his pocket, for the sake of a couple-hundred baht.

Lily made it to the arrivals hall and let out a huge sigh of relief. Checking her watch, she realised there was still an hour and a half until he even landed. That was quite alright for her though. She knew she didn't know where she was going, so deliberately left with plenty of time, because she couldn't be late for him. Apart from her two-minute panic after getting off the train, she'd made it there in one piece and without too much drama.

Hunger rolled in her stomach, so she checked a restaurant menu but the prices were all so high. She checked a few others and they were all the same. She couldn't understand it and didn't appreciate that airports were always more expensive. She did have enough money to buy something, but decided to wait. Perhaps Archie was hungry too and they could eat together. There was plenty time to kill, so she had a look around and stumbled across a convenience store. There was food there and the prices were more or less okay, so she bought something small just to tide her over.

She received a message: "Hello my love! Guess who's in Thailand?" She was so thrilled that she could hardly write back, but channelled her energy into constructing a coherent reply. "Wow, I'm so excited to see you teerak!" *Teerak* was a Thai term of endearment equivalent to darling or sweetheart.

"We just landed, I'm still in the plane. I need to go through passport control and get my bags. Probably another half an hour or something. Did you eat yet?" He knew her so well.

"I just eat something small. I don't know if you want to eat or not."

She had patiently passed most of the wait by sitting on a bench close to one of the air conditioners, but it was finally time to go and find him. Even though Archie was updating her with his whereabouts, she didn't really understand what 'passport control' was or where 'baggage claim' was. But from the moment she knew he had touched down, she checked each and every face in the airport waiting to see him.

She asked someone where the arrivals came out and stood with her posy of flowers whilst people wheeled their cases and carts past her. She'd dreamt of the moment for months and imagined it something like a movie. He'd appear and she'd be able to run and jump into his arms. She'd feel his embrace and be complete once again.

The glass at arrivals was mirrored from the outside, which meant Archie could see Lily, without her seeing him. She had a black vest on with a white shirt over it which hung loosely and draped off one of her shoulders. A sudden rush of euphoria filled him whilst he watched her scan like a woman on a mission. Even in her normal plain day-to-day clothes, she looked remarkable to him. His heart started thumping in his chest as he suddenly started to anticipate their reunion.

Ever the prankster, he timed himself with a horde of Chinese tourists and hid behind them as he came out onto the concourse. Knowing where she was enabled him to do it perfectly. He snuck around the back and approached her as she was still diligently checking faces. 'Excuse me miss.' She turned around already knowing the voice and let out a yelp. It bounced up and around the terminal building.

'Archie!' She remarked something in Thai which he guessed was related to the fright he gave her. 'Ooi! Welcome back na, teerak.' She gave him the flowers before he wrapped his wanting arms around her. It felt so good. Although he'd been travelling a long time and was a little sweaty, she could still pick out his scent. That was something she really missed. And the place her head would fit on his chest was like home to her. It wasn't the run-and-jump reunion that she had in mind, but she didn't mind one bit. He broke the embrace only to kiss her hello.

'Flowers?' he said. 'You're so sweet.'

'I don't know what else I can bring for you.'

'I have my Lily. That's the only flower I need.' He caressed the side of her face lovingly and told her: 'I missed you so much.'

'I miss you too.' A teardrop gathered and overflowed from the corner of her eye. She couldn't help it. It was merely a release of a few months of anticipation and longing.

She didn't feel the distance that he went from her, only how close he was getting every day. To wait for him was not a chore or a hardship, it was just part of course for her. Of course, there were nights where she'd feel low and lonely and she'd really wish that he was by her side, but they always passed. And with each one that passed, he grew closer still.

Before returning to sea, he told her to expect the internet to go off sometimes, but the first time it happened she'd forgotten all about it. She got mad and upset and irrational. She allowed herself to get worked up and sent him angry messages asking what he was doing and why he wasn't talking to her. Then she switched to lonely and told him how much she missed him and begged him just to reply. Eventually, she started to worry that something had happened and tried to search online for any accidents involving ships. She didn't know what she was looking for though, so it just confused and distressed her even more. She found some disasters, but didn't know if they were relevant or not.

All she did was scare herself and fear the worst. The last resort was to ask some of the other girls whether they'd heard from him, but he wasn't really in regular touch with them anyway.

She eventually sent messages along the lines of: "If you not love me anymore it's ok, just tell me if you're ok! Please!" It was a long three and a half days for her and she felt so silly when he finally replied and reminded her that the internet went off at times. A huge weight lifted from her and she looked back to check what she wrote (particularly in the angry stage) and was quite embarrassed. "I'm so sorry teerak, I just really start to worry when you not reply." He loved how she'd behaved because it proved that she really did love him. The fact that she didn't give up writing to him was nothing but a positive sign too. She didn't lose interest or forget him even when he was unable to reply.

On the following instances of no internet, she had to exercise patience, but paranoia would always set in. It would feel as if he'd forgotten about her and that he wasn't thinking about her, even though she knew it wasn't the case. It was probably a very normal feeling for someone in a long-distance relationship when messages were your foremost way of maintaining the bond with each other. At least there was no chance of him going out to bars or sleeping with any women whilst he was at sea. Knowing that was just enough for her to keep calm whilst she waited for him to have some signal again.

When he couldn't reply, she'd continue to send messages updating him about her day, because it was her habit. Not only did she not want him to think that she was up to something, she simply couldn't handle a day without messaging him – regardless of whether he'd reply or not. He was the only one she wanted to tell everything to. As soon as the internet would come back, she'd get his reply and feel instant relief. But no matter how uncomfortable it may have been for her without his replies, it was even harder for him sitting alone in his cabin not being able to talk to her.

As she sobbed softly in the terminal, he dried her tears with one hand and held the flowers in the other.

'Oh, baby, why are you crying?' he asked.

'I don't know, I'm just so happy to see you. Thank you for coming back to me.'

'Lily, there's nowhere else in the world I'd rather be. And thank you…for being here waiting for me. I can't believe you came here to meet me too.'

'Of course, I come here. I will be here every time you come back.'

'Okay.' He smiled tenderly at her and lifted his pinkie towards her. 'Promise?'

'Yes, I promise,' she happily linked her little finger with him and the pinkie promise was made.

They made their way to the taxi rank and rode into the city. The ride from the airport was becoming second nature to him, yet it was the first time he'd had someone with him, and the first time Lily had ever done it. He thought it was unusual for him to know certain aspects of Thailand better than a Thai person, but that's just how it was.

Everything was arranged for the condo, and all he had to do was sign some papers and hand over some cash when they arrived. He decided to stay for two months. It was the longest time he'd spent there in one go, and he'd need to get an extension on his visa, but that wasn't a big deal.

The roads gradually became more familiar on the other side of the taxi window and he knew he was approaching home. They arrived at the building on the other side of the road from where he usually stayed. There was a doorman there who helped to take his cases and place them safely in the foyer. He escaped around the corner for a moment to use the ATM and Lily waited patiently with the bags. She then led him to the office, or 'Juristic Person' as it's known. She handled everything for him again and he had no idea what was discussed, but he knew she was taking care of things.

The juristic person took them up to room. It'd been a few weeks since Lily had seen it, and she was so worried about whether he'd like it or not. Of course, he did. She'd done well to find a lovely condo in the place he loved and at a reasonable price. He was very proud of her, since he knew it would have been something which took her well out of her comfort zone.

He took a shower and felt the griminess of travel and ship dissolve from his body and drain away down the plughole with all the soapy suds. Lily waited for him to emerge from the bathroom in order to hand him a bottle of water. 'Are you hungry mai? she asked.

'I'm...so hungry...' He took a sip of water whilst eyeing her up with animalistic desire.

'What you want to eat?' she asked innocently.

'You...'

Archie and Lily spent every moment together. Morning, noon and night, they were by each other's side. He'd come to her bar when she had to work, but it wasn't like work at all, just hanging out in the same place every night. Lily usually had a Monday off each week, but arranged to work the previous two months straight so she could save up eight days off. Archie did mention that he'd like to take her for a holiday, but that wasn't why she did it. She just wanted to not have the bar interfere with the time she could spend with him, as far as was possible. Lily would have been happy enough even if they just stayed in Bangkok.

Having an aunty as the manager did have its' advantages. It's not that she was getting something for nothing however. She'd worked for her days, so it didn't create any animosity with the other girls, but saving up days off was not normal practice. They browsed hotels on different islands and he checked out travel plans before deciding to split the eight days into two holidays.

She noticed the condition of his hands after being at work. It looked as if they were dirty, but she knew that could not have been the case. As they sat at their table, she wanted to inspect them more closely.

'Can I look your hands, please?' she asked.

'I know, they look terrible.' She took hold of them and turned them round like rocks she'd found on the ground. Dirt and oil were ingrained into them, there were cuts, grazes, abrasions and the skin was so rough. 'After a week or so, they come back to normal,' he said.

'Why it's like this?'

'Just from work. It's very intense on the hands.'

'Ooi, you work so hard na. But you not have before.'

'Yeah, because I didn't see you straight from work last time.'

'Ah, okay. But you need to put lotion. Or I think maybe I not let you touch me anymore. Okay?' She was getting better at teasing, yet he was still better at it.

'You didn't mind this afternoon though…' he said as he stood up pretending to leave the bar.

'Where you go?' she asked.

'Well, I need to go and buy some good hand cream *right now!*'

She laughed her pure laugh that he so missed. Her sense of humour was simple and straightforward and reflected the wholesomeness of her. It reminded him how sincere and unspoiled she was. Even his deliberately crappy jokes were hilarious for her. Words couldn't express how glad he was to be in her sweet presence again.

Amm was still working there, and they'd manage a polite 'hello' and 'goodnight' when they were coming and going, but that was it. She was behind the bar rather than out front. Amm and Lily were civil to each other but they were no longer friends. They avoided one other.

Things had calmed down for Amm after her bad night and she had a talk with her boss. She told him she didn't want to work there anymore, at which point, he offered to put her behind the bar on a slightly higher salary. He didn't want to lose her, even though he knew that their 'special arrangement' was no longer valid. He was fine with that, because he could easily replace her with some other unsuspecting girl. After all, with all the young girls trying to make ends meet, what was the point in having the same one all the time? He didn't love Amm in any way and just wanted to have a paid mistress to fuck when he didn't fancy fucking his wife. It was truly disgusting though, that she could be shared among friends like a commodity. Of course, after what happened, she let herself be a commodity no more.

For holiday number one, Archie and Lily flew down to Phuket. He arranged a hire car, which was just as well, because there was not the same transport available as in Bangkok. They arrived in the afternoon and picked the car up at the airport before driving to the hotel. It was a lovely hotel with a beautiful room. It was perhaps a little older than how it looked in the photos, but it was still good. On the top floor there was a roof terrace with a restaurant, swimming pool and bar. It was their base to explore the area and the beaches for a few days.

It was her very first time in the sea. The extent of her swimming experience was the pool at Ploy's ex-boyfriends' condo. They'd hang out there whenever they could, but she'd never been in the open sea at all. Ploy had planned to take her to Pattaya a few times, since it was only a few hours from Bangkok, but in the two years she'd been there it never happened. Her desire to go to the sea grew considerably after Archie went back to work, even if it was just to stand on the shore. If she could look out and imagine Archie somewhere over the horizon, then she'd surely feel closer to him.

Feeling the sand between her toes and the swirling strength and saltiness of the currents around her was incredibly exciting. She splashed and jumped and giggled through the waves. The beach was something she'd only ever seen in pictures and videos. The delight on her face was palpable now that she'd finally made it there in her early-twenties. It was yet another new experience for her which Archie had made happen and that gave him such satisfaction.

When they weren't out playing in the sea or in restaurants or bars or markets, they were in the room making love. They made love like there was no tomorrow. With previous relationships, he'd expect a couple of times at night and maybe once in the morning, but they were enjoying each other at least a dozen times each night. Every time was a mutual satisfaction. She developed a veracious sexual desire which she never knew she had in her, but it was only for him. He certainly had no interest in anyone else either. He knew he'd never connected with another girl in the same way before and only ever had eyes for her.

They visited Phuket's big Buddha and it was an interesting drive for him. They had some trouble to find it because it wasn't well signposted. He could see it perched high up on the hill and he tried a few side roads, but always came round in a circle or to a dead end. He asked Lily to be his navigator and help him to look out for signs. Through teamwork, they eventually found themselves on the right road and started their ascent. The road was littered with deep potholes, but most of the other drivers – particularly the tour vans – were very impatient and hogged the road or overtook him on blind corners, inviting disaster to come their way. He was hardly a dawdling driver, but he was worried about destroying the suspension in his rental car or shaking their eyeballs out of their sockets, so took it easy. It wasn't like they were in any rush anyway.

There were plenty interesting things to look at on the way up, which gave him another reason to not drive too fast. Not only did he want to see, but he wanted to let Lily see too, since it was probably a bigger deal for her. There was a tour group on quad bikes and he had to wait behind them until a long enough stretch opened up before passing. By the time they got to the top, the view was outstanding. Towns and cities sprawled out down below interspersed with lush green. The mountains in the distance bounded the beautiful blue sea. Boats dotted the water and the sun shone gloriously down on it all.

It was an active temple and they were continuously maintaining it. There was a spot where visitors could donate or buy souvenirs to help raise funds for maintenance and one of the options was to buy a tile which would be used in the building. Behind the desk there was a man, and behind him were stacks of tiles in two sizes. 'Shall we get a tile?' Archie asked. She looked to see what he meant.

'Yes, and we can write our name.'

'Big or small?' he asked.

'I think big one is better.' It was the first time she wasn't her modest self, but she wanted to write their names as big as she could to be cast into the body of Buddha. A small one just wouldn't do. 'It's okay?' she asked.

'Yes, it's okay,' Archie confirmed with a soft smile. The man hurriedly produced a tile and pen for them whilst he juggled several visitors at one time. 'Can you remember my name?' he joked.

'Yes,' she laughed, 'I think I never forget you na.'

She wrote her name, his name, the date and a love heart before handing it to the man. 'Please take care of it,' she told him in Thai.

The holiday was like heaven on earth for Lily. It was a comfortable atmosphere, she could eat, drink, relax and make love, and she really didn't need or want anything else. Her mind and soul were being opened up by all the new things she was seeing. Each experience filled her heart with sheer joy. It was so great to be far away from the bar too, yet she knew that reality would rear its ugly head and she'd have to return there eventually. She thought about how to circumvent returning and wanted to discuss it with Archie. Up until now, she'd gotten used to just accepting what came to her, but Archie gave her the ability to speak up and better herself. She pondered steadily in the background to make a plan and was waiting for an appropriate time to discuss it with him.

It came to their last night in Phuket and they went to a beachfront restaurant a few minutes walk from the hotel. They stayed local so that Archie didn't need to use the car and they could enjoy a bottle of wine and maybe a few whiskies together. The restaurant was outside in a strip along the beach and right next to the road. It was perhaps a little too close to the road for Archie's liking, but it was fine. A cool onshore breeze flicked her hair around like a model on a photo shoot and she battled to keep it out of her face.

She worried if Archie was okay because there were no seats. The tables were very low and they had to sit on brightly coloured mats on the ground – very Thai style. He stared out to sea, but it wasn't clear because of the background lights from the restaurant and seafront. She stared at him and inspected his every movement and was eternally happy. 'Archie?'

'Yes, teerak?'

'I don't want to go back to work at the bar.' His feeling was the same. Even though he trusted her, he didn't trust other people. It wouldn't take much for someone to buy her a drink and maybe drop something inside to make her very sleepy. Of course, Ploy would be there to take care of her too, it's not like she could just be led off like a stray sheep. Yet, the mere thought of other men objectifying and eye-humping the love of his life was unacceptable for him.

'So, what do you want to do? Do you have any ideas?'

'I don't know,' she fibbed. She just didn't know how to say it, because it would require financial support from him. It wasn't something she ever wanted to come into their relationship, but that was just the reality of it. If she was to make a break from the bar then it was essential. 'Maybe I can go home, but I will not have salary. Or maybe I can go to college. But college I will have to pay, and I don't know how I can.' She brushed the hair out of her face. 'Maybe I can work more one year and save money and I can go to college.'

'But...' he searched for the right words so he could express himself as sensitively as he could, '...you don't make much money there, how can you manage to save anything? Or even if you can, it might not be enough.'

'Yes, I don't know how I can do. Maybe I can change to another bar and have higher salary.'

'But it's just the same. This bar, that bar, there's no difference. And I'd rather you stayed with Ploy.'

'Yes, I know. Me too.'

They were interrupted by the food as it descended onto the low table, and that took them off-subject. They both thought about bringing it back up but it was their last night of the holiday so wanted to keep it light. She was glad she managed to get it out and give him a chance to think about it more, and Archie was glad she found the courage to bring it up by herself. She always found money so vulgar and really didn't want to be the same as so many other bargirls who saw boyfriends as an ATM. Most of those girls had several boyfriends too, which meant several ATM's. There were some couples who were faithful to one another, but the relationship was completely dependant on the financial support that the boyfriend or husband could provide. That was basically a matrimonial prostitution. Lily wanted a real relationship because her love for Archie was real. Anyway, they could discuss it in more detail once they got back home to Bangkok.

They sat hand-in-hand at the departure gate, waiting for their flight to Bangkok. She'd followed him diligently around the airport, trying to learn as much as she could from her seasoned traveller of a boyfriend. Airports mesmerised and confused her, but Archie explained how it all worked and took some of the mystery out of it. He was trying to train her in case she'd ever have to fly alone some time in the future.

She'd had the most amazing time of her life and was thoroughly delighted with all the things she'd accomplished during her holiday. All the excitement had worn her out though. They'd done so much since he arrived back, not to mention how she was quite exhausted from their night-time activities too.

Whilst Archie was away, her normal routine was to go to work around 6 p.m. and work until 2 a.m. She'd eat something before heading home, then play on her phone or chat to him, perhaps watch a Thai drama and sleep around 3.30 a.m. Then she'd sleep right through until 4 p.m. the next day. There were a few exceptions, for instance, when she was searching for condos, but mostly she slept a clear twelve hours every night. But she wouldn't trade the time spent with Archie for more sleep, because it was more valuable to her than anything else in the world.

She slept most of the flight and the taxi journey home. All the while, she was snuggled into her safe haven in Archie's chest. The drivers' phone rang at one point and she stirred. She peeked her head up just to see where they were, before checking on him. It was early evening, and rain lashed down on the Srirat Expressway as well as the rest of Bangkok – from the temples and palaces, to the shopping malls and condos, to the lady bars and massage parlours. She settled back into her spot again. Without looking back up at him, she uttered tenderly into his chest:

'Khob khun ka, teerak. Chan rak khun.'

'You're welcome, my Lily. I love you too.'

Chapter Twenty

บทที่ยี่สิบ

'Can I use your computer please? I want to look at dresses.'

'Sure.' He was cooking breakfast in the afternoon and came across to start the computer and open the internet for her. 'Is your phone okay?' He wanted to enquire because she'd usually look for things using that.

'Yes, I just want to see it big.'

'Sexy dresses?' he asked light-heartedly.

'Ka!' *Yes!* she confirmed.

Lily enjoyed his breakfasts. It wasn't something that she ever bothered with before, but they meant a lot to Archie. They'd formed the habit of eating together to start their day, regardless of whether it was already a few hours into the afternoon or not. He served her, poured orange juice then brewed coffee for himself in a cafetiere. Afterwards, he went for a shower whilst she resumed browsing dresses. They were going to have a look around the mall and then maybe grab a bite before taking her to work. There probably wasn't enough time for a movie that day.

She showered after him and whilst she was in the bathroom, he opened his computer again. He wanted to look at what style of dress she was interested in so he might expand the kinds of things that he could buy for her. He'd brought her a purple tartan mini kilt from Scotland and she wore it as often as she could. She loved it. He remembered trying to figure out what size she was when he was in the shop, before realising that actually he knew the circumference of her waist very well indeed. She thought that a man who could buy clothes without any prior instruction was a rare thing – especially when it was so much to her liking.

He checked his browser history as he started his reconnaissance. The first page she looked at was a search for 'wedding dress Scotland.' He clicked the other history entries and she'd clearly been browsing wedding dresses and trying to find out about traditions and customs for a Scottish wedding. She probably was unaware about the history, or forgot about it completely. Or perhaps she was entirely aware and knew him well enough, so was trying to plant the seed. They hadn't been together long but she was already sure that she wanted to spend the rest of her life with him. She wished they could make it official, to put it gracelessly – to make sure that he couldn't get away. He was shocked at what he found, but it was a good shock. Deep down, he wanted it too. Lily was everything to him and she worshipped the ground he walked on – why wouldn't he want that for the rest of his life? He closed the screen not wanting to see anymore, because after all, it was bad luck to see her wedding dress before the big day.

Archie was already snoozing a little by the time she emerged from the bathroom. She was wearing nothing but her underwear and flaking her hair out with the towel. With his recent discovery, she looked even more beautiful more usual. Her pure and delicate nature was beyond anyone he'd ever known before. That was the moment he was sure – he wanted her to be the only one he'd make breakfast for, or have emerge from the shower. It wasn't just about how sweet and innocent and beautiful she was; it wasn't just the perfect body and the incredible sex-life they shared; Archie loved the way she loved him, above everything else. He knew that she'd stand by him and wait for him, no matter what. He knew she was going to be the new constant in his life and that day-in and day-out, she'd be the one he can share everything with. That was the thing he wanted most in life.

'Hi,' he said brightly, with a bigger than usual smile on his face. She looked at him perplexed.

'Hello?' she said coyly. 'Why you smile?'

'Nothing…just you.' He was still lying on the bed. 'Come here please. Five minutes.' She approached his outstretched arms, knowing it was a request for her to fill her spot. That was a request which she'd never deny. 'I really love you, Lily. You're everything to me, you know?'

'No, I don't,' she teased, 'you can tell me again please?' She loved to hear it.

'Pom rak khun.' *I love you,* he said.

After a few minutes, she made to get up. 'No!' He locked his arms around her. 'I'm sorry, you cannot leave here.'

'But teerak, I need to make up na.'

'But I need your cuddles more. Just five more minutes please.'

'Okay.'

'So, did you find any nice dresses?' he enquired.

'Not yet. I will look more later.'

'Lily, I want to ask you,' he paused as he tried to formulate the words in his head first, 'what are your plans for the future?' He then realised she may have thought he was asking about college. 'I mean for us,' he added.

'I don't know. Up to you na.'

'No, it's not just up to me, I'm pretty sure you have an opinion about it too.'

'You can tell me first?' she asked.

'Well…' He slid his hand up from her back to stroke her hair, whilst they lay together tenderly. 'I want to have a family. I want to settle down and just have a nice life. I want one girl to stay with forever.'

'Okay.' She said. 'You…' she hesitated, '…you have some idea who?'

'Yes, I do.'

'What you want and what I want, it's the same. You think...you want to be with me?'

'Yes. Of course you, who else? I love you Lily.' He turned to look her straight in the eye. 'You've got everything I want and more. I want to spend the rest of my life with you.' There was no great outward reaction but her world exploded with celebration.

'I want to be with you forever too, teerak.'

'Just promise me that you'll never ever change.'

'I never change na. Promise.'

'So...you want to do it? Spend your life with me?' he asked.

'Yes. I want.'

'Okay...'

There it was. The most casual and laid-back proposal. Well, they maybe were not yet engaged and it wasn't a proposal as such, but it was a betrothal. They'd promised that they'd be together and start a family, but the formal proposal still had to happen. His brain raced off trying to plan a perfect one for her.

When they got to the mall, they were both a little quiet with one another. It wasn't an awkward silence, it was more that they were both preoccupied. He was trying to plan the proposal down to the last detail, and she was running scenarios in her head of how it might be – the proposal, the wedding, the next fifty years or so. She thought about where they'd settle, and was attracted to Scotland. Of course, she loved Thailand and her family were there, but she often felt as if they didn't really care for her. They always pressured her to work and bothered her about money. Archie was the only one who'd truly loved her, let her be herself, supported and listened to her. She'd be quite happy to follow him wherever he may go. And they could always travel back every now and then so she could see her family. She thought about any children that they may have too and supposed they'd have much better prospects growing up in Scotland rather than Thailand. Particularly if she had a daughter – she wanted her to be educated and successful. She didn't want her to end up working in bars like she did.

They continued wandering the mall and looked at clothes. She had been very discreetly altering his style, one garment at a time. She liked how he dressed, but often he was too formal. Then the rest of his clothes were too casual or outdoorsy. He was either going for a fancy dinner or going for a trek or adventure somewhere. He didn't have anything for the in-between – that being, going around malls and stopping at coffee shops in the afternoon or looking round markets. They browsed some shirts and she picked one out, laying it along his back to check the size. She then tucked the hangar under his chin to check how it looked from the front. 'Wow! So handsome!' she giggled.

'Oh, I shy!' he made an impression of her.

She paid for the shirts, despite his objection. It was important that she bought them for him. He'd already spent so much money on her, and she'd been trying to save some money to buy him something. The money she'd budget for food whilst he was away was repurposed as *Archie money* once he was back, seeing as he would pay for everything when they were together. She just wanted to give back what she could and it meant the world to him.

Lily went to the toilet, which gave him a good chance to look for rings and things on his phone without being discovered. He couldn't find any rings online in Bangkok, well, no decent ones. He supposed he'd have to go to look in person, but there was no shortage of jewellery shops anyway. He knew he'd have to take her so that she could pick the style, but just wanted to get some ideas because he was excited. He then searched for hotels and dates for her remaining four days off that she had. They didn't manage before, but if he'd been smart, he could have stuck the four days on the front or back of her Monday off so that they'd have five days away.

She'd been in the bathroom a while and he had long finished looking at what he wanted to for the moment. Sometimes she'd take a while, but he never thought about it much before. He checked, and she wasn't online. He sent a message: "Are you okay? Did you get lost?" There came no reply, and he had to wait a further five minutes for her to come out.

'Teerak, are you okay?' he asked. 'You were a very long time. I thought maybe you go out the window or something!'

'Yes, I'm okay ka, I just sometimes have pain in my stomach.'

'Pain? And you've had this before?'

'Yes, but I think just from alcohol.'

'But we've not been drinking much recently.'

She patted his shoulder and smiled reassuringly. 'It's okay na, you don't worry.'

That evening, they did the usual sitting and drinking at her work, but he suggested she didn't drink alcohol. She suggested the same for him, so they sat in a bar drinking an orange juice for her and a coke for him. It seemed entirely pointless for them to go, because she never spoke to any other customers. When Archie was there, she'd just sit with him all the time. Other than bringing out some food orders, collecting glasses and helping clear up at the end of the night, she wasn't really working. She still got her salary from that of course, so it had to do in the interim. On occasion, she'd collect a few drinks here and there from some regulars, but then she'd make her excuses to return to Archie's side.

It had been a pivotal day. They both knew where they were going and their desires, hopes and dreams matched. Now they just had to make a plan to bring it about. Whilst sitting at their table, they browsed and settled on a hotel on Koh Lanta and managed to work it so that they had the five days. He booked there and then. He had also settled on his idea for a proposal, but supposed that he'd have to enquire when he got there. The hotel choice had to coincide with the proposal idea, and if that hotel couldn't do it, then he'd just have to find some other place that could. It was a very fancy hotel though and some of the guest pictures included birthdays and weddings and more, so he was sure that they'd be able to action his request. It wasn't that he was in a hurry, but at the same time, he didn't want to wait any longer. They were both sure that they wanted each other, so why waste any more time?

Koi, Wan and a handful of the other girls turned up at Sport Spot. Lily and Archie moved to a table outside to join them, because it was the only place big enough. It was nice for Lily to have a catch up with her old workmates. They all talked in Thai of course, and discussed Archie most of the time. It was a good chance for Lily to boast about him too. The girls were all happy for her, because they knew how much the bar life wasn't for her. It was one of the end goals for bargirls though. To work in a bar until they manage to find a farang to take care of them. There was still the perception that all white people were vastly wealthy. That meant they just needed to find one and then enjoy being a trophy wife.

Many of them took it too far though. Once they can sniff money, they become greedy, and nothing is ever enough. It was common for foreigners in Thailand to work overseas, which meant that their lady was free for a while. That freedom was then used to fraternise with new men, because she could get more money again. They'd tell their sad story of poverty and hardship and win the sympathy of kind men who just wanted to help. Tears were always the most effective weapon that a woman had to get her way. A bargirl who could turn on the waterworks was a very dangerous creature. So long as there was a steady stream of money it didn't matter about the moral compass. Money was everything in Thailand.

Not all of them were like that, of course. For every ruthless money-hunter, there was a genuine one too. Lily, for example just wanted to be a good and faithful wife and make her husband happy. She may have hated working in bars and hardly made any money at all, but it turned out that the bar life actually worked out for her. Meeting Archie was the luck that was going to change her life forever.

The girls chatted over him at the table, but he didn't mind to be excluded from the conversation. He accepted that by not being able to speak Thai. He was just thrilled because he knew that Lily was boasting about him to all the other girls. He watched her as she smiled and giggled and was a contributor to the conversation, rather than the shrinking violet that she was before. The girls could hardly recognise her because she had come out of her shell so much in such a short time. The wallflower was blooming at last.

Their outside table was along the roadside. It was obviously hotter there, but there were fans to help keep him cool. They were much closer to the action there though. Taxis and motosais passed close by. Even the occasional coach would squeeze its' way down the soi, as well as all the tourists and locals going about their business. Archie was approached by a homeless guy, but he didn't realise until one of the girls had already chased him away. He just heard him say 'gin kao' which literally meant 'eat rice.' He timidly tried a few more tables as he carried on down the road, making an eating gesture and asking for some help to get himself a meal. Archie felt so sorry for him, and sorry that he didn't even see him before it was too late. It was funny though to see how some of the girls looked down their noses at a homeless guy. Had it not been for their pretty face, nice tits and the fact she was happy to open her legs, then it could be her not knowing where her next meal was coming from.

Lily had really enjoyed her night at work. It was nice to hang out with her old friends, especially since all her circumstances had changed. Each night at work, she was quite happy to go, because Archie was always by her side. She felt safe, protected and content. The girls were going out clubbing and they invited her and Archie along, but all she wanted was to have a bite to eat then go home with him. Once the bar was closed, they wandered along to the end of the road. There was a convenience store there and Archie wanted to nip in for a few bits and pieces. He spotted the same homeless guy again, in a quiet corner at the shopfront. He was curled into a ball, hanging out with the stray dogs – or soi dogs, as they're known. It must have been a very pitiful existence trying to find some scraps to eat. And trying to sleep in a place with reasonable footfall and lighting to avoid being attacked, as they were often at risk of that.

Archie selected the shopping that he needed. 'Is there anything else you want, teerak?' he asked Lily.

'No, it's enough.'

Archie then picked up a few extra bottles of water, soft drinks and opened the food fridge. The convenience stores in Thailand were able to prepare the ready meals. He picked a stir-fry chicken, hot dog and a sandwich and asked the assistant to heat them up. Lily asked him: 'Teerak, I thought we go to eat na?'

'Yes, my love, we'll go to the end of the block for food. But this isn't for us.'

She was confused, but she hadn't even noticed the guy curled up in a sorry state outside. He asked her to hold their bags for a moment and when they got outside, Archie went into the corner where the guy was huddling. 'Sawatdee khap,' he said. The guy flinched and seemed frightened of Archie. It seemed perhaps he had a slightly low IQ, or perhaps he was simply terrified by his street life. 'Gin kao,' Archie said. It took a few seconds for the guy to catch on, but Archie opened the bags to let him see. He also left a few hundred baht on top of the food too. It wasn't going to solve all the guys problems, but it was going to help him for a while. The guy then made a wai with his hands and thanked Archie profusely: 'Khob khun mak mak khap.'

'Teeraaaaaak!' Lily wanted to say something but wasn't sure what.

'I saw him earlier,' Archie said, 'he was searching for some food.'

'Ooi, teerak…' Lily linked her arm and snuggled him on the street as he took their shopping bags back from her. 'My husband so good man. My husband so kind.'

They flew to Krabi for holiday number two, and rode a minivan to the ferry pier. There was a marketplace outside selling souvenirs, beach wares and of course food. More minivans and coaches and taxis drove in and out, turned around and dropped off and picked up people. It was organised chaos. The scene inside was much the same – teeming with travellers from all around the globe, trying to find tickets, or the correct place to wait for their boat. They bought their tickets and had a look around the market. She bought a sarong and two straw hats with her own money, one for her and one for him. He bought some essentials like water and snacks for the journey, because he knew she'd get hungry. Lastly, they bought some ice creams, found a spot of shade and sat together patiently waiting for their boat to board.

The boat was slow and wobbly. She felt very intrepid on her voyage out to sea. 'So, what about this one? It's same your work?' she joked.

The sun thumped down on them as they sat outside on the top deck. A few young backpackers sat next to them, playing reggae music on a portable speaker. Archie didn't think it was particularly authentic to Thailand, but he was hardly going to be a buzzkill and correct them. It reminded him of Natasha, and how she'd read all her travel blogs which apparently made her an expert on Thailand. It was funny to compare that to what Archie was now, having all the experience he did – about culture, class and real Thai life.

The crossing was very peaceful with the sea breeze, the spray and the gentle rocking motion from the boat. Lily enjoyed the sensation. He'd been worried about her not feeling well, because she sometimes got a little car sick, but it looked like she was having the time of her life. He enjoyed the journey too. He'd always loved being at sea which was why he chose the job he did, but a lot of the romance and enjoyment had been squeezed out of it with the pressures of work. If he was ever out on deck, he'd have to wear a boilersuit, boots, helmet, gloves, safety glasses and it was not comfortable at all. It was nice to be out on the sea and not be working for a change.

They arrived on the island and rode a tuk-tuk to the hotel. As they checked in, they were greeted with a cool refreshing drink at the reception. It was some kind of fruit juice, but Archie couldn't identify it. It was absolutely delicious though. There wasn't enough time to ask what it was though, since he could see that Lily was tired. Never one to complain, Lily was silently suffering and he knew she wanted to reach the room as quickly as possible. That bond they had was what made them special; being able to understand how tired she was and what she needed, without either of them having to say a word. She was still not accustomed to travelling, but didn't want to moan to Archie, like another girl might. Even though she was completely out of power, she just waited patiently, because she knew Archie was taking care of things.

After concluding the check-in, they were led to their incredible room. There was a large lavish bedroom and en-suite with luxurious décor. Beyond the en-suite was a sitting area with a TV and fridge. Beyond that, there was a balcony which overlooked the pool and ocean. The main event though was the small plunge pool and daybed on the balcony. It was private, and whilst they could look down on the main pool, no one else could look up at them. Finally, the only other sight before them was miles of sea rolling off over the horizon. It was paradise.

He had big plans to action during his four nights in paradise. Despite having no doubts about her whatsoever, he was still nervous. Given the amount of time they'd been together, he worried what his family and friends would say. Nobody back in Scotland really understood his life in Thailand. They assumed that he was just there like any other scumbag, going to strip clubs and sleeping with prostitutes every night. They had the impression that all Thai women were only interested in money. A few of his friends told him to be careful and his dad had advised him to *keep his hands in his pockets*. For a lot of Thai women, they were perhaps right, but he had Lily and she was his perfect little flower.

He told her to lie down whilst he unpacked the suitcase. She brought what seemed like a hundred bikinis. 'So…I'm going back after four days. But how long are you planning on staying here?' he chuckled.

'But…maybe I want to change sometimes.' At least they didn't take up too much space in the suitcase, he supposed. Despite having a lot more changes of clothes than he did, the case was still about a fifty-fifty split, because all of her outfits were of much less material. He was always very smart at travelling and planned what he'd wear for each day in order to bring just the exact amount, plus a little extra as a contingency.

He found there was a certain pleasure in seeing her clothes in his suitcase. Usually, it was filled with clothes for months at sea; uniform, ear defenders and other work essentials. It'd been round the world many times, dragged through heat, snow, rain, sand, everything. It'd been pulled up and down ships sides dozens of times, miles offshore and in rough seas. To have bright bikinis, sexy tops, cute jean shorts and bras and panties in it was a sight that he took real pleasure in.

After a quick shower he changed into a vest, shorts and flip-flops so that he was island-ready. 'I'm just going to go and ask about hiring a motosai. And maybe they have a map,' he said.

'Okay, I want to take a shower. And I feel tired. Maybe I can have a nap before we go to dinner?'

'Sure. But wait for me before your nap. All new beds must be checked under an engineer's supervision,' he joked.

He went to the reception to enquire about his grand proposal plan. The receptionist called the duty manager through, and they had a quick discussion about it.

'Yes, it's no problem. We can do for you, anything you like.'

The discussion distracted him so much that he almost forgot to ask about renting a scooter. He could hardly go back empty-handed, because his plan had to be a complete surprise. He initially planned on renting just one, but when they went out to look, there was a blue one and a pink one of the same model parked next to each other. He knew she could drive a scooter; in fact, she was better at it than he was. He'd only ever really driven cars, whilst she'd driven scooters around her hometown and the farm since she was young. He thought it'd be nice to have his and hers vehicles to explore the island together. It was to protect her too. In case he somehow lost control of the scooter, he didn't want to take her down too. He filled out the paperwork and paid a deposit before they handed him two keys.

After their very enjoyable 'bed check,' they got ready to go to dinner. They still didn't know the area, so decided to head back to the town where the ferry port was. There was definitely good scope for a decent place to eat there, as well as things to see and do. He took her out to the scooters and handed her a key. She saw one in his hand too. 'You get two?' she asked.

'Yes,' he replied excitedly whilst walking along the line of parked scooters. 'This one is mine,' he then pointed to the one next to it, 'and that one is yours.'

'Oooooh…' The bodywork was mostly black, but she saw the coloured detailing, one with pink and one with blue. She spoke in Thai and he knew that she'd said it was so cute. Lily rode behind him on their way into town. She was worried about him riding because she knew he wasn't very experienced. But then again, he was quite good with machines, and was a fast learner. He wasn't really a liability, just a little green behind the ears, but it was better if he set the pace. They approached the town and it had a nice cosy ambiance in the night time. There were lots of people milling about and plenty of life and activity on the streets, but all in a cool relaxed way. It wasn't the same frantic relentlessness of Bangkok.

They drove on past the markets and along the main street towards the port. There was space enough for them to park up side-by-side along the beach front. The waves lapped up against the shore and the atmosphere was calm and tranquil. He stopped the bike and flicked out the kickstand whilst she very smoothly and accurately pulled in to the gap next to him. They meandered past the restaurants hand-in-hand and perused some menus, whilst the front of house for each place stood at their respective entrances vying for business. They found one which went out over the water on pontoons and she checked the menu. After her approval, they took a table. She'd always ask him what he wanted to eat, but he didn't mind. He could always find something suitable on the menu. He was more concerned about giving her what she wanted because she'd had much less opportunity in her life to enjoy fancy meals. As long as the restaurant had a romantic setting, it was fine for him.

They ordered a whole steamed fish, somtam and she asked for oysters. They were not something that were particularly appetising to him, but he was quite happy for her to enjoy them. She'd always liked them, but was usually too reserved to ask because she knew they were more expensive. But she was on holiday and knew he wouldn't mind. 'You know they're aphrodisiacs?' he asked.

'Huh?' she didn't understand the word.

'Aphrodisiac means…it's like a food that makes you want to have sex.'

'Oh,' she giggled. 'But you never eat it, so how you can do it so many times?' Her sweet goofy laughed disturbed some of the other diners. She had just prepared her oyster to be eaten and offered it to him. 'Here, you can try?'

'No, I don't think so. Maybe I'll just have a red bull or something,' he joked.

The food was incredible. The fish was thick and soft and succulent and the somtam was sweet and sour and spicy. Everything was perfect. Before leaving, she slipped off to the toilet and he searched online for things to do and places to see on the island. She took her time again. He was beginning to get concerned, because it had happened a few times already. It was really a seriously long time she spent in there. The paranoid part of his psyche flared up and suggested that she was spending so long in the toilet perhaps to talk with someone else. He remembered how she'd always arrange a time to talk with him when he was away. But then again, that was more for him and his work times. And also, her toilet breaks were totally in keeping with their actions. There was no way that she'd be able to predict what time they'd finish eating in order to call someone. What's more, if they'd ever manage a short video call, she was never in a toilet cubicle. He had to trust her, but there was some damage done to him which meant that he couldn't help but be suspicious.

Eventually she returned to the table. 'Teerak, is everything okay?' he asked.

'Yes, I'm okay. Just my stomach sometimes.'

'But it's really a long time to be in the toilet. Maybe you should go to see a doctor?'

'No, it's okay. Doctor is expensive.'

'Lily, it's your health. You can't put a price on that.'

'But I don't have problem. Just sometimes my stomach no good. Not everyday na. You don't worry please.' She smiled reassuringly at him before taking her phone out of her bag, which had been at the table with him the whole time.

He certainly should never have jumped to such a rash conclusion about what she might have been doing, only for her phone to have been three feet away from him the whole time. He knew it was bad of him, but he couldn't help it and it wasn't his fault. What a relief he was proved wrong though, because he'd already started the ball rolling on his proposal plan. It did make him more worried, however, because it meant that she was actually using the toilet for that length of time. He supposed that she could get an upset stomach from time to time though. She ate so many random and spicy things, plus she'd been travelling that day. Her body wasn't used to travel, so perhaps it was just that.

They walked around and looked in shops, browsing souvenirs. Lily bought a fridge magnet for herself and one for Ploy. She wanted a modest reminder to keep at home and remember her time there with him. Her feet began to ache again so they stopped for a drink. Lily

286

uploaded some pictures to her profile and started to collect likes and comments. The first comment read: "Wow, so nice you two. Have a good time." It was from Amm.

Each day they saw a new place and a new beach. Each evening they'd make use of the plunge pool on the balcony to watch the sun go down over the horizon. They'd make love as the birds rustled and squawked and nested down in the trees for the night.

They discussed the next move for her after he'd leave Thailand. He thought about just sending her some money so she could go home. If she started college then she'd be in Bangkok alone and still have to pay for her rent. Not to mention how if she was still there, then her family would be expecting her to work. If she started college she'd also be tied there for a few years, but the intention now was after maybe another year or so they'd be married and would move to Scotland. That would make all the time she spent in college a complete waste. There were colleges back at her hometown where she could enrol, but they still had the attendance issue so put that on the back burner. He'd be happy enough just to send her money so she can relax in her hometown and help out around the farm for the time being. She'd be far away from the bar but also, and more importantly, she'd be happy.

They talked about him going back to her hometown to meet her family. Of course she wanted him to meet them, as did he, but she dreaded it. She was wary about the attention he would bring. She'd be the talk of the town and people may jump to the wrong conclusions about them or start to ask for money. All her distant relatives would no doubt wriggle out of the woodwork in an attempt to glean money from them and she always had difficulty in saying no to her family.

He'd also been researching about Thai wedding traditions and found something called *sinsod*. It was similar to a dowry paid to the girls' parents in order to be with her. He wanted to ask about it, but decided to wait until after the proposal. There would be plenty of time to discuss it then. He also didn't want to mention anything specifically matrimonial, because it was important to keep the proposal as a big surprise. If he'd been talking about it everyday or asking about *sinsod*, then she'd probably know it was coming soon. Instead, he decided to keep it all under wraps, whilst she was waiting patiently for it to come one day in the future, with a big fat 'yes' locked and loaded on her lips.

Their last morning on Koh Lanta came around. Archie was dressed a bit more sharply than usual with a nice shirt and fisherman's pants on. It was quite a smart yet relaxed look – a hybrid of formal and Thai clothing. He suggested to her that they'd go for a walk along the beach after breakfast and take some photos, but that was a cover. He encouraged her to dress nicely too and wear a little makeup for what was coming. Not for him, of course. He loved her with or without makeup; she was always his gorgeous little flower. But if there were photos to be taken, he knew that she'd regret not being done up when she looked back. He really thought of everything.

They walked the winding path through from the room and he had his big camera with him. When they reached the restaurant, Archie spoke to the staff at the desk and made a wai with his hands, 'Sawatdee khap. Is my breakfast ready?'

'Yes, khun Archie.'

Lily was puzzled. They never usually greeted them like that. He would just tell them the room number and they'd sit down. Someone brought out a blindfold on a tray and asked her politely in Thai to put it on. She looked at Archie and he smiled enthusiastically. 'It's okay, put it on.' He handed the camera over to a staff member before lifting her and spinning her round a few times to disorient her. She screamed and other breakfasters looked on as Archie shushed her. He carried her down to the beach and she really didn't know which way they were going – back through the trees to the room, down to the beach or out of the hotel – but when he descended the couple of steps from the hotel to the sand, she could sense the sea was near.

He walked her all the way out into the water. She heard splashes as he stepped through the waves and screamed again, thinking he was going to play some kind of prank and drop her into the sea. 'Archie! My phone in my pocket na! Don't put me in the water!'

'Don't worry, teerak, only your feet. Are you ready?' He removed her flip flops and threw them towards the shore before gently placing her down again. He wanted to create a sensory element and the first thing she could recognise was the cool morning sea lap around her ankles, and the soft sand between her toes. He turned her round and removed her blindfold to reveal a table and two chairs sitting in about ten inches of water. There were flowers and fruits and the table was decorated beautifully. Their breakfast was laid out and they had their own private buffet out there in the water. 'Oh my God, Archie. It's so beautiful!' A couple of staff members were appointed to them, one for photographs and one to attend them for food. He helped her sit down, but it was hard to push her chair in because of the sand.

When he took his seat opposite her, Lily's eyes were glossy. She managed to keep her composure, but she was continually amazed. The things he did for her were like real fairytales. She thought maybe only celebrities or really rich people could enjoy things like that. Those sorts of things didn't happen to her – except they did now, and all because of him. They collected spectators on the beach. Some people that were walking past and a few of those that were disturbed by her screams at breakfast, came down from the hotel and took photos of them. As much as she hated being centre of attention, for the first time in her life, she loved it. Every second and every photo taken of her, made her feel like she was really someone. Lily was no longer just the shy, quiet, retiring girl with no opinion. She had grown more in the few months with Archie than she had in the rest of her life so far.

Once she calmed down and took a hundred photos with her phone, they started to eat. She was full of things to say, yet she was speechless. It was so perfect that she didn't ever want to leave. She was always slow to eat and whilst he usually didn't mind, he really wished she'd hurry up that morning. Lily was taking her time however, because she wanted to savour the moment for as long as possible.

Eventually, she rested her cutlery down and gave a sigh of fulfilment. It was the moment he'd been waiting for.

'Are you finished eating?' he asked.

'Yes, teerak. It's so amazing. Thank you so much ka.'

'Oow!' he cried, jerking his foot up.

'Ooi, teerak, what happened?'

'I don't know, I felt like something bit me!' It was a ruse. Nothing bit him. He got out his chair to 'tend to his foot' and pretended to follow something along the seabed, right the way next to her chair. He was already crouched, and proceeded to put one knee down into the water as he reached her side. He presented the ring that he'd been clutching tightly for the past week.

'Lily,' he began, 'I love you with all my heart. You're the sweetest and most wonderful person I've ever met. You satisfy every part of my mind, body and soul. I'm the luckiest man alive to have you. I hope you don't think it's too early, but I've already decided I want to spend the rest of my life with you. So…I was wondering…will you marry me?'

'Teerak! Oh my God! Yes! Yes!' She broke down as he slipped the ring on her finger. He stood up from the water to embrace her as she wept tears of joy into his chest. She knew it was early too, but she was more than ready. Archie was the most perfect man and she loved him fiercely. He was all she wanted. He opened doors for her and gave her a life beyond anything she could ever envisage before.

After their initial talk about the future, they looked at a few rings whilst passing through malls, so he knew what style she liked. He didn't know what ring size she was, but thought he'd ask Ploy if she knew. It just so happened they were the same size. After that, he had all the information he needed. He then had to request that Ploy invite her for a movie and a catch up one day, just so he had the opportunity to go out and buy it. He'd managed to keep it safe and secret the whole trip.

There were cheers, hoots and applause from the shore, followed by a pop of a champagne bottle by the staff. It was a total shock for her. She *was* expecting it, but he deliberately told her that they'd buy the ring together, so she really wasn't expecting it any time soon. He'd been in Thailand a month already and still had one to go. She thought it'd most likely be after his next trip away. She certainly wasn't expecting it at breakfast. But for him, breakfast was always more intimate. People can go for dates and have dinner the first time they meet and then never see each other again. Breakfast was had after spending the night together and waking up in each others arms.

Archie had arranged a special dinner for them that night. He would tend to use her time spent in the bathroom or napping for all his secret research and endeavours. He found a restaurant with a lovely setting and contacted them. Not only was it a restaurant, but it was also a cooking school, ran by a foreigner. It was not so big, with only a couple dozen tables downstairs. There was a small upstairs with just eight tables that would be opened for engagements or when the downstairs was busy. Archie booked the upstairs for the night. He'd explained the story in an email and the female owner thought it was all incredibly sweet and romantic. She said there'd be a modest charge for decoration, but she'd only charge him for the hire of the space if it got busy and she had to turn people away.

When they arrived, the staff called the owner. She greeted them warmly before ushering them upstairs. She was a lovely American lady who'd been living on Koh Lanta for the past fifteen years. She met Lily and spoke perfect Thai to her. She showed her the ring and they exchanged a few more pleasantries before they were left to their own devices. It was decorated with white chiffon suspended from the ceiling and fairy lights and candles all around as per his request. Thankfully the owner had enough of a vision in her decorating skills as she did with her cooking and the place looked beautiful. They had manoeuvred the other tables out of the way and placed one in the middle, close to the edge of the balcony, overlooking the sea. Personalised menus had been printed with love hearts and the date as a keepsake. That was a really nice touch, they both thought, especially since Lily loved to hold on to keepsakes.

'Archie?'

'Yes, my love?'

'You know, I am so happy I meet you. My life before…it's so boring and I'm so tired every time. Many times I feel no good about my life. Now…I feel happy every time.' She reached for his hand over the table. 'You give me so much, and I don't have anything to give you.

Maybe I can work and help with money. But you are so good to me and I love you so much.'

'Lily, all I want is for you to wait for me each time I go away, be faithful to me, and stay your sweet little self. The only thing you need to give me is your heart and your loyalty, forever.' He kissed her hand.

'Yes, you have it already na. I will love you always.'

'Just promise me Lily...promise you will never leave me.'

'I promise na. I will be with you forever.'

'And I hope you know I don't go away because I want to, but I need to,' he added. 'But when I'm home we can do things like this. We are free to travel and do anything we want and I'll give you a good life. You're my dream come true.'

They ate dinner as the sea washed up and down on the sand below them. Coming and going, ebbing and flowing like a heartbeat, washing away but always returning back. Other diners chatted and laughed downstairs, oblivious to the two of them upstairs in their little private slice of heaven. Together, just the two of them.

Chapter Twenty-One
บทที่ยี่สิบเอ็ด

They returned to Bangkok and to the usual life, but it felt different. He'd continued to patronise the bar every night with her, but there was another element to it now since they were engaged. She wasn't one to brag, but was only too happy to show off her diamond to the other girls. It wasn't about the ring itself, it was about what it represented. In five weeks, they'd been on two holidays, got engaged and made love uninterrupted. The latter was a something of a concern.

She wanted to discuss it privately but she never had the courage to bring it up because she was worried and didn't know what to say. Plus, with the holiday, she'd just never gotten round to it. It'd been on her mind however, and the longer she thought about it, the bigger it grew as a concern for her. He could tell that she wasn't quite right that night and caught her staring into space a few times. 'Lily, is everything okay?'

'Yes. Why?'

'Just…you look…not a hundred per cent?'

'Yes.'

'Well, what is it?'

She supposed it was as good a place as any to discuss it. She knew him well enough to know he was hardly going to make a scene. Plus, he'd noticed something was up, so it was time to come clean. 'It's about…my period. I not have for long time.'

'Oh. Yeah. I was sort of wondering that actually. How long is it?'

'Six weeks. Last one finish one week before you come back.'

'Okay. Maybe it's just late, sometimes that can happen right? We've been quite…active. Maybe it's…disrupted your pattern or something? I don't know though.'

'Yes, sometimes I'm late before, but this time not same.'

'Okay, well…we'll go to the pharmacy and get a test in the morning. Or…do you want me to go now?'

'No. Tomorrow is okay.' She didn't want to bother him. Neither did she want to do the test at work. Waiting another twelve hours wouldn't make any difference in the long run anyway.

In the morning, he went out to the pharmacy and bought a couple of test kits. They nervously waited the few minutes for the result to develop. The condo was silent. They didn't want any distraction from the TV or music as they sat together on the sofa. *Pregnant*, it displayed. They both didn't know how to react. Of course they dreamed of having a baby together one day, but he only had a few weeks left in Thailand, they were unmarried and had no real plan of how to bring a baby into the world. She checked the instructions again, looking at the accuracy and tried to factor in all the things that could alter the result. 'Okay,' he said reassuringly. 'You can check again later, but I think we should go to the hospital and get it checked properly.'

'Yes. But I think, maybe I feel like I *do* have baby.' She turned to look at him. 'What can we do?' she asked.

'If we do, then we'll raise it and love it and cherish it. If we don't, then I'm still the luckiest man in the world.'

'But it's so soon.'

'I know. But we'll manage. I love you Lily, and this is going to be okay, whatever happens.'

Following a formal test at the hospital it was confirmed that she was indeed pregnant. She explained to the doctor how she also *felt* that she was pregnant, and he explained there were no physiological traits that she could pick up at that stage. 'But I can feel it in my heart,' she told him. They'd had time to think and talk about it, and the fear started to subside. Archie was supportive and kind. His excitement was starting to pass to her, but she was still worried. They had to formulate a plan about her and about his work. College looked like it was out the window now for sure, but that was fine. Certainly, working in a bar was too.

Archie and Lily decided it'd be best if she just went home where she could relax and be free of stress. She had to break the news to her parents and tell them she was coming home, which wasn't easy for her.

Their reaction wasn't great – in fact it was terrible. They told her she was not welcome at home and that she had to continue working at the bar. His heart ached for her as he picked up the pieces following that phone call. She cried and cried in his arms and was totally lost. Her parents were always so unfair to her and she couldn't understand why. She was so happy to have Archie's baby inside her, but she was so scared that she'd have to do it all alone now. He couldn't stay all the time, he had to go to work. She could no longer work too, and couldn't even go home now. She had no idea what to do.

'Okay,' he said, 'you can just stay here in Bangkok. Let's find a nice condo, comfortable, two bedrooms, maybe closer to Ploy. And we'll arrange private healthcare at the hospital.' The healthcare in Thailand was good, and private care was only a fraction of what it would cost in the UK. But for him, money was no object anyway. He couldn't put a price on her health and wellbeing. It meant that he'd have to shell out every month, but it didn't matter. Things were different now, they were serious, and this was important.

'But what will I do when you go to work?' she asked.

'You just have to be strong, my love.' He clasped her head in both hands. 'You are an amazing, clever young woman – you can do it.'

'I want to be here for you too,' he continued, 'so we'll have to see what I can do. Maybe I can do a longer trip and then I'll have more time off to help you when the baby arrives. And I'll maybe take some more time off after that anyway. We'll need to be more careful with money now. No more holidays or fancy restaurants for a while. I'll work hard, and I'll take care of you.'

'But I need you here when the baby comes.'

'I will be. I promise to you, when our baby comes along, I'll be right by your side. Don't worry.'

She never went back to the bar. It was the perfect excuse to escape, and having such a slim frame, it probably wouldn't take long before she started to show anyway.

Ploy called after speaking to Lily's parents once more. They were still furious and accused her of being lazy by not helping them at all. They said that she'd got involved with a farang for nothing. What they meant by *nothing* was for no money. She was carrying his baby, but seemingly she'd gotten nothing from him, and neither had they. They more or less disowned her and she was devastated.

Archie and Lily attended appointments and had long, detailed conversations with the hospital staff. They carefully explained the situation and how he wouldn't be around all the time. The staff were all very nice and helpful, so she started to feel a little more at ease, despite knowing that none of them could ever take the place of Archie. But she had to face up to the fact that she was going to have a child. Deep down she was delighted, and the more she thought about the actual baby, the better she felt. It was her and Archie's baby. It was *their* baby. It may have been a little bit overwhelming for both of them, but it's what they wanted. Even though things were happening incredibly quickly, they had no doubts about each other. They both had sensitive and genuine hearts and their feelings for each other were unadulterated, unconditional, and unshakable. They found strength in each other and were eager to start their journey together. It was scary, but they knew they would manage it together.

They had a look around at condos with a second bedroom and found one to rent longer term. It was easy enough to get to the hospital from there too and it was closer to Ploy's place. It was going to be their home, at least for a while – most likely until they were married and moved to Scotland. She could go to college there if she wanted, and live there with him for the rest of her days. Other than Ploy, she felt like she no longer had anyone left in Thailand. Things with her parents were already hanging by a thread and after their reaction she just wanted to leave it all behind. Archie was her family now.

He had his family in Scotland too, who were supportive and loving and looking forward to meet her. If he was still to work at sea after the baby came or after they were married, she wouldn't need to be alone. She'd have people who loved and cared for her, and a good network of support. It was ideal. She just had to get through the pregnancy unscathed and then it would be all plain sailing.

The rest of his time there was spent making plans. They went out and bought some gender generic baby clothes together and some of the equipment that she might need. It was still early perhaps, but they wanted to do as much of it together as they could. Archie asked her if she wanted him to stay longer, or to come back again after visiting home. She rejected the idea, because she wanted him to save money on flights. He was very tempted to book a flight back, but decided it'd be better if he went back to work earlier and then towards the later stages of the pregnancy, he'd be there to support her when she'd need it the most. He also thought about just staying in Thailand until he went back to sea and not going back to Scotland at all, but could hardly just neglect everyone at home and send a message to say, *Hey, I got engaged*, and then, *Hey, I'm having a baby, see you when I see you.* He knew that his next leave and beyond would just be about Lily and the baby, so he had to go home for a while, otherwise it'd be a long time without seeing his family and friends.

The trip at sea was very hard for him. He couldn't help thinking about how he ought to be there with her and felt guilty about leaving her alone. He wished he could share in every moment and take good care of her, but she'd send nice messages saying that everything was okay and not to worry. She was his rock. She told him she understood him and didn't hold anything against him for going away and working hard everyday to provide for her and give her a good and comfortable life.

She also knew how hard it was for him. Life at sea was a very solitary one. He didn't have any opportunity to wind down – even during down time, he was still at work. He was always on standby for a fire, grounding or even piracy. It certainly wasn't as if he was partying all the time when he was away. If his work wasn't so isolated then perhaps it would have been harder for her to stay so strong. She'd heard of many girls with foreign boyfriends who 'went to work' when in actual fact they went back to their wives and families, or they were simply out partying and sleeping with other girls in another city or country. Archie never did any of that. He struggled and strived everyday – for him, for her and for the baby.

She often felt that he was too good to be true, which gave her a fear that all of a sudden, he might just disappear. Yet, he was fiercely loyal. All he wanted was one girl to love and settle down with and start a family, and there was no way he would do anything to jeopardise that.

Lily was lying to him though. The pregnancy was hard as hell on her. She had morning sickness, as well as afternoon sickness and evening sickness. There were so many times that she'd want to tell him what she was going through, but she couldn't. There was nothing either of them could do about the distance, other than be patient. She was particularly worried about his safety out there on the ocean deep. That was why she didn't want to load him with more stress and distract him whilst he's at work.

She'd had a few scares, with intense pain in her abdomen and other occasions where she'd bleed. She was taken into hospital several times for unscheduled check-ups and scans. She was so concerned that there may be a problem, but she had to keep it to herself. The doctors ran tests but could never find anything out of the ordinary. Now and then, Archie would get a particularly forlorn message saying how much she wished he was with her and how much she missed him. He was under the impression they were just a routine thing, perhaps a rough night. He had no idea that in reality, she was lying alone in a private hospital bed without anyone by her side.

The only choice for her was to persevere. It wasn't going to be like that forever and he told her about jobs that he'd been applying for in Thailand, even just as an interim for a year or so until they moved to Scotland. He promised that he wouldn't always be away. And then they could start a fresh life together. She clung to that dream and it was the only thing keeping her going every day and night.

He signed off the ship and flew straight back to Thailand. She was six months pregnant and found it hard to move. Because of her tiny frame, she already looked so huge, and was forever in a state of discomfort. She wanted to meet him at the airport again but he insisted that she didn't.

"But last time I promise you I come every time."

"I know, but we didn't know you'll be pregnant last time. You'll be there at home and that's all I care about."

It would be too uncomfortable a journey for her, and it was better for everyone if he just got a taxi by himself. He didn't want to worry about her going on and off trains, being squeezed between people in a hurry, or even sitting in a taxi through all the traffic. It'd only delay their reunion by about an hour, after several months apart.

It was a very restless night for her and she'd already vomited twice on his morning of arrival, but of course she was so excited for his return. She'd cooked in anticipation, and awaited his message. "I'm about 5 mins away teerak." She slipped her sandals on, made her way to the lobby and waited patiently. His taxi pulled up and the door opened. He looked slimmer, tired, his hair was long and he needed to shave, but she'd never been so delighted to see anyone ever before. She rolled herself up from the sofa and waddled towards the door as he was retrieving his bags from the taxi. The glass double doors slid open and he dropped everything to rush and embrace her. He had to alter how he held her because she was a completely different shape from the last time he had her in his arms. 'Oh my God! Look at you!' he said. He kissed her before crouching down to kiss her bump. 'You've no idea how happy I am to see you. I've missed you so much.' The taxi driver waited patiently because he still hadn't been paid, but could appreciate what kind of reunion was going on, whilst the doorman kindly collected the bags unprompted and placed them in the lobby.

Lily cried. The sight of him just washed over her and the strength that she'd had to find over those months suddenly released all at once. This time it had been more serious too and she started to worry that she'd lied to him about everything being okay. There hadn't been a problem for about a month though and the doctors said everything was fine, so it seemed that there'd be no need to tell him anything at all.

'I miss you too, Archie. Everyday I miss you.'

'Thank you for being so strong. And I've never seen you looking so beautiful.' She thought that he wouldn't find her attractive because of her big belly. Big blue veins ran along her abdomen and there were

304

sometimes smells and leaks that were never there before. She felt unattractive and grotesque, yet he loved how she looked. But all she'd had to go on was the media and celebrity pregnancies which never showed the real side of it. She didn't have anyone else with her to tell her it was normal or what to expect. Ploy was the only one she had and she'd never been pregnant. 'I'm so proud of you Lily, for doing this by yourself. But I'm here now. I'm going to take good care of you.'

'But you just finish work and I know you're tired, you have to relax.'

'Don't worry. To take care of you is a pleasure for me. It's not hard work and it won't make me tired.' He kissed her hard on the forehead as she looked up at him timidly through her wide brown eyes. Now that Archie was there, she could finally breathe a sigh of relief. Not that she could relax, but she knew she'd have the help that she'd need and he'd always be by her side.

Archie spent his days tending to everything that he could. He took care of Lily, fetching and gathering for her. They went shopping for nursery furniture and he'd build it as she sat in the chair and watched in adulation. Archie had brought a few things from Scotland via the ship, and was arranging them in the room. There were a couple of small books and Lily lifted them to have a look.

'Archie, where you get this one?' she asked.

'From Scotland.'

'No, it's bad luck. So bad luck.'

It was a children's book with an elephant on the front. He thought it was cute, and given the association between Thailand and elephants, he bought it. Lily took it and left the room. It was the fastest she'd moved lately, as she exited the condo with the offending item. He watched her head along the corridor and place it in the garbage room.

He stood at the door waiting for her to return. 'What's wrong?'

'So sorry na, but elephant cannot have...' she didn't know the word for *trunk*, so gestured with her arm at her nose as they walked back through to the nursery.

'The trunk?'

'It cannot be down. It's bad luck.' He grabbed an elephant soft toy which they'd bought a while ago at chatuchak weekend market. 'What about this one?' he asked. 'The trunk goes down.'

'Yes, but it's going up on the end.'

'So, the end needs to point up? Okay. I'm sorry, I didn't know.'

'It's okay na, but we cannot keep it.'

She was tired all day every day and he worried about her, but that was hardwired into him. Even from the days when they were nothing significant to each other, he'd see her milling around the bar with a glum look and he'd want to buy her food and a few drinks, simply because he cared about her. From the time he took her out to eat and paid her rent without any expectations, and to where they were now, he'd always worried about her. Now the stakes were so high. She wasn't just a sweet girl that he cared about anymore; she was his wife-to-be, the mother of his unborn child, his future and all his hopes and dreams in one. She was his entire world.

He had completed a longer trip and missed her terribly the whole time, but not only did it ensure he was home at the more critical time for her, it meant he had a much longer leave. He would also still be drawing salary for several more months, which in turn meant he didn't need to start a new job – or go without salary – for a while yet. He did it to maximise the amount of time he could dedicate to her. What's more, once he did start his new job, at least he'd be home with her every night.

He bought a car for the initial purpose of taking her to the hospital when the time came. He couldn't imagine how else to get her there. If they were caught at the wrong time of day, an ambulance might take a long time to reach them through all the traffic. He'd seen some of the Metropolitan Bangkok ambulances in his time too. Most of them were minivans and some were pick-up trucks. He supposed the pick-ups were perhaps just the ambulance technicians themselves, like first responders. Either way, he didn't want to rely on them to pick up his Lily once she'd began labour.

He was going to need a vehicle for his new job anyway. It was with a global engineering and facilities company as a service engineer. The salary was much less than what he was previously on, but it didn't matter. He'd be going around servicing and fixing back-up generators in condo buildings, malls, hospitals and the like. He bought a big SUV since he'd need to travel around with tools and spare parts. Of course, he still had to sort out his visa and apply for a Thai driving licence, but except for the few times he'd have to attend somewhere in person, he'd manage all his affairs in the morning before she would wake up. That way, he didn't need to take any time away from her.

He'd always thought there was never be any point in having a car in Bangkok because of the traffic and availability of taxis, but actually it came in very useful indeed. Since it was a big car, they could bring all the furniture back home for the nursery, and she sometimes liked to venture out for a change of scene. He could load her in the car down in the parking garage and drive straight to the mall. She'd apologise sometimes for being a burden and preventing them from having the same kind of lifestyle as before; going out to eat and drink, being free and travelling wherever they liked. 'Are you kidding?' he'd say. 'This is the life I want. I couldn't be happier. And it's not like it's your fault, I think I had something to do with it too.'

He always knew how to reassure her. As much as she'd grown in the time she'd been with him, now and then she was still the same timid girl who'd over-think things and feel unworthy. She just sometimes couldn't believe that she'd managed to find herself such a genuine man. In the low points of her hormones she'd get upset thinking about how it'd been so fast and surely he was going to leave her because she was 'fat' and 'unattractive' now, and they couldn't make love like before. But there was no way that he'd leave her.

Ploy came to visit one day and he cooked for them. They ate and talked for a while before he resumed pottering around in the nursery, which gave them a chance to have a catch up. Not that he'd understand what they were saying, but he wanted to give her a bit space to just have a talk with the only member of her family that she had left. All of a sudden, Ploy shouted through to him. 'Archie! Come!' He rushed through from the next room to find Lily bleeding profusely from between her legs. Ploy was searching for something to use to stop the blood and grabbed some paper towels, but Archie had already lifted her and was taking her to the door.

'Ploy, the door…and my car keys are there.'

She opened the door and grabbed the keys. He didn't know what was happening. Maybe she was going into labour, but there was still six weeks to go. But it didn't look like labour, it looked like something much, much worse. Archie was horrified. He'd had fought fires, been through typhoons where he had to try and sleep in his lifejacket, but nothing was as tarrying as this. His heart raced and he could feel it thump in the back of his throat as he loaded her into the back of the car. Ploy helped him with the doors before climbing in next to her. It was afternoon and the traffic was not too heavy. He raced the car along the road and forced his way in and out between other vehicles. The hospital was usually around a five-to-ten minute drive, but he'd managed it in three-and-a-half. When they arrived, Ploy ran in whilst he took her out of the car. She reappeared with a staff member and a wheelchair into which Archie gently lowered her. They rushed her off and he tried to follow but was told that he couldn't leave the car where it was because he'd stopped in the ambulance bay. He quickly moved it into the car park and ran back inside. He found Ploy, who had been told to wait behind and they'd come back to update them when they could.

'Oh fuck, what the hell was that?' he exclaimed.

'It's same like before, this is what happened to her. But they never find something wrong.'

'Before? This has happened before?'

'Yes, I think…four or five times already. She don't tell you anything?'

'No, I had no idea.'

'I think she don't want to worry you when you go to work.'

He was distraught, frantic, and anxious. He was upset that she'd kept it from him, but understood she was just trying to protect him. He knew there was no malice in her intention, but he still wished he knew.

'So, what…have they done tests or something?'

'Yes, they check her before, but cannot see anything wrong.'

'But there must be other things they can check for, or maybe another doctor?' He paced up and down the waiting room.

'This is why she don't tell you. She know you will be so upset. And you on the ship, it's nothing you can do. Maybe she don't want you to worry so much. It's not bad that she lie. But I think she tell you already.'

'I know.' He stopped pacing for a moment. 'She's not bad. She's never bad, my Lily. But there's maybe more that could have been checked. I don't think that's normal.' He was fraught with worry about the love of his life and the baby.

'Archie...go to the bathroom. Go to wash yourself first na.' He was covered in blood, as were the back seats and steering wheel of his new car. But that could be washed off the synthetic leather with no lasting damage.

Not knowing exactly how much time had passed, it felt like forever until the doctor came out to update him saying that she was stable and both mummy and baby were okay. He asked if they found what caused it but it was apparently the same as before. All tests came back inconclusive and he suggested it was just some inflammation and then a subsequent escape of blood. 'Can I see her please?'

'Follow me please.'

Archie and Ploy followed the doctor to her bedside. 'Lily, oh my God. Are you okay?'

'Yes, I'm okay ka,' she said softly with a smile on her face.

'Why didn't you tell me about this before, teerak?' She paused because she thought she'd get away with it, but now she'd have to own up to the fact that she deceived him.

'I just don't want you to worry. I don't want to make you more tired. Are you angry with me?'

'No.' He cradled her hands in his and kissed them. 'I'm not angry, I could never be angry with you. But you should tell me everything, we're a team, everything together. I was so worried about you.'

'I'm sorry.'

'It's okay, I understand. But you and the baby are what I care about the most. I have to know everything. Please, Lily.' Guilt and regret washed over him. 'I'm sorry I wasn't here before. I know it's my fault to put you in that position.'

'No, Archie. Not your fault. You always do so good for me, everything.'

'I'm never going to leave your side again,' he professed, 'for the rest of your life. I promise you, teerak.'

Ploy sat in the corner of the room watching Archie and her niece exchanging comfort and kisses whilst on the other side of the window, the sun set over Bangkok. It descended between the temples and high rises whilst the day came to an end. Unrelenting, coming up and going down everyday, overseeing the progress of the eight million lives of the city. Time marched on and brought with it joy, fear, good times and bad times. But in their private hospital room, there was an entire world on the cusp of being. A nucleated existence of two people who grew up six thousand miles apart but somehow found each other at last, and the new life they were about to bring into the world.

Chapter Twenty-Two
บทที่ยี่สิบสอง

She was back home in the condo. With the nursery complete and all the baby equipment anyone could ever want, they were more or less ready. After her last scare, he'd tried to convince her to get a second opinion but she assured him it was nothing to worry about. He desperately wanted to check elsewhere, but ultimately respected her decision. It was *her* carrying the baby, and it was *her* body. He didn't want to force her because he knew she was uncomfortable being prodded and poked like a piece of meat.

There was just under a month to go and they filled their days just relaxing and sometimes researching baby things. Mostly they stayed at home because she was so low on energy, but that was fine for him. On the long nights spent at sea, he yearned just to relax with her, and now he had it. Ploy was in their hometown and tried to talk with her parents again. They still maintained their despicable attitude towards her. Ploy thought that it may have been nice for Lily's parents to come to Bangkok for when the baby arrived and was sure that Archie would help them with travel and accommodation, but they refused.

For some reason they'd really got it stuck in their heads that she was no good and didn't care about them, so why should they care about her? Never mind the fact that they forced her to go and work in bars when it was the last thing she really wanted to do. There was another girl in the village who'd married a farang and her parents suddenly had an extension on the house, a new car and some walking around money. Lily didn't provide any of that, so she was clearly no good. Of course, that girl was in her twenties and her husband was pushing sixty. It was not a real love, it was a matrimonial prostitution.

It's not even that the girl was unhappy in the relationship though, because she was. Whenever she wanted something, she'd click her fingers and he'd come running. She had a great power to manipulate the divorced older man and make him comfortable in parting with a lot of money. In return, he could have sex with a girl he'd have no hope of getting in the real world. There was no room for him to question whether or not her parents needed whatever thing she was asking for, because she'd just say it was 'Thai tradition.' Should he go against anything she said then it would apparently be seen as a big insult to her family, not to mention risking her running off with one of the many guys she chatted with everyday but who she claimed was her 'brother.'

It wasn't all girls who did such things, but it tends to only be those ones that everyone hears about. When he eventually comes home early and she's sleeping with someone who she finds attractive but has no money, then he blasts every Thai girl online and to his friends. And that's how that single image of Thailand is spread around the world. The man with a good girl who's loyal and faithful has no reason to take to the internet to complain, so it's never represented.

Likewise, in her village, the few girls with real boyfriends who quietly support their family are never talked about. Money makes the world go round, but it's also vile and warps people. It breeds jealousy in those who don't have what someone else has, especially when it's something obtained because of the farang husband. Lily's parents had nothing to show for their daughter's farang. They felt hard done by, but it was their own fault.

She had an older brother who was the main breadwinner for the family, but he was killed in a road accident. That's when they pushed her to Bangkok without any consideration for her life. They were grieving, as well as being flung into financial turmoil. Lily was grieving too, yet she was shunned from her family and forced to stay in a big, noisy, dirty city and talk with dirt-bag foreigners. That's the reason why over the past few years she'd felt further and further from them.

Each time she was home they weren't interested in how she was or what she'd been doing – they were only interested in how much money she could give them. Lily hated money and hated the pressure they put on her. It would make her miss her brother even more, knowing how much he supported them and sacrificed his own wants and needs just to provide for them. There was no way she could fill her brother's shoes, yet she was always expected to. Subsequently, she felt inadequate and worthless not being able to contribute in the same way. He was the first child and the one they invested money in for education. For him to be taken from them was entirely unfair, but it certainly wasn't Lily's fault.

Being in the condo all the time allowed him to have daily video calls with his own parents in back Scotland. Previously, Archie and Lily would always be out and about and it'd just be a few messages each day with maybe the occasional video call. They'd 'met' Lily over video call and she was so pleased to see smiling faces and receive well wishes and be told how welcome she was there and how beautiful she was. She was so excited to go. She tried to avoid being seen at first, but began to feel awkward hiding away when he'd call, and she didn't want them to think badly of her. Once she'd said hello and stayed on the call, it just felt completely normal for her.

'Archie, your family so lovely na.'

'Yes, they are, and they can't wait to meet you. And the baby.'

'But…what they think about me?' She was also aware of the reputation that Thailand had around the world.

'What do you mean?'

'I mean…they think I'm good or not?'

'Teerak, they love you.'

'But…they never meet me yet.'

'But they know how happy you make me, and that's all that matters.'

To be loved by a family was something new for her. She was always second best, the underachiever compared to her brother. She never got the good food or the nice presents, if any at all. She finally felt good about a family, and soon she'd have her own with Archie. It finally felt like things were working out for her at long last. She imagined him as a father and knew he would be the best in the world. She could feel herself pulling further and further from Thailand in her heart. As much as she loved her roots and her culture, it seemed like there was nothing left to stay for anymore.

'And how long is Ploy staying at home?' he asked.

'I think three days more, or four,' she said.

'Will we go to pick her up from the bus station? Or maybe just me?' She didn't answer. 'What do you think?' She still didn't answer but winced her face. 'Lily, what is it?'

'Nothing, just have a pain.'

'Can I get you something?'

'No. I...' She let out a yelp and he knelt down in front of her. He could recall the image of her bleeding profusely. It had haunted him since it happened and now he was just waiting to see it happen again. She felt a big thump in her stomach and a searing pain. She screamed again.

'I think the baby coming!'

'You've still got three-and-a-half weeks!' Before he had time to panic, he lifted her and took her to the door again. Without a word, she picked up his keys and opened the door whilst he cradled her, it was true teamwork. They rushed to the hospital once more and he got someone to bring a wheelchair once more. He was panicking, but tried to reassure himself it would be alright. They'd been through it before, so he'd just have to keep his calm and ride this one out too. He thought for sure he'd force her to get a second opinion now though. Whilst she was wheeled off, he ran back to move the car without a prompt from staff this time. He called Ploy and she told him not to worry and that she'd be okay as he circled the waiting area again.

A few hours passed and then a few hours more. He was starting to go out of his mind with worry, especially without Ploy there to keep him calm. Why wouldn't they just let him in to see her? Why was it taking longer this time? He was beginning to get angry with the doctors. He was under the impression he was paying for the best healthcare he could get, but that didn't seem to be the case. It was probably too late to change now though because there was so little time to go. It'd be too much upheaval for her. But they were certainly going for a second opinion now for sure.

The doctor came through the double doors and called out: 'Khun Archie.'

Archie stood up and rushed to his side. 'Can I see her now?'

'Follow me please.' He was led into a small room and told to sit down. There wasn't much in the room except from a sofa, a small table with tissues on it and a couple of Thai countryside and temple photos on the wall.

'What's going on? Where is she?'

'She have some complications and we have to deliver the baby by emergency caesarean. Your daughter is fully healthy and we have no concerns for her. But of course, because she's premature, we have to keep her in for a while for observation.'

'Oh my God! The baby's here?'

'Yes.'

'So, can I go to see them?' His frustration at the doctor was mounting even more. He grew very agitated and couldn't understand why he was dragging his feet.

'Sorry, there's more. Lily suffered a lot of internal bleeding and unfortunately...we are not able to stop it. She passed away in theatre. I'm so sorry.'

Archie went numb.

His whole world crashed around him.

He paused for a moment, wondering whether he heard it right or not. But he knew what he heard. His heart felt like glass struck by a hammer. He felt it shatter and scatter into a million pieces, as the whole of heaven and the sky above seemed to fall on his head.

Outside the small room, people could mutedly hear someone scream and scream and absolutely lose his mind. He smashed his hands on the table until they bled. The doctor didn't interfere with his reaction and let him get it out of his system. Archie was usually always calm and peaceful, but he was still a very powerful man. Not that the doctor felt threatened, but it was unwise to walk into the path of tornado. The screaming and the *noes* went on for a few minutes until he could regain his composure.

'You mean to say...she's gone?' Archie asked. 'My Lily is gone? But she can't be. She can't!'

'I'm afraid so,' the doctor replied. 'I'm so sorry for your loss.' Archie was in disbelief. It was too much for him to handle. And his baby was there too? How was he supposed to take care of her alone?

Eventually, he slumped into the sofa in a pile of his own tears. The doctor knew the tornado had passed so offered him a tissue. There was a great pressure in Archie's head and it felt like blood was pooling in his ears. He felt a compulsion to smash his head off the wall because if he split it open, maybe that might let some of the pressure out. The doctor continued to speak, but Archie couldn't hear a thing. It was useful information and advice on how to seek support for his situation, but none of it mattered. He didn't want tissues. He didn't want support or advice. He didn't want leaflets. He wanted Lily.

Since they got over the initial surprise of the baby, he'd pictured an image in his head. It was of the three of them, happy healthy and smiling in the hospital, after the baby was born. He wanted to be there during the delivery to hold her hand and soothe her through the whole thing. It was what drove him everyday since they found out, and now he would never have it. Lily was concerned that she'd be alone, but he specifically promised her that he'd be by her side when the baby came. It seemed like he broke his promise – through no fault of his own. In breaking his promise, his heart was broken, as well as his spirit, and his mind. He couldn't understand it. He always tried his best and showed kindness, even to random strangers. He couldn't comprehend what was wrong with his karma to bring about such suffering.

All he wanted was to settle down and have a family, like everyone else does. Even all the scumbags and shit people managed that, so why not him? He was so, so close, but it appeared as if it wasn't meant to be. Now his baby girl would never know the most amazing, beautiful and faithful woman on the planet. The fact that she'd never know her mum broke his heart perhaps even more than his own loss.

Lily endured all that time alone when he was away. She'd struggled alone without a single complaint and she never even got to meet her own baby too. It wasn't fair. None of it was fair. And it didn't make sense to him. He was filled with questions and anger and dread. He wanted to scold the doctor, but deep down he knew it wasn't his fault.

The doctor could sense that nothing he was telling Archie was going in, so he left him for a while. 'Just take your time. Please wait here and I will come back. If you would like some water or something just please tell one of the nurses.' Archie nodded an acknowledgment and with that he was left alone in the small room, whilst he had no idea what was going to happen next.

He'd relieved the tissue box of several tissues. He wiped his tears as well as the blood from the heel of his hands. He remembered how susceptible Lily was to crying. It was only because since she met Archie, it was the first time in her life she'd ever truly loved and been loved. Archie was her day, her night, her whole world, and she worshipped him. Everything regarding him was so sensitive for her. Inside her was always a mix of eternal happiness and fear of losing him, but the latter was negated with the knowledge that he'd never leave her – to which she was infinitely grateful and felt even more emotional about. Being such a melting pot of love, subdued fear, and gratitude was what made her so close to tears all the time. He heightened all her emotions, opened doors for her and enabled her to feel and live life. She was also truly thankful for the way he had elevated her consciousness and feeling of self-worth, and was so excited to spend the rest of her life with him.

Archie's thoughts became dark and he felt as if he'd killed her. If they'd never met, he wouldn't have got her pregnant. Perhaps she'd still be living her meagre existence at the bar, but at least she'd still be alive. He should have never taken her out for something to eat that night and helped her out. He should never have taken her out with Koi and Wan. He should never have fallen in love with her, because he killed her. And now he had a baby to raise without her. What a mess.

He should have just gone home after Mam and lived a meagre existence himself. He'd maybe have missed out on a special love, but then he'd never feel such devastating, soul-crushing agony. He was there in Thailand and had nobody except his premature baby who he'd never even seen yet. That bond he always felt he had with Bangkok seemed to disintegrate all at once. He suddenly felt a very long way from home indeed.

Ploy tried to call a few times but he didn't answer. She wanted an update, but how was he supposed to tell her that? To repeat the words would only confirm his worst nightmare. Perhaps there was still a chance that the doctor had made a mistake or there was a misunderstanding. Maybe he'd come back into the room and tell him he could see her. And he'd occupy the space at her bedside and the baby would be there too and he'd fulfil that image he had of the three of them. Meanwhile, Ploy supposed they were already back home and he was fussing over her and taking care of her and just hadn't had a chance to pick up his phone yet. He was still in disbelief, but eventually found the power to call her back to break the bad news. She told him she was on her way to the bus station and she'd get the very next bus back to Bangkok.

The doctor eventually came back in and Archie stood up expectantly. 'Khun Archie...if you'd like to see her, I can take you there now.'

'What?'

'If you'd like to see her before we take her out the room.' The doctor was trying to avoid saying *move her to the morgue*. It was morose, but Archie had to go. It was his last chance to say goodbye.

She was in another private room. They'd 'prepared' her body and made her acceptable to be seen. Archie dropped to his knees at the door as his sweet flower lay there in her eternal sleep, cut from the earth in her prime. She looked so peaceful. She looked so beautiful. He managed to pick himself back up and cross the room to be next to her.

'Oh, Lily! Oh, my Lily! I'm so sorry! I'm so sorry!' He looked to the doctor and gestured whether he could take her hand or not. The doctor intimated a nod that it was fine. He held her hand like he always did. He intertwined his fingers with hers and stroked her forehead one last time. He could sense how the temperature was already starting to go from her fingers, but then she always had cold hands when she was sleeping. 'What am I going to do now?' he asked her. 'What am I going to do without you?' It was the first time she'd never responded. He stooped over her and kissed her gently. It was also the first time he'd kissed her without there being any reaction from her. No squeak, no whimper or tremble down her spine. There was no release of breath or flicker of her eyelashes like usual. There was nothing. She was gone. And she was never coming back.

He could have stayed there forever but the doctor eventually had to usher him out. Archie asked for a final minute so he could say his parting words: 'Wait for me once more please, teerak. I'll see you when I get to heaven…or in the next life. I'll find you again, I promise.' He placed a final kiss on her forehead. 'I love you Lily...I will always love you.'

Tears streamed from his eyes and he blinked repeatedly to keep as clear a view of her as possible. He slowly backed out of the room, knowing it would be the very last time he would ever lay his eyes on her. The doctor was waiting and held the door open for him. 'I'm very sorry for your loss,' he repeated. 'Maybe you want to take some time and then I'll take you to see your baby.'

'No, I want to see her now.'

'Okay, follow me please.'

She was in the premature ward and he wouldn't be able to hold her. The doctor took him there and he had to meet his baby through the glass. A beautiful baby girl. She was *so* beautiful, just like her mum. She cried and wailed in her little glass cot. She cried for her mummy, and cried for her daddy; the baby who came into the world alone. She already didn't have her mum, and her dad was somewhere outside. He wanted to be there but he didn't know what was going on and he still couldn't even get close to her yet.

Archie and Lily had talked about names and had a strong shortlist. They wanted a hybrid Thai-English name – a Thai name that when shortened would sound English, or some kind of combination that'd serve her well in both countries. It was whittled down to two choices: Jenjira, which would become Jen or Jenny, and Mayuree, which would become May. They wanted to give her the very best chance at achieving everything she could even from the very start.

When Archie saw her though, all their previous ideas came to nothing. 'Hello, Little Lily,' he said.

Chapter Twenty-Three
บทที่ยีสิบสาม

Word had started to spread around Bangkok of the terrible news. He received sympathy from all of his friends, both from Thailand and from Scotland. His parents thought about going across to help, but somehow he didn't want them there. If they were going to come, it'd be to meet her. He and Lily would pick them up from the airport and they could go for dinner. They'd all be together and get to know one another and it'd be amazing family time. He could have really done with their support but didn't feel comfortable in having them come. He still felt that he'd killed Lily so he didn't deserve their help. He was the one that went off chasing a life in Thailand. He'd made his bed, now he'd have to lie in it – alone. Although, he was not completely alone now.

Little Lily stayed in the hospital for a while until Archie was well enough to take her. She was fully healthy and there were no concerns over her prematurity whatsoever. The doctor said not to worry about how long, but after several days of crying and neglecting himself, he couldn't stand not being with her. She was the only piece of Lily that he had left, so wanted to keep her close.

He needed her there too, because staying alone in the condo was absolute torture for him. One evening, he took one of Lily's dresses out of the wardrobe, sprayed it with her perfume and held it close to him as he imagined her in his arms again. He put on one of their songs and swayed with it as he looked out over a callous and empty Bangkok. He had collected her belongings when he left the hospital and immediately put her engagement ring on his pinkie finger with the intention of never removing it again. It persisted in shining, even though he felt that all the sparkle had gone from his life.

As he danced with her empty dress, the thought crossed his mind about jumping off the balcony. He was always a good man, yet the universe still dealt him such a tragic blow. What was the point in staying in a world like that? He could have clung on tightly to her dress and leapt the twenty-one floors to the street below, then he'd be with her again. But Lily was always patient, and she didn't mind waiting for him – no matter how long it might take. He knew that she'd be heartbroken if he came to her early, and there would be no way he could explain how he left their baby alone. Had it not been for their daughter, there was every chance that he would have gone through with it, because he couldn't handle the pain. He had palpitations in his chest, light-headedness, shortness of breath and inexplicable shooting pains around his body. He couldn't help the physical symptoms which manifested from his broken heart.

His parents called very frequently. They were very worried about how he'd be with the baby, but he told them that her family was there and he didn't need any more help. Of course, her family were *not* there, apart from the occasional check-in from Ploy. But she had her own life and it was not her duty to be tied down to take care of both the baby and of Archie. He had to be strong and do it alone, but at any time of the day, he ached for her.

As bad a shape as he was in – there was not a single moment of neglect for little Lily. He doted on her and took as good care of her as he did her mummy. He'd tell stories about her mum and rock her to sleep in his arms. He would sit watching the baby in the chair where Lily used to watch him build the furniture and arrange the place. She was supposed to nurse her in that chair.

She was a good baby. She slept peacefully and frequently, unlike her daddy. He was so tired. He never slept in the bed anymore. Without Lily there with him he just couldn't. Plus, he didn't want to let little Lily out of his sight even for a second. Sitting by the cot, he'd usually fall in and out of sleep in the chair. He sometimes had nightmares and would wake up with a start, but little Lily rarely flinched.

On top of everything he was also faced with a lot of paperwork. He felt like he couldn't stay in Thailand, and couldn't start his new job. He had to somehow research about how to bring the baby back to the UK, as well as if he could bring Lily back too. Considering her family were well out of the picture, he wanted to take her to Scotland like they'd talked about, but didn't know if it was possible. He thought she should come home with him so that he could visit her, and take her daughter to visit her too. He wanted to keep Lily's memory alive, so that little Lily never wondered why there was a big mum-shaped hole in her life. Of course, it wouldn't be anything like the same, but it was as much as he could do, and he had to do as much as he could.

He just didn't have the power for paperwork however. He watched the baby twenty-four hours a day and had absolutely no chance to conduct the research that he needed to. He'd sometimes open the computer and try to read up about it, but his head was so full that the words simply didn't make any sense to him.

He was receiving lots of messages and often didn't have any chance to reply, mostly because he didn't know how to. Every occasion that he had to recount the story would make him relive it and cause it to sink in more, and he still didn't want it to be true. He was still hoping that he'd wake up from his nightmare. One message he received did manage to grab his attention however.

"Hi Archie. I'm really so sorry to hear about Lily. I didn't know if it's okay that I send you a message. That's why it's little bit late. But I just want to tell you I'm so sad to hear about it. If you need something you can always ask me. I will help you if you want." It was Amm. He left it for a while before deciding to reply.

"Thank you Amm. I just can't believe that she's gone. I can't believe that she's not here with me and the baby. Life isn't fair."

That was a sentiment to which she was certainly familiar.

"I know. You and Lily look so perfect. I also cannot believe this can happen to you. Lily was so good girl and you are so good man." After a while she sent another message. "But you are okay mai? You eat and take care of yourself?"

He didn't expect to start chatting with her, but it was the first non-generic message he'd had. "Well, I'm not the priority. But I'm taking good care of the baby. I don't have any choice. If something happened to her, then I really don't know what I'd do."

"But if you don't take care of yourself, how you can take care of her?" She made a good point. He mostly only prepared formula for little Lily and would forego making food for himself. He'd mastered the two-minute shower and dry so that he didn't need to leave her unattended too long. He maintained his hygiene at least, but that again was more for the baby, since he was going to be in close contact with her all the time.

"I know. I'm okay. Thank you for thinking about me."

"Did you eat something today?" He hadn't. He was a little torn and felt confused to be talking to her again, but then again, she was the only one really reaching out to him. Staying merely with the baby, he hadn't even seen anyone else at all, so there was a desire in him just to talk to another human being, and it just so happened it was Amm.

"Well, no, not really."

"And if you get sick, then who can take care of the baby?"

"But I never have the time to. And I can hardly go out, so it's just difficult."

"Yes, I understand you." She followed up with: "Today I'm free. If you want, I can bring you some food."

He wondered what the hell was going on and why she was suddenly being so interested. He got the impression that she felt guilty and wanted to make it up to him. Lily sometimes fed him select snippets from Koi about how she regretted the way she treated him. In the first few months of him and Lily, he'd occasionally receive a drunken text from Amm directly, apologising for everything she did wrong. He wasn't keen to invite her back into his life. But it would have been nice to have something real to eat, he supposed.

"No, it's okay, I'll be fine. I don't want to disturb you on your day off. Just enjoy yourself. Thank you for the messages." He was trying to bring it to a close and could have simply started to ignore her, but he also wanted her to know that he didn't have any problem talking with her, as if he was the bigger person. Not to mention the fact that he still cared for and respected her, so didn't want to ever just ignore her.

"It's not disturbing me. I'll bring you some food na. You're still in the same place? What number your room?" Lily had told Koi, who'd of course told Amm about which condo building they were in.

He had no time for stupid games, but regardless of that he still loved Lily as much as ever and had absolutely no interest in anyone else. If it was completely off the table then it might be alright just to use her to bring some food. It's the least she could do. It also looked like she was determined too, so it'd be the easiest way to bring the messaging to a conclusion so that he could focus on the baby again.

"Ok, if you're sure, then I'm still in the same building. It's 21/2."

"Ok, see you soon ☺"

More than an hour had passed and it was beginning to look like she was never going to show up, which would just be true to her character, he thought. Why should she change her ways now? Maybe it was for the best though. There was some kind of sense of betrayal letting Amm into his home – particularly when Lily was no longer there. Something didn't sit right with him about letting her see his gorgeous baby, whilst at the same time, he was desperate for a chance to show her off. He was proud of her. He may have felt the guilt and responsibility of killing the love of his life, but it was not at all down to the baby. She had no say in anything that happened. She blindly passed each day with daddy, not knowing mummy, and not knowing that anything was wrong. Her world existed only in the condo building off Sukhumvit Road in Bangkok.

In actual fact, Amm had been running around gathering supplies for him until she was caught in traffic. The taxi eventually made it to his building and she struggled with all the shopping she brought. The doorman came to assist her. He didn't recognise her, but it was a big building with a lot of people coming and going. Considering all that she'd brought, it seemed pretty clear she had a genuine purpose to gain access to the building. 'What room, Miss?' he asked in Thai, before pushing for the lift, helping her in with the bags and pushing the correct floor. She ascended to the twenty-first floor and knocked on Archie's door. Meanwhile the guard switched his camera to the hallway outside Archie's condo, to make sure she was received and was genuine enough.

'Amm…how did you get in?'

'Guard.'

'Okay…Long time no see…' Archie said.

'Yes…long time,' she replied with a smile.

'What's all this?' he asked. She had multiple shopping bags and he helped her as she entered. She slipped her sandals off and he placed the bags on the counter. There was cooked food, plus some food shopping for him, water, juice and a couple of baby things including a little plush toy and a snugly blanket. She'd done well. 'Wow, this is too much. I thought you were just bringing food?'

'No, not too much.'

'Well, thank you very much.'

'No problem na, Archie,' she said gladly.

He put some things away and she asked where the plates and cutlery were so that she could serve up dinner. He was uncomfortable at how comfortable she was. It was just strange being in such close proximity to her again, especially given the circumstances. He tried not to over-think it though. It was evident how much he needed a good feed. He'd become so weak and forgotten about himself, so just kept that in the forefront of his mind. Given everything in the past, he supposed it may not have been easy for her to come too. Perhaps she just wanted to make amends and repair her karma. He was happy enough to allow her to do so. Beyond that, Archie was truly struggling alone. The grief and solitude were destroying him and there was absolutely nobody that he could turn to. He just needed someone to help, and it didn't matter who.

She laid the food out on the kitchen table whilst he checked on little Lily. He appeared back in the doorway and spoke softly. 'Do you want to see her? She's sleeping, but you can see her.'

'Yes, I want to, if it's okay? But it's up to you.'

'Come on.'

She was a little scared to wake or disturb her, so crept quietly into the room and lowered herself next to the cot. 'Oh my God! She's so beautiful, Archie,' she whispered. He couldn't contain himself and burst into floods of tears. It wasn't fair. She *was* beautiful. She was his perfect little baby. Amm comforted him with a nice platonic rub of the shoulder-blade. 'It's okay Archie. You will be okay. You're clever man and so strong. If anybody can do it, you can.' He hastily dried his tears.

'I'm sorry. It's just too much sometimes.'

'You don't need to be sorry to me. Let's go to eat something na, I think you so hungry already.' He complied, but wheeled the cot softly and gently to the side, where he could maintain line of sight with little Lily as he sat at the table.

Amm never forgot his preferences for food, so everything was to his liking. 'Thank you for this,' he said. 'I really appreciate it.'

'You're welcome. It's no problem.'

'How much do I owe you for all this?' he asked.

'Oh, it's ok…it's my treat, you already have many things to think about.' She curled noodles around her spoon with her chopsticks. 'You know, I don't know if you're okay with me, but I just feel so bad about what happen to you. You always good to everyone, you always do good, but you get some really bad luck in your life. Ploy tell me about her family also, about what they do.'

'Yeah…'

'I just feel like I want to help you. Because I do some of the bad things in your life too.' He didn't know what to say. At least it wasn't some kind of shitty scheme to get back in with him which was what he feared.

Ultimately, he came to realise that everything she did before was in an attempt to protect him. She pushed him away, because she knew that she wouldn't be able to be the girlfriend that he wanted or deserved. She had her agenda about making money, but Archie caught her in her transition and it threw her way off course.

'Well…what's past is past,' he said. She nodded as she chewed her noodles. With the air clear between them, he began to appreciate her company. He had many friends in Bangkok, but they were mostly girls. And whilst he wasn't 'involved' with them, those friendships were focussed purely on socialising. It was not really a deep and sincere friendship.

The Amm that turned up to his condo was more like the real Amm. She was calm and polite and thoughtful and he was certainly very glad that he didn't have to spend another evening alone with only his thoughts. It helped him to talk things through and there was a different level of understanding with her. Having worked with Lily, and given Archie and Amm's history, she could comfort and console him from a different and more profound angle than others. She said the words that he needed to hear, rather than generalised words of sympathy from well-wishers. It did a lot to help his state of mind and refresh him, if even just a little.

During the evening, she revealed to him that she'd quit her job at the bar. An opening came up at her sister Joy's work, who then managed to convince her boss to give Amm a shot. She trained her up very well and she was performing nicely in her new position. She'd never look back at bars and the other things that she'd done. She was on an upward curve, having been at rock bottom. Archie told her it was great that she was taking control of her life and doing something positive with it. He noticed she was wearing the bracelet he bought her for her birthday too. Out of all the gifts and offerings from her customers and admirers, it was still one of her most prized possessions.

Little Lily had stayed peaceful all evening. Amm did hope for a cuddle, but she was still scared. It was a little awkward for her too, to be there with Lily's baby.

'Okay, so I think I will go, and you can have some rest. How many hours you can sleep in the night?' she asked.

'Oh, I dunno. Not much. Sometimes I kinda fall out the chair and I give myself a fright.'

'The chair?'

'Yeah, the chair in the nursery.'

'You not sleep in the bed?' The answer was already apparent.

'I'm scared I'll miss something. I don't want to be far away.'

'But your bed is not far away. And I know you will wake up if she make some noise. But it's up to you na, I just say.'

'Yeah…' He knew she was just trying to help, and also that she was probably right. He just wasn't ready to either leave little Lily alone, or to sleep in the bed alone, and didn't know when he would be. Sometimes he'd lean over the baby whilst she was sleeping, just to check that she was still breathing, or adjust her position to make sure her breathing could never be obstructed. Considering his fiancée was cruelly taken from him without warning, he was continually terrified that something bad was going to unexpectedly happen to the baby, and that he'd lose her too.

They stood up and Amm made her way to the door to slip her sandals back on. 'Well, Amm, thank you so much for tonight. I really needed the food and…to talk to someone. Thank you.'

'Welcome na Archie. Maybe, if it's okay, I can come again? Or if you need something you can just tell me. My day off different every week, but evenings I'm free…if you need something.'

'Okay. I'll keep it in mind. Get home safe, please.'

'Yes, thank you.'

He didn't realise how late it was and he did start to feel tired. Perhaps because it was the first time he'd had to metabolise food for a while too. He wasn't sure if he'd invite her back again, but it certainly was a better evening than usual, or rather it was just *less bad* than usual. She sent a message after a while: "Hi, I'm home now. So good to see you. So happy we can be friend now. Goodnight. X"

"Yeah it was good to see you, and thanks again for the food and everything. It was such a big help to me. Have a good sleep." He truly meant it. He had no plans about her and was just doing everything he could to get through the days, even if that meant spending time with Amm again. What else could he really do?

Chapter Twenty-Four
บทที่ยีสิบสี่

Despite Amm's encouragement, Archie still couldn't sleep in the bed. He was building up a huge sleep debt, what with caring for the baby and just generally being tormented by his own guilt and heartache. It was finally starting to take its toll, however.

He made himself some dinner with the food she brought, and he wished he was able to sleep. He didn't feel great physically. His immune system was down and he had no energy at all. His nose was runny and he developed a persistent cough, which he started to worry about, being in such close proximity to his premature baby all the time. He'd been going non stop for a couple of weeks and never even allowed himself to properly grieve for his late fiancée. He had all his paperwork still to do too, and meanwhile, the time was passing. He had to really get a move on, because he had to arrange something for her.

She couldn't just stay in the morgue forevermore, she deserved much more than that. It was so hard for him to face.

It was a couple of days after Amm had been, and he woke up in his chair. It was still the middle of the night and he had been so restless, even more so than usual. He was dizzy, running a fever and the cough had worsened, so he thought he should ask for help. Even if he'd just manage a few good hours of quality sleep he'd surely feel better. It would be much more than what he was currently getting. He was only human after all and couldn't act like a machine forever.

Once it reached a reasonable hour, he sent a message: "Hey Amm, how are you? I was just wondering if you'd be able to come round some time just to watch the baby for a while? I'm just so tired all the time, and I'm not feeling great at the moment. You won't need to do anything really, I just want to catch some sleep, and if she needs something you can wake me up."

She replied immediately. "Hi. Yes I can. When you want me to come?"

"Well, just let me know when you can spare some time."

"I can tonight. What time?"

"Ok, that's great. Any time is good for me." He wasn't expecting her to manage that night, but he was glad that she could.

"Ok, and I'll bring dinner again," she told him.

"No, you don't have to."

"It's ok, I want to ☺"

During the rest of her working day, she imagined him alone in that lovely condo with his baby. It was really a sad state of affairs. Between her calls and administrative tasks, she'd think about what to bring for him, and where to get it from that was on the way.

The guard recognised her from her previous visit, opened the door with a smile and called the lift for her.

'Hey Archie. How are you? You okay mai?' she asked. He looked like shit. He knew it and felt it, but he wasn't trying to impress her so it didn't matter. She gave him a quick hug despite his symptoms, and slid her shoes off. Little Lily was awake and he brought her through to meet her.

'Lily, this is your aunty Amm, she's going to help take care of you tonight.' Amm didn't have any experience with babies, but she was keen to learn. He taught her how to hold her and they took to each other straight away. Lily fell fast asleep in her arms.

'Oh my God Archie, she's so cute!' He just nodded humbly. 'So, do you want me to stay tonight?' she asked.

'No, it's okay,' he was a little shocked, 'You don't need to stay, just let me sleep for a few hours. Just watch her for me. That's all I need.'

'Archie, it's not enough. You need to sleep, really.'

'But I don't have anything for you to stay on.' It was far more than what he'd imagined. There was a bed which hadn't been occupied by anyone for a few weeks, but that certainly was not for her. Lately, it hadn't even been for him. Other than that, there was the chair in the nursery or the sofa in the living room. It didn't overstep the mark *per se*, but it was too much, he thought. He stopped thinking about it for a while as they sat down to have something to eat. He fed little Lily before feeding himself. 'This is great again Amm, thank you.'

'It's okay,' she smiled.

He showed Amm how to put the baby down and got ready to sleep himself. He'd been mentally preparing himself for the bed. Since Lily was gone, he only ever ventured into the bedroom for fetching clothes and then storing them again after washing. He knew he had to cram as high a quality sleep in as possible though and it was stupid to try and sleep anywhere else. That didn't mean it wasn't hard as hell for him. 'So, if she needs something, just wake me up. And just help yourself to anything, make yourself at home.'

'Don't worry. Go to sleep, everything will be okay,' Amm said reassuringly.

'Thank you for doing this, I know it's a huge favour. And I'm sorry if I ruined your night.'

'No, you didn't,' she said with a smile.

He gently shut the door and lay on top of the covers. He wasn't ready to get inside just yet – he needed to reacclimatise himself first. He closed his eyes and could feel the presence of his deceased fiancée next to him. He sensed the slight indentation of her slim body in the mattress by his side. He reached over like he usually would, but she was no longer there. Amm could hear him sobbing heavily through the door and felt so sorry for him.

She took it upon herself to help him through it. She had no real expectations, but it'd be a lie if she said she didn't still have feelings for him. In fact, she'd loved him all along but just had so much trouble with herself that she'd never come to terms with it. She knew she was foolish and childish and impetuous before. She also knew she had no right to him anymore and didn't want to mix him up any further than he already was. She simply wanted to be there for him, whilst trying to keep a little distance.

Amm was quite content relaxing in the nice chair in the nursery. She quietly watched videos on her phone with just one earphone in, and took glances at the baby every minute or so. She hoped that Lily's daddy was sleeping as sweetly as she was.

A couple of hours passed and Amm started to hear some commotion from Archie's room. He was talking and sounded distressed. He was in a cold sweat and panic as he was suffering a nightmare. She knocked gently on the door and spoke his name softly. He didn't reply, so she tried once more but without success. She pushed the door open and he was tossing and turning in bed. She didn't know what to do. Should she wake him? She couldn't stand to see him like that. It was as if he was fighting an invisible demon. But she was in his bedroom and recognised that was not the kind of distance she was trying to keep. She went back outside, closed the door and knocked on it a little louder. 'Archie? Archie? You okay mai?' She knocked again and the commotion stopped. There was silence for a moment so she tried again. 'Archie?' He shot up out of bed and came to the door thinking little Lily needed him.

'What is it, is she okay?'

'Yes, she okay, but I think you are not. You are so loud when you're sleeping. You have bad dreams?'

He came out the bedroom to check on his daughter and Amm followed.

'What happened?' she asked.

'Just exactly that. Bad dream. But…' he took a breath and sighed heavily as he recalled it, '…it just felt so real, and I was really trapped. I couldn't stop what I was doing, I was like…crazy. This is really killing me.' His eyes welled up and teardrops spilled over onto his cheeks as he sat down in Lily's nursery chair.

'You can remember what happened? You want to talk about it?'

He did and he didn't, but perhaps it'd help to talk it through with someone, because keeping it bottled up was going to destroy him. 'I was with Lily. And I was…' he hesitated, '…stabbing her in the stomach. Over and over.' He held his head in his hands. 'I killed her Amm. It's all my fault.' She came across to the chair and kneeled next to him.

'It's just a bad dream na, Archie,'

'No, I mean, I *really* killed her. This is all my fault. If it wasn't for me, she'd still be alive.' He stooped forward and could feel that pressure in his head again but didn't know how to let it out. Tears fell gently onto the soft carpet and each drop turned it from its light fawn colour to dark caramel as Amm rubbed his back gently.

'No, it's not your fault. Don't talk like that. And you don't think that.' She shifted her position and sat crossed legged on the floor in front of him.

'You know, Lily was so happy. You give her everything. But...even me I learn this now...it's not about money or what you can buy, it's about heart and love and caring. And you care for her so good.' He looked up to face her. 'I know Lily almost three years, because of Koi, and I never see her smile one time before she is with you. And when she get pregnant with your baby, she is feeling one hundred per cent complete in her life.'

The image flashed through his head of setting her into the wheelchair before she was carted away. That was the last time he saw her alive and it tore a hole through him not being able to properly tell her goodbye, or at least tell her he loved her one last time. He knew deep down Amm was telling the truth, but he couldn't help how he felt. 'Everybody know you never do anything wrong to anybody. So why *you* don't know?' Her words were kind and did something to quell the fire that raged inside him. It wasn't anywhere enough to extinguish it, though.

'What am I going to do now? And I've not done anything about a funeral or about bringing little Lily back to the UK.'

'Oh, so you think you'll take her back to your home?'

'Yeah, I don't have anything here now, only hurt and pain. She'll always be with me, but…I don't know. I don't feel comfortable here anymore. And I can give the baby a much better life in Scotland. And my family is there and everything. That was our plan anyway.'

A few cute gurgles came from Lily and he wiped his tears as he rose from the chair. Amm leaned to the side to let him past and check on his daughter. 'Archie, I think you should try to sleep more.'

'What time is it anyway?'

'Now ten o'clock.'

'Okay, but do you not need to get home?'

'Don't worry about me, I can stay more, you go to sleep first na.'

'Okay, maybe just another hour then. Wake me up when you need to go.'

He returned to the bed and slept on top of the covers. He knew he wasn't ready to sleep under them yet. Amm returned to her post, watchful of Lily, concerned about Archie. Eventually, she fell asleep too.

Morning broke over the city and into his bedroom window. He woke up, and for a moment forgot about everything. It was as if he didn't know where he was – it being the first time in weeks he'd woken up in that bed. When he stirred in the morning, he would often search for and hold Lily's hand under the covers. His arm extended like habit and when no one held it in return, it all came rushing back. When he realised it was already morning, he panicked. Was Lily okay? Was

Amm still there? He jumped out of bed and went through to the nursery. Amm was asleep in Lily's chair whilst little Lily was awake and kicking her legs into the air. She gurgled when he picked her up and it woke Amm. 'Hey, so you stayed?'

'Yes.' She wasn't sure if he was upset about it or not. He also wasn't sure. 'I hope it's okay,' she said.

'Yeah, it's fine, I just didn't think you'd stay. I'm sorry I've taken up so much of your time.'

'No, you don't. I just want to help you.'

He had to take a quick shower to freshen up from his cold sweat the previous night, before performing his morning routines with the baby. Amm watched him intently, trying to learn as much as she could. 'Are you working today?' he asked.

'Yes,' she checked the time on her phone, 'but I still have a few hours before I go to work.'

'Okay, well, can I make you breakfast or something?'

'Sure.' He gave her the baby to hold as he prepared breakfast. They sat down together all three of them and ate – well, Lily got her bottle first and then Archie ate. He'd never had breakfast with Amm before. It felt strange, but he also drew some comfort from her presence there. He hated himself for it, but then there wasn't much he didn't hate himself for lately. She asked him more about his long-term plans about returning to Scotland and could understand him. For some reason, she assumed and hoped that he'd just stay in Bangkok. But it made perfect sense for him to return home. 'So, what about your papers and things? When you can do it?'

'I don't know. But the time is just going now. I really need to make a start. I just…I can't even get my head around it.'

'Well…tomorrow I have day off, I can come to stay with her and you can do your papers. And what about tonight?'

'No, it's fine, you've already done so much.'

'But…I think you still look not okay. Better if you sleep again tonight and then tomorrow you will feel good and you can do everything you need to do.' He couldn't really argue with her sound reasoning and she'd also managed to invite herself round again. The taboo of her was beginning to fade a little as she'd just been there to help him. He was desperate for some assistance and there was no other way he'd be able to complete the paperwork otherwise.

'Well, if you don't mind. And you're sure you're not doing something else better?'

'No. Now I stop all partying. I don't like it anymore. And I just stay alone in the room. Koi, she have boyfriend, so she always with him. And I don't like to stay alone.'

'What about a boyfriend or something for you?'

'No, I don't have and I don't want.' She didn't want to be out there on the market, because she knew what Bangkok had to offer. Archie was the best man she'd ever met by a long shot, and even if it came to nothing, she just wanted to spend more time with him.

Especially considering that by the time he got back to Scotland, she'd probably never see him again.

'Well, I always appreciate your help.' He gently put his finger on little Lily's chin and made it look as if she was talking, 'Yes, thank you aunty Amm.' It was his first joke in weeks and the first smile he'd made. His face almost ached, having forgotten how to use those muscles.

He insisted on driving her home. He'd hardly been out at all, other than nipping along the street for provisions, with Lily in the baby carrier. He secured her in the baby seat and Amm sat next to him in the front. The rest of his day was free of course, so he drove baby Lily home the long way, and showed her places that he'd been with her mummy. They came along the road from Amm's place and made a right-turn onto Sukhumvit Road. 'When I first came to Bangkok, I used to stay there,' he pointed to the hotel on the left, 'and I used to take your mummy for food there,' he pointed to the right, 'and then we lived there for a while,' he pointed again to the right and then up towards the high rise condo. 'You were made in that building...or maybe Phuket actually...' Lily's bright eyes looked unwittingly to the left, to the right and she had no idea what daddy was saying. It didn't matter though, because he was doing something else rather than sitting at home feeling depressed. He didn't even realise that he was out enjoying some quality time with his daughter, and loving every second of it.

The ache of losing his fiancée coloured even his joyful moments with a dark black. But he was trying his best for the baby and didn't ever want to let her see how much distress he was in. He made sure her life did not start in strife, because even if she wasn't able to understand, he believed she'd be able to feel it. He watched her in the extra mirror he put in the car. She'd sometimes look at him with her gorgeous brown eyes that she'd inherited from mum. They would always wash away some of the darkness in him. He had to protect her now, because she wasn't just his daughter, she was the only thing he had left of Lily.

He took her into a big supermarket to look for a blow-up bed for Amm, since he couldn't expect her to stay in the chair again. She was doing him a big favour, so he should at least make her feel comfortable. He bought another duvet and sheets and some other essentials, as well as stocking up on food. It was time to take control of the situation and move forward. He suddenly realised that he'd probably never have achieved that without Amm's intervention. Her intent was probably much simpler, just to make sure he could eat and sleep – but it was far reaching. He could no longer waste time and energy in not going forward. He owed it to his baby, and he owed it to his late fiancée.

He had to make arrangements for Lily, whatever he could. Her parents weren't interested since they didn't want to bear the cost of what needed to be done. They merely told their story of woe about a brainwashing farang who stole their daughter away and never allowed them any access whenever they reached out and especially after her death. That pandered to their strengths anyway. Ploy was the one who tried to negotiate everything because his Thai was very basic. She was the one who told him to give up after the first couple of weeks. Of course, they were truly devastated to lose a second child tragically, but the way they handled the whole issue was appalling.

They'd held vigils in her hometown with candlelit photos of her and flowers upon flowers. Monks attended and people made merit, and the one thing that was lacking from the whole thing was the truth. Archie was blamed for all the bad things that happened to her. According to her parents, he didn't let her see a doctor when she felt unwell, and that's what allowed her condition to worsen. He was apparently a control freak who'd threaten her into compliance and was continually stingy with money. They made false representations in order to blame their shortcomings on him. He was demonised so that they could milk as much sympathy as they could. It was all about saving face.

Ploy still talked with him most days to see how he was doing. She never revealed the bogus rumours that were being spread about him in Lily's hometown. He had enough on his mind already, after all. She stuck up for Archie a few times only to be called names from her so-called family. Her pleas were falling on deaf ears however. In the end, it wasn't worth the hassle, so she had to block it out.

He hadn't told her about Amm, mainly because there was nothing really to tell. Ploy was busy with work and tired from life too. She loved Lily very much and thought that she finally had a chance of a great life with Archie. She had a lot of difficulty coming to terms with Lily's death. She let him know that she would be there any time, but it was hard for her to see him and little Lily. Amm however, insisted on it and he was grateful that she did.

Rain fell hard outside the condo. He slid the balcony door and left it open to feel the fresh cooling effect of the raindrops sweeping against his building. He could hear the drops pulsate against the glass, whilst far below, people tried to duck and dive in vain. The rain always fell so hard and there was no way to avoid it. It was as if to purge the city of filth every once in awhile, washing layers of muck into the sewers. It would never last, however. In Scotland it could rain all day, but rain in Thailand would come down hard, but usually stopped as quickly as it started.

Meanwhile, he cradled his daughter and thought about her mum. He remembered how she'd send him photos of rain whenever she was caught at work and was waiting with Ploy for it to pass before going home. He remembered an occasion they got caught out themselves after coming home from the mall. It was only a couple of minutes between the BTS and their door, but they were both soaked to the skin. He remembered how they tried to run hand-in-hand but after she lost a shoe in a puddle, he carried her the rest of the way. She felt like a damsel in distress being rescued by her knight in shining armour. He remembered the shower they took together to warm up after that, and how gorgeous she looked with her hair wet and clinging to her perfect face. He could also remember how she felt in his arms as he held his baby as lovingly as he held her before.

After gathering his composure, he cleared a little space in the nursery to try out the new airbed. It looked fine and he hoped Amm would be okay on it. Looking at the inflated velveteen mattress, he thought it was a bit unusual to be cohabiting with someone else, particularly Amm, but he needed it. He'd started to think of her like a live-in nanny as opposed to an ex-girlfriend or anything else. Once he'd come across that mindset it became a lot easier for him to accept.

When evening came, he offered to pick her up but she insisted on taking the BTS. Not only was the traffic terrible, but she wanted to go home first to get a few things before making her way there. He'd prepared the food this time and cooked everything in time for her arrival. They sat to eat and she asked if she could feed Lily. 'Sure,' he said. Amm was a natural. Lily had been restless that evening whilst he was trying to cook since she presumably wasn't used to daddy cooking. But once she was in Amm's arms getting her bottle, she was quite happy. Amm had really bonded with Lily and absolutely adored her.

They all watched TV together. Archie and Amm took turns holding the baby until they put her down for the night. It was the first time he'd actually let her stay alone in her room unattended and as such, the first time the baby monitor was put to use. Despite that, and despite being only around ten feet away, the TV was kept down low so they wouldn't miss her cries.

They talked comfortably and he started to feel a little more human again. They talked of Lily and her hometown. He complained about the way her parents had handled the situation and Amm explained that sometimes it happened like that, but it was very unfortunate nonetheless. She told him a bit more about her family too and about how she never knew her dad, and how lucky little Lily was to have a dad like him who cared so much and would never ever leave. Whilst she talked quite casually about her absent father, he could sense that it had an impact on her life. It dawned on him that it may have had something to do with her state of mind and the way she viewed men.

Given that her first relationship also broke down on a count of her boyfriend having a family, how else would a sensitive girl react? Being downtrodden and miserable is one, and flipping out was probably another. She'd done both at different times of course.

What she'd learnt from her experiences of men before him was that all they could do was cause her harm. She was very close to her mum, particularly because she was the youngest daughter, and she'd always ask about her dad. She'd see other girls at school or around and she always felt like something was missing. Her mum of course didn't have anything positive to say about him, because there simply wasn't anything positive to say.

He came to a much higher level of understanding of her because they were building a real friendship based on respect and concern for one another. It was the first time that she was truly honest and open since they'd first met. She talked candidly and didn't mind revealing private things about her life to him. She'd been a closed book before because she felt she had to be tough and survive by herself. But she'd come to realise that life is sometimes much better if its' shared with someone, so long as that person was worthwhile.

There was nothing she'd rather do now than spend the evening with Archie and Lily, even as friends. Yet, they were getting closer all the time. He was the only person who would qualify as worthwhile to her and was so glad that he didn't shun her the way that she did, considering how she treated him before. That was the true measure of him.

Chapter Twenty-Five
บทที่ยี่สิบห้า

Amm had been staying every night for a week which allowed Archie to come on leaps and bounds. She herself had progressed from just feeding Lily, to changing her nappies and doing everything that Archie would. He was meticulous in the way he took care of Lily and so taught Amm the exact same way. He'd filled out all his paperwork and was waiting for various replies. He would need to attend an interview at some point, but knew he could work it in because he had Amm's support. He trusted her to stay alone with Lily should the need ever arise. They'd also enjoyed each others company and Archie had broached the subject to Ploy. He kept it low key and told her that she'd been round a few times to help and not that she'd been staying over all the time.

Ploy's response was a positive one. She'd noticed how when they'd talk, he was telling her more about Lily's progress and sending her photos captioned *Hello aunty Ploy*, rather than the *I don't know how I can live, I wish I died instead of her* messages. If that was down to Amm, then it could only be a good thing. She knew about Amm's true feelings for Archie too and that she only ever had his best intentions at heart. Even before, all she was trying to do was protect him. It was just the way in which her feelings manifested that was completely diabolical. "It's good she can help you, but don't give yourself any more problems." Ploy advised.

"It's not anything like that. Lily is my true love and she always will be. It's nice now that we can just be friends. I'm not interested in finding anyone else, I just need someone to help sometimes."

"Yes, but also one day you will need someone. You shouldn't stay alone forever. You are still young! Lily will want you to be happy!" He cried for a few minutes before he could reply to that message.

"But she was my happiness. Now I just have to try to be okay and do my best for the baby. That's all I care about. I don't see how I can recover from this damage. I'll never be the same again."

"But nobody knows the future." That was the understatement of the century. "If she is doing good, you can just keep her close. Don't think too much. You are a good man."

It came to bedtime again and everybody settled into their own beds, but he couldn't sleep. He sat awake and looked at photos and videos he'd taken of Lily on his phone. Hours passed but he didn't realise. He turned on the TV after cycling the photos for a second time. He put the movie channel on as a distraction, but that was a mistake. They were showing the same movie he watched with Lily in his hotel room the first time she stayed over with him. He couldn't believe the serendipity. He remembered his clever invite and how she'd just been eagerly waiting for it. He cried out loud as he couldn't contain his sorrow.

'Archie?' Amm appeared at the door in a slouchy t-shirt, jogging bottoms and her hair up squintly. She didn't wait for a response before coming in, but opened the door slowly. She saw the movie playing and light flickering around his room, the same way it did in his hotel room that night. 'What happened? You okay mai?'

'Nothing…just the same. I miss her so much!' She came into the room and sat gingerly on the edge of the bed. That was Lily's spot, but he had to realise that she was never going to fill it again. In his gut, he wanted to reprimand Amm for daring to enter Lily's place, but that wouldn't help anyone. Amm had been nothing but amazing and she wasn't to know how sacrosanct he held that part of the condo.

'I understand. I don't know how bad you must feel really. But you still have good things in your life. You have your lovely daughter now. And you have me. Is there something I can do?'

He looked to her with pleading eyes. 'Can you bring her back?'

There was a pause before she shuffled further onto the bed. 'Is it okay?' she asked. He shrugged his shoulders. She may not have been Lily but he was tired of that space being empty all the time. Truthfully, he didn't know if he was okay with it, hence, he shrugged his shoulders. He switched the movie off, which he immediately regretted because it plunged the room into darkness, except from a little light leaking in from the hall.

'Archie, I don't know what I can do to make you feel better. But one day you will. I remember also, not long time ago, I feel like I'm going crazy. I know it's not the same thing happen, but my feeling na…it's like I have nothing and…I just want to die. Now I'm okay. Now I try to bring my life up, I try to do good things. But…' she sighed, 'I don't know…maybe there's no point.'

'What do you mean?'

'I mean, I think maybe my life supposed to be bad. Even when I'm younger, I have a bad luck. Maybe it's just like this for me.' It was hard for her to discuss, but she always found it easier to be completely open in the dark.

'What happened?'

'When I'm teenager, I have cyst…in my ovary. I have operation and they take it out, but they said I cannot have a baby. It's so hard for me, because I feel like I am not good. Every girl just dream to meet a good man and have a family. But I cannot. I feel like only half of a lady.' By the tone and anguish in her voice, it suddenly dawned on him – that was actually what she meant when she said he wouldn't like her once he got to know her. Being only half a lady, her worth would be continually limited no matter what she did. 'And then I meet someone, but he is older. Thai guy, you remember. And I feel so scared to tell him about it, but he said it's okay. And then I know why it's okay, because he already have children with his wife. He never care about me, or serious about me. But I'm so serious about him. I think we can get married.'

'And that's when you started cutting yourself?'

'Yes.' She paused. 'And then when I meet you, I really have strong feeling, but…you work far away, so I'm sure you have family already. And I'm so scared you will hurt me. But now I know really the truth about you. But I'm still stupid then and I'm so bad to you every time.' She sighed deeply. 'Archie, I do a lot of bad things.'

'I know.'

She thought it'd maybe make its way back to him because he had almost as many friends in Bangkok as she did and many of them were the same people. But she wanted to be sure they were on the same page, because she was coming clean.

'About stay with farang?' she asked.

'Yes. I actually figured it out. You know, one night I came to see you, and you weren't there, because you were out with someone. I'd have to be stupid to not realise what was going on.'

'I never think you are stupid.'

He remembered how heavily offensive that word was for her. 'I know, it's just…an expression.' She went from her seated position to lie down at the very edge of the bed because she started to feel too conspicuous sitting up looking at him.

'And that was the first night I spent time with Lily, you know? We went for something to eat. And it took off from there.'

'Yes. I am happy when you meet her, because she is really good girl. And I think you two are so nice for each other. At first, I really hurt and feel jealous, but I know it's my fault. Then I just want you to be happy. But I'm so sorry for what I do before. I know I really hurt you.'

'Well, it's in the past now. And you've more than made up for it now by helping me out. So, if you're trying to make it right with me and fix your karma, then you've done it. I forgive you and I release you of your burden,' he said jovially, 'you don't need to come anymore.'

'But I want to,' she said.

'It was probably partly my fault too,' he admitted. 'I know sometimes I'm too intense and I pushed you. I was always about to go home too, so there was always pressure.'

'No, it's not your fault. You just loved me and you try to be with me. Everything is so sweet what you do. I never see you do anything wrong.'

'Then,' he sighed, 'if I never do any wrong, why would such a bad thing happen to me?'

She searched for the answer then searched for his hand in the dark. She could only find the latter. 'I don't know.' She squeezed tight and didn't let up. It was comforting for both of them.

'I'm sorry about what happened to you when you were younger,' he said. 'You didn't deserve that.'

'Yes, and then I know nobody will want to love me. I cannot be a mother. I cannot have a family. That's why I'm bad to you also,

362

because I know I cannot give you what you want. You deserve someone better than me.'

'But you never know Amm, that was a good few years ago, things may have changed for you, it may still be possible. There's maybe things they can do now too.'

'I don't know, it's just what they tell me. And if I want to check, it's so expensive. And I think still not easy na.'

'Nothing's easy these days...' he said.

Her cyst was a huge blow for a young Amm, and then being the 'bit on the side' made her feel like she had no worth. That was the main reason why she wanted to push Archie away and finish working at the restaurant to start having the kind of encounters that she did. It's not that she had a plan to go with customers as such, but neither had she ruled it out. She just wanted to shift to that environment for the money, because she considered herself to be an empty shell – except she wasn't. She was a vibrant, caring and thoughtful young lady who'd been given a bad hand in life. She reacted badly for a while but she'd picked herself back up at last.

'That's sort of, why I want to help you with the baby too,' she continued, 'because it's the closest I can get. I don't know if it's okay to say na, but it feels little bit like a family for me. That's why I like to stay here. I don't know how I can get this feeling from somewhere else. It's only chance for me, even if just for short time. And when I stay here, you don't look at me like...working girl, even though I was. You always look at me different than someone else.' She let go of his hand as she thought she may have been pushing things a little.

He thought about what Ploy said. He was in no way ready for something to happen between them, but he certainly couldn't imagine how he'd manage without her now. It was a broken home with mum gone, but it seemed a little less broken with Amm there.

'You need to give yourself some credit, Amm. You're a sweet and caring person and you have a lot to give. I only wish you could see yourself through my eyes,' he said. 'Then you'd know how much worth you have.'

'Thank you na, Archie.'

They both hurt, in different ways, but were trying to find the strength to carry on. 'I can wait for you. I was stupid before but that time I'm not really me. I hope you can understand. I know it's not the right time, but I just want to tell you, I'll always be here for you now. Even if you want to tell me no later, it's okay. I'm here if you want me, and even if you don't want me.'

He thought about his response. It *was* perhaps quite early to say something like that to him, but he could understand that she just wanted to be upfront about her feelings. Considering the fact she was sleeping there too, it was probably better to be upfront about everything. She wanted to right the wrongs she made before and do things differently. She never revealed any feelings before, so this was her new approach, because she was making positive and genuine changes in her life. It seemed to him like she'd done a lot of growing up in the past little while.

He didn't have space in his heart to love her yet. Like he told Lily before, he's either one hundred per cent or nothing at all. He'd have to wait for that space to open up first before letting her in. Of course, a big portion of that would be occupied by Lily forevermore, which would be an issue in moving on. Someone new might not appreciate that, but Amm could already understand and accept it.

'I'm not saying yes, but I'm not saying no,' he said. 'I know you're just telling me and that's okay. But you'll have to wait a long time, and I don't even know if I will ever be ready. All I know is this would be ten times harder without you. You've turned things around for me Amm, and I really appreciate all you've done. Maybe you weren't there for me before, but you definitely are now.' He reached to take her hand back again. 'But I have to know that I can trust you. I mean, I trust you with Lily, but I mean about your fidelity, because you broke it before. Because it's not just me that you'd hurt now. I let you hurt me over and over, but I will not let you hurt little Lily.'

'Yes, I know. But I would never do like that again. Just take your time because I'm happy to wait for you. I don't want anyone else na Archie.'

'But I can't promise you anything. I also don't want to hurt you or waste your time. I just don't know if I'll ever reach that day.'

365

She turned on her side to face him. 'That's okay. I just want to be here with you now and with Lily. For me it's okay, and later if you don't want something, then we will always be friends.'

'Okay.'

She reached over to him and they held each other comfortingly. By the way of some devious destiny, it was someone else's head that rested on Lily's pillow, next to the man Lily loved, late at night in Lily's condo, in Lily's corner of Bangkok.

Epilogue
บทส่งท้าย

He sat at the airport waiting for his flight home. This was it. He was finally leaving Thailand and didn't know if or when he'd be back again. He sat with baby Lily on his knee and looked out at the aircraft pushing back, approaching gates or being replenished. The following week it'd be her second birthday. Her first birthday was so hard for him, and would always be. That day wasn't just her birthday, it was also the day he lost her mum. It was a cruel twist of fate that he'd have to live with for the rest of his life.

The taxi ride there was an emotional one. The sun hung low and cast deep and bright oranges over the sky as he sat quietly taking in the last of Thailand that he could. He'd been to and from that airport many times, but the taxi driver told him he would take a different route because of the traffic. It was the back way, and he'd never been that way before. It seemed fitting that he'd go a different way and it made it feel more final.

Much to his regret and heartache, his application to take Lily's body to the UK was refused, so he laid her to rest in Thailand. Her family didn't want anything to do with it, despite Archie's efforts. The papers for little Lily were accepted, but after that he simply wasn't ready to leave. He took his interim job in the end and stayed in the condo for a while just trying to get on with his life.

He found a great nursery for Lily which was part of an international school, for whenever he was at work. He hated having to leave her and the first few months were so terrible for him. He'd call the school every spare moment he had. The teachers were sympathetic and understanding because he'd explained his circumstances when he first took her there. But he had to learn that he couldn't be with her every moment. Life kept going and bills had to be paid. He had to keep the roof over her head and food on the table, so he couldn't just stay at home.

He recalled the first few days of dropping her off and how he'd weep inconsolably in his car for several minutes before being able to make his way to work. Of course, it gradually became easier. Being at work did help him sometimes, particularly when he'd have a complex problem to solve and needed to use all of his brain power. He'd stop tormenting himself and stop realising his crushing pain, at least for a while. But the days couldn't pass fast enough until he could pick up his little angel again and spend the evening with her.

He'd go to visit Lily's grave frequently. He'd take little Lily with him and talk to both of them, but neither of them spoke back.

Time passed and he learned how to get to grips with things. The pain never left him, but he just managed to cope with it better. If anything, he hurt more every day, since every moment that passed took him further from Lily and there was no way to reverse that. He'd found a new routine though, and whilst it was not the one he envisaged, he had to make it work. His parents wanted to come so badly but he'd always fobbed them off and told them he was going to come back soon and of his own accord. They had been trying to encourage his return but could understand that he needed to reach a point where he was able to leave. It made sense for him to take baby Lily to Scotland in time for her second birthday so that he could celebrate it with family, or rather, they could celebrate it with her and he could sit in quiet contemplation about his departed fiancée.

Eventually, he realised that Lily wasn't there anymore, but she'd always be with him in his heart, so it didn't matter where in the world he was. That realisation took almost two years to come about though.

He checked the time and there was still about forty minutes before the flight would board. He rearranged his bag and brought the essentials for Lily to the top. 'Do you have everything you need?' he asked.

'Yes, I do,' Amm replied.

After about a year of being an unpaid nanny, they'd become suitably close and she'd proved her loyalty to him. All she did was work and spend time with them. Sometimes she'd see her sisters, but she'd always send photos of what she was doing and video call him and Lily to prove it. For all intents and purposes, they were already in a relationship, except nothing had happened between them physically. She was determined to wait for him, and wait she did.

He came to the point where he couldn't stop himself from going forward in life and as much as he missed Lily, he'd thoroughly enjoyed having Amm with him. It started with her just sleeping in the bed. Then after a while, some cuddles, then kisses. Then after another while, full intimacy. It was very different the way he thought about her this time, however. He'd say that he loved her, but it wasn't a magical, fantastic and spectacular love like he had with Lily. Their love, whilst being true enough, was now based on friendship and caring and companionship. They understood each other and could appreciate the difficulties each other had, so staying together was the ideal situation and beneficial for both of them. Over time, they'd built up trust and spent that time to get to know each other, just as she wished they could before.

There was no one else in the world who'd be quite so aware of the delicacy of his situation or as understanding of his feelings as Amm would be. For her, there was no one else who made her feel whole like he did. She loved baby Lily like she was her own and in spite of her problems, she already had the family unit up and running.

They'd filled out all the necessary paperwork for Amm to stay in the UK too. She was going to attend college there and study hospitality, just as she'd been working in Thailand for two years. She wanted to get a job and help support him financially as well as emotionally and psychologically.

From the outside, no one was to know they were not a 'natural' family, so it just made sense. She also wanted a chance at a better life. The thought of Archie leaving was too much for her to bear and she'd have done anything to go with him. He also didn't know how he'd cope without her. Everything she'd done for the two years was for Archie and Lily. The two girls had also bonded so much that he simply couldn't part Lily with the only significant female in her life.

Amm took Lily for a while whilst Archie took a walk around the shops via the bathroom. He looked at the souvenirs and remembered the first time he went there. He realised that he was taking home the biggest souvenirs anyone ever could – a baby and a partner. It didn't quite work out the way he'd expected and there had certainly been a lot of very upsetting twists and turns along the way, but he had his family. He missed Lily as he always did, but in a way, he felt things were going to be okay.

As the plane took off, there was a sudden rush which overwhelmed him and he couldn't help but weep. Amm held his hand and wiped his tears as he held little Lily tight.

'You okay mai? Please don't cry. Everything is okay. I love you na, Archie.'

He could hardly talk, but he did manage to place a kiss on her hand. She then placed his hand between her legs like she always did. Lily was safe enough sitting on his lap and cradled into his chest, smiling up at him with her big brown eyes.

'She is always with you,' Amm said. Archie nodded. 'And I'm always with you too.'

He wept tears for the loss he suffered, and for knowing how fortunate it was to have things come back around with Amm. At lease he finally had the real her who was caring and supportive. He wept to be leaving behind the biggest influencer in his life and to close the door one final time. From a simple holiday, nobody could ever imagine all the things that transpired. And as the nose lifted on the plane and the wheels broke away from the tarmac, he realised he'd wept the last of his Bangkok Teardrops.

'Amm'

November 2015/พฤศจิกายน 2558

She's the favourite t-shirt you refuse to not wear, even though the threads are unravelling
She's the cold you don't want to ever recover from
She's your favourite movie that no one else has seen and can't relate to when you talk about her
She's the unwritten pages of your book

She's the quiet before the storm
She is the storm itself, but you'd rather let your ship go down than navigate away
She is the flood, she is the drought
She is the famine and she is the feast
She's everything you dream about yet she haunts you as you sleep
But never do you want to wake up from her

She's a car without brakes
She's a skydive with no parachute
She's a compass with no needle, yet you know which way you're going
She's the waterfall that drowns you and she is the kiss of life

She's the air that fills your lungs, yet she takes your breath away

She's the drug to which you're addicted

She's buried treasure no man before could find

She's a diamond in the riverbed

She's your first thing Monday morning and your Friday afternoon

She's the song that's forever stuck in your head

She's every boundary you've ever faced and she's the key to unlock every door

She can take on half the world and she can be stuck hiding beneath her covers

She can wound with a look and heal with a touch

She's thunder, she's lightning, she's the rainbow that's bound to follow

She is the universe, she's every star in the sky

She's a ray of sunshine and the dark of the night

She's every secret you've ever sworn to keep and she's the word you can't help but spread

She's the teardrops on your pillow

She's your wonderwall

She's everything that you hold in your heart

She's your desire to self-destruct and your realisation of eternity

She insists she's imperfect, but she's perfect to you
She's the reason you exist

She's the chaos in your life, the discord in your brain
She is your pain, she is your joy
She is your peace and harmony.

Printed in Great Britain
by Amazon